THE

MYSTERIES OF

OLD FATHER THAMES.

𝔄 Romance.

Mighty river—oh! mighty river,
Rolling, in ebb and flow, for ever,
Through the city, so vast and old—
Through massive bridges—by domes and spires,
Crowned with the smoke of a myriad fires ;
City of majesty, power, and gold :
Thou lovest to float, on thy waters dull,
The white-winged fleets, so beautiful,
And the lordly steamers, speeding along,
Wind defying, and swift and strong ;
Thou bearest them all on thy motherly breast,
Laden with riches, at trade's behest—
Bounteous trade, whose wine and corn
Stock the garner and fill the horn,
Who gives us luxury, joy, and pleasure,
Stintless, sumless, out of measure :
Thou art a rich and a mighty river,
Rolling, in ebb and flow, for ever.

                                    MACKAY.

LONDON:

W. CAFFYN, 31, OXFORD-STREET, MILE-END;

AND ALL BOOKSELLERS.

THE MYSTERIES OF
OLD FATHER THAMES,

THE

MYSTERIES OF OLD FATHER THAMES.

PROLOGUE.

HAIL, Father Thames! Spirit who presidest over London's mighty river, hail! Attend unto my call, and reveal the mysteries which thy rippling waters have witnessed and concealed.

Thou shouldst have much to tell, Old Father Thames. Alike of the hoary past and the vivid present would thy revelations teem with interest, and prove the assertion, that "Truth is stranger than fiction." What fearful mysteries couldst thou not unfold! What appalling revelations couldst thou not disclose! Thou hast borne upon thy bosom the pirate, the smuggler, and the mutineer— the convict and the emigrant have descended thy broad stream—the press-gang has invaded thy banks—and thy rippling waters have received the corpse of the suicide, weary of the troubles and cares of the world, and the victim of midnight assassination, thrown in from dock and stair and sedgy bank, or floated down with the filth of the sewers.

River of many mysteries! who can gaze upon thy waters without reading upon every wave which ripples thy glassy surface, as in the mirror of olden necromancer, some story of the loved and lost, of sin and sorrow, of misery and remorse? Say, Old Father Thames, is there one house past which thy silver waters flow, from which thou bearest not the sighs of the forsaken, the moan of the conscience-stricken, the wail of the mourner, or the anguished cry of despair?

Softly flow thy pellucid waters from their tiny spring, gliding with a pleasing murmur over their pebbly bed, as they meander through green meadows and umbrageous woods, where the feathered choristers raise an everlasting thanks-giving to the Omnipotent Spirit of the universe, and by straw-thatched cottage and baronial hall, giving health and vigour to the swain and the peer, and visiting the hovel of the over-wrought labourer and the ancient towers of Victoria's palace.

What a crowd of legendary associations and historic reminiscences rush upon the mind as we descend thy stream, and gaze contemplatively on tower and spire, mansion and grove, as the various objects rise on either hand. Have thy willows never wept for the betrayed and deserted maiden, the victim of man's treachery and her trusting heart?—and are not the loves and hopes, the griefs and trials of humble life as pregnant with interest as the follies and inanities of the fashionable world?

Do no reminiscences of interest linger about thy palaces and halls? Has Windsor no untold secrets to reveal? Has Kew no revelations to make?—no hidden crime that hitherto has baffled inquiry, and feared to meet the public gaze? Have the groves of Richmond treasured up no secrets since they heard the whispered loves of Alice Pierse and the third Edward? Thy waters roll on, and make no response, and a voice mingles with the zephyrs that gently agitate the drooping branches that kiss thy rippling waters, murmuring that the time has not yet come to lift the veil from the crimes and frailties of the great and titled.

Roll on, proud river, to where arise, side by side, in a contiguity which excites most serious reflections, palaces and hovels, churches and barracks, workhouses and prisons! Strange association! We have arrived at a city of contradictions—a very Paradoxopolis!—a metropolis which unites the extreme phases of barbarism and civilization! Here is a splendid palace, in which resides a single family, and that the least important in the nation, since it contributes nothing to the national resources; and there a dirty hovel, inferior in comfort to the wigwam of the Indian, in every room of which two or three families are herded together, without regard to either decency or health. Here is a church ostensibly reared for the preaching of peace and love, and there is a barrack for the teaching of war and hate, and a workhouse and a prison for the victims of social error.

Strange anomalies are these, and worthy of fictive illustration. And as we float onward, the scenes on either bank of the mighty river thicken with marvellous interest; for, though the seeker after horrors will no longer find food for his morbid appetite in the gory heads of traitors and rebels which formerly were wont to *adorn* old London-bridge, and the fleshless skeletons of mutineers and pirates which formerly swung from the gibbets of Blackwall-point; yet, to those who, Asmodeus-like, can penetrate the abodes of vice and misery, the shores of Old Father Thames are as rich as ever in the materials of romantic lore.

Night draws her sombre mantle over the sleeping river, and the midnight hour booms sonorously from the cathedral, the dark outline of whose cupola is dimly visible through the fog which hangs continually over London—fit hour for the contemplation of the dark mysteries of Old Father Thames!

My spells have evoked the spirit of the river! Old Father Thames is before me bodily, to portray the secrets of his watery realms, and a thin mist ascends from the dark bosom of the river, in which is revealed, as in a dim phantasmagoria, the mysteries of the Thames.

Faint shrieks and groans reverberate along the misty air, and the river gives up its unsepulchred dead! From the dark and silent water below the bridge of Waterloo, a figure slowly rises: the form is that of a young girl; her countenance is pale, and stamped with an expression of misery and despair, and the water drips from her dishevelled hair.

The next form that rises from the dark bosom of the Thames is a wild-looking figure, with dark staring eyes and long black hair—tall and gaunt, with remorse and horror impressed upon every lineament of his haggard countenance.

Lo! another comes—a robust and martial figure, but with countenance distorted by pain and suffering, and head bowed down with the recollection of shame and anguish.

Another comes!—one clad like a mariner, with hands held up, as if for help and succour; and now a ragged, famished, misery-crushed wretch, with glassy eye and hollow cheek, and emaciated form.

Faster and faster rise the disembodied spirits of the unburied dead of Old Father Thames—the suicide and the victim of midnight crime, and all whose last resting-place has been his muddy bed. But again the old cathedral booms the hour upon the silence of the night, and the misty curtain draws up from the broad stream—wharf and pier loom through the fog, and every airy form has vanished. The hour has passed when the wandering and unquiet spirits of the unsepulchred dead are permitted to revisit the earth, and the rushing murmur, as they seek their cold and watery graves, faints away with the last echoes of the cathedral bell.

CHAPTER I.

ST. KATHERINE'S-DOCKS.

On a fine spring morning, in the year 1815, now thirty-three years ago—the memorable year of Waterloo, the last decisive battle of the world, and we trust the last which history will ever record, which cemented the throne of the Bourbons with the blood of France's best and bravest sons, and restored to Europe the blessings of peace, of legitimacy, and the Jesuits—a man of colour, who had arrived in London the evening before, from the East, came out of a lodging-house in Old Gravel-lane, and sauntered towards St. Katherine's-docks. He was a Malay, one of a race distinct from both the Hindoo and the African, and regarded by those who have deeply studied the physical history of the human race as superior in mental organism to both the negro and the aboriginal American, occupying a place in the scale of intellect between those races and the more civilized nations of south-western Asia. The man in question was evidently young, though it were vain to guess at the years of a native of the equatorial climes, born and reared under the burning sun of the torrid zone, where the human being springs to early maturity, and the deepest and darkest passions of our nature are aroused to vigour and activity, and where love and hate, and jealousy and revenge, receive an intensity in accordance with the clime.

The Malay was of moderate stature, slight of frame, and well-proportioned; his long straight black hair fell upon his shoulders, and small moustaches of the same hue adorned his upper lip. His eyes were small and very dark, and seemed incessantly in motion, roving from one object to another as he walked along the extensive range of warehouses in the rear of the docks. His complexion was a deep olive colour, his nose aquiline, and the general arrangement of his features good; but there was a deficiency of mind in the upper part of his countenance, and the restless motion of his dark eyes marked the grade which his race occupies in the chain of nature, as one removed more by form than by habits and modes of thought from the shaggy denizens of the forest. He was attired in a tunic of faded pink silk, and trousers of the oriental fashion; he wore a turban of dingy white linen on his head, and a sash begirt his waist, in which he carried that inseparable weapon of the Malays, a long finely-pointed *creese* or dagger, and a bamboo pipe for inhaling the fumes of opium, having a long stem and a very small bowl.

Entering the docks, the Malay regarded every object about him with the keen curiosity of a savage set down for the first time in his life in the midst of civilized society, and glanced from vessel to vessel, and from one man to another as men of every nation passed and repassed him. There were the sallow Russians, in their thick dreadnoughts and fur caps, unloading their cargo of hemp and tallow—Germans, redolent of tobacco-smoke, bringing corn to a land where millions of acres lie uncultivated, while starving labourers cry, "Give us work! let us till the land, lest we perish!"—swarthy Spaniards, smoking their *cigarillos*, or paper cigars, while they unloaded their wine and fruit—and passing and repassing along the wharves were Frenchmen, Danes, Italians, Greeks, Hindoos, Africans, and our trans-Atlantic brethren, whose stars and stripes might be taken as emblematical of liberty, did not the latter remind us of the slavery of the negro.

Gazing on the forest of masts, and permitting not the Babel of sounds around us to disturb us from our reverie, we might wander for hours through St. Katherine's-docks, meditating on the mighty events which arise in the dim future from trivial causes, and the progress of that civilization which, emanating from the docks of Old Father Thames as from a common centre, radiates in every direction throughout the known world, and plants its flag on the distant shores of China, penetrates the mighty rivers of Africa, and extends to the islands of the Pacific, beautiful offspring of the volcano and the coral insect! It is true that our commercial system is vicious, but it is a phase through which society must necessarily pass to a better state: we admit that the present generation of Chinese have little to thank our traders for, and we have no hesitation in declaring our conviction that the virtue and temperance of the savages of Polynesia were preferable to the drunkenness and prostitution which have accompanied civilization, and that the worship of Oro was purer than that Christianity which planted its cannon against Tahiti, introduced war and dissensions, and broke up the ties of home and kindred with its intolerant dogmas. But we may ask, with the optimist, whether these evils will not tend to the evolution of a greater good? Our commercial intercourse with uncivilized people will soon enable them to make but one step from barbarism to civilization, instead of passing through the intermediate stages which have marked the progress of the European nations. We know that the aborigines of America are rapidly approaching extinction, and unless a remnant of them be preserved by intermarriage and the adoption of true civilization, we have no doubt that all the inferior races of mankind will ultimately disappear from the earth, and give place to their superiors in the scale of intellect, in the same manner as the

megatherium and the enaliosaurians of our early planet's existence were replaced by the dog, the horse, and the sheep.

But from this digression let us return to the Malay, whom we find regarding
with much attention a fine vessel which had only that morning arrived from
the East Indies. Some of her hardy crew were aloft, furling her ample sails,
and longing to escape from the duties of the ship; some to their homes and their
families, their sweethearts or their wives—others to the grosser and more selfish
pleasures of the tavern-concert, the pipe and glass, and the society of the
nymphs of Wapping. Several Lascar sailors were shivering about the deck,
which was strewed with bales of goods and coils of rope; and the captain, a
gentlemanly-looking man, about fifty years of age, was giving directions to the
mates respecting the unloading of the cargo. While the dark eyes of the Malay
wandered over the stately vessel, a passenger came on deck, followed by a
young woman and a child, and, after a few minutes' conversation with the
captain, crossed the gangway, and walked towards the entrance of the docks.
The Malay started involuntarily when he saw the gentleman ascend from the
cabin, and shrank within the shade of the tall warehouses to avoid observation.
As the party left the ship, his eyes gleamed with vindictiveness at the gentleman—his teeth were set, as if to restrain the violence of the fierce emotions
which were raging in his breast, and his hand wandered almost mechanically
to the dangerous weapon in his sash. But he subdued his feelings, of whatever
nature they were, for fear of exciting the attention of the many sailors and
labourers about him, and, emerging from his ambush, he followed the party at
a little distance.

The gentleman was about thirty-five years of age, of the middle height, and
well made; his countenance was bronzed more by exposure to the weather and
a tropical sun than by nature; for his hair was brown, his features regular and
not unhandsome, and his manners something between the rough joviality of the
seaman and the more refined habits of the gentleman. His attire was of the
semi-nautical description usually adopted by the masters of merchant-vessels of
the first class; but all that we can at present inform the reader concerning him
is, that he had come as a passenger in the vessel he had just quitted, from
Singapore.

The child was his daughter, a little girl scarcely more than a year old, a
smiling cherub whose dark eyes and complexion seemed to indicate that her
maternal progenitor must have been a native of that far-eastern land where the
golden-plumed bird of Paradise hovers among the aromatic shrubs, and the
fire-flies glitter along the banks of every river. The little innocent was dressed
in clothes of the finest India muslin, and borne in the arms of her *ayah*, or nurse,
a young woman of pleasing exterior, and attired in the simple costume of a
Hindoo female of the *coolie* or labourer class.

The Malay followed the gentleman who had quitted the vessel with the child
and nurse, and saw them enter a hackney-coach at the entrance of the docks,
which was immediately driven off in the direction of Tower-hill. With all the
acuteness of his race, the Malay had taken such a rapid but complete observation
of the hackney-coach and its driver, that when he saw them return in a few
hours afterwards, during which he had loitered about the neighbourhood of the
docks, he had no difficulty in recognising them.

" Well, *sahib*," said he to the driver, in his best English, " where have you
taken the gentleman and the little child, and her *ayah*—nurse ?"

" What's that to you, darkey ?" said the jarvey, with the usual civility of his
class. " I say, are you the chap as a peice of chalk won't make a white mark
on ?"

" You are a pleasant fellow, *sahib*," returned the Malay, showing his white
teeth as he affected a conciliatory smile. " You could not drink a glass of rum,
could you ?"

" Just try me !" exclaimed the driver, grinning as he dropped the reins on the
box.

The Malay smiled, and waved his hand towards a public-house opposite the
dock-gates, upon which the hackney-coachman descended from the box, and
they both entered.

" Well, where did you drive that party to ?" inquired the Malay, when the barman had placed two glasses of rum before them; and his mode of eliciting the information he desired showed that he possessed a fund of natural shrewdness which more than counterbalanced his ignorance of the vicious usages of civilized society.

"Well, I druv 'em to Camberwell, a place over the water, and the gentleman did the 'andsome, and no mistake about it," replied the jarvey, as he smacked his lips after swallowing the alcoholic fluid, and wishing his Asiatic acquaintance "good day," he mounted his box, and drove off.

The Malay then returned to his lodgings in Old Gravel-lane, from which he emerged again on the following morning, with a small bundle under his arm; on reaching Ratcliffe-highway he turned to the left, and threading his way through groups of tarry sailors and low prostitutes, Irish labourers and applewomen, he proceeded towards Tower-hill. Crossing that spacious area, the scene of many a legal murder in bygone ages, he passed up Eastcheap, and at length finding his way to London-bridge, he crossed over into the borough of Southwark, and from thence proceeded direct towards the suburban town of Camberwell.

He stopped on the vacant space which existed opposite the Duke of Clarence, at the top of Southampton-street, before the shops were carried out to the pavement, and began blowing a small trumpet which he took from his bundle. We need not remind our readers how easy it is to collect a crowd, and when the Malay had thus far accomplished his object, he laid down the trumpet, and drew from his bundle five brass balls and the same number of knives, such as are used by jugglers in the exercise of their profession. After exhibiting a number of feats with the knives and balls, which are so common as to require no explanation, he went round his spectators with a small japanned box, and collected halfpence to the amount of sixpence. He then went on to Camberwell-green, where he gave a similar exhibition, and at its conclusion inquired of a bystander the residence of Captain Hastings. Having received the information which he sought, the Malay proceeded towards the nearest public-house, where he remained smoking his long bamboo pipe, and sipping from a glass of rum, until a late hour.

CHAPTER II.

THE STOLEN CHILD.

WE must now return to the passengers who had arrived from the East Indies, in the vessel then lying in St. Katherine's-docks, and, as we have seen, had taken a hackney-coach to convey them to Camberwell. Captain Hastings, with his infant daughter and her Hindoo attendant, alighted at a genteel, villa-like house in the Grove, the occupants of which were an elderly widow lady and her two daughters, the mother and sisters of Mr. Hastings, who was more usually called Captain Hastings, on account of his having been the master of a vessel trading to various parts in the East. Four years had elapsed since they had seen each other; and this absence having been unexpected, Edward Hastings had been mourned by his relatives as dead, as it had been ascertained that his vessel had been wrecked, and nothing had been afterwards heard of the crew. The joy of his mother and sisters may therefore be readily imagined, and when a score of questions had been asked in a breath, and the relatives had gazed their fill on each other, the attention of the sisters was turned from Edward Hastings to the smiling infant which he had brought with him.

"Oh, what a pretty child!—whose is it?—is it yours, Edward?" were the simultaneous remark and questions of both his sisters, and the eldest took the little cherub from its nurse, and caressed it fondly.

"Yes, it is mine, Julia," returned Edward Hastings, smiling; and then he added, in a more pensive tone: "She lost her mother before we left India, and I did not like to leave it among strangers, poor thing!"

"What a sweet little creature!—what pretty dark eyes she has!—do give her to me, Julia," said Adela Hastings, a blooming girl of seventeen, with long auburn ringlets; and, receiving the child from her sister, she lavished upon it a display of fondness equal to what it had received from the fair Julia.

" Poor little thing!—how old is she?" said Mrs. Hastings; and, much pleased at the reception and admiration which the little innocent had met with, Edward replied that she was just turned twelve months old.

" What is her name, Edward?" inquired Adela.

" Lolah," he replied.

" What a strange name!" observed his eldest sister.

" It was her mother's name," said Edward Hastings, glancing with the affection of a parent at the child; " and though she has been regularly admitted by baptism into the fold of the church, and her mother worshipped the god of her forefathers, I see no objection to the name. All our Christian names are equally of heathen origin, and I believe our creed has not furnished us with a single name."

After dinner, Edward Hastings related to his mother and sisters the circumstances connected with the wreck of his vessel, and his subsequent adventures in the East.

The vessel which he commanded, and of which he was part owner, had left England about four years previous to the date at which our tale commences, and had a fair and prosperous voyage to Calcutta, from which port they proceeded towards the coast of China, their destination being Lintin and Canton. But, in the passage between the shores of Malacca and the large island of Sumatra, a tremendous storm came on, and such was the fury of the gale, that the masts had to be cut away to lighten the strain upon the vessel; all night the vessel was buffeted by the wind and waves, and at daybreak she struck upon a reef, and immediately went to pieces. Some of the crew perished in the waves, and the rest escaped in the long-boat; Edward Hastings was one of the fortunate survivors of the wreck, and under his direction the boat was steered for the coast of Sumatra. They entertained hopes of reaching the English settlement at Bencoolen, but they were too far to the eastward, and when they arrived on the coast they were almost famished for want of food.

Having found a spring of fresh water near the coast, and partially appeased the cravings of their stomachs with some wild fruits, they laid down underneath the boat, which they drew upon the sand, and went to sleep. During the night they were much alarmed by the growling of tigers close to the boat, and could even hear their breathing, as they snuffed about round the boat, where they found the prints of their feet in the sand on the following morning. Having dried their powder, and loaded two or three muskets which they had saved from the wreck for their defence, they left some of their party to guard the boat, and walked up the country. Passing a ravine which opened into a valley, where they were rejoiced to see a native village, they were startled by hearing a scream proceed from the jungle, on the skirts of which they were travelling; and, looking round, they beheld a large tiger, preparing to dart upon a young female. Captain Hastings discharged his musket at the ferocious animal, which immediately rolled over in the agonies of death, and then hastened to the assistance of the young female, who had fainted.

She was young and beautiful, and dressed in the style of the superior class of natives. In this country her years would have entitled her only to the appellation of a child, but maturity is dependent on climate, and not on the lapse of years; for the physical development of females born in the sultry lands of the tropics is as perfect at ten years of age as that of an English girl at fifteen. The lovely Sumatran was about twelve years of age, slender in figure, yet admirably proportionate; her long silky hair was black and glossy, her eyebrows superbly arched, and her dark eyes gave increased piquancy to her clear olive complexion. Edward Hastings bent over her with enraptured eyes, as he strove to restore her to consciousness; and having sufficient knowledge of the Malayan language to converse with the natives of the Indian Archipelago, the terrified girl informed him that her father was a chief, and lived in the village.

The Sumatran chief received them hospitably, and after a stay of two or three days to recruit their strength, during which Edward Hastings became more and more enamoured of the charming Lolah, the crew set out for Bencoolen. The young officer parted with reluctance from the hospitable chief and his daughter, whose manners and disposition were calculated to strengthen the

impression made by her transcendent beauty of countenance and figure. But on their way they were attacked by a strong body of natives from the interior of the island, who had rebelled against the authority of the Rajah of Achen, and many of the shipwrecked mariners were slain, and the remainder taken prisoners. Captain Hastings was among the latter, but contrived to effect his escape, and never heard of his companions in misfortune again; after wandering about for several days, suffereng from hunger and fatigue, and exposed to the attacks of wild beasts, as well as to the danger of being retaken by the insurgent natives, he found his way back to the village where dwelt Lolah and her father. The manner in which the charming Sumatran received him convinced Edward Hastings that the passion which he had conceived towards her was reciprocated, and her father having desired him to consider his house as his home, it need not excite surprise that he was in no hurry to set out again for Bencoolen.

The young man was not slow in declaring his passion, and Lolah blushingly acknowledged the reciprocity of the attachment; but he soon found he had a

2

rival in the person of a Malay named Alompra, who was supposed to be a spy of the Dutch government. With the passion of his countrymen for a roving and adventurous mode of life, Alompra had in early youth joined the crew of one of those piratical prames which infest the Indian seas; after this he had served in the army of the Dutch East India Company, and had signalized himself by his desperate courage in the defeat at Batavia. Subsequently he had been employed as a spy, and sent in this capacity to Sumatra to excite the natives to make war upon the English, and attack their settlements; but the alliance between this country and Holland was unfavourable to his projects, and he became a wanderer about the country, no one knowing precisely how he obtained his living. He had conceived a violent passion for the beautiful Lolah, which was not reciprocated, and hence he burned with jealous and revengeful feelings against Captain Hastings. Thwarted in a bloody attempt upon the Englishman's life, he fled to Achen, and was not seen for some time; during this interval Edward Hastings and Lolah were united in marriage, according to the rites of the country, and shortly afterwards removed to Bencoolen.

Alompra soon traced them out, and secretly introduced himself into their house, with the intention of assassinating his successful rival, but being discovered and arrested, he was thrown into prison; he obtained his release, however, by making some important disclosures of a political nature, and, through his artful intrigues, Captain Hastings was ordered to quit the country. He accordingly proceeded to Singapore in an English vessel, and his young wife accompanied him; he now determined to return to his native country, but the state of Lolah's health, which had been delicate since the birth of their daughter, compelled him to delay his departure. His wife never recovered, but died a few months after her *accouchement*, and Captain Hastings engaged a Hindoo nurse for the little Lolah, and immediately commenced his preparations for returning to England. The Malay had followed him to Singapore, and, having learned his intentions, embarked privately in another vessel, and, as we have seen, arrived in London the day before Edward Hastings and his infant daughter.

It was on the first hour after their arrival, and darkness yet reigned over the earth, and silence uninterrupted by a single sound; the infant daughter of Captain Hastings lay sleeping in her cot, by the bedside of her Hindoo attendant, who was also fast asleep. The deep silence which prevailed was all at once broken by the hour striking from the tower of Camberwell-church, and scarcely had its vibrations ceased upon the stilly air, when, had Azalie been awake, she might have heard a slight noise at the chamber window, and the head of a man indistinctly visible amid the darkness. In a few minutes the grating sound ceased, and the window was gently raised, and the man stepped softly into the room, and approached the cot of the sleeping child.

It was the Malay, who had resolved to wreak a profound vengeance upon his successful rival, by stealing the child, and keeping the father in dread uncertainty as to its fate, until an opportunity offered of giving the finishing stroke to his revenge by murdering both. He softly raised the infant from its cot, and wrapping it up in a large shawl belonging to Azalie, which he found upon the nurse's bed, he tied the ends about his neck—requiring both hands to effect his descent from the window—and made his exit as noiselessly, and in the same manner as he had his entrance. The child did not awake, and thus Alompra accomplished his aim successfully; and when the nurse awoke and missed the child, not a trace could be perceived of the manner in which the abduction had been effected, and, as Captain Hastings had no idea of the presence of the Malay in the metropolis, the whole affair was involved in the deepest mystery, to which not the slightest clue could be obtained.

CHAPTER III.

THE MIDNIGHT MARRIAGE.

ON the same night, and almost at the same hour as the mysterious abduction of little Lolah Hastings from her grandmother's residence in Camberwell-grove, an event no less extraordinary and startling in its nature occurred at the mansion of Lord Clanrobert, situate near the village of Erith, on the banks of the Thames.

It was past midnight, and the moon had sunk to rest, leaving that portion of the earth veiled in darkness, and every light had long been extinguished in the peaceful village; the only sound which broke the solemn stillness of the night was the occasional and distant barking of some watchful house-dog, and the low murmuring of the wind as it agitated the foliage of the trees. Yet at that hour of silence and darkness, when all nature seemed hushed in repose, two men and a female quitted one of the cottages at the outskirts of the village, and proceeded towards the mansion of Lord Clanrobert. All the party were evidently young, and the men wore the garb of mariners, but little could be distinguished of their features amid the darkness; the female was neatly dressed, though in a humble style, and walked between the two men. Not a word was spoken when they emerged from the cottage, and they walked on in silence until they came near the mansion above mentioned, when they were joined by another, an elderly man, dressed in a shabby suit of black.

" Well met, sir," said the eldest of the two men, in a respectful tone. " I began to fear that you had repented your promise, and would disappoint us."

" No, young man," returned the old man; " a promise should be sacred; my yea is ever *yea*, and my nay *nay*."

" If all men would act like that, there would be no necessity for this affair to-night," observed the young man.

The female sighed deeply, but spoke not.

" Men do evil because they are so morally purblind that they know it not from goodness," said the aged man. " They know not what they do, but the day shall come when their eyes shall be opened, and in that day, they will learn to distinguish the good from the evil, the true from the false."

" May it come speedily," sighed the young woman.

" Amen," responded the stranger; and, at that moment, the party reached the lodge gates of the mansion, which one of the young men opened with a skeleton key, and the party proceeded in deep silence towards the house.

" Now, if Ned Pearce has served us well and truly, we shall soon be in the house," observed the youngest of the men, alluding to one of the male domestics of the household.

" All right!" said the other, as he found the fastening of the door had been removed inside; and, having opened it, the whole party cautiously entered, closed the door behind them, and proceeded with noiseless steps to the drawing-room, the female acting as guide, and being apparently well acquainted with the internal topography of the mansion.

When they were all assembled in the drawing-room, one of the young men procured a light from a phosphorus-box, and proceeded to ignite two of the wax candles which had been left in silver candlesticks upon the table. The sudden light revealed the countenances of the group who had thus strangely, and with extraordinary object, effected an unlawful entrance into the mansion in the dead of night. The two young men were of the respective ages of seventeen and twenty-six, fair and florid in complexion, but browned by exposure to rough weather in many a tempestuous voyage; they wore blue pea-jackets and trowsers, and checked shirts, and from the pockets of each of their jackets obtruded the butts of a brace of loaded pistols. An air of calm yet stern determination pervaded the features of both; and the quiet, collected manner in which they proceeded with the purpose which had brought them to the mansion, showed that they were resolved to execute it at whatever risk might be incurred.

The female, who, from the resemblance in the general expression of their countenances, appeared to be their sister, was about twenty years of age, and evidently in a situation shortly to become a mother. She was slightly pale, sighed frequently, and pressed her hand upon her heart, as if to restrain the agitation of mingled fear and hope, which alternately paled and flushed her fair cheeks; and she watched every movement of her brothers with breathless interest.

The old man, who had joined them on the way to the mansion, was a little, withered, sallow-visaged sexagenarian, with long white hair hanging on his shoulders, and grey eyes, which seemed to retain all the brightness and animation of their youth. He was dressed in a worn and faded suit of black, but his linen was scrupulously clean and white, and, despite his venerable appearance, his voice was as full, and his movements as quick as those of a man twenty years younger. Yet there seemed, at times, a wildness in the gleam of his dark grey eyes, which increased the strangeness of appearance imparted to him by his long white hair, and impressed the observer with the idea of a visionary or a fanatic.

Having lighted the candles, the two young men pulled off their boots, and silently ascended the stairs to the chamber of Lord Clanrobert, the locality of which they had previously been made acquainted with by their sister. The younger brother placed the candle which he had brought with him on a chair, and then they approached the bed of the sleeping nobleman, who was about the age of the elder of these daring disturbers of his rest.

"Awake, Lord Clanrobert!" said the elder of the brothers, in a low, stern tone, as he rudely shook the young nobleman by the shoulder.

Lord Clanrobert instantly awoke, and, starting up in the bed, looked from one to the other with amazement and alarm.

"Arise, my lord!" exclaimed the elder brother, with a glance of cool determination.

"Who are you?" demanded the young nobleman, in a tone of surprise not unmingled with alarm.

"The brothers of Charlotte Corbett, whom you would have brought to shame and disgrace!" replied the brother of the young girl, looking sternly on the seducer.

"What is your purpose here?" demanded the aristocratic nobleman.

"To witness the performance of a solemn act of justice," replied the elder Corbett. "Arise, therefore, and dress yourself, my lord; the bride is below, and all is prepared for the ceremony."

"Are you aware, rash man, that you have committed an offence which would consign you all to the penal colonies?" exclaimed Lord Clanrobert.

"No words, my lord," returned Corbett; "we have no time to spare for useless talk. You have seduced our sister, and you must marry her or die!" and the brothers each drew forth a loaded pistol, and deliberately cocked it.

Lord Clanrobert made a sudden movement to reach the bell, but the younger Corbett anticipated his intention, and placed the rope out of his reach.

"I am willing to compromise this unfortunate affair in a handsome manner, but marriage, as you must be aware, is totally out of the question," observed the baffled peer. "What sum will satisfy your sister?"

"None!" exclaimed Corbett, indignantly. "You hesitated not to make her your victim, and, as you thought not of your dignity when you seduced her, you have no right to make it an excuse for not repairing the injury you have done her. You have only one alternative: choose between an honourable atonement and instant death."

Lord Clanrobert turned pale, and a cold perspiration stood on his forehead; he was averse to entering the matrimonial state with one who had lived in his service in a menial capacity, even though she had shared his bed, and would soon bring into the world an infant of which he was the father; and yet, with a loaded pistol on each side of his head, he was not in a position to refuse performing the act of justice required of him. But he thought that this marriage might afterwards be set aside for illegality, and the Corbetts be got rid of on the charge of burglary; and he thought it unlikely that they would insist upon more than the performance of the marriage ceremony, for the purpose of legitimising the child of which their sister would shortly become the mother. These thoughts ran rapidly through the brain of the libertine nobleman, when he found himself completely at the mercy of the resolute brothers of his victim, and he soon decided upon the course which he intended to pursue.

"If I agree to marry Charlotte now, as you require, you will not, I presume, insist upon our immediate cohabitation?" said he, getting out of bed, and preparing to dress.

"We have no wish to interfere with your lordship's domestic arrangements, after you have performed this act of justice towards our sister," returned the elder Corbett; "but your own sense of honour and right should teach you what is due to one who has sacrificed her all for you."

Lord Clanrobert made no reply to this observation, but hastily dressed himself, and descended to the drawing-room, preceded by young Corbett with the light, and followed by the elder brother with the pistol still in his hand.

"Let this mummery be concluded as speedily as possible," said Lord Clanrobert, in a haughty and petulant tone, and without deigning to notice the poor victim of his libertine arts.

"This is no mummery, my lord," said the elder Corbett, sternly; "Mr. Ashdowne is a regularly ordained minister, though not of the established church, and a special license having been procured, nothing will be wanting to render the ceremony legally binding."

Mr. Ashdowne then began reading the marriage ceremony, during which the libertine nobleman bit his lips with vexation and suppressed passion, and Charlotte Corbett sobbed audibly as she thought of his unkindness, while her brothers stood by, calm and stern, to witness the due performance of the ceremony. The ring was placed on the finger of the trembling bride, the vows of love and constancy were spoken, and at length the ceremony was concluded; but what vows can bind a heart not tied by the links of love?—chains of adamant cannot bind the inconstant, and the true require only the rosy garlands of love.

Mr. Ashdowne gave Charlotte Corbett a written certificate of the marriage, signed by himself and the witnesses, and then the party prepared to take their departure from the mansion.

"Have you not one word for me, my lord?" faintly articulated the bride, as Lord Clanrobert turned to leave the apartment; and she laid her hand on his arm in an imploring manner.

"You have acted unwisely, Charlotte, in forcing me to this step," said the young nobleman, in a hesitating manner.

"It was not my wish, George—indeed it was not! I would have trusted to your honour to do me justice," replied the weeping girl.

"You would have trusted to a broken reed!" exclaimed her brother. "There was no means, but this marriage, of saving your own honour, for Lord Clanrobert, but a few minutes since, declared his union with you impossible, on account of the disparity of condition."

The libertine peer felt the blood mount to his face, at the tacit reproach of Charlotte's confiding affection, and he hastened from the room, while young Corbett endeavoured to console his weeping sister.

"Come, let us go, Charlotte," said her elder brother. "He is unworthy of so much love; and you are now Lady Clanrobert, for he cannot undo this marriage, and your child will be heir to the title and the family property."

The party then quitted the mansion in the same manner as they had entered it, and returned to Erith; Mr. Ashdowne parting with them at the gates, and going in a contrary direction.

CHAPTER IV.

CHARLOTTE CORBETT.

CHARLOTTE CORBETT, who, with her brothers James and Edward, figure so conspicuously in the preceding chapter, was the daughter of a small farmer in the county of Kent, who, after struggling hard to bring up his family respectably, was dispossessed of his farm by the proprietor, who added it to others of which he had deprived the holders, and farmed it himself, tempted to this injustice by the high price which wheat was then realizing, and the consequent profit attending agricultural operations at that period. Farmer Corbett was so crippled in his pecuniary resources, through his little capital being sunk in improvements upon the farm of which he had been dispossessed, that, though he took another, he was uable to conduct his operations with advantage, and being obliged to give it up, he gradually sank to the condition of an agricultural labourer. Grief soon terminated the old man's existence, and his wife speedily followed him to the last resting-place of all human kind, the " bourne from whence no traveller returns." His two sons had previously taken to a nautical life, disgusted with farming, by the reverses of their father, and the monstrous injustice with which our agrarian system is replete; and his daughter, just emerging into womanhood, went to service.

James Corbett had made several voyages to the West Indies, previous to his father's death, but afterwards made short trips to various parts of the continent, which are more profitable than long voyages to the seaman, and he also increased his means of living by small ventures in the contraband trade. The death of a distant relative having placed a considerable sum of money at his disposal, he and some others purchased a small light vessel, and engaged largely in smuggling transactions, sometimes running to Hamburgh, but oftener to Cherbourg or Flushing. There were two causes, at that period, which led to the extent to which the contraband traffic was then carried on—the heavy duties imposed by the legislature on foreign and colonial produce, in order to meet the ruinous expenses of the liberticidal war with France, and the risk to which our merchant-vessels were exposed of being captured by French privateers, and the consequent high price of the produce of foreign countries and our colonies. The purchasers of contraband goods were tempted by the high price of the commodity upon which the duty had been paid; and the large profits derived from the traffic were sufficient inducement for men to eagerly engage in it, while the adventure and excitement attending upon it made it as attractive as the army or the navy.

Edward Corbett embarked in the same traffic with his brother, who had married a year or two previous to the date at which our tale commences, and whose wife occupied the cottage at Erith, from which we have seen the brothers and sister issue at the commencement of the preceding chapter. Charlotte was at that time in the service of Lord Clanrobert, a gay young nobleman, who had recently succeeded to the title by the death of his elder brother, who had been thrown from his horse, while riding a steeple-chase, and killed on the spot. The late lord had never been married, and hence his brother succeeded to the title.

Lord Clanrobert was what is termed in fashionable society—that sphere in which every thing bears a false name—a *gay man*. How lightly is that word often used, and yet how many vices does it not often gloss over! How often is it the synonyme for the swindler of honest men and the seducer of virtuous women!

"A fellow-feeling makes us wondrous kind;"

and it may be a tender consideration, based upon the principle that those who live in glass houses should not throw stones, which prompts the use of the phrase in aristocratic circles. But such considerations are unfelt by us, and should ever be disregarded by those whose necessity is caused by aristocratic selfishness and profligacy. Byron represents the devil as enjoying a sinecure, since mortals damn themselves fast enough of their own accord; and sure are we that no effort of ours is required to bring the aristocracy of this country into that contempt which their own conduct is rapidly drawing upon themselves. The newspapers of the last few weeks have teemed with the records of aristocratic turpitude. One noble lord appears at the bar of one of the metropolitan police-courts for stealing a slipper—another, a scion of the noble house of Paget, is outlawed for omitting to surrender as a bankrupt—and, to put a climax on the whole, a third noble lord, a cabinet minister, is summoned for neglecting to pay his wheelwright's bill, a paltry sum of about seventeen pounds! And these are the hereditary legislators of our country! The reflection makes us feel ashamed of the name of Englishman.

We have said that Lord Clanrobert was a gay man: had we said that he was a man who, in the pursuit of pleasure, was restrained by no consideration that did not affect his own safety or convenience, we should not have exaggerated the selfishness or profligacy in which he was steeped. The unassuming loveliness of Charlotte Corbett attracted his attention from the moment that she entered his service, and, from the frequent opportunities he had of being alone with her, he anticipated a speedy surrender of her chastity; but the young girl was proof against all the allurements which he held out to her, with the view of tempting her from the path of virtue; and had he not at length obtained an ally in her own heart, he would never have succeeded in his dishonourable intentions. But a deep and passionate attachment for the handsome but unprincipled young nobleman stole insensibly into the guileless heart of Charlotte Corbett, and her misplaced affection betrayed her: the libertine took advantage of the deepest and holiest feelings of our nature, and the maiden's ruin was accomplished; the tears of the recording angel blotted out the register of her frailty, and the seraphs folded their wings over their eyes, that they might not behold the wickedness of men.

Then came a brief period of tenderness and dalliance; and, though marriage had never been spoken of by either, Charlotte relied on her seducer's sense of honour to repair the wrong he had done her, by making her his wife, which every right-minded man would have considered as the implied condition of the intimacy which existed between Lord Clanrobert and Charlotte Corbett. But that which was overlooked by the poor victim of aristocratic profligacy, in her ardent love, and by her betrayer in his selfishness, was soon forced upon Charlotte's conviction by the discovery that she was in that condition which would soon publish to the world her lapse from chastity; and, with mingled hopes and fears, she revealed to her seducer the result of their illicit love. Then was the sunshine of life's morning clouded with doubt and sorrow—Love's myrtle nipped by the chilling frosts of fear, and the withered roses scattered on his altar. Lord Clanrobert received the intelligence with ill-concealed vexation, and he coldly advised her to leave his house, and take lodgings in London, but said not a word of marriage.

Charlotte saw at once that her hopes were wrecked, and that the idol which she had taught her heart to worship was but a cold and selfish profligate, to whom the softer feelings of the heart were all unknown; but she neither remonstrated with her betrayer, nor reproached him with his perfidy and cruelty, for no promise of marriage had been made to her; and though she reflected bitterly on the wind-shaken reed to which her heart had clung, pride came to her aid, and she left the mansion of her seducer, and sought an asylum in the cottage of her elder brother, to whose wife she confided the secret that preyed upon her heart. Mrs. Corbett then, unknown to the afflicted girl, had an interview with Lord Clanrobert, and urged him to repair the wrong he had done her sister-in-law, by marrying her; but the libertine treated with contempt the idea that he would compromise the dignity of his family by wedding one so far beneath him as Charlotte Corbett. The kind-hearted woman then besought him, at least, to settle an annuity on his victim, and provide for the future maintenance of the child, which he declared was out of his power, and added that he had doubts whether the forthcoming child was his own. At this heartless insult to her husband's sister, Mrs. Corbett withdrew from his lordship's presence; and, as her mission had been productive of no good result, she forbore to inform Charlotte of her visit to the mansion of her betrayer.

But when James Corbett and his brother became acquainted with the seduction of their sister by Lord Clanrobert, and the manner in which she had subsequently been treated, they were deeply indignant at his profligate and unmanly conduct, and resolved, at all hazards, to compel him to marry the victim of his wiles and her own tender and too trusting heart. Hence the midnight visit to the mansion of Lord Clanrobert, whose union with Charlotte was solemnized, as we have seen, by a clergyman named Ashdowne, with all the necessary forms of law. The minister whom the Corbetts had procured to perform that strange marriage had formerly been the admired pastor of an Independent congregation at Deptford, but had seceded from that church, and had for several years rambled about the country, addressing large congregations in the open air, and enunciating, with the most fervid eloquence, doctrines peculiar to himself, in the advocacy of which his enthusiasm sometimes rose to fanaticism. By some he was called the " Mad Parson," and indeed it was often hard to say whether genius or insanity most predominated in his discourses; but his admirers held that there was method in his madness, as there was in Hamlet's, and that his preaching was considered insane only by those to whom his doctrines were unpalatable. His usual theme was the Last Judgment, which he declared was near; and he called upon all to repent of their iniquities, abandon all worldly considerations, and fit themselves for heaven by prayer and self-denial.

On the day after the marriage, under such extraordinary circumstances, of Lord Clanrobert and Charlotte Corbett, the young bride received a note from her husband, requesting her to meet him at a certain hour and place, and proceed with him to London. What this might presage, Charlotte knew not, but her heart beat with re-awakened hope; and when she met Lord Clanrobert, and he spoke to her, as he handed her into his barouche, with something like his former tenderness, she felt that she could love him as tenderly as ever, if he behaved kindly to herself and the hapless babe to which she would shortly give birth. There was a constraint upon the manners of both towards each other at first, but it soon wore off, and, after gently reproaching her with the scene of the preceding night, a perfect reconciliation seemed to be effected. Lord Clanrobert even acceded to Charlotte's wish to reside at Greenwich; and, instead of taking her to London, as he had originally contemplated, he took comfortable furnished apartments for her in that town, and promised to acknowledge her as his wife, on the death of an uncle, which he represented as being probably near, and from whom he had large expectations. Charlotte was overjoyed with this apparent revival of regard on the part of her husband, and they separated on good terms, Lord Clanrobert returning to Erith the same night.

CHAPTER V.

THE CHRISTENING PARTY.

NEARLY twelve months had elapsed since the singular marriage of Lord Clanrobert and Charlotte Corbett; the occurrences of which period of time may be related in a few words. No clue had been discovered to the missing Lolah Hastings, though her father had been indefatigable in his search; and Charlotte remained on the same terms with Lord Clanrobert as we left her in the preceding chapter. She had given birth to a charming boy; and as her husband's uncle had not yet given up the ghost, she continued to pass as Mrs. Macrae; which was the family name of Lord Clanrobert.

It was a cool night in early spring, when a numerous and joyous party were assembled in the parlour of the White Hart, in Ratcliffe-highway, now called St. George-street. One of the group—and, perhaps, the most important, since he was the unwilling cause of all the revelry—was a chubby boy of about six months old, the first-born of one Sam Skelter and Mary his wife. The said Sam Skelter was a mariner; and the child having been born during his absence from England, on a voyage to Quebec, the christening had been deferred until his return to share in the festivity of the occasion. Sam Skelter was a thick-set, big-whiskered fellow about thirty years of age, with a devil-may-care expression upon his sun-burnt countenance, and small grey eyes twinkling with hilarity and grog; his wife was a few years younger, and had formerly been bar-maid at the tavern in which they had now met to celebrate the christening of their first-born. The lodgings of the happy couple were at Rotherhithe; but as the bantling had been admitted into the fold of the Protestant church at Stepney, where its parents had been united in the bonds of matrimony about twelve months previously, they had agreed to keep the christening at the White Hart; where they thought they could be more comfortable than at their own lodgings.

The rest of the party consisted of the sponsors; who were Mrs. Skelter's sister, a merry, blue-eyed girl of twenty summers; and her lover, a young sailor, whose accomplishments consisted in being able, in the words of one of Dibdin's inimitable sea-songs,

> " To dance and to sing, and to play on the fiddle,
> And swig, with an air, his allowance of grog."

We must not forget the nurse, a portly dame, smelling strongly of gin, who would have deemed herself slighted had she not been invited to the christening

LOST MY BLESSED LEGS IN THE FROZEN OCEAN

of the little squaller whom she had assisted to usher into the world. In addition to these, there were present half-a-dozen jolly tars, the shipmates and boon companions of Sam Skelter, and as many bright-eyed, rosy-cheeked young women, who either had lovers among the sailors aforesaid, or were exerting their utmost powers of pleasing to obtain them. The men were smoking long pipes, and imbibing deep potations of divers compounds of ardent spirits, hot water, and sugar; and the young women laughed and chatted, and sipped from the glasses of their companions; while the joke, the song, and the toast went merrily round the festive board.

"Let's drink the young 'un's health," suggested a red-nosed tar; and he forthwith raised his glass to an angle of forty degrees, and poured the potent contents down his throat.

"The health of Samuel Skelter, junior; and may he be as good a man as his father!" said the nurse, with much gravity; and having drank the toast, the good woman hiccupped, as if the liquor did not agree with her.

"And may we have such a one before this time next year!" was the addition

3

made, in a whisper from the godfather to the godmother, the lively sister of Mary Skelter.

"Get along with you, do!" returned Caroline, blushing and smiling at the same time, as she bestowed a hearty slap on the young sailor's shoulder.

"Messmates!" said Sam Skelter, rising, with his glass in one hand and his pipe in the other; "in rising to return you thanks, on behalf of the young 'un, for the honour you have done him in drinking his health, I ought to tell you the reason why this sprinkling business has been deferred until this occasion. You must know, then, that when I went out in the Gally-te-a, Poll and I had been married about six months, and consequently we had laid the keel——"

"Come, sit down, Sam, and drink your grog," interrupted his wife, pulling him into his chair, amid the laughter of the sailors, and the suppressed titter of the young women.

"Well, who will give us a song?" exclaimed Sam Skelter; and without waiting for a response, he began:

> "One night came on a hurricane,
>   The sea was mountains rolling;
> When Barney Buntline turned his quid,
>   And says to Billy Bowling——"

"Oh, I am quite sick of that," observed Mrs. Skelter; "do try something else."

"Ned is going to sing us one," said Caroline; and the young sailor by whom she was sitting threw his arms round the young woman's waist, and sang the following stanzas:

> "The glowing maids of Grecia's isles
>   Have charms a king might prize;
> And none can tell the lovesome wiles
>   That lurk in their dark eyes.
> But dearer far to the British tar,
>   Though far and wide he roam,
> The cheeks so fair, and light-brown hair,
>   Of his own little girl at home!
>
> Oh, brightly beams the maiden's eye,
>   On Coromandel's coast,
> Whose burning glances might outvie
>   Golconda's sparkling boast.
> Their charms so rare might well compare
>   With Venus from the foam;
> But dearer far to a British tar,
>   His own little girl at home!"

The young sailor concluded his song amidst the applause of all the company, except one weather-beaten old tar with an anchor marked on the back of each hand, who declared that "it warn't half so good as 'Bound 'prentice to a coasting ship,'" which he began singing at the top of his voice, but was compelled to desist by the females of the company.

All the sailors had now decidedly got as much grog aboard as they could stagger under; and though we will not be so ungallant as to say so much of the young women, yet even some of them began to see four candles where there were only two; and the old nurse was in that state of obliviousness in which she began to talk of old friends and old times, and to exchange vows of friendship, over the snuff-box, with every one who was unfortunate enough to be near her. At length Sam Skelter suggested, that as they had to cross the river, and it was getting late, they had better be getting under weigh; then the young women put on their bonnets, and Ned helped Caroline with her shawl, and at last all were prepared for their departure.

"Heave ahead, my hearties!" exclaimed Sam; and then he led the way to the street in a zigzag fashion, followed by his wife and the rest of the party.

The adieux occupied some time, and more than one kiss was exchanged between the sailors and the young women; and then the joyous party separated; and Sam Skelter described a curious line of beauty across the street, followed by his wife and the nurse, and plunged into the dirty streets of Wapping.

Ratcliffe-highway was through a densely-populated portion of the ancient parish of Stepney—which formerly comprehended Shadwell, Limehouse, and Poplar; and from thence to the waterside is a maze of little streets, courts, and blind alleys, forming a dark, dirty, vice-infested region, as little known to the inhabitants of the west-end of the metropolis as the unexplored plains of Central Australasia. At the corner of almost every street is a public-house or a gin-shop, blazing with gas and plate-glass, and adorned within with fixtures of mahogany and polished brass, forming a strange contrast to the abject poverty and squalid misery in the very midst of which it rears its head. The other houses are principally those of pawnbrokers, most of whom also cash the advance-notes of seamen; marine-store dealers, who drive a profitable trade with the river-pirates; crimps, who derive large profits from their dealings with our hard-working and generous-hearted seamen; tobacconists, who retail tobacco at a lower price than the wholesale rate of manufacturers in other parts of the metropolis; and ship-brokers, who appear to break their ships very small, or to be in a very small way of business. These, with outfitters and ship-chandlers, make up the principal occupants of the better streets. The cross-streets and courts are very dirty, and badly lighted; and there is a necessary accordance between the dirty, undrained, and badly-ventilated dwellings, with the stagnant gutters before the doors, and the black puddles which stand amid the broken pavement, and the minds and morals of those who inhabit them. The dark and pestiferous lanes and courts abound with houses let out in lodgings to labourers of the lowest class, and women and girls who sell apples, oranges, and roasted chesnuts, or make sacks for the corn-factors in Mark-lane. The lower part of these houses is often a coal-shed, a fried-fish warehouse, or a marine-store repository. The darkest and dirtiest courts harbour that numerous class of degraded females with which, like all resorts of shipping, this part of the metropolis abounds. In this quarter, one of these females will serve as a type of the whole—short, stout, slatternly girls, who parade the highway, and haunt the taverns, of Wapping and Shadwell, with bare necks and bosoms, and without bonnets.

Through this region of material filth and spiritual depravity, Sam Skelter staggered along, followed by his wife with the nurse and child; and at length they reached the stairs at which they intended to take a boat to convey them to Rotherhithe. The night was dark; a mizzling rain had begun to fall, and the wind howled and moaned among the chimneys, and caused the sails to flap mournfully against the masts of the vessels lying on the river, and the blocks to creak with a dreary and depressing sound. A mass of black and threatening clouds overhung the river; and the opposite shore would have been invisible amid the darkness and the mist, but for the lights which glimmered along the line of buildings near the water.

"Steady!" cried the waterman, as Sam Skelter almost tumbled into the boat, and his fare having taken their seats, began pulling with a will towards Rotherhithe.

CHAPTER VI.

THE MURDER ON THE RIVER.

ON the same evening that Sam Skelter and his friends celebrated the christening of the infant Skelter at the White Hart, in Ratcliffe-highway, Mrs. Macrae, as Charlotte Corbett called herself, until she could assume the title of Lady Clanrobert, accompanied her husband up the river as far as Battersea. Lord Clanrobert had hired a boat for the purpose, and rowed himself, as the weather was fine, and the air mild, in the earlier part of the evening. Charlotte took her baby with them; and they repaired to the celebrated Red House, where they took tea, and from the front windows of which they gazed on the river, with its old wooden bridge, the narrow arches of which scarcely afford room for the passage of the Richmond steamers and the boats and barges which are continually passing up and down.

During the evening, the manners of Lord Clanrobert towards his wife were the same as they had been since their marriage—tender, attentive, yet less so than during the period of love's sunshine which preceded the ill-omened night of their strange nuptials. But when night came on, and they embarked at Battersea to return to Greenwich, his manner was perceptibly changed, and he sat moody and reserved, rowing slowly, as if he wished to prolong the voyage.

As the shades of night gathered over the river and the city, symptoms of a coming storm were visible, yet Lord Clanrobert made no exertion to accelerate the speed of the boat: dark clouds were gathering up from all parts of the heavens; the wind howled and moaned like a chorus of infernal spirits; and, to add to the discomfort of Charlotte and the child, it began to rain. She entreated her husband to pull to the Lambeth shore, and obtain a hackney-coach to convey them to Greenwich, instead of continuing the journey by water; but he sullenly refused, and continued to row slowly down the river.

The storm continued to increase; the wind and the heavy rain, which now poured down in torrents, raised the river into waves, and the little boat was tossed up and down, as if it had been on the open sea. Charlotte wrapped her shawl around the little innocent in her arms; but it began to cry, notwithstanding her attention; and its father's brow grew more dark and gloomy as the sounds reached his ears.

" Throw that squalling brat into the river!" he exclaimed, suddenly; and Charlotte started violently, not less at the nature of the command, than the savage tone in which it was delivered.

" Good God! what is the matter, George? you frighten me!" exclaimed Charlotte, trembling and turning pale.

" I will frighten you a little more, presently," returned her husband, brutally; and he seized the child, and attempted to snatch it from her.

" No, no, George!—dear George, you will not harm our child!" screamed Charlotte, endeavouring to retain the child.

" Give it up!" cried Lord Clanrobert, fiercely; and dragging the screaming child from its mother's grasp, he struck her violently on the temple with his clenched fist, and she fell into the foaming river.

The howling of the wind drowned the shriek which burst from the pale lips of the unfortunate young woman; and the darkness which overhung the river concealed the foul and dastardly deed from every human eye.

" Loathed image of thy hated mother, thou too must die!" exclaimed Lord Clanrobert; and raising the innocent child with one hand, he flung it into the river, and then pulled rapidly towards the Surrey shore.

The part of the river where this brutal and deliberate murder was committed was opposite Rotherhithe-wall; and at that time a waterman's boat was conveying Sam Skelter, his wife and child, and the nurse, across the river in that direction. They had not witnessed the double murder attempted by Lord Clanrobert; but, as the waterman pulled across the stream, they beheld the bodies of the mother and child floating down with the tide.

" Hulloa! here's a woman and a kid—hold hard!" cried Sam Skelter; and the more than half-intoxicated seaman leaned suddenly over the side of the boat, and attempted to clutch the garments of the unfortunate Charlotte; but the sudden lurch upset the boat, and the whole party were precipitated into the river.

Sam Skelter was a good swimmer; and his wife clung to the boat, and screamed as only a woman can scream; but the old nurse and the child were gone. Sam swam towards the boat, and attempted to right it; and at that critical moment, another boat, with a man in it, was rowed to the spot. He was a waterman returning with his boat to Wapping Old Stairs, from landing a fare at Rotherhithe, and had already picked up a child; but the old nurse he had not seen. Sam Skelter was nearly sobered by his immersion in the river; and, between them, the boat was righted, and Mrs. Skelter assisted into it: her clothes were dripping wet; but she eagerly caught up the child which the waterman had saved, and which, in the excess of her joy, she did not perceive was not her own. The waterman was picked up in a few moments after; but the poor old nurse had disappeared, and was never heard of afterwards.

Skelter's waterman pulled over to Rotherhithe-wall, where they landed; and all three had a stiff tumbler of grog at the nearest public-house; then Sam and his wife hastened to their lodgings, to remove their wet garments as quickly as possible. Sam turned into bed; and Mary Skelter undressed herself and the child, and, in so doing, made the startling discovery that they had got the wrong child.

"Why, Sam, look here!" exclaimed Mrs. Skelter, in a tone of unfeigned surprise; "this isn't our child! Look at the clothes—they are better and finer than ours!"

"Why, that must be the little chap as I capsized the boat in grabbing arter!" said her husband.

At that hour of the night, and on a night so dark and stormy, there was no probability of the life of the other child having been preserved; and though poor Mary Skelter was for some time almost distracted for the loss of her own little boy, she could not deny the little innocent who had been, in such a singular manner, consigned to her care, the nutriment which it required. Having lost her own, she felt the more tenderly towards the foundling of the Thames, and drawing it to her bosom, wept herself to sleep.

We must now return to the river, and relate what became of the unfortunate Charlotte and the hapless infant of Mrs. Skelter. The blow which Charlotte received from her ruffian husband rendered her insensible; and in this manner she was carried along with the tide, the infant following her at a little distance behind. The waterman who came to the assistance of the Skelters picked up the child of Lord Clanrobert without seeing the corpse of its murdered mother, and, having witnessed the capsizing of Skelter's boat, rowed swiftly to their assistance, naturally supposing the child which he had saved to be theirs.

In the meantime the unfortunate nurse had sunk to the bottom of the river, in spite of the child's caul, which she had secured about her previous to leaving home, under the impression that it would prevent her from being drowned—a superstition which is now nearly exploded, and of the fallacy of which the fate of the poor old lady was a striking instance. At the time when Skelter's boat upset, another boat was coming up the river, in which was a man wearing a blue pea-jacket, checked shirt, and full blue trousers. It was James Corbett, the elder brother of the murdered wife of Lord Clanrobert.

Seeing the body of a woman coming towards him, he seized it by the dripping garments, in the humane hope that life might not yet be extinct, and dragged it into the boat. Scarcely had he accomplished this, when he observed the child, the progeny of the Skelters, and was fortunate enough to get it likewise into the boat. He then pulled swiftly towards a lugger which was lying outside the coasting-vessels moored off Rotherhithe, and which he hailed as he came alongside. A rough-looking seaman made his appearance, and assisted Corbett to get the bodies on deck, and convey them into the cabin.

"Gracious God!" exclaimed the smuggler, starting violently, as the light fell on the pale countenance of the murdered woman, whom he had placed upon the table. My sister!—and dead, too! Can there be murder in this? or is it possible she can have committed suicide? My heart misgives me strangely. Ah! a bruise on the temple: what can this mean? It might have been caused by accident, if she fell from the bridge; or it might have been the consequence of a stunning blow. And the child, too—does it breathe, Caleb?"

"Yes, the young 'un's all right, Mr. Corbett," replied the man. "See, he has opened his eyes. Shall I go ashore for a doctor?"

"It is useless, Caleb—she is quite cold," said James Corbett, in a choking tone; "and yet I scarce know how to act. I wish Ned was here——"

At that moment another boat thumped against the side of the lugger, and Edward Corbett seized a rope which hung there, and in another minute was on the deck.

"You keep a blind look-out here, Caleb," said he, as he descended to the little cabin; "the Custom-house sharks could have boarded the lugger as easily as I have. A drowned woman!" he continued, with a slight start, as he entered the cabin, and saw the corpse of his unfortunate sister lying on the table.

Struck with the saddened countenance of his brother, he quickly advanced to the table, and immediately recognised the features of the drowned woman.

"Charlotte!" he exclaimed, starting back in horror and surprise.

"I found her in the river," observed his brother, with deep emotion. "I picked up the child, too; but that is living. Look, Ned, at that bruise on the left temple, and say if this be suicide or murder."

"This is strange, and fills me with fearful thoughts," returned Edward Corbett, shuddering; and then, leaning towards his brother, he whispered: "Murder!"

"Retire, Caleb, and when Tiller comes aboard, prepare to get under weigh," said the elder Corbett; and when the sailor had left the little cabin, he turned a look of eager inquiry upon his brother.

"I saw Lord Clanrobert but just now landing from a boat at London-bridge stairs," said Edward Corbett, in an agitated voice. "He was alone, and called a waterman to take charge of the boat, and take it to Greenwich; but I did not hear the name of the person of whom he had hired it. But here is proof that he hired a boat at Greenwich, and rowed himself up the river: now we must ascertain whether Charlotte accompanied him, and take our measures accordingly."

"Then do you hurry down to Greenwich, and make the necessary inquiries," said his brother; and when Tiller comes aboard, we will drop down with the tide as far as Erith, where you will await us."

James and Edward Corbett then went on deck, and Tiller having now returned, James gave orders for getting the lugger under weigh immediately, and Edward and Caleb jumped into the boat, and rowed ashore. Leaving the sailor to return with the boat, Edward Corbett ran to the coach-stand in the High-street of Southwark, which was nearly deserted; and having elicited from one of the drivers, that a man answering to the description which the young man gave of Lord Clanrobert had hired a coach off the stand a short time previous, to take him to Greenwich, he jumped into the vehicle, and told the man he would give him a guinea if he overtook the other coach. Thus incited, the man scrambled to his box, and, by dint of various devices, such as getting up and sitting down, dropping the reins on the back of his bony horse, whipping and chirruping, the animal was persuaded to gallop down the Dover-road and along the road to Greenwich, with as much alacrity as if he had been going to his stable.

"There's t'other coach right ahead," said the jarvey, bending his head down to the window. "Am I to pass it, or keep behind?"

"Keep behind, but near enough to see where it stops," replied Edward Corbett; and when the two coaches entered Greenwich, the first was seen to stop a few minutes at the house where Charlotte had lodged, under the name of Macrae, where a gentleman got out, and, on returning to the coach, was again driven along the main Kentish-road.

"Hold hard!" cried young Corbett, as his coach came opposite the same house, and leaping out, he knocked at the door, and, on inquiring of the servant if Mr. Macrae had not just been there, she replied in the affirmative, and informed him that he had called to say that Mrs. Macrae had been taken ill in London, and was staying with some friends there.

This was strong presumptive evidence of the guilt of Lord Clanrobert; but Edward Corbett was unwilling to take any steps towards his apprehension or punishment, without consulting his brother; and as the rain had now ceased, he gave the coachman his stipulated reward, and, hurrying from the town, walked quickly towards Erith, which he calculated upon reaching nearly as soon as the lugger.

CHAPTER VII.

THE MURDERER AND HIS VICTIM.

HAVING a favourable wind, and the advantage of the tide, the lugger reached Erith before Edward Corbett, and her commander immediately went ashore, taking the poor little infant with him, and knocked up his wife, to whom he communicated the sad fate of his sister, which he strictly enjoined her to keep secret, and to whose affectionate care he consigned the child. Edward Corbett called at the cottage before going aboard the lugger, and between them a scheme was devised for securing the succession of the child to the title and estates of Lord Clanrobert, which was rightly considered as better than taking vengeance upon the murderer in a manner which would leave his supposed offspring unprovided for. In pursuance of this scheme, Mrs. Corbett accompanied her husband and Edward on board the lugger, taking the child with her, and the voyage was then continued as far as Gravesend. A brief epistle was then written, and having been addressed to Lord Clanrobert, was posted early in the morning, the lugger lying-to off the town until the evening.

Lord Clanrobert arrived at his mansion after midnight, and immediately retired to rest; and, despite the foul deed that he had so recently committed, he did rest. Wherever conscientiousness is imperfectly developed, there may we find a life of crime attended by as much equanimity of mind as if the offender were the most amiable and virtuous person in existence. Remorse and horror are not the invariable attendants of the guilty, but depend upon the individual's greater or less development of conscientiousness: those in whom the organ is large, and the other qualities in harmony with this, will feel more acute remorse for the inadvertent crushing of a worm, than those in whom the organ is deficient will experience after the commission of an atrocious murder. Its development is usually in proportion to that of the moral faculties generally, and as we can readily suppose that the brain of the libertine Clanrobert afforded but a low standard of these, we may infer from thence that there was a deficiency of conscientiousness in the same ratio.

At noon on the day following the murder, Lord Clanrobert received a letter, the contents of which filled him with consternation and dread. It bore no signature, and ran as follows: "All is discovered! Fly from Erith the moment you receive this, and at nightfall a boat will await you on the banks of the river, opposite the chalk-pits at Northfleet. A friend has engaged a lugger to carry you to the Continent. Ask no questions—hesitate not; your life depends upon your compliance with these suggestions."

Lord Clanrobert turned pale, and trembled, and a cold perspiration stood upon his forehead, as he perused these lines; and when he had concluded, the letter fell from his hand, his knees smote each other, and he remained with his eyes fixed on vacancy with a horrible and stony glare. Thus he sat for some time, as if suddenly struck into marble; and then, comprehending all at once the necessity of instant flight, he started up, thrust the letter into his pocket, and telling his housekeeper that he was going away for a few days, he quitted the house, and hurried towards Northfleet. He avoided the high road as far as was practicable, and, on reaching the above village, he went into the "Leather Bottle," and engaged a private room until the evening, saying that he had many letters of business to write. It was not until ten o'clock that he ventured from the alehouse, and stole like a guilty thing down to the shore near the chalk-pits, where he found a boat lying, with two men who were strangers to him, and apparently common sailors.

Tiller and Caleb (for they were the rowers) touched their caps to the young nobleman, and, without speaking, Lord Clanrobert stepped into the boat, which they immediately pulled towards the lugger. Pale and agitated, and wondering who his anonymous friend could be, and how the murder had been discovered, he sat trembling in the boat, as it was swiftly propelled over the rippling surface of the Thames, and in a few minutes they were alongside. He looked eagerly around him as he gained the deck, but no one was there; Tiller then touched his cap, and informed him that his friends were in the cabin, to which he led the way.

Lord Clanrobert started, as if he had trod upon a serpent, when he entered the little cabin of the lugger, and there encountered the stern glances of James and Edward Corbett, who, with loaded pistols in their belts, stood behind a table on which lay some object covered with a piece of sailcloth, which hung down like a funeral pall. A convulsive shudder agonized his frame at this scene, and, clasping his hands in wild consternation, the murderer's eyes were fixed, with a terrible presentiment, upon the object covered with the pall.

" Lord Clanrobert," said James Corbett, addressing the guilty man, whom terror seemed to have deprived of the faculty of speech, in a voice at once deep, calm, and stern, " knowest thou the features of the dead ?"

As he spoke, he raised the sailcloth pall, and revealed the inanimate remains of his murdered sister. A cry of horror burst from the white lips of Lord Clanrobert, and he recoiled from the ghostly object which his own hand had made, and would have rushed from the cabin, had not the door been closed and fastened. The blanched cheeks of the corpse, the fixed blue eyes which seemed to glare horribly upon him, the long light-brown hair with whose silken tresses he had often dallied with a lover's admiration, the cold blue lips which his own had often pressed with passionate warmth, formed a spectacle which chilled the murderer's soul with horror.

" Take it away !" cried he, in a tone of fear and dread. " I did not do it !— she fell into the river !"

" Fearest thou to look upon thine own work ?" said James Corbett, slowly dropping the pall, and fixing his keen glance on the horror-stricken countenance of the murderer. " If such sudden consternation seize upon your guilty soul at this moment, how will you stand at the bar of God, when the victim of your treachery rises to brand you with the charge of murder ? You thought that, because no eye saw the fatal blow, and no ear heard the dying shriek of your ill-fated victim, that your crime would remain for ever unknown and unpunished. Vain, presumptuous, guilty wretch ! there is a Providence over all ! Though none saw that blow—none heard that dying shriek, yet that overruling Providence, without whose special knowledge not even a sparrow falls to the ground, directed its instruments to the detection of the foul deed ; and, before the body of your victim was cold, the avengers of the innocent were on your track !"

" Spare me !" cried the wretched Clanrobert, averting his face, and speaking in a thick, husky voice. " I am guilty !—I confess the crime—but spare me !"

" Ask mercy of God, whose creature you have robbed of that gift which you can never restore," returned James Corbett, solemnly. " What mercy had you for her who is here?—she who loved you with all the passionate devotion of which woman's nature is capable, who had been the partner of your bed, and who was the mother of your child. And yet all those ties, the dearest which man can know, and which even the most savage beasts respect, you ruthlessly snapped, and sent mother and child to eternity without a moment's preparation ! Perhaps it would be no more than your crime deserves, were I to hang you, like a dog, to the yard-arm of the lugger ; but I wish not to arrogate to myself that power over life which should remain with Him who gave it. I wish, too, to render your life productive of good, while your death would be but a vain and sterile example. You have committed a crime which a long life of penitence can never fully atone for, for tears of bitterest anguish will not restore your victim to life ; but I thirst not for your blood, and I leave you to the judgment of the Almighty. You are free—' Go, and sin no more.' "

" On one condition, you are free ; but that condition must be complied with," said the smuggler.

" What is it ?" gasped Clanrobert, recovering his faculties. " I will do anything you require of me, so that you spare my life."

" By suffering you to escape from the penalty of your crime, I throw you upon society, to follow the promptings of your evil passions, without having any power or control over you," replied James Corbett. " That power I must have ; you must, therefore, write, to my dictation, a confession of your crime, and I pledge my word never to use it, unless you again sin against me or mine. There are writing materials ; kneel down, and write upon the chair."

Lord Clanrobert was glad to escape an ignominious death, even by this humiliation ; and, kneeling down, he penned the following confession, with a trembling hand, from the dictation of his stern judge :

" Upon my knees, in the cabin of James Corbett's lugger, off Gravesend, I confess that, on the night of February 10th, 1816, I murdered my wife, Charlotte Macrae, by throwing her into the Thames below London-bridge, from a boat in which I had rowed her from Battersea."

"Sign it," said James Corbett; and the culprit completed the document by affixing his signature.

"Write again," continued the smuggler, folding the confession, and placing another sheet of paper before Lord Clanrobert, who, with visible astonishment in his features, wrote the following lines to the dictation of James Corbett:

"I hereby declare that I was legally married to Charlotte Corbett, as set forth in the register of the Rev. Robert Ashdowne, and that George Macrae, the only issue of that marriage, and who was born at Greenwich, and whose baptism is duly registered in the parish-church of that place, is my true and legitimate heir."

"Does the child live?" inquired Lord Clanrobert, with a start of surprise.

"Sign the declaration," said James Corbett; and when the nobleman had done this, he and his brother affixed their signatures as witnesses.

"The child does live, my lord," said James Corbett; "and now you may guess why I required the confession, for that is a guarantee for the future security of the child, which is under my guardianship; and, until he attains the

4

age of manhood, I shall keep a watchful eye upon him. I have pledged my word that the confession shall never be divulged, unless you compel me to take that step by your machinations against the future interests of the child; and I trust that you will take warning by the events of this night, and endeavour, by a life of usefulness and goodness, to atone for the evil you have already committed. Go, my lord—you are free!"

Lord Clanrobert had risen from his suppliant posture while James Corbett was speaking, and, when he had concluded, he turned and left the cabin, humiliated by the position to which he had reduced himself by his crimes, and yet scarcely knowing whether he were dreaming or awake. The voice of James Corbett came upon his stupefied sense of hearing like the sounds that we hear in a dream; and it was not until he stood upon the deck of the lugger, and the cool air of night fanned his cheeks, that he felt fully awake. Edward Corbett followed him on deck; and, in obedience to his orders, Caleb rowed the young nobleman ashore, landing him at the same point from whence he had been taken off. Caleb then returned to the lugger, which immediately got under weigh; and Lord Clanrobert, after walking along the beach to compose the intense agitation of his mind, proceeded to Gravesend, and there hired a post-chaise to return to Erith.

CHAPTER VIII.

THE CHANGELING.

The lugger proceeded on her voyage to Hamburgh, and on the third night after the murder on the Thames, the body of Charlotte Corbett was taken on deck, sewed up in a hammock, to which were attached several cannon-balls, to insure its sinking, preparatory to its being consigned to the bottom of the ocean. It was a wild and stormy night, and the light vessel of the smugglers rushed over the foam-crested billows, under the impulse of the gale; and so dark was the sky, that the waves seemed to mingle with the clouds, as if nothing separated the darkness of the heavens from the darkness of the ocean. The brothers of the deceased, with Mrs. Corbett, and Tiller, stood around the bier, which was covered with the ensign; and Caleb having taken the wheel, James Corbett began to read the service of the church for the burial of the dead at sea.

During the performance of this last act of respect to the memory of their ill-fated sister, the gale increased to a perfect hurricane; the masts bent, the wind drove the lugger deeper into the water, and she cast the spray from her bows as she dashed along, leaving in her wake a long line of white foam upon the dark bosom of the ocean. Tiller glanced more than once at the straining rigging of the vessel, with an air of anxiety, during the reading of the burial-service, and, when it was concluded, the ensign was removed, and the body of the murdered Charlotte was consigned to the waves of the German Ocean, amid the creaking of the masts, the snapping of cordage, and the rattling of blocks, as the topmast-yard bent like a whip, and, snapping in two, fell upon the deck with a crash, bringing the sail with it.

"Furl everything!" was the loud command of James Corbett, immediately the ceremony was concluded; and his brother and the seaman Tiller sprang aloft to execute the order with the rapidity necessary to insure the safety of the vessel.

The wild career of the lugger was thus checked by the removal of the strain upon her rigging, and the wind no longer drove her with irresistible speed through the water, but whistled through her shrouds and naked masts. Towards morning the force of the gale diminished, as if its fury was expended, and the lugger reached Hamburgh without the occurrence of any other incident worth recording.

Mrs. Corbett had sailed in the lugger with her husband, in order to insure the safety of the child whom the latter had rescued from the Thames, until some steps could be taken to obtain from Lord Clanrobert a sufficient guarantee for the succession of the child of his hapless victim to the peerage. Some accidental resemblance between the two children who had been immersed in the river on the night of the murder, caused the mistake of one for the other; natural enough under the circumstances, when we consider the equality of age, the resemblance, and the almost general likeness which pervades the features of children of that tender age. We have seen that Mrs. Skelter discovered the mistake when too late to rectify it; but, as the Corbetts had not seen the child of their sister sufficiently often to distinguish it, under the peculiar circumstances of the case, from any other child, it was naturally concluded by them that the infant which James Corbett had picked up in the Thames could be no other than the offspring of Lord Clanrobert and their ill-fated sister. Thus, while the heir to an ancient title reposed beneath the humble roof of Sam Skelter, the seaman's child was tenderly nurtured, and regarded as the son and heir of Lord Clanrobert. In order, therefore, that future portions of our narrative may be fully understood, we shall call them by the names by which they were respectively known in the widely different spheres in which they were to move: the peer's offspring must be called by the name given to the lost child of his adopted father, and the seaman's child regarded as the son of Lord Clanrobert.

On the return of the lugger from Hamburgh, it was decided that the child should remain for the present in the charge of Mrs. Corbett, who waited upon Lord Clanrobert, taking with her the infant, to ascertain his intentions with reference to a provision for its maintenance. The nobleman seemed somewhat embarrassed by Mrs. Corbett's visit, but, by allowing her to open the business of the interview, he gained time to recover from the agitation caused by the reflections on the scene, on board the lugger, which her presence excited. He offered to make a handsome allowance for the child's future maintenance, and gave Mrs. Corbett a twenty-pound note for her present use. But when she unfolded the shawl in which she had enveloped the infant, in order to protect it from the cold, and Lord Clanrobert glanced at the countenance of the little innocent, he started slightly, and a strange expression stole over his features, which the smuggler's wife ascribed to the recollection of his dastardly attempt on the life of his offspring, after the murder of Charlotte.

But when Mrs. Corbett had quitted the room, that expression became more strange and sinister; and as Lord Clanrobert stood before the fire, musing on what had caused that sudden start, he gave an half-audible utterance to the reflections which were passing through his mind.

"This is most strange!" he muttered, in an abstracted tone. "I dare not look upon it as an interposition of Providence in my behalf, and yet no accident ever happened more opportunely than this mysterious coincidence. I could scarce endure to look upon the brat, and yet how fortunate was that momentary glance which enabled me to make such an unexpected discovery! The child of that girl did really, then, meet the fate which I intended for it, and found a watery grave in the Thames, and this brat is some luckless changeling. Can some accident on the river have caused it to be mistaken for *her* child, or is it but an imposture devised by her brothers? May it not be the child of that woman and that amphibious skipper of the lugger? Yet these people seem honest and upright, and the child may, after all, be some infant lost in the Thames on that night which rid me of wife and heir in one brief moment. I can take time to mature my plans, for I feel assured that these Corbetts will deal honourably with me; and surely they will not insist on calling the child mine, if I can prove that it is not the offspring of that ill-starred amour."

Thus mused this bad man upon the discovery which he had made, and which he resolved to make subservient to some plan for emancipating himself from the thraldom in which he feared he would be held by the smugglers, through their knowledge of his guilt in respect to the murder of their sister. Released from the terror inspired by the scene on board the lugger, which he never recalled to his mind without a shudder, and assured of personal safety by his victim's brothers, who alone were cognisant of his atrocious crime, this inveterately selfish man sought not to follow the counsel given him by James Corbett on that terrible night, but rather to release himself from their influence, and plunge anew into a career of sensual profligacy. The period of which we are now writing was not one which abounded in moral examples in that class which we are taught to look up to with respect and reverence; the reigning sovereign,

George III., by his private marriage with Hannah Lightfoot, whom he afterwards repudiated for a princess, had set an example which his eldest son soon followed, and sowed in his youth the seeds of disquietude, which caused him many a pang in his declining days. His daughter, the Princess Sophia, formed an illicit connexion with her half-brother, the offspring of her father's private union with Hannah Lightfoot, without being aware of the relationship, and the result was a child, now on the pension-list of this over-taxed country. The Prince Regent, that modern Heliogabalus, had been privately married to Mrs. Fitzherbert, whom he afterwards repudiated for the unfortunate Caroline of Brunswick; and, in addition to the beautiful Fanny Robinson, the list of his adulteries and seductions would fill a volume. His next brother, the Duke of York and *Bishop of Osnaburg*, revelled in the charms of the haughty beauty Mrs. Clarke; and his third brother, the Duke of Clarence, lived with Mrs. Jordan in the quiet seclusion of Bushy-park, endeared to him by the affection of one whom he afterwards deserted, and left to perish in poverty and neglect.

Lord Clanrobert was, therefore, a type of the morality of the day, and only reflected the vices of the superior luminaries of society, as the planets reflect the light thrown on them by the sun; but the sun in this comparison was only a parhelion.

But all the base and selfish schemes of the profligate young nobleman were frustrated, and his career suddenly terminated, by an attack of apoplexy, about twelve months after the murder of his wife. As his marriage with that ill-fated young woman had hitherto been a profound secret in the fashionable world, a claim to the peerage was preferred by a cousin; but on the evidence of the marriage being produced in the committee appointed by the House of Lords to examine the conflicting claims, the legitimacy of George Macrae was fully proved; and as the property appertaining to the heir was very considerable, the infant was made a ward of the Lord Chancellor.

James Corbett destroyed Lord Clanrobert's confession of the murder of his wife, as soon as he heard of that nobleman's decease; but the declaration of his marriage, as well as the certificate of the marriage, he preserved, in case any event might arise which should require their production. Lord Clanrobert, as we shall in future term the foundling of the Thames, remained under the guardianship of his maternal relations until he was old enough to be placed at a preparatory school, from whence he was in due time removed to Eton-college to complete his education. With this statement, we must take a leap of ten years, premising that nothing occurred during that period to affect the situations of the two children who were changed in such a remarkable manner, on the night of the murder on the Thames; and that the fate of Lolah Hastings still remained unknown to her father, as if it were for ever to be involved in mystery.

But there is ever a moral revolution in the affairs of mankind which accords with the orbital revolution of the earth in its appointed track through the boundless regions of space; and though error and injustice may prevail for a time, truth and right will ever be triumphant at the last. Let this reflection teach us not to despair, but look forward with faith and hope to the good time coming.

CHAPTER IX.

THE LOST HEIR.

ONE fine evening, about ten years after the date at which this tale commenced, a middle-aged man and a boy were sitting by the side of the road in Ratcliffe-highway—not seated on the pavement, but on the roadway, so as to face the passers-by. The man had a bronzed and weather-beaten countenance, in which, however, a physiognomist might have detected an expresssion of cunning and dissipation: he wore an old straw hat with a blue ribbon round it, a tattered blue jacket, and dirty white duck trousers, tied round the stumps of his legs, both of which had been amputated at the knee. The boy was about ten years old, and was likewise dressed in a blue jacket and white trousers, a straw hat on his curly head, and a belt round his waist, to complete the picture of a "man-of-war's man" in miniature. Before them lay a vividly-coloured representation, on canvass, of a ship among the icebergs of the Polar Sea, with a boat's crew attacking a whale, which was spouting water to an amazing height; and on a large piece of floating ice were two white bears, looking very ferociously at the adventurous seamen. Underneath this picture was written—"Lost my blessed legs by frost in the Frozen Ocean."

"Come, Sam, let's hook it—we've got enough for to-day," said the legless sailor to the boy, raising himself on his wooden stumps as he spoke. "Come, gather up the pictur', and let us be off home."

The boy folded up the canvass, and he and the sailor trudged eastward along the highway; but they had not gone far when they saw a crowd collected in one of the streets leading to the Commercial-road, and the boy lingered to see the cause. An itinerant juggler, clad in the oriental costume, and having the olive complexion and straight black hair of the Malayan race, was tossing in the air and rapidly catching a number of brass balls, while a little girl was collecting the halfpence of the spectators, in a small tin plate. The beauty of the little girl seemed to draw forth many a coin, which the dexterity of the Malay would not alone have obtained, and a smile of pleasure pervaded the countenance of the little sailor-boy as he appeared to recognise her.

She was, indeed, a beautiful little girl : her long black hair fell in spiral ringlets, silken and glossy, upon her bare and gracefully-sloping shoulders, and her eyes, dark as night, and lustrous as its stars, were replete with expression, and derived an additional charm from the long, dark, silken lashes which fringed them, and the black and superbly-arched brows under which they had shone like twin stars. Her complexion was scarcely darker than that of the brunettes of southern France; her features accorded with the strictest rules of female beauty, and the symmetry of her form was equal to the loveliness of her countenance. She appeared not more than eleven years of age, but an artistic observer would not have hesitated to decide upon the faultlessness of her figure, when a few more years had developed it into the ripeness of womanhood. Her charming head was bare, and also her arms, on which she wore gilt armlets and bracelets; the body of her dress was of black velvet, covered with spangles, and the skirt of white muslin, as proportionately short at the knees as the body was low at the bosom; stockings of flesh-coloured silk completed the characteristic attire of the itinerant danseuse.

"Come along, don't stand gaping at that little darky, you sir!" growled the sailor, turning round to look after the boy, who had lingered behind.

The sailor-boy took a last look at the beautiful little dancer, and then ran after his adopted father, whom, we doubt not, our readers have already surmised to be no other than Sam Skelter. The boy was the offspring of the secret marriage of the late Lord Clanrobert and the unfortunate sister of James Corbett, and had been brought up by the Skelters as their own, after the loss of the little Skelter in the Thames; the latter child being now at Eton-college, and supposed by all to be the true Clanrobert. The accident which had deprived Sam Skelter of his legs occurred while stepping from one lighter to another to reach his ship, and, being very much intoxicated at the time, he slipped between them, and broke both his legs. He was removed to one of the hospitals, where amputation of both legs was found necessary; and, when he came out of the hospital, being much inclined to a lazy and dissipated mode of life, he adopted the profession of a mendicant, which he found as remunerative as the toil and danger of a seaman's life. His pictorial appeal to the benevolence of the passengers was an after-thought, and so completely successful was the imposture of the cunning seaman, that he never was without a shilling in his pocket, unless when he got drunk at night, and spent the whole proceeds of the day. His present abode was in a narrow, dirty street at Shadwell, and thither he and the boy were now wending their way.

"Come, light the fire, Sam, and put the kettle on," said he; "I am going to the Duke of York to have a drain of rum, for I ar'n't had a drop to-day; and mind the kettle boils when I come back, or it will be the worse for you."

We must here inform the reader that, during the interval of ten years which had elapsed since the loss of her child, Mrs. Skelton had eloped with the master of a trading vessel, and had not been heard of since. This was after the accident which deprived her husband of his legs, and Skelter had only refrained from abandoning the foundling of the Thames to the tender mercies of the parochial officers, on account of the many services which the boy was able to perform for him in his disabled condition. Yet the boy not unfrequently received, for all his services and attentions, what Skelter termed "monkey's allowance;" and, as the dissipated fellow only kept the boy to serve him as a slave, he was cuffed and snubbed about in a manner which would have crushed his spirits, had they not fortunately been as buoyant as cork, and as elastic as India-rubber.

The lame sailor hobbled off to the tavern, and Sam proceeded to light the fire, and prepare the evening meal, and, by the time they usually had it, the kettle boiled, and everything was ready. But Skelter had not returned, and, after waiting an hour, Sam went in search of him. Not finding him at the "Duke of York," he knew that it would be useless to run all over the neighbourhood in quest of him, and accordingly returned to their lodging. Hour after hour passed away, and, knowing by experience that his adoptive father would most probably return in a state of lamentable intoxication, he put away the bread and butter, and sat down by the fire to await his return.

Presently he heard the silvery voice of the little dancing-girl calling his name in a soft and subdued tone at the bottom of the stairs, for the Malay juggler and his *protégé* occupied the lower part of the house, and his eyes brightened as he advanced to the door, and stole softly down the stairs.

"What is the matter, Lolah?—you have been crying," said Sam, starting with surprise, as he beheld the red and tearful eyes of the little *danseuse*.

"Father has made himself mad with opium, and has turned me out, and threatened to kill me," replied the little girl, sobbing. "He is quiet for a moment now, but he will be raving again presently."

"Can't you sleep somewhere to-night, and perhaps he will forget it when he comes to his senses again?" suggested Sam.

"Oh! I can never go back, for he is flourishing his terrible creese, and he does terrify me so with his wild speeches," returned Lolah, with a shudder.

"Here comes father, drunk as usual, so I must get up-stairs," said Sam, in a hurried whisper; and he ran up the dirty stairs, and gained the room just as Skelter staggered to the door, holding the wall as he came along, to preserve his equilibrium.

"Sam," cried the drunken sailor, as he hobbled up the stairs with some difficulty, "you cantankarous young willin, where are you? So you have pretty nigh let the fire out, have you? You young wiper, you have been playing with that little imp of darkness down stairs, instead of making the kettle boil. I owes you a rope's-ending, don't I?"

"What for?" said Sam, in a tone of mingled deprecation and remonstrance.

"Oh, never mind what for," returned Skelter, looking about for some instrument of punishment; if I don't owe you one, I'll give you one against I do. Oh, here's the rope's-end—now, pull off your jacket, sir!"

"I tell you what it is," said Sam, in a resolute tone; "you are not my father—for you have told me so yourself many a time—and I am not going to be wollopped for nothing; so, if you touches me with that rope's-end, I hooks it; and then you will have to shift for yourself."

"Mutiny!" cried the drunken fellow, flourishing the piece of rope; "I'll soon flog that out of you, my man!" and he hobbled about the room after the boy, who dodged round the table, and easily evaded the blows intended for him, as Skelter was obliged to hold by one hand to keep his perpendicular.

"Come, stow it, I say!" cried the boy, as the end of the rope just reached his shoulder; and as Skelter had removed the table to have a clear deck for their action, as he expressed it, he began to think of putting his threat into execution.

"I shall have you now, sha'n't I?" exclaimed Skelter; and he raised the rope to inflict a severe blow on the back of the orphan.

"When you have caught me," returned Sam, made bold by desperation; and suddenly throwing down an old chair, the drunken sailor pitched headlong over it, and fell prostrate on the floor.

Sam ran down stairs, regardless of the fierce oaths which his adoptive father hurled after him; and in another moment he was in the street. He now began to think of what he was to do; and he found his situation by no means comfortable or encouraging for a boy of ten years old. But boys of the neglected class to which he unfortunately belonged by adoption, acquire, as a natural consequence of their position, an independence of action unknown to those more happily placed in the social scale; and young Skelter possessed a heart as light as a feather. He lingered about the street for a moment, and wondered whether the dancing-girl had gone away; and then he strolled towards Stepney-green.

It was growing late; but the principal streets were full of people, and the public-houses were blazing with gas, and from many came sounds of music and revelry. Drunken sailors were reeling about; and shameless women, with bare shoulders and bosoms, steeped in profligacy from their very childhood, were seeking their prey in every tavern, and lying in wait in every court and alley. But young Skelter was accustomed to these scenes, and they excited no remark: he kept on towards Stepney-green, and on arriving there found it, as he had expected, a scene of drunkenness and riot. The annual fair was to commence on the following day, and all the booths and stalls were already erected; and the former were filled with the very dregs of the population from all parts of the east-end of London. Drinking and singing within the booths, fighting and shouting outside, prevailed in all parts of the green; and laughter, screams, oaths, and yells formed the horrible and discordant din which arose on every side. It seemed as if all the demoralizing elements of the district were there concentrated.

Young Skelter roamed amid this saturnalia until the revellers gradually disappeared as the neighbouring clocks gave notice of another day; and when the scene of riot and dissipation had become comparatively deserted, he crawled under one of the caravans containing Wombwell's celebrated menagerie; and lying down on a heap of straw, he sank insensibly into a sound sleep.

CHAPTER X.

THE MALAY.

WHEN the Malay juggler and the dancing-girl returned to their lodgings in Shadwell, the former laid down on his bed; and having lighted his long bamboo pipe—in the tiny bowl of which he had previously placed a small piece of opium along with a little of the light, dry tobacco of Turkey—he began inhaling the narcotic fumes, and puffing them through his nostrils. He had long been in the habit of indulging, in a slight degree, in the use of this pernicious drug; and latterly he had become more and more addicted to it, and every night took his pipe as soon as he reached his lodging, and wafted his thoughts to Paradise upon the wreathing fumes. The effects of opium upon the constitution are baneful in the extreme—and it supplies the Orientals with the false and unnatural excitement which the nations of Europe seek in ardent spirits: it makes the muscles rigid, dries up the blood and emaciates the frames of its votaries, and not unfrequently causes delirium of the most violent kind. Yet a few years only have passed away since the government of this highly christian country, with a full knowledge of its life-destroying and demoralizing effects, made war upon the Chinese, because their government, more careful of the people than our own, refused to allow the importation of opium into their country.

Opium drew the mind of Alompra from brooding over his jealousy and revenge, and transported him, in the strange visions which it inspires, to the realms of bliss; and in the amaranth bowers of Paradise a thousand houris contended for his favour, each more voluptuously beautiful than the lovely Sumatran. Such are the fascinating effects of this narcotic, when taken in moderate quantities; but when it is indulged in to an excessive degree, the voluptuous languor and pleasing dreams are changed for wild ravings and fits of delirium; and to that point had the Malay frequently reached in his latter indulgences. On the present occasion, he had already taken several glasses of rum during the day; and thus his head was unsettled before he applied himself to the pipe. He took a dozen whiffs, passing the smoke through his nostrils, a process which aids the effect of the opiatic fumes, and then he began talking to himself in a wild and incoherent manner.

"Now for paradise!" said he, with his eyes half-closed, and leaning back upon his pillow. "Now to sit in the shade of that glorious tree which grows by the throne of Allah, and listen to the songs of love which the zephyrs waft at night from the fragrant bowers of Amberabad ! But where is Lolah ? There shines a star brighter than the diamond turrets of Shadukiam, but her home is not there : where have they hid the bright-eyed maiden of Achen ? I have sought her among the unnumbered rubies of Chilminar, and in the secret depths where the genii hid the jewelled goblet of Jamsheed ; but Lolah flies me still. Dwells she in the islands of perfume below the waters of the sun-bright ocean of the south, or have evil genii changed that lovely form into one of those gorgeous birds which float among the spice-groves of Molucca ? Ah, she comes ! —is it her, or one of the fair and erring line shut out from paradise for sin ? It is Lolah, the lovely maiden of Sumatra ! Had houri ever such soft black eyes, which seem to melt the soul, and fill space with light ? Her warm breath fans my cheek like the aromatic gales of Arabia ; her rounded and graceful limbs entwine about my own, and I feel the beating of her heart against mine, and the thrilling contact of her firm exuberant breasts, heaving with the soft tumult of love's delight !"

The voice of Alompra had become fainter as he proceeded with his rhapsodic reverie, and at length he ceased speaking, his eyes closed slowly, and he seemed to sink into an uneasy and troubled sleep. Lolah, the little dancing-girl (whom our reader will recognise as the stolen daughter of Mr. Hastings) stood in one corner of the room, watching the Malay, whom she believed to be her father, and listening with a feeling akin to awe to the strange rhapsodies in which he indulged. Seeing him sink into sleep, she prepared to repose in her own little bed in the corner of the room, when suddenly the Malay leaped from the bed into the middle of the apartment, his dark eyes rolling wildly, and his whole countenance strangely agitated.

"Man the ramparts !—make fast the gates !" he cried, in a fierce and excited tone ; and he glared like a maniac round the room, until his glance rested on Lolah, whom he immediately recognised, though the piercing shriek which the terrified girl uttered when he sprang from the bed did not appear to have attracted his attention.

"How like her mother !" he soliloquised, as he fixed his serpent-like eyes upon the cowering form of the young dancer. "How much more like she might have been had *she* been mine ! But that pale-faced spawn of Eblis snatched her from me, and this girl——Avaunt ! or I will fling thy body to the ghouls !"

Lolah shuddered at the terrible menace of the juggler, and her dark cheeks became pale with fear ; she moved slowly towards the door of the apartment, still keeping her eyes fixed on the form of the Malay, but before she could reach it, the madman snatched his long creese from his sash, and sprang towards her like a fury. His dark eyes gleamed with insane and demoniac ferocity, and the veins in his temples were swelled by the unnatural excitement of the narcotic drug, and stood upon his dark skin thick and rigid as cords. The terrible weapon of the Malay gleamed before Lolah's eyes, and with a bound of terror like that with which the antelope springs from its resting-place at the shot of the hunter, she gained the door, and closed it behind her, just as the creese was plunged through the panel by the violence of the blow.

"Kill ! kill !" shouted the frenzied wretch, in a tone of fierce excitement, and no longer hearing or seeing, save through his distorted or distempered fancy, which peopled the apartment with enemies, he continued to strike madly with his creese at every object within his reach.

He thought not of pursuing Lolah, who had reached the bottom of the stairs in safety, but struck furiously at the enemies who rose up on every side, and scored the partition with his sharp creese in this imaginrry warfare of extermination. Raising at intervals the cry of "Kill ! kill !" he continued to lay about him, regardless of the injuries which he received when he came in violent contact with the furniture or the walls, until he was overthrown by the violence of his onset against a fresh host of imaginary foes, and fell, stunned and senseless, on the floor.

It was at this time that Lolah, who had remained at the bottom of the stairs, listening with fear and trembling to the sounds of violence which reached her from the apartment of Alompra, hearing the din no longer, ventured to ascend

the stairs cautiously, to take counsel with young Skelter. Their interview, as we have already seen, was interrupted by the return of the drunken sailor, and Sam was obliged to retreat to his room; and poor Lolah descended the stairs, saddened and depressed, and uncertain of the best course to adopt. She had on her dancing-dress, and had fortunately caught up, when first menaced by the juggler, the shawl which she wore over it when walking; this she now folded about her, and resolved to make an attempt to obtain an independent subsistence by dancing in the streets, which she had been accustomed to almost from her infancy. The children of the lower orders of society, compelled as they are to seek their own living, almost as soon as they can walk, early acquire a feeling of independence of their parents, and the habit of acting for themselves. This is particularly seen among the girls working in the cotton-mills of Lancashire; and in the metropolis there are thousands of children, of nine or ten years old, getting a living apart from their parents, buying their own stock in trade, and spending the proceeds as they please. That this throwing of children upon their own resources almost invariably leads to vicious courses, is undoubted; for,

5

placed upon a social equality with their parents, by the necessity of competing with them for a subsistence, they acquire prematurely the cares and feelings of advanced life, and practise the habits and vices of their elders.

Lolah Hastings experienced a feeling of diffidence at making the first essay without the protection of the Malay, and without his means of gathering an audience; she, therefore, sauntered about the streets some time, and had she had the means of paying for her lodging, she would have deferred her purpose until the morrow; but she had not the smallest coin in her possession, and, with some hesitation, she ventured into the tap-room of a public-house in Lower Shadwell. It was a large room, and filled principally with mechanics and labourers employed in the neighbourhood and about the docks. She had been induced to enter this house from seeing an old man go in, a moment before, carrying under his arm a violin, in a green bag.

" Would you like a tune, gentlemen ?" said the old man, glancing round the room.

" Ay, give us a tune," returned one of the topers; and then, turning to Lolah, he said : " And what are you going to do—sing ?"

" No, sir; but if this good gentleman will play the violin, I will dance," returned Lolah, taking off her shawl.

" You don't belong to one another, then ?" said the man.

" No; I do not know the girl," returned the fiddler, with a little asperity in his tone.

" It is the little girl that goes with that darky," observed one of the men; " she is a stunning little dancer."

" Come, play up, music, and let us see the girl dance," said another; and, thus abjured, the old fiddler drew his instrument from the green bag, and gave a preliminary scrape, like the sharpening of saws.

" Slow, if you please," said Lolah Hastings; and when the old man commenced playing, in very good style, the well-known " Flowers of the Forest," a pleasingly plaintive Scotch air, she began one of the oriental dances taught her by Alompra.

The great charm of these Eastern dances consists in the graceful and voluptuous attitudes assumed by the performer, who follows the slow and plaintive movements of the music, and depicts every feeling and passion represented in the composition, which is generally expressive of the varied sensations of the heart under the influence of love. Lolah's performance drew forth the energetic applause of the company, and the collection which she made at the conclusion amounted to a shilling. She gave the whole to the old fiddler; for she felt that she could not successfully exercise her abilities independently. The man gave her fourpence back, and when she quitted the house he followed her out.

" Will you come with me to another house, my dear ?" said he. " You are a very good dancer, and we can do better together than alone."

Lolah hesitated a moment, and then acquiesced in the proposed arrangement.

" Do you always go about alone ?" asked the old man.

" No; I used to be with my father, till to-night," replied Lolah; " but he has turned me out, and threatened to kill me."

" What is your father ?"

" A coloured man, that plays with balls and knives, swallows a sword, and eats fire," replied Lolah.

" A low connexion, my dear," said the violinist, shaking his head. " You will do much better with me, and we shall make our fortune in the fair to-morrow."

They had now come to another public-house, and, going into the tap-room, Lolah executed the dance which had been so much admired at the other house; and the languishing movements and graceful abandonment of limb which she displayed were again rewarded with a goodly collection of halfpence.

" You have got fourpence for yourself, and I'll pay your supper and lodging out of what we have got here," said the old fiddler, who again acted as treasurer, when they had left the house. He then conducted her to a tramps' lodging-house, situated up the court adjoining the public-house which they had just left; and, after supping off bread and cheese and onions, and a pint of porter, they went to bed. The room, one of three thus occupied, was a small one, and contained only two beds, one of which was empty, and this was assigned to the old fiddler. The landlady, with a sense of propriety not always to be met with in houses of this description, recommended Lolah to the other, which was already occupied by a Flemish girl, whose tambourine lay at the foot of the bed. Thus Lolah Hastings passed the first night after her flight from the terrible guardianship of her adoptive father.

CHAPTER XI.

STEPNEY FAIR.

THERE were few people moving about around the booths and caravans when Sam Skelter awoke, and looked about him with some surprise on finding himself reclining under one of Wombwell's caravans; and, before he had awoke to a full consciousness of his position, and how he came there, a loud roar, which shook the wooden cage above him, caused him to start with terror from the ground. Looking about him, and beginning to understand his situation, the boy strolled round the booths, and then from street to street, until he reached the Commercial-road. Only a few of the shops were opened, such as taverns and coffee-houses, and those of bakers and grocers; rosy-cheeked Welsh girls were going their rounds with milk, and the household drudges of the shopkeepers made their appearance with pail and brush. Those rosy, smiling little Welsh women have often attracted our attention; for we believe that for industry and virtue they are, as a class, unexcelled by any in the world. They rise at an hour when most of their sex are in bed, they work hard, their duties are often prolonged until a late hour in the evening, they have little time for rest, and none for recreation and mental culture—even Sunday brings them no cessation of toil—and yet they are almost invariably neat, clean, and contented; and, notwithstanding that they are brought from the hills and vallies of their native country, where the simplicity of manners exceeds that of even the most remote of the rural districts of England, and set down in a city abounding with temptations, yet, as a class, they are patterns of sobriety and chastity.

Sam Skelter began to feel hungry, and he asked charity of several passengers, but he got none; and his mendicancy having previously been of a passive nature, he soon became disheartened, and sauntered back to Stepney-green.

"Halloa, Sam! what are you arter?" said one of a knot of three or four boys, a few years older than himself, who were walking round the booths.

"I have been trying to cadge a penny, to get something to eat; but it is no go," replied Sam, in a doleful tone.

"Come along—don't stop talking with a cadger!" said one of the boys, with a ludicrous attempt at dignity.

"I say, what a fool he is—ain't he?" said another, pointing derisively at the little sailor-boy; and then they all laughed heartily, and went on.

Sam sauntered about, hungry and disconsolate, until the green became gradually covered with people, and the amusements of the day commenced. Canvass was removed from the fronts of stalls and booths—the excellent band of Wombwell's menagerie began playing—the pictorial representations of living prodigies and *lusæ naturæ* were unfolded to the gaze of the gaping throng—and famous old Richardson was beating a gong with all his might. Merry laughter resounded from the swings, in which sailors and their sweethearts were taking an aerial flight; and boys were shouting from the roundabouts, as only boys can shout. A Babel of sounds arose on every side, and the strangest articles were offered for sale, from "a cigar and a light for a penny," to "all the fun of the fair," in the shape of a little wooden instrument of mischief much patronised by romp-loving young women. Sam Skelter forgot his hunger for a time, as he walked round the fair, and looked up at the canvass representations of giants and dwarfs, Albinos and Hottentots, monstrous snakes and learned pigs, six-banded armadillos and children with two heads; and from them to the comedians, dancers, and acrobats who figured on the rival stages of Richardson and Gyngell, Cook and Scowton, and others less renowned, in the day when the canvass theatre was in the zenith of its fame.

Having passed the shows, and come to where the crowd was less dense, Sam saw Lolah Hastings dancing in the midst of an admiring throng, to the music of the old violinist, and he stopped to gaze at the lovely dancer. Having concluded, and levied contributions on the generosity of the bystanders, Lolah and her companion went into a public-house, near the green, to dine; and Sam sighed involuntarily, as he wondered how he was to obtain the means of breaking his fast.

On the strength of the anticipated receipts of the day, the old violinist, when they had dispatched their bread and cheese, called for a pot of ale and a pipe; and, having got into friendly conversation with a clarionet-player, he became so oblivious, under the joint influence of the ale and the pipe, that Lolah began to be impatient. Standing at the window of the tap-room, beating time to the music in the booths with her pretty feet, she saw the Malay juggler (whom she now suspected was not really her father, from his incoherent observations the night before) approaching the house; and, while she stood, pale and trembling, at the window, she saw him enter, and shuddered as she thought he must be in search of her. Quickly opening the window, she swung herself into the street, and disappeared in the crowd which was entering the fair, just as Alompra entered the tap-room.

His countenance was wild and haggard, an unnatural brightness shone from his dark, snake-like eyes, and a hectic flush tinged his cheeks, even through the deep olive of his complexion. He was a doomed man; for when the use of opium is carried to the point of excess which we have described, it is almost impossible to abandon the fatal habit, and in ten or fifteen years, at the utmost, it terminates the existence of its emaciated victim. He had not seen Lolah at the window, and he seemed suffering under the nervous debility and lassitude which the use of opium never fails to induce. The violinist had now discovered that the clarionet-player was a native of the same town as himself, and from this resulted the discovery that they had been schoolfellows, and so many reminiscences were thereby awakened, that they became intoxicated before they had fully compared notes.

Lolah Hastings, in the meantime, had returned to the fair; and while pondering on what was best to be done, and gazing listlessly at the plumed and bucklered heroes on the stage of Richardson's theatre, she felt her shawl twitched by some one, and a hoarse voice whispered: "Ain't you the little girl as was dancing in Ratcliffe-highway last night?"

Lolah started, and turned quickly round. The speaker stood on the steps of one of the minor shows, and was dressed like a clown or merry-andrew, with his face rubbed over with chalk, relieved with lamp-black and red ochre.

"Yes," replied the dancer.

"Along with a cove as eats fire?" continued her interrogator, making a grimace.

"Yes," again returned Lolah; and she removed the shawl which she had thrown over her shoulders.

"Oh! ain't you a duck? Do come along with me, and Mr. Allens will make you the star of the ballet," exclaimed the clown, with a gesture of ludicrous admiration; and, catching hold of the girl's hand, he led her up the steps to the platform erected in front of the theatre for the external performances.

Mr. Allens, whose real name was Allen, was a tall man about forty years of age, wearing a shabby black frock-coat, black stock, velvet waistcoat of the same colour, and plaid trousers, strapped very tight to conceal a hole in one of his boots. At that particular moment he was engaged in inviting the audience, in a stentorian voice, to come and see real merit in the shape of the wonderful performances of the India-rubber Brothers, three youths in flesh-tights and scarlet smalls, who were performing a variety of acrobatic feats. The rest of the company were the proprietor's daughter, a young lady who figured, in her papa's verbal announcements of the performances, as Mademoiselle Carolina, and a lad wearing a little oilskin hat, striped shirt, broad belt, and white duck trousers, who did the nautical at this Olympic temple.

"Oh! this is the fairy dancer, is it?" said Mr. Allen, turning to Lolah and the clown. "Well, my dear, would you like to dance on these boards?"

"Yes, sir, I would rather dance here than in the streets," replied Lolah.

"Well, you must do your very best, because mine is a very select establishment; and we will see about your salary afterwards," said the proprietor: and, taking the gong, whose brazen tones drowned every lesser noise for some distance, he proceeded, in a most energetic manner, to invite the gaping throng to witness the performance of the dancing-girl of Delhi, the only real oriental dancer in the three kingdoms.

Lolah then commenced one of the dances which she had so often practised in the streets, the clown beating the drum as the musical accompaniment. Again her performance elicited the rapturous applause of the spectators; and, as they crowded up the steps, Mr. Allen mentally calculated the extra shillings which the acquisition of the lovely dancer would bring into the treasury. The interior performances, which Lolah witnessed from the steps leading from the exterior platform to the temporary pit of the canvass theatre, consisted of posturing and tumbling by the acrobats, tight-rope dancing by Miss Allen, and a nautical hornpipe by the young gentleman in the striped shirt. Caroline Allen was a fair, well-formed girl about fifteen years of age, with long light-brown ringlets, and wore a white muslin dress, very short, and low at the bosom, with short sleeves, and silk stockings encasing a foot and leg of most admirable symmetry. She had travelled with her father as a tight-rope dancer from her earliest childhood; and though possessing personal attractions of no common order, and exposed to innumerable temptations, as a necessary consequence of her profession, yet her conduct had hitherto been marked by the strictest observance of propriety.

Lolah Hastings was standing in front of the exterior platform, conversing with Caroline, during the performances of the India-rubber Brothers, when she observed the old violinist, whom she had left at the public-house, taken to the watch-house in a state of helpless intoxication; and this circumstance confirmed her in her intention to remain, for the present, in the company of Mr. Allen. The green was now thronged with people; and the inspiring strains of the music from the booths and shows was mingled with the Babel of discordant sounds which arose in every direction. The conductors of wax-work and fantoccini-exhibitions were burning blue and red fire, firing pistols, and bawling through speaking-trumpets to attract attention; and from every part of the crowd came shouts and laughter, the whistling of bird-calls, and the squeaking of penny-trumpets.

Sam Skelter was gazing with surprise at the elevation of Lolah to the boards of the Olympic temple, when one of the boys who had accosted him in the morning approached and asked him, ironically, if he had had his dinner yet.

"No! nor yet my breakfast," replied Sam, with a languid smile.

"Why, what a muff you are!" said the boy, with something of contempt in his tone. "Why, I've had breakfast, dinner, and tea; and presently I am going home to supper. Cadging is a poor trade, Sam: I speaks feelingly; for I was a cadger myself once: besides, it's so low. Come along with me, and have a bit of supper; and I'll put you up to a better dodge than that."

Sam followed the boy without speaking; and, leaving behind them the riot and din of the fair, they crossed the Commercial-road, and proceeded towards the densely-populated district of Whitechapel.

CHAPTER XII.

THE SCHOOL OF CRIME.

In the purlieus of Whitechapel is a narrow court called Baker's-arms-alley, having a dead wall, as high as the houses, only two yards from them; which renders the alley at all times dark and gloomy. The court is intersected by others extremely narrow, into which it is almost impossible for a breath of air to penetrate. Close to the dead wall, and between that and the houses, is an open gutter full of stagnant water and putrefying matter, the effluvia from which is very offensive, and fills the close air of the court with malaria. At the top of the courts which intersect Baker's-arms-alley are receptacles for rubbish, which are usually full of decaying vegetable and animal matter in every stage of putrefaction, the stench of which is intolerable to those not accustomed to it. There is no lamp in the court; the houses are old, dirty, and dilapidated; and the very atmosphere is a dense fever-mist, in which the germs of disease are constantly floating. Seldom does a summer pass without this court, in common with many others in this densely-populated district, being visited by the demon of pestilence, especially when a wet season is followed by great heat; and as seldom does the dread visitant fail to carry off a fifth part of the entire population of this filthy and typhus-generating neighbourhood.

Sam Skelter followed his companion up this dark and dirty court, and into a house in one of the side passages diverging from the main alley, where a tall middle-aged woman, of coarse and masculine appearance, was sitting at a deal table in a dirty and miserably-furnished room.

"Here's a fresh catch'd 'un, Mother Brown," said the boy, with a jerk of the head towards his young companion.

"That's the ticket, Jem," returned the woman, staring at Sam Skelter. "Why, what a pretty little sailor-boy! Where do you come from, my man?"

"His old man has give him the dirty kick-out," said Jem; "and the poor boy hasn't had a mouthful of grub to-day."

"Who is his father?" inquired the woman.

"That lame buffer as comes the pictur' dodge in Ratcliffe-highway," replied Jem.

"Well, we'll have supper when t'other boys comes in; and then he can have a snap with them," observed Mother Brown; and, putting a large fryingpan on the fire, she placed therein a quantity of beef-sausages, or rather what were sold under that designation by the butchers of the neighbourhood; for it would be hazarding too much to assert what the contents really were.

"Turn out what you have got, Jem, and then fetch two pots of beer," continued the woman; and the boy proceeded to draw several silk handkerchiefs from between his trousers and shirt; which Mother Brown carefully examined, and then placed in a basket with some others.

Jem then ran out for the beer; and, when he returned, he was accompanied by three other boys about twelve or thirteen years of age, all of whom were thieves in the employ of the woman Brown, who received and disposed of the produce of their larcenies, and by whom they were lodged and boarded, and supplied with pocket-money. Jem was a couple of years older than the rest of the gang, and acted as Mother Brown's recruiting-serjeant; in which capacity we have seen him inveigle Sam Skelter to the filthy den of the female fence. A variety of plunder was brought in by these boys, consisting of several silk handkerchiefs, a silver gravy-spoon, a purse containing a sovereign and some silver, a silver snuff-box, and a pocket-book containing several bank-notes and bills of exchange. These Mother Brown was in the habit of disposing of, at a large discount, to a Jew in Rosemary-lane, who sent them to an agent at Amsterdam, for circulation on the continent.

Mother Brown then gave each of the boys, Sam included, a sausage on a slice of bread; and they helped themselves to the beer as they liked. When the supper was disposed of, Jem was sent out for pipes and tobacco, and to get the pewter replenished; and as Sam declined taking a pipe with them, the other boys annoyed him by puffing the smoke in his face. Sam bore the affront as long as he could; and then his indignation boiled over suddenly, and he struck one of the offenders a smart blow on the cheek. The boy dropped his pipe; and, both springing to their feet, a pugilistic encounter took place, to the great delight of the other boys. But Sam, though two years younger than the other, was nearly as tall; and after three or four rounds, he was declared the victor. After this, Sam was no longer annoyed by his companions, who complimented him highly on his *pluck*, and prophesied that he would be as good a man as Jack Sheppard.

Just as this fracas was concluded, two girls about fourteen years of age came in, singing the rolling chorus of a flash song. They were both slatternly, impudent-looking creatures, with unkempt hair and unwashed countenances. One was of sallow complexion, with hair of a dingy yellow hue, and large grey eyes. The other was a well-formed girl, on whose cheeks dwelt colour which vicious habits and the pestiferous atmosphere of that vile den had not yet dimmed, and the faultless beauty of whose features dirt and untidiness had marred, but not destroyed. Her hair, though rough and carelessly arranged, was of the hue of the raven's wing; and in her dark eyes was an expression which seemed to indicate that all the better feelings and higher aspirations of the human heart were not obliterated, but only dormant, like seeds sleeping in the soil, and that they only required culture to develop themselves in that perfection which constitutes the glory of humanity. The germs of good exist in the heart of every human being; and albeit they are choked by vicious and deteriorating circumstances, they will spring up and bring forth fruit when placed in the proper conditions, like the bulbs found in the tombs of Memphis, which germinated after a lapse of three thousand years.

The girl with the sallow countenance and yellow hair took the pewter pot from the table, and, having drank, handed it to her companion; then they sat down, and began questioning Mother Brown and the boys respecting Sam Skelter, in whose good opinion both seemed desirous of ingratiating themselves.

"You must pick the marks out of them handkerchers to-morrow: mind, you have done nothin' to-day," observed Mother Brown to the two young girls, rising and taking the key of the door from a nail near the fire-place. "I am going to the Baker's Arms, and you have got your beer and 'bacca; so I shall lock the door."

With that she went out, locking the door behind her; and the inmates of that school of crime and profligacy continued to amuse themselves with singing flash songs, telling tales of successful roguery, and drinking and smoking until the evening's supplies were exhausted. One of the girls then produced a greasy pack of cards; and, as Sam Skelter had no money, the other girl took him as her partner, agreeing that their winnings should be divided, if they were successful, and that if they lost, Sam Skelter should pay his share of the loss when he got some money, which they assured him would not be long. Sam and his partner were among the losers; and, about midnight, the latter proposed that they should go to bed, which was unanimously approved, and two old mattresses were laid upon the dirty floor, with a couple of dingy blankets for covering. Mother Brown occupied the room above, and the boys and girls slept upon the two mattresses down stairs. Ancient travellers mention an Indian tribe, the women of which were allowed a plurality of husbands, thus reversing the polygamous system of Mahomet; and a corresponding order of things existed in the school of crime in Baker's-arms-alley.

A dispute, therefore, arose between the two girls, as to whose mattress their new companion should occupy; for as they had no doubt that he would succumb to the views of Mother Brown, and become a thief, each was desirous of obtaining an influence over him, to be hereafter exercised for their own advantage. Sam Skelter was allowed no choice in the matter, and his partner at cards was determined to keep him to herself; but the yellow-haired girl protested against such a monopoly on the part of her companion, and they would have fell to scratching one another had not Jem interfered, and proposed a compromise, to which the dark-eyed girl reluctantly assented. Such were the vicious habits of the inmates of this sink of depravity—such the examples to whose contaminating influence Sam Skelter was now exposed. This picture of early profligacy is no imaginary one, as the unsophisticated reader may be inclined to suppose; unfortunately, it is but a faint delineation of the state of the morals which exist among large numbers of the juvenile population of our overgrown metropolis—a state which the magistrates and police are fully cognisant of, but which mere penal enactments are inefficacious to remedy.

It was one o'clock in the morning, when Mother Brown returned to Baker's-arms-alley in a state of beastly intoxication; and having groped her way up the broken and dirty stairs, she laid down on the bed in her clothes, which she was too drunk to remove. The coming day was the sabbath, but its observance was unheeded by the inmates of that vile den, whose religious sentiments were as imperfectly developed as those of morality. The most refined ideas of religion are ever found in company with the purest and most philosophical morals, and as we descend in the scale of intelligence and morality, we see religion become grosser and more material.

To the dwellers in the country, the sun had risen some hours, dispersing the misty vapours from the hills, and shedding glory on the valleys and plains; but only a dim light struggling through the almost opaque windows, announced to the degraded population of Baker's-arms-alley the dawn of another day. One by one the companions of Sam Skelter arose from their mattresses; and, true to the animal instincts which swayed them, their first thoughts were of breakfast.   Without waiting to dress, one of the girls proceeded to light the fire, and having finished dressing while it burned up, she went up to Mother Brown for money to buy coffee and other articles for breakfast.   When the morning meal was concluded, the two girls sat down to do the work which they had neglected the day before—picking the marks out of the handkerchiefs stolen by the boys, and the latter went out to pursue their avocations.   Sam Skelter was sent out in company with Jem, to make his first essay at picking pockets—of the criminality of which he had no other idea than, that if he were detected he would be sent to prison.   The low standard of morality which he had imbibed from the wooden-legged sailor had not enabled him to form any other; and the fear of punishment was more than counterbalanced by the good living which he had witnessed among his new companions, and the vivid representations which Jem drew of the penny theatres and other resorts of the juvenile criminals of the metropolis.

CHAPTER XIII.

THE FIRST LESSON.

SAM SKELTER and his companion wended their way towards Stepney-green, and, on arriving at that spot, the latter looked about him to see if there was a chance of exercising their profession.   Knots of idle boys were playing in various spots, and, in the largest open space, a considerable crowd was collected, consisting principally of working men and women.

"Come along, Sam," said Jem; "here's a fellow holding forth, and while the soft 'uns are turning up the whites of their eyes, we can draw 'em of their wipes, and p'r'aps nipper a yack and inguns."

"What's that?—anything to eat?" asked Sam.

"How precious green you are," returned Jem, grinning; "but never mind now.   When I nudges your elbow, and points out a green bird, pick him neatly, and pass the swag to me—then nammus like blazes."

"What?" Sam's ignorance of the flash lexicon again compelled him to ask.

"Why, shove your trunk—cut away, to be sure," replied Jem, with a look of sovereign contempt for the boy's ignorance of the phraseology in common use among the thieving fraternity.

The cause of the crowd was a venerable old man, with long white hair, who, in a strain of fervid eloquence, was preaching to his motley audience from a text referring to the last judgment; the preacher was Robert Ashdowne, the perambulating clergyman who, as we have already informed the reader, had acquired the name of the mad parson.   The crowd was principally composed of unshaven mechanics and artizans, scarcely recovered from the debauch of the previous night; dirty and half-intoxicated coal-heavers, sailors who had just quitted the houses of infamy in the courts and lanes of Wapping, the wives of working men, lingering on their way to the butchers, and, mingled with these, a few men of higher standing in society, whom the preacher's strange but eloquently-delivered discourse had attracted to the spot.

"What means the howl of poverty, and the insensate laugh of the rich?" said the preacher.   "What are they but the preludes of destruction, the faint murmurings of the coming storm on the distant horizon?   We have been preserved from the horrors of war, in our own country, by our insular situation, and we have shown our gratitude to Providence for this immunity, by our eagerness to spread those horrors over nations less happily situated.   In the midst of safety at home, we have raised or joined the yell of war abroad.   Shall such wickedness pass unpunished?   Are we better than populous No, that was situated among the rivers, that had the waters round about it, whose rampart was the sea?   Ethiopia and Egypt were her strength, and it was infinite; Phut

and Lubim were her supporters. Yet was she carried away—she went into captivity; and they cast lots for her honourable men, and all her great men were bound in chains. And if such was the fate of mighty No, what shall be the end of this country, whose wickedness is so much greater? The central fire of the earth shall burst forth, upthundering from the deep, and this great and mighty city shall be swallowed up; and, in the words of Nahum, 'all that hear the report of thee shall clap the hands over thee, for upon whom hath not thy wickedness passed continually?'"

"You don't mean to say as how there'll be an earthquake?" exclaimed an unwashed coalwhipper, removing his short black pipe from his mouth, for a moment.

"Ay, and fiery comets shall shoot athwart the sky, heralding the final destruction," continued the preacher. "The sun shall wane, the stars shall fall down, and the comet-smitten earth shall leave its orbit, and rush flaming through the infinite fields of space."

"Lor! what will become on us all?" observed an old woman to a neighbour.

6

" All that 'ere won't be in our time, will it, master ?" inquired a lad.

" This generation shall not pass away until all the things of which I spake are fulfilled," returned Mr. Ashdowne, solemnly. " Wherefore I call upon you all to repent of your sins, and prepare yourselves, by prayer and self-denial, for the kingdom of heaven. Pray, pray while you have yet time, that you may be fit for life everlasting ; for when earth and comet rush to the embrace of ruin, and the red-eyed fiend Destruction spreads his fiery wings over a lost and blazing world, it will be too late. Now is the appointed time for salvation—now is the day of grace !"

" How shall we know when these things are going to happen ?" asked a stout, well-dressed man, in a tone of evident alarm.

" When the next comet appears, the end of all things will be near," replied Mr. Ashdowne, with solemn emphasis. " But those who wait for that sign of the coming day of wrath, will have waited too long, and they shall be swiftly arrested in their wickedness. Repent, then, quickly, lest you be cut off—repent and pray, that you may be worthy of immortality."

" I do not know that I have much to repent of, and I pray every Lord's day," observed the stout man, who was a member of a dissenting congregation at Limehouse.

" Every day is the Lord's day, and every one has much to repent of," returned Mr. Ashdowne. " Therein you are in error, friend. Have you clothed the naked, fed the hungry, visited the sick, and comforted the prisoner ? Inasmuch as you have not done all these things, you have much to repent."

The stout man shrugged his shoulders at this address, took a pinch of snuff, and walked away, striving to reconcile to his conscience the difference between the primitive and the modern churches. A tall, thin man, with a long nose and straight back, and wearing a shabby suit of black, was about to put a question to the mad parson, with the view of raising a theological discussion, when he suddenly felt his silk handkerchief leaving the pocket in the tail of his coat ; for Sam Skelter, in obedience to a signal telegraphed from the knowing Jem, was cautiously drawing it out. Turning quickly round, the reverend gentleman—for he was the minister of the chapel frequented by the stout man—seized Sam by the collar, and called out for a constable. Jem took to his heels, and Sam kicked and wriggled to get away, but a constable came up, and he was given into custody, for attempting to pick the pocket of the Reverend Malachi Muddlepate.

The constable immediately hurried Sam off to the watch-house, which was already pretty full ; for the reader must remember that not only had the preceding day been Saturday, but also the first of the fair. Sam glanced around him, on being thrust into the cell, with mingled curiosity and fear ; both emotions springing from the same cause—the novelty of his situation ; and when the constable in charge of the watch-house had turned the key, he sank down on the settle in one corner. In the opposite corner were a group of noisy sailors, scarcely recovered from the intoxication of the preceding night, and in another a knot of disorderly prostitutes of the lowest grade, while seated on the settle near him were two boys playing at shove-halfpenny.

" I say, what game have you been up to ?" asked one of the juvenile delinquents, turning with a knowing grin to Sam Skelter.

" Nothing particklar," returned Sam, with assumed indifference.

" Ain't you one of Mother Brown's boys ?" said the other.

" What of it ?" asked young Skelter, evading the question.

" Cos she'll pay a cove to gammon the beaks, and send Tom the Coster to swear an *alibi*," replied the other youngster.

" Who is Tom the Coster ?" inquired Sam Skelter.

" Mother Brown's fancy man," replied the boy. " He keeps a moke, and sells apples, inguns, and fish, 'cording to the season. Oh, he's such a downy cove !—ain't he Bill ?"

" I b'lieve you !" ejaculated Bill, with a grin.

" Wouldn't he just make a prime counsellor !" observed the other. " Why, he'd gammon the best twelve men as never was—blest if he wouldn't. If he only had the tin, what an out-and-out parliament cove he'd make, wouldn't he, Bill ?"

" Wouldn't he !" exclaimed Bill.

" Arter all, Bill," continued the young vagabond, after a pause, " what's the mighty difference between us and them as governs us, and makes the laws ? Suppose you and I, and Tom the Coster, and Hearthstone Bob, was to make the laws, wouldn't we lay on the taxes, and help ourselves pretty tidy, and get pensions for flash Carry and Ginger Sall; and don't they do the same ? First, there's the king, and he takes the first pull out of the swag, and a tidy pull too, like Jonathan Wild, the prince of prigs ; then comes the nobs, and they answers to swell-cracksmen, buzz-gloaks, and macing-coves ; and arter them is the rooks us devours and picks up everything—I mean the bishops and parsons, who are the worsest of all, and puts me in mind of a flock of noisy crows, for they robs us while we lives, and prey upon us arter we are dead. These parish-prigs answers to magsmen, for they have got the gift of the gab, and comes the honest dodge—trying to persuade the people as how they're all sucking-doves, and wouldn't do any thing wrong not for never so much. Walker !—eh, Bill ?"

" I b'lieve yer !" responded Bill.

Sam Skelter listened with much attention to the edifying discourse of his new companion, and an idea was gradually and involuntarily forced upon his mind, that all society was a vast combination of villany, or rather a series of classes, rising above each other, and each preying upon those beneath it ; which forced the lowest class in the social pyramid to live in poverty and misery, or turn and prey upon those above it. And a very little reflection will serve to convince us that the animadversions of the juvenile vagabond were not very far from the truth. Every idler is a robber ; every one who produces nothing, robs the industrious producers of every thing. While tens of thousands of honest, virtuous, and industrious men are standing in unwilling idleness, and hundreds of thousands are receiving only from seven to ten shillings per week, look at the incomes of the pampered idlers, the gilded idols of Britain's insensate worship. While Victoria and her husband are allowed an annual income of nearly half a million sterling, there must necessarily be great numbers unable to obtain a crust of bread to save them from death. The famine in the cottage is a necessary effect of the lavish expenditure in the palace. It is not long since a larger sum was granted for the improvement of the royal stables at Windsor, than the annual vote for national education ; and now a hundred and fifty thousand pounds are demanded for enlarging the palace at Pimlico ; and yet Victoria, who must be either the most ignorant or the most guilty woman in the nation, has already house-room enough for all the household troops. Why are our poor allowed to sleep on the cold steps of the metropolitan workhouses ?—because the wards are full of misery and destitution, when the palaces erected with the nation's money would accommodate them all ! Why should one family, and that the least useful in the nation, have half-a-dozen palaces to reside in, while those who build the palaces, and are taxed to maintain the pampered idlers who dwell therein, are houseless and destitute ? Not room enough for the royal Anthropopagi at Pimlico !—and in St. Giles's, in Shoreditch, and in White-chapel, one small room is often the sole habitation of two or three families. Away with this horrible system ! Well might Franklin say that royalty was as great a crime as poisoning ; for it works ruin and destruction wherever it exists. Away with it, then !—let the millions determine, that while there is no comfort in the cottage, there shall be no peace in the castle, and take a lesson from the land of Arago and Lamartine.

CHAPTER XIV.

TOM THE COSTER.

THE conversation between Sam Skelter and his young companions in the watch-house continued in the same strain until late at night, when they laid down on the hard settle, and went to sleep. The manner in which prisoners are treated in this country is a proof of the fallacy of the legal aphorism, that " every man is considered innocent until he is proved guilty;" for, so far from this being the case, every suspected person is treated as a criminal. Let a man, however innocent he may be, be accused of a crime, and he is dragged through the streets in a ruffianly manner, locked up with the vilest characters in a filthy cell, perhaps from Saturday night until Monday morning, when he is taken before a magistrate; then he is, perhaps, committed for trial, and undergoes two or three, or it may be six months' imprisonment, and when brought to trial he is acquitted. During this time, besides the degradation, and perhaps loss of health, his family endure great anxiety, and are probably reduced to starvation, or compelled to seek refuge in the parish bastile; yet, when the unfortunate comes out of prison, what recompense does he receive for all this degradation and misery, for his loss of time, and perhaps of future employment? "Oh! he may bring his action for false imprisonment—the law is open to the poor as well as the rich," exclaims some sleek, well-fed *respectable*, who thus gives utterance to another common legal fallacy. "So is the London Tavern," observed Horne Tooke, when the remark was once made in his presence; but the charges in either case close it against the working-man.

Our whole system of jurisprudence is, in fact, false and anomalous, and clogged with the barbarisms of a past age; our sole idea of justice is that of punishment, whereas an equitable and enlightened system would seek to reward virtue while it punished vice, and not proclaim the prison, the hulks, and the scaffold as the penalty of crime, and poverty and wretchedness as the meed of the virtuous poor. For the wicked, chains and torture—for the virtuous, poverty and neglect!—such is the formula of the present. True justice requires, not only the restraint of vice, but the reward of virtue—and, indeed, such a course would be the best preventive of crime; but our legislators and our spiritual instructors point upward, and tell us that the virtuous shall have their reward beyond the grave. How inconsistent, then, to punish crime on earth; if the reward of virtue be left to Providence, why not the punishment of vice?

In the course of Monday morning, Sam Skelter and his fellow-prisoners were taken from the watch-house, before the magistrates presiding over the district of Stepney; for this was before the establishment of the Thames-police. In those days, the only protection of property on shore were the local constables and the night-watchmen, and on the river the boats of the men-of-war which sometimes laid off Blackwall or Woolwich. When Sam was placed at the bar, he looked eagerly round, to see if he could recognise any one present as him whom the vagabonds at the watch-house had denominated "Tom the Coster;" but he beheld only the two magistrates, their clerk, his reverend accuser, and the constable who had arrested him.

"What is the charge against this boy?" asked one of the magistrates; and, as he owned a great number of houses about Stepney and Mile-end, his tone was proportionately arrogant and peremptory.

"Picking a pocket, your worship," replied the constable, deferentially; for the magistrate who had spoken was one of his best customers, he being a tradesman in the neighbourhood, as the constables of that period frequently were.

"Ah! a precocious young vagabond!" exclaimed the magistrate, looking sternly at Sam Skelter; "I can see it in his looks. He has stood there before."

"I never was in custody before in my life!" said the boy, in an indignant tone.

"Hold your tongue, sir!" vociferated the magistrate, sternly. "I am sure he has been here before, constable."

"Well, your worship knows best, of course; but I do not remember having him before, your worship," observed the obsequious constable.

"Humph! he will again, then, I warrant," said the uncharitable magistrate; and, vexed at having been at fault, he determined to punish the boy as severely as possible. "Where is the complainant?"

"Malachi Muddlepate!" shouted the crier; and the reverend gentleman immediately entered the witness-box, and took the oath.

"Now, sir, state the particulars of this robbery," said the magistrate.

"I will, your worship," returned Mr. Muddlepate, in an oily tone. "I am the minister of Ebenezer-chapel, in Limehouse-fields; and, being yesterday morning on Stepney-green, where the carnal-minded hold one of their profane assemblages, which the ungodly call a fair, I beheld there a large crowd of sinful creatures gathered about one who expounded the blessed Gospel."

"What has all this to do with the robbery?" asked the magistrate, with some asperity; for, being a rigid churchman, he regarded as heretics all who differed from the rubric of the Church of England, and would very gladly have sent Sam and the minister to prison together.

"I am coming to the robbery, your worship," continued Malachi Muddlepate. "The preacher was expounding the Word in a strange and unevangelical manner, and I felt moved by the Spirit to speak, lest, the blind leading the blind, they should fall together into the ditch. But just as I was about to speak, I felt a hand in my pocket, and, turning quickly round, I caught the boy at the bar in the act of drawing out my handkerchief. I seized the evil-doer at once, and called for a constable, when this good man came up, and took the graceless sinner to the watch-house."

Just as the reverend gentleman concluded his account of the robbery, a middle-aged man elbowed his way up to the witness-box, and entered it when Mr. Muddlepate quitted it. He was about the middle height, and had whiskers and hair of the colour vulgarly called carrotty; he wore a dark velveteen jacket, with large metal buttons, corduroy smalls, and speckled stockings; a yellow silk handkerchief was tied carelessly round his neck, and a battered white hat surmounted his head.

"Who are you?" demanded the magistrate.

"Tom Smith—leastways, Thomas Smith; but my pals calls me Tom the Coster, 'cause, you see, yer worship, I deals in wegitables," replied the witness.

"Are you a witness in this case?" asked the clerk.

"Yes, a witness for the prisoner," returned Tom the Coster.

Sam's looks brightened up a little on the opportune appearance of the costermonger, to whom the clerk administered the oath in the usual careless manner.

"Now, tell their worships what you know about this case," said the clerk, as he resumed his seat.

"Well, yer worships," began Tom the Coster, "I was on Stepney-green yesterday morning, and I was standing close to the genelman as had his pocket picked, when I sees a boy trying of it on, and at last he drawed out the handkercher, and then the genelman turned round."

"Was it the boy at the bar?" asked the magistrate.

"Lord bless you, no!" yer worship," replied Tom the Coster, with apparent sincerity. "That boy as stands there, yer worship, is as honest a boy as any in the parish of Stepney—ay, or Limehouse either; but he was standing by, yer worship, and d'rectly the genelman turned round, the young wagabone as drawed him of his handkercher shoved it into this poor's boy's hand, and nammussed away like one o'clock."

"Do you know the boy who you say picked the gentleman's pocket?" asked the other magistrate, looking up from the morning newspaper, in whose ample folds he had hitherto been concealed.

"Lord, no! yer worship," said the costermonger, in a deprecating tone. "I'm a honest fellow as keeps a donkey, and sells apples and inguns, and peas, when they're in season, and cowkimbers, or any thing as I can get a honest living by, yer worship; and I 'peals to the court whether it's likely as I should know a wagabone boy as picks genelmen's pockets."

The magistrate looked earnestly at Tom the Coster, as if he doubted his assurances of respectability; and then, turning to the constable, he asked if he knew the witness.

The constable looked steadfastly at the costermonger for a moment, and then replied in the negative.

"Please your worship, I know the man well," said another constable, who had been examining Tom with much attention; "he lives somewhere about Whitechapel, and, though ostensibly a costermonger, he is the constant associate of well-known thieves, and has been two or three times summarily convicted of petty larcenies, and assaults on the watch. He lives with a woman named Brown, whose house is a notorious resort of juvenile criminals; and yesterday morning I saw the prisoner in the company of a boy whom I immediately recognised as a well-known thief."

Before the constable had spoken a dozen words of this disclosure of the real character of Tom the Coster, that individual had hurried from the witness-box, and was soon out of court.

"If we required any corroboration of your testimony as to the witness's character, his precipitate retreat would be sufficient," said the magistrate, addressing the constable; and then, turning to the prisoner, whose countenance had become much more elongated than when the costermonger entered the witness-box, he added: "Your witness has damaged your case, rather than served it; for, instead of this being your first offence, as I was at first inclined to believe, it appears that your associates are well-known characters, and that you are not the novice in crime which you would have us believe. You stand committed for one calendar month, and if you come here again, I warn you that you will not escape again so easily."

Sam was then removed from the bar in the custody of the constable who had him in charge, and in a few hours afterwards he was in prison. This was the first robbery he had ever committed, and he resolved that it should likewise be the last. The charm with which Jem had invested the existence of a thief was broken when the boy found himself in prison; and, in spite of the contaminating influences by which he was now surrounded, he never swerved from the resolution which he had formed. The young thieves confined in the same prison jeered and laughed at him; but Sam remained inflexible, not from any fixed principle of honesty—for we have already shown how lax were his notions of right and wrong—but on account of the punishment, and the risk of its frequent repetition, with increasing severity, unless he quitted the path of life upon which he had entered. He had no very definite ideas of what he intended doing when he left prison, but at any rate he had determined not to be a thief again; and in this salutary state of mind, in which skilful treatment might have effected a complete cure of this moral patient—for such we hold every criminal to be—he remained until his release from prison.

But a criminal prison is not a moral hospital, and a turnkey is not a moral physician; hence, nine in every ten of their patients leave with the moral disease more deeply confirmed, instead of its being eradicated. True, something has been done of late years, by Lieber in America, by Sir Richard Phillips in England, and by Quetelet in Belgium; and the classification of prisoners, which their labours have effected in those countries and in France, is a step in the right direction. But much yet remains to be done. Crime must be treated as moral disease before it can wholly be eradicated; and instead of prisons for its punishment, we must have hospitals for its cure. Theft results from a diseased state of the organ of acquisitiveness, or an undue development of that organ, and murder from a similar state of the organ of destructiveness. The brain is the apparatus of thought as much as the stomach is the apparatus of digestion; and surely it is as irrational to punish a man for having a diseased or imperfect brain as it would be to punish him for having a weak digestion. It is quite possible for the brain to be diseased without insanity, or malformed without idiotcy; for those mental derangements arise from disease or malformation of the intellectual faculties, while crime results from a similar state of the moral sentiments. Any one well acquainted with the science of Gall and Spurzheim will bear me out in these views, and also that crime is as liable to be constitutional and hereditary as gout or scrofula, or any form of mental derangement.

CHAPTER XV.

THE MUD-LARK.

At length the day arrived on which Sam Skelter completed his term of imprisonment; and while he yet stood near the gates of the prison, undecided which way to go, or what course to adopt, he was accosted by his former companion, the elder of the Baker's-arms-alley gang.

"Well, Sam, how is yer, my boy?" said he. "You don't look any the better for being lummed up. Come to Mother Brown's, and put a beaf-steak and a penny bu'ster and a pint of heavy into you, and then you'll do."

"No! I shall not go back to Mother Brown's any more," returned Sam, firmly. "I've had a sickenin' of prigging; and I mean to take to something more respectable than picking pockets."

"It's very easy talking about being honest, and all that," observed Jem, with some bitterness in his tone; "but how do you mean to live? Take my word for it, it ain't so easy to be honest and 'spectable as it is to talk about it. Suppose you were to go back to the old man, and took to cadging again, why, the old 'un would give you a good flogging for cutting away from him; and as to cadging, it's as bad as prigging, and a precious sight meaner. Then, if you tried to get a sittivation as errand-boy, or anything of that sort, every one you went to would tell you, there are plenty of boys to be had as are used to the employment, and even if this wa'n't the case, who, do you think, would take a boy as had just come out of prison?"

"Then I will sell apples, or oranges, or chesnuts, or something of that sort," returned Sam, moodily, for the gloomy but true picture which Jem had drawn, of the difficulty attending the efforts of a boy in his situation to return to the path of honesty.

"Where's your money to come from, to buy your first stock?" asked Jem, in a jeering tone.

"Well, I will go into the country and get some flower-roots and moss, and sell them in Covent-garden market," returned Sam Skelter.

"Better be sucking in a hot supper at Mother Brown's, than digging up flowers in the woods, and then padding the hoof up to town, with your basket at your back, through the pelting rain," observed Jem. "Come, let's go and have a pint of heavy, and talk it over."

Sam followed the lad into a public-house in the neighbourhood; and, sitting down in the tap-room, Jem called for a pint of porter, and then taking a short pipe from his jacket-pocket, he filled it from a brass tobacco-box, and began to smoke.

"You just try to be honest, and you'll soon find out it ain't so easy as you think for," said Jem, after taking a draught of the porter, and pushing it across the narrow deal table at which they sat, to Sam Skelter. "Just take a spell at honest poverty for a month, and if it agrees with yer, so much the better. But I'll bet yer a bob to a mag yer comes back to Baker's-arms-alley afore the time's up."

"Agreed!" cried Sam Skelter, quickly.

"No, yer won't come back, perhaps; but how shall I know what game you are acting of somewheres else?" responded the cautious Jem.

"I just now told you what I mean to do," observed Sam.

"Yes! I know. Over here!" said Sam, grinning, as he pointed over his left shoulder. "Come, mop up the heavy, and come down to Whitechapel with me."

Before Sam Skelter could make any reply to his companion's invitation, the door of the tap-room was opened, and two constables entered, with their staves in their hands; at sight of which Jem grew pale, and his countenance became wonderfully elongated.

"Come, my man! we have nabbed you at last, you see," said one of the constables to Jem. "You must come along with us; and this time you will go over the herring-pond."

"What for?" said Jem, with an assumption of innocence. "I ar'n't done nuffin'. Sarch me, if yer like."

"Oh! we do not want to search you, because the gentleman can swear to you," returned the constable.

"What's it for, then?" asked the lad.

"That little job at the silversmith's in Aldgate," replied the constable. "So come along with us. Your goose is cooked this time, and no mistake."

"It's all up, Sam; they've nailed me at last," said Jem; and having emptied the pint pot, he was seized by the constables, and taken away in their custody.

A little old man, who had been sitting in one corner of the tap-room with a half-pint pot and some cheese-parings before him, rose from the settle, as Jem was led out in custody, and sat down by the side of Sam Skelter. He seemed about sixty years of age, and his sallow and unwashed countenance bore the traces of deep misery. From the appearance of his beard, he was not in the habit of using a razor; and his garments betokened the most abject and squalid wretchedness. An old, shapeless hat, with the crown almost out, was slouched over his careworn brow; his coat was extremely ragged, and patched with a variety of colours; his lower habiliments were in the same condition, and his legs were encased in very muddy high boots much too large for him. It was really a marvel how the old man contrived to get on his ragged coat; but, most probably, he never took it off, for his whole appearance was indicative of squalor and destitution.

"Ain't yer got no browns?" said he to Sam Skelter, in a low, hoarse voice.

"Not a blessed mag," responded Sam.

"No home?" said the old man, interrogatively.

"No."

"No friends?"

"No."

"Poor devil!" ejaculated the old man. "Come along with me." And, rising from the settle, he quitted the public-house, followed by Sam Skelter.

The old man shuffled along the busy streets of the city, ever and anon turning to the left as he proceeded towards Blackfriars, until, at length, they reached the river. It was then low water; and, dropping from a coal-wharf into the mud which the receding tide had deposited along the banks of the river, the old man began picking up bits of coal, coke, wood, old iron, &c., which he placed in a twig basket hanging at his back, while he was assisted in his search by a stick with which he walked.

"Boy," said he, pausing in his occupation to address Sam Skelter, "this is the way I provide myself with firing; and the old iron that I pick up and sell to the marine-store dealers finds me in money to get a bit of bread and cheese, and sometimes a half-pint of beer, or a penn'orth of gin. By-and-by, I will show you where I lodge; but my lodgings cost me nothing. Sometimes I picks up pieces of copper and copper nails that have come off ships; and sometimes something more valuable, that has been dropped in the mud, or washed down the sewers. How shall you like the life?"

"Oh, anything for a honest living!" returned Sam, cheerfully, as he picked up a piece of coal and threw it into the old man's basket. "Then you are what they call a mud-lark?"

"That's it," said the old man; "and a rare lark it is, to see the rats scamper away when I walks up the sewers."

"Up the sewers!" repeated Sam, looking up with evident amazement.

"Ay! that's the way home," replied the old mud-lark, with a dry laugh.

"The devil it is!" thought Sam; but he made no remark, and continued to search about in the black mud for the mineral treasures there deposited.

"Come, we'll go home now, if you ain't afraid," observed the mud-lark, when his basket had become filled with coals and old iron; and Sam Skelter followed him towards the outlet of one of the main sewers near Blackfriars-bridge.

The old man entered the arched subterranean, and Sam unhesitatingly followed him into the dark and pestiferous thoroughfare below the streets of London. Knee-deep in the filthy stream, the boy and the old mud-lark groped their way along, supporting themselves by stretching their hands against the damp walls on either side; for, in the main sewers, and particularly the one of which we are writing, the current is sometimes very strong and rapid. Onward went the old man, without any other light than what came through the iron gratings over the gully-holes in the streets above; onward followed Sam Skelter, often starting as some huge rat splashed in the water, or swam between his legs.

The sewers of London form a far-spreading labyrinth of subterranean ways extending from the Thames to Islington, and from Hyde-park-corner to Mile-end-gate; and that branch where the wanderers were then traversing runs from north to south the whole of the above distance. The walls and arched roofs of these buried lanes are damp and slimy, and exhale a noxious and pestilential vapour. The only living creatures which inhabit them are scores of large black water-rats, whose lives are passed in darkness and filth. These dark and silent passages contrast strangely with the bustle and animation of the streets above. Along the gloomy and pestiferous sewers of London no sound is heard, save the squeaking and splashing of the huge rats, and the gurgling of the fetid stream; but above resound the rattle of carriages, the cries of itinerant traders,

and the thousand noises of the modern Babylon. In the city above are the shops of the traders, the haunts of the gay, and the mansions of the noble by descent; but in the dark and silent city below, all is solitude and filth.

After proceeding some distance along the gloomy and pestiferous passage, the old mud-lark turned to the right: and here the sewer was narrower, the fetid water less deep, and the current less strong and rapid.

"Do you know where you are now?" said he to his young companion.

"No," replied Sam Skelter.

"We are now underneath West-street, close by Smithfield-market, you know," said the old man. "I know the city underground as well as the city above; and if the sewers were only dry, I would live there in preference to a house, for here there is nothing to remind me, by the contrast, of my own wretchedness. But here we are, at home."

Sam looked up in surprise, and saw the mud-lark ascend a rude and clumsy set of wooden steps; and he prepared to follow. The old man raised a trap in the half-rotten planks above his head (for many of the houses in this locality

7

are built over the sewer without any intervening arch of brickwork), and passed through it. Sam followed, and found himself in a desolate-looking apartment without any fireplace, with the shutters closed over the broken windows, and the moisture exuding from the bare walls of plaster, discoloured with the exhalations from the filthy stream below. Had not Sam undergone a preparatory training by his passage through the sewer, he could not have borne the stench which pervaded that damp, chilly, and dreary-looking room.

"Close the trap, boy," said the old man, setting his basket on the floor, and placing his stick in one corner of the desolate apartment.

"Do you really live in this miserable place?" asked Sam Skelter, as he closed the trap-door and glanced round the chilly and mournful-looking place.

"No, I only exist," replied the aged mud-lark. "But the room overhead is where I sleep, because it is drier, although the wind blows through the shattered windows sometimes, and the rain too. But then I doesn't pay no rent; so I s'pose I mustn't grumble. The house has had no other inhabitant than myself for the last fifteen years, and is fast falling into decay. But damp walls and rotten floors would not prevent its letting, in a neighbourhood where every house overflows with its human load; but there is another cause, for the house is said to be haunted."

"Haunted!" repeated Sam Skelter, starting.

"Ay, and well it may be," responded the old man; "for this house has been the haunt of infamy and crime—these walls have echoed the wild revelry of the burglar and the assassin, and the death groans of the victims of midnight murder: ay, in this very room have been held the orgies of the vilest miscreants in this overgrown metropolis; and when some hapless stranger was decoyed here by their female associates in profligacy and crime, he was plied with drink, in which a strong narcotic had been infused, and, after being robbed, was plunged into the black and fetid stream that rolls beneath. Thus the miscreants were assured of impunity, for the next tide carried the corpse down the river; and, even if it were discovered, there would be no marks of violence, and the victim of murder would be regarded as a suicide."

"Horrible!" exclaimed Sam, with a slight shudder. "Are you not afraid to live here all by yourself?"

"No, boy," returned the old mud-lark; "the terrors with which superstition has invested this old house are my protection against annoyance or ejection. But let us go up-stairs; it is not so chilly and dismal-looking there."

"How long have you lived here?" asked Sam, as they ascended the broken stairs, which creaked and trembled beneath their weight.

"About nine years," replied the old man. "Some day you shall hear my history; I wrote it one day, from a strange whim, and there it is in the closet. I was not always a mud-lark; there was a time—but no matter. Do you think you can get your living, like me, by groping in the sewers and along the mud of the river?"

"Yes," returned Sam; "but can we not go in and out any other way than the sewers?"

"Yes; at night we can slip out unperceived, sell our old iron, or whatever we can pick up, and have a bit of supper," replied the old man. "I have all my meals at the public-house, for the rats would speedily demolish any thing that was brought here."

The old mud-lark then struck a light, and, having lit his pipe, sat down on the broken floor. Sam followed his example, and they passed the time until evening, in talking of the tragedies that had probably been enacted within the four walls of that ruinous dwelling.

CHAPTER XVI.

THE MINIATURE.

It was towards the close of a fine evening in the summer of 1826, when Sam Skelter, who had then been domiciled with the old mud-lark about twelve months, was pursuing his way and his avocations in the sewer which, passing under Fetter-lane, empties its filthy stream into the Thames near the Temple-gardens. Suddenly he stopped, for some glittering object caught his eye, lying half-imbedded in the filth on one side of the arched passage. He stooped and picked it up, and wiped it on his dirty trousers; but, in the glimmering light which came down the iron grating of the gully-hole above, he could only perceive that it was some trinket or ornament, and, thrusting it into his pocket, he continued his subterranean journey. The rolling of carriages in the busy streets above was but faintly heard, and the quick steps and voices of the passengers became lost in the distance, or only reached the ears of the young mud-lark as a low and confused murmur. Sam Skelter hurried along the damp and gloomy passage, assured that he had found a greater prize than had ever rewarded his researches in the sewers before; and at length he gained the outlet near the Temple-gardens. It was low water, and, standing over his ankles in the mud of the river, he hastily examined his glittering prize.

It was a miniature of a young female of exquisite beauty, and clad in the picturesque garb of the nations of southern Asia. Sam Skelter was immediately struck by the resemblance of the miniature to the little street-dancer, the adopted daughter of the Malay juggler; and the thought which that resemblance caused to enter his mind was, that he must be gazing on the portrait of Lolah's mother.

The miniature was set round with diamonds, and was consequently of considerable value; but Sam was so impressed with the idea that thereon hung the secret of Lolah's birth, that he determined to restore it, if he could find a clue to the owner, and trust to that person's generosity for his reward. This determination, which he arrived at while paddling through the mud towards the nearest stairs, rendered him fearful of returning to West-street, lest the old mud-lark should discover his prize, and insist on converting it into beer, gin, and tobacco. He had no money in his pocket, and the temptation to obtain from a pawnbroker an advance on the miniature was very great, but Sam withstood it, and wended his way towards Blackfriars-bridge, musing on the necessary steps to be taken to obtain a clue to the owner of the miniature.

Crossing the unsightly-looking bridge of Blackfriars, Sam wended his way along the Commercial-road, towards Waterloo-bridge. The thoroughfare we have named runs close to the river, having a row of small private houses on one side, and on the other coal and timber wharves, extending as far as the bottom of the Cornwall-road, which runs down from the New-cut, where it takes the name of the Belvidere-road, and, passing under a dry arch of Waterloo-bridge, is continued as far as the foot of Westminster-bridge. The dry arches of Waterloo-bridge form the nightly resort of numbers of shivering and houseless wretches, the neglected children of society: the arch protects them from rain, and thus forms an agreeable variationto the cabbage-leaves of Covent-garden and the cold steps of St. Martin's workhouse. In summer, many of these homeless outcasts prefer the shelter of the trees in St. James's-park, on account of the cold breezes from the river; but the excellence of the roof causes the bridge to be selected by the experienced in wet weather.

Waterloo-bridge, though decidedly the most beautiful structure of the kind which spans the noble river which flows beneath, is one abounding in painful interest; as if it were not enough that its very name should conjure up reminiscences of that day of blood, the baneful effects of which have not yet ceased, it has acquired a melancholy renown as the spot from which so many unfortunates have taken a plunge into the darkness of eternity, seeking refuge from remorse, or misery, or shame, beneath the rippling waters of Old Father Thames.

Perhaps there is not a stone of the balustered recesses of that handsome bridge, whose piers rise white and graceful in the moonlight from the dark bosom of the silently-flowing river, which has not been the last resting-place of some poor wretch whom intolerable grief has made weary of life—some lovely unfortunate, shrinking from her misery and shame—some unwed mother, forsaken by her seducer—some victim of persecution—some wretch bewildered by remorse. Yet how few of the thousands who daily cross that bridge, in quest of business or pleasure, ever think of these things, or bestow more than a passing thought upon the shivering outcasts who cower beneath the dry arches, or the unfortunate females who nightly throng the pavement, in the hope of attracting some passenger returning from the theatres. The melting glance, the bewitching smile, and the laugh of forced merriment, are all that meet the eye and ear; but these are but the effervescence on the surface, while in the silent depths of the heart lies the canker that preys on the springs of life—the recollections of home and childhood that rise in the hour of their apparent gaiety, like corpses floating on the sunlit river.

These associations give a melancholy interest to the bridge which derives its name from the crowning carnage of the war of royal legitimacy; and as we stand upon its level footway, and gaze on the mighty flood that rolls beneath, we cannot fail to be forcibly struck with the truthful lines of Charles Mackay:

" Mighty river—oh! mighty river,
Rolling, in ebb and flow, for ever,
Through the city, so vast and old—
Through massive bridges—by domes and spires,
Crowned with the smoke of a myriad fires;
City of majesty, power, and gold:
Thou lovest to float, on thy waters dull,
The white-winged fleets, so beautiful,
And the lordly steamers, speeding along,
Wind defying, and swift and strong;
Thou bearest them all on thy motherly breast,
Laden with riches, at trade's behest—
Bounteous trade, whose wine and corn
Stock the garner and fill the horn,
Who gives us luxury, joy, and pleasure,
Stintless, sumless, out of measure:
Thou art a rich and a mighty river,
Rolling, in ebb and flow, for ever.

" Doleful river—oh! doleful river,
Pale on thy breast the moonbeams quiver,
Through the city, so drear and cold—
City of sorrows hard to bear,
Of guilt, injustice, and despair;
Thou hidest below, in thy treacherous waters,
The death-cold forms of Beauty's daughters,
The corses pale of the young and sad—
Of the old, whom sorrow has goaded mad—
Mothers of babes that cannot know
The sires that left them to their woe—
Women forlorn, and men that run
The race of passion, and die undone;
Thou takest them all in thy careless wave—
Thou givest them all a ready grave:
Thou art a black and a doleful river,
Rolling, in ebb and flow, for ever.

" In ebb and flow, for ever and ever,
So rolls the world, thou murky river—
So rolls the tide, above and below;
Above, the rower impels his boat—
Below, with the current, the dead men float.
The waves may smile in the sunny glow,
While above, in the glitter, and pomp, and glare,
The flags of the vessels flap the air;
But below, in the silent under-tide,
The waters vomit the wretch that died.
Above, the sound of the music swells
From the passing ship, from the city-bells;
From below there cometh a gurgling breath,
As the desperate diver yields to death.

Above and below, the waters go,
Bearing their burden of joy or woe,
Rolling along, thou mighty river,
In ebb and flow, for ever and ever."

Sam Skelter passed the night under Waterloo-bridge, and, with the early dawn, went shivering forth from that refuge of the destitute, and wandered towards the foot of London-bridge, musing upon the resemblance of the miniature to the lovely dancing-girl, and the steps to be taken to establish the identity. At that hour the great city is in its most composed and quiet state; and it is the only one for calm contemplation of its many strange scenes and unfathomable mysteries. A grey mist hangs over the river, the sparrows twitter on the housetops, and ever and anon the pavement echoes the tread of some approaching policeman. It is light as day, and yet the streets are silent and deserted, as if it were a city of the dead. The honest and industrious are buried in the repose necessary to prepare them for the cares and toils of the coming day; the theatres have disgorged their multitudes, and the taverns and concert-rooms are deserted, even by the latest revellers; the burglar has done his work, and slinks to his lair like some night-prowling depredator of the woods; and even the houseless destitute seek repose, though it be under the shelter of the trees in the immediate vicinity of that costly royalty which is housed so well at their expense. The first hour after daybreak is therefore that which presents the greatest solitude and quiet which so vast a hive of humanity can know.

It is only for about an hour that this quietude in the midst of a city swarming with life can be experienced. Soon is heard the rattle of tradesmen's carts proceeding to market, then the hurried tread of labourers who have a distance to go to their employment; and these come thicker and faster until they mingle with the cheerful, rosy-cheeked Welsh women with their milk-cans, and old men with water-cresses. Then smiling housemaids and servants of all-work appear at the doors, and the keepers of taverns and early coffee-houses begin to take down their shutters; these are soon followed by the bakers and grocers, and the streets begin to exhibit that busy and bustling appearance which they present during the day, and, with very little diminution, until after midnight.

CHAPTER XVII.

THE VICTIM OF OPIUM.

SAM SKELTER passed over London-bridge, usually so thronged with vehicles and passengers, but then silent and deserted, and turning down Thames-street, sauntered towards Tower-hill. He looked up at the white walls of the old fortress—vestige of Norman feudalism—which were beginning to reflect the first slanting rays of the morning-sun; and passing over the spacious area in the midst of which it stands, he proceeded down East Smithfield. He was guided by no definite purpose in the way which he took, but was drawn on, as if instinctively, towards the scenes amid which he had passed his early childhood.

He had reached Ratcliffe-highway, wiling away the hours by loitering about and gazing at the shop-windows, and it was now near the meridian hour, when a sudden outcry and confusion on the opposite side of the street drew his attention, and he beheld a man in the oriental costume running along the pavement brandishing a long dagger, and crying fiercely: "Kill! kill!" The terrified passengers sprang into the road, as the excited wretch rushed madly along; and one poor fellow, whom he had stabbed with his formidable weapon, was taken up, bleeding profusely, and carried into the nearest surgeon's.

With countenance pale and haggard, with eyes wild and staring, the Asiatic rushed madly along the street, raising his murderous cry, and menacing all whom he encountered with destruction; but all at once his career was terminated by the courage and dexterity of a gentleman who happened to be passing, and flinging his stick between the legs of the Oriental, he was thrown down and speedily disarmed. He was almost stunned by the violence of his fall, his head having struck the pavement; and two or three constables being immediately on the spot, he was taken at once before the magistrates, followed by a great concourse of people.

As soon as Sam could obtain a near view of the fellow's countenance, he recognised the Malay juggler who had passed as the father of the pretty Lolah; and this circumstance induced him to follow with the crowd to the court. As soon as the case was disposed of which was then before the magistrates, Alompra was placed at the bar, and the gentleman who had been instrumental in effecting his capture entered the witness-box. The mad and furious excitement of the Malay—the result of excessive and habitual indulgence in opium, which he had now acquired the habit of chewing as well as smoking—had now given place to an apathetic stupor: he trembled violently, as if every nerve had been shattered by the deadly drug; his countenance was haggard and distorted; the veins on his temples had the appearance of dark cords, and his whole frame was frightfully emaciated.

The constable who had taken the charge against the prisoner having stated it to the magistrates, and the oath having been administered to the gentleman in the witness-box, the latter gave evidence to the following effect:

" I am master of an Indiaman now lying in the London-docks. My name is Hastings. Passing along Ratcliffe-highway within the last half-hour, I saw the prisoner rushing along the street with a long dagger in his hand, crying: " Kill! kill!" and striking at all whom he encountered. Having been much in the East, and witnessed the manner in which the police arrest the muck-runners of Batavia and Achen, I threw my stick between his legs and tripped him up. The creese or dagger was then taken from him by a butcher, and two or three constables coming up almost immediately, he was taken into custody; and I then heard that a young man had been stabbed by him."

" You did not see the man stabbed ?" said one of the magistrates, interrogatively.

" I did not."

" Call the next witness."

Mr. Hastings left the witness-box, but remained in the court, attentively scrutinising the sinister countenance of the Malay.

Two labouring men then deposed to seeing the prisoner strike a young man with his creese, and to picking up the unfortunate man, and carrying him to the surgery of the nearest medical man. The constables then gave their evidence, which corroborated that of Mr. Hastings; and by the time these witnesses had been examined, the surgeon arrived who had dressed the wound of the victim of Alompra's murderous frenzy. He deposed that the young man had received a severe wound in the region of the stomach, that much loss of blood had ensued, and that the unfortunate man was unable to give evidence, and was in a very precarious state from the nature of the injuries inflicted by the Malay's weapon.

" I know the prisoner, your worships," said Mr. Hastings, re-ascending the witness-box as the surgeon quitted it. " Thirteen years ago, I first saw him in the island of Sumatra, off the coast of which I was shipwrecked, in the year 1813. The prisoner was then in the service of the Dutch East India Company, and, having an imaginary prior claim upon the affections of a young lady whom I married at Achen, he conceived a deadly antipathy to me, and twice made an attempt on my life. My wife having died at Singapore, I returned to England, in 1815, bringing with me my child, a little girl about twelve months old. Until to-day, I have not seen the prisoner since I left Singapore on that occasion; but, on the very first night that I slept in England, the child was stolen in a most incredible manner, and I have endeavoured in vain to discover her from that day until now. If the prisoner be remanded for a week or two, as I presume he will be, inquiries might be made as to the time of his coming to England, and whether he has ever been seen with a child, which may elicit information of an important nature."

Sam Skelter eagerly drank in with his ears very word of the above statement, and then, pressing forward, he touched the arm of one of the constables, and whispered: " I know the darky, and can tell a good deal about him."

" Please your worships," said the constable, here is a boy who has evidence to give respecting the prisoner, which may be of consequence to this gentleman's case."

" Let him be sworn," said the magistrate.

Mr. Hastings again withdrew from the witness-box, and Sam Skelter entered it; and, after being duly questioned as to his knowledge of the nature and obligation of an oath, he was sworn.

" Now, state what you know concerning the man at the bar," said the magistrate.

" I have known him as long as I can remember, and I am about eleven years old," deposed the boy, with a side-glance at the Malay. " Part of the time, he lived in the same house as me and my father, and used to go about doing tricks with knives and balls; and a little girl used to go with him, and dance in the streets."

" How old was the little girl?" asked the magistrate; and Mr. Hastings waited with intense anxiety for the boy's reply. As for the prisoner, he seemed to have sunk into a listless stupor, in which he was scarcely conscious of what was going on around him.

" About two years ago, she told me she was ten years old," replied Sam.

" Describe her features."

" She was as much like that as one pea is like another," said the boy; and he produced the miniature set with diamonds, which he had found in the sewer.

" Where did you obtain this miniature?" asked the magistrate, suspiciously.

" I found it in the sewer which runs under Fetter-lane, down to the river near the Temple-gardens," replied Sam Skelter.

" What business had you in the sewer?" inquired the magistrate, with increased suspicion.

" I am a mud-lark, and get my living by groping in the sewers, and in the mud of the river at low water, for old iron, or anything that gets lost," replied Sam; " and I found that picture in the sewer, as I just said."

" Do you know this miniature, Mr. Hastings?" asked the magistrate.

" I do; it is mine—it is the likeness of my wife!" exclaimed Mr. Hastings, with emotion. " I lost it a few days ago, but where, or in what manner, I am unable to say. When did you find it, my man?" said he, turning to the young mud-lark.

" Yesterday evening, sir," replied Sam.

" And where is the girl of whom you spoke just now?" continued Mr. Hastings.

" I have not seen her for twelve months, sir," returned the boy; " for she ran away from home at that time, and went away with some show-people, last Stepney fair."

" Why did she leave her home?" inquired Mr. Hastings, in a tone of painful anxiety.

" She said that the juggler threatened to kill her, when he was mad, like he is to-day, and told her that he was not her father," replied Sam.

" I can no longer doubt that the girl of whom this boy speaks is my daughter," said Mr. Hastings, addressing the magistrates. " The prisoner must have stolen her, and brought her up as a dancing-girl, to gratify his malignant feelings against me. Come with me, honest lad," said he, turning to Sam Skelter, " and I will reward you for the restoration of the miniature."

Mr. Hastings and Sam Skelter then left the court, and the Malay was remanded until the man whom he had stabbed was able to attend and give evidence against him.

The merchant-captain and the young mud-lark repaired to a coffee-house in the neighbourhood, and, on Mr. Hastings finding that the boy had fasted since the preceding morning, he ordered him a plentiful meal of coffee and bread and butter. When Sam had satisfied the cravings of his stomach, he related, in detail, all that he knew of Lolah and the Malay, every circumstance of which tended to impress Mr. Hastings more and more with the conviction that the dancing-girl was his long-lost daughter. But Sam had not seen her for rather more than twelve months, and most probably she was no longer in London. Where then should he seek her? In a few moments he had decided on the first step; for his impatience to recover his lost daughter would brook no delay: he determined to seek the assistance of the police-officers of Bow-street, whose shrewdness and perseverance in tracing out criminals and fraudulent bankrupts were well known to him. He accordingly called a hackney-coach, and, desiring Sam to accompany him, ordered the driver to take them to Bow-street.

Alighting at a public-house near the court, which at that time was much frequented by the thief-taking fraternity, Mr. Hastings discharged the coach, and entered the parlour, followed by the young mud-lark. Here he found the famous Ruthven, the officer who arrested Thistlewood, the leader of the Cato-street conspirators; and to him he related the circumstances attending the abduction of his child, and the manner in which she had been reared by the Malay juggler.

"There is a fair held this very day at a little place in Essex, about ten miles out of town," observed Ruthven, after a pause, during which he had been pondering on the singular nature of Mr. Hastings' statement. "What say you to a drive down, sir?—and we'll take this kinchin with us to 'dentify her."

"With all my heart; and if you succeed in recovering her, I will give you fifty pounds," said Mr. Hastings.

Ruthven then desired the waiter to call a hackney-coach, into which the party got, and were driven rapidly round the corner, into Long-acre.

CHAPTER XVIII.

THE LOST ONE FOUND.

THROUGH the city went the hackney-coach containing Mr. Hastings, Ruthven, and Sam Skelter, down the Whitechapel-road, through Mile-end and Stratford, and along the dull, flat road leading to Romford. At length they reached the village where the fair was being held, and, leaving the vehicle at the only inn in the place, the party walked towards the village green, while the driver solaced himself with a pint of Calvert's XXX and a pipe of tobacco. Down one side of the green were a dozen drinking and dancing-booths of greater or less pretensions, and on the other side were two or three shows, including a scenic exhibition of the battle of Waterloo, a collection of living curiosities, and, conspicuous above all, the canvass theatre of Signor Alleno, to which that individual was making tremendous exertions to attract the gaping rustics.

"We shall soon see whether she is here," observed Ruthven; and scarcely had he spoken the words when the faded green-baize curtain which hung in front of the entrance from the external stage was raised, and a beautiful girl of twelve years old made her appearance. A garland of artificial roses was twined about her raven locks, and her short dress of white muslin contrasted well with her clear olive complexion.

"There she is!—that is her!" exclaimed Sam Skelter; and a thrill of joy pervaded the heart of Mr. Hastings.

"The very image of her mother!" said he, gazing upon the lovely dancer, who had begun one of the voluptuous Eastern dances which Alompra had taught her.

"Let us wait till she is done dancing, and then go up," said Ruthven. "It is of no use to make an unnecessary hubbub about the affair."

Mr. Hastings consented to wait; but, unable to restrain his feelings, he returned to the public-house, leaving Ruthven to negociate with Mr. Allen for the release of Lolah from whatever engagement she might have entered into. Ruthven was not sorry to have succeeded so easy in their search after the lost girl, and, when she had concluded her dance, he ascended the steps leading to the platform in front of the theatre, followed by Sam Skelter.

"Can I speak a word to this young lady in private?" said Ruthven, addressing Allen, and indicating Lolah by pointing his thumb over his shoulder.

"What is the nature of your business, sir?" asked Allen, looking sharply at the officer.

"My business is private, sir," returned Ruthven. "My name is Ruthven, and I am a Bow-street officer."

"Well, the theatre is empty; you can speak with her there," said Mr. Allen, upon whom the announcement of Ruthven's name and profession made an evident impression in his favour.

"My dear, I want just one word with you, if you please," said the Bow-street officer, turning to the beautiful dancer; and he forthwith raised the curtain of faded green-baize, and motioned her to enter the canvass theatre.

"With me!" ejaculated Lolah, shaking her jetty ringlets from her forehead, and opening her brilliant eyes with surprise.

"Yes," responded Ruthven, as he and Sam Skelter followed the beautiful girl into the theatre. "Do you know this young gentleman with the dirty trousers?"

"Sam Skelter!" exclaimed Lolah, clapping her hands joyfully, and then extending them to her former play-fellow."

"Yes; how glad I am we have found you!" said Sam, taking the girl's hand in his own.

8

" Do you know anything about your father, young lady?—that is what we have come about," observed Ruthven.

" My father! I only know Alompra, and I am sure he was not my father, for he threatened to kill me; and he said so himself," returned Lolah, shrugging her beautiful shoulders.

" Well, there is a gentleman up at the Feathers as says he is your father, and you was stolen from him when you was a infant," said Ruthven; " and he commissioned me to make the journey pleasant with old Allen, and take you away with me. Now, are you bound any way to stop with Allen for a certain time?"

" Oh, no; I can leave him when I choose; but he will expect me to finish this fair with him," replied Lolah.

" Well, we can arrange that, I dare say," observed Ruthven; and, raising the curtain, he returned to the platform with Sam Skelter, while Lolah hastened to acquaint her friend, Caroline Allen, with her good fortune.

" The father of that young lady has commissioned me to release her from her professional engagements with you, sir," said the Bow-street officer, approaching the proprietor of the theatre. " I suppose a sovereign will amply recompense you for the loss of her services during the fair?"

" Why, yes," returned Mr. Allen, taking the proffered coin. " There's a trifle of money due to her, but as she leaves me at rather an inconvenient time——"

" We will forego that, Mr. Allen," interrupted Ruthven.

" Who is her father?" inquired Allen.

" All I know of him is, that he promised me fifty pounds to come down from London after her," replied the Bow-street officer; " so he must be a trump-card, and no end of a brick."

Lolah was now ready for her departure, and, having bid adieu to her friend Caroline, she tripped down the steps after Ruthven and the mud-lark. They were not long in walking to the Feathers, and, entering the parlour, they found Mr. Hastings waiting; but as the room was full of farmers and their wives and daughters, and holiday-making people from the surrounding neighbourhood, he checked his parental feelings, and hurried Lolah into the hackney-coach. The half-shabby and half-flaunting style of the young girl's dress caused some of the pleasure-seekers lounging about the inn to make some not very charitable remarks upon the morality of Mr. Hastings; but they were unheeded, and the whole party were driven off in the direction of the great metropolis.

The mother of Mr. Hastings had been for some time dead, his charming sisters were married, and he now lived, a lonely widower, in the neighbourhood of Stratford, a little removed from the noise and bustle of the city, and yet sufficiently near to the river and the docks. Here the driver of the hackney-coach was ordered to stop, and wait to take Ruthven back to Bow-street, and the party entered the house.

" Now, Mr. Ruthven, what expenses have you incurred on account of this business?" said Mr. Hastings.

" Why, sir, I gave Allen a sovereign to release the young lady from her engagement with him; and, as for other expenses, we'll say nothing about them," replied Ruthven.

" Well, there is the sovereign, and there are notes to the amount I promised you—two twenties and a ten," said Mr. Hastings, taking the sovereign from his pocket, and the bank-notes from his cash-box, and laying them on the table.

Ruthven was not slow in transferring the notes to his pocket-book, and, thanking Mr. Hastings for his liberality, he left the house, and returned in the hackney-coach to Bow-street.

" As for you," said Mr. Hastings to Sam Skelter, " you have done me a greater service than even the officer, since from you came the clue which led to the recovery of my daughter. I owe you something, too, for the restoration of the miniature. Your reward shall therefore be in proportion to your services. You shall be a mud-lark no longer. Henceforth, I take upon myself your future welfare, and I will clothe and educate you, so that, when you are old enough, you shall be able to get your living in any way that shall be most agreeable to you."

Sam Skelter expressed his gratitude in the best manner that he was able, but for the moment could hardly believe in the reality of his good fortune. Mr. Hastings then turned to Lolah, and overwhelmed her with questions relative to Alompra; and the answers of the pretty dancer convinced him more than ever that she was the child who had been stolen in so remarkable a manner, on the night of his return to Camberwell, after his long absence in the East. In the evening, he took her to his eldest sister, who resided in Aldgate, and in her care he left her, that she might be clothed in a manner suitable to her improved prospects; and he then took Sam Skelter to a clothier, and fitted him out in a decent manner.

On the following day, Sam was placed at a respectable boarding-academy at Mile-end; and, in a few days afterwards, the delighted Lolah was taken by her aunt to a genteel seminary near Hackney, Mr. Hastings having to leave England in a few weeks.

On the second examination of Alompra, the written deposition of the young man whom he had stabbed, taken at the hospital, was produced in evidence, together with the certificate of the surgeon, stating that he was out of danger, but unable to be removed. This being deemed sufficient, the Malay was committed for trial, on the charge of cutting and wounding with intent to do some grievous bodily harm.

He underwent his trial at the ensuing Middlesex sessions, and, the evidence being complete and conclusive, he was sentenced to seven years' transportation; but, as only convicts for a longer term are sent to the penal settlements in Australia, he was removed to the *Euryalus* hulk, lying off Woolwich. Some convicts, sentenced to five or seven years' transportation, are sent to Bermuda; but though many prefer remaining in England, on account of the difficulty of returning from a transmarine station, the condition of those sent to Bermuda is far preferable. They are assured of food, clothing, and lodging; they work no harder than they would have to do in this country, and they have quite as much freedom as the labourer who trudges to his work at daybreak and returns to his wretched home at sunset. Happy fellows! they have not to walk about, hollow-eyed and hungry—willing to work, but finding it not; they have not to go for relief to a board of guardians, and be refused it, because they have been offered employment at six shillings per week by one of the guardians, and have declined it. They have not freedom; but what a mockery it is to talk of the freedom of the labouring classes in England! Free to do what? Free to starve —free to choose the ditch they will die in; that is the sole freedom which class-legislation has left the industrious working-bees of this country. The convicts of Bermuda and the slaves of Maryland are as free as they.

CHAPTER XIX.

THE CONVICT-HULK.

Two years had the Malay passed at Woolwich, working hard by day and confined on board the convict-hulk at night, still brooding over his long-cherished projects of vengeance, his desire for which had been sharpened by the reflection that he owed his capture and present punishment to his old enemy, Mr. Hastings. Day and night he brooded over his imaginary wrongs, and watched with the vigilance of a savage for an opportunity of escape. But the convicts were so well watched and guarded by the marines, both on shore and on board the hulk, that more than two years passed away without an opportunity of escape presenting itself.

Towards the close of a fine afternoon, while the last rays of the setting sun illumined the rippling bosom of the Thames, a private of the artillery approached the Malay, and seemed to wish to speak to him, but afraid of being observed.

" You are about my height, friend," said he, at length; " what say you to a change of clothes?"

Alompra looked hard at the soldier, who was a fine martial-looking young man; the latter smiled faintly at the convict's surprise, and repeated his proposal.

" We shall be seen," objected the Malay.

" We are not observed, and you can reach the marsh in no time," whispered the soldier, looking cautiously around. ."Away into the marsh, and I will follow you."

Alompra hesitated no longer, but darted into the marsh. The young soldier glanced hastily around, and then sprang after him, with rapid strides.

" I only want your trousers," said the soldier, as each hurriedly threw off his garments ; " your coat would be as bad as my own. They have refused me leave of absence, to see a sister who is near her death—the wretches ! If you can get away, so much the better; if you are found out, you will be no worse off than you are now. They will never see me any more; they would never have had me at all, if starvation had not driven me into the army. There—I shall look like a man leaving his work, or a poor devil on tramp. As for you, you had better hide in the marshes till it is dark, and then be off to London."

The metamorphosis was now as complete as, under the circumstances, it well could be : the soldier had lost his military appearance, and looked, in his own words, like " a poor devil on tramp ;" but the Malay found himself under the necessity of passing for either an escaped convict or a deserter from the army. The young soldier who had thus taken the liberty which the tyranny of his officers had denied him, strode with rapid steps through the marsh, leaving Alompra to adopt whatever course might seem best to himself. Avoiding the high road as much as possible, the soldier pushed on to Greenwich, where he purchased a flannel jacket and a cloth cap, and took a boat to the opposite side of the river.

The Malay, in the meantime, had pulled on the soldier's trousers, and as his own coat would have betrayed him, he took it off, and concealed it among the rushes and rank grass of the marsh. To have put on the red coat and military cap of the young soldier would have been equally perilous ; he therefore determined to abandon them, and take his chance of being suspected through the trousers. He then thought of the advice of the soldier, relative to waiting in the marsh until night; but he feared that, if he waited for the darkness, his escape would be discovered, and the marsh searched for him; while, if he started off at once, he could almost reach London before his absence would be discovered.

Impressed with this conviction, he quitted the marsh, and struck into the bye-roads, intending to proceed to Lewisham, as he shrewdly calculated that, when his escape was discovered, his pursuers would take the London road in search of him, as the metropolis is the general resort of escaped prisoners and convicts, and criminals flying from justice. The reason is obvious : in the metropolis, a stranger is no more regarded than a drop of water in the ocean ; in a country-town or village, he is immediately recognised as such by the whole population. He had scarcely left the marsh, when a countryman came up to the spot where he had left the soldier's clothes ; and, after staring a few minutes at them in mute amazement, and scratching his head, as if puzzled to account for their appearance there, his broad unmeaning countenance relaxed into a grin, and, tucking up his smock-frock he put on the scarlet coat, and buttoned it over his rustic habiliments ; then, putting the military cap on his head, he strutted out of the marsh, very much pleased with his martial appearance, but looking as much unlike a soldier as it is possible to conceive. The foolish fellow promised himself some rare sport in his disguise ; and, chuckling over this anticipation, he proceeded towards a public-house about a mile from Woolwich, on the road to London.

The escape of the Malay was discovered when the roll was called, and a party of marines was immediately dispatched in pursuit of him. After searching in the neighbouring marshes, they proceeded towards Greenwich, but failed to obtain any tidings of the runaway convict. The absence of the young soldier from his barracks was not discovered until a later hour; but when it was found that he was missing, the officers immediately concluded that he had deserted, and ordered a serjeant to take a file of men, and go in search of him. The picket having already visited every public-house in Woolwich, the party set out at once towards Greenwich ; and, on entering the first tavern they came to on the road, they found the countryman wearing the coat and cap of the deserter, and half-intoxicated.

"Come, old boy," said the serjeant, "you must come along with us."

The rustic's countenance fell, and he became sober all at once, at this termination of his adventure.

"Oh, lor! I didn't mean any harm, Mr. Serjeant," said he; "I ain't a soger at all—it's only a lark, sir. I'm a civil'un, if you please."

"You are either a rogue or a fool," rejoined the serjeant, with some asperity. "Where did you get those things?"

"Found 'em, sir. I'm a fool—as maister often tells me—but I never knowed it afore," said the chop-fallen countryman, scratching his head.

"Fetch a constable, landlord," said the serjeant. "We will soon see if this fellow has told the truth."

"O dear!—O Lord!" said the terrified rustic, falling on his knees. "Pray doan't send me afore the justice. I found the things in Woolwich marshes, and just put 'em on for a lark."

"After all, it may be as he says," observed the serjeant. "You are a foolish fellow, and I have a great mind to have you locked up. Why did you not bring those things to the barracks, when you found them? Come, take them off, sir."

The rustic was glad to escape so easily; he took off the red coat and cap, and surrendered them to the military party, which immediately left the public-house, and proceeded towards Greenwich.

Alompra had, in the meantime, reached Lewisham, a long straggling village, near the skirts of Blackheath, and from thence he walked on to Sydenham, where he entered a public-house, and solicited charity in the tap-room. Having gathered a few halfpence, he rested himself, and partook of some slight refreshment, and then continued his journey. He passed through Dulwich and Camberwell, and, about midnight, entered a low lodging-house in the obscure quarter of Lock's-fields, weary and fatigued, and with only just enough halfpence to pay for one night's lodging, even in that miserable place.

But two powerful feelings sustained him, and rendered him heedless alike of danger and fatigue; the first was, the sense of freedom which he experienced, when he strode from the marsh, and found himself at large, though the ban of the law was still upon him; and the other, which now chiefly absorbed him, was his insatiate longing after vengeance. And yet how different, and how opposed to each other in spirit, were those two feelings; for the love of liberty is a natural and inalienable aspiration of the human mind, while revenge is one of those dark and evil passions engrafted in man's nature by the wrong impulse which a perverted state of society has given to his best feelings. It is the child of selfishness—the prolific mother of all sin, and is totally repugnant to the genuine spirit of Christianity.

Yet it was this dark and merciless feeling which now held permanent sway over the heart and brain of the vindictive Malay, and he ground his teeth with repressed passion, as he thought of the beautiful Sumatran maiden whom Mr. Hastings had snatched from him, of the manner in which the offspring of that maiden's union with his rival had escaped from the vengeance which he had meditated the infliction of, and of the recent punishment he had undergone through the instrumentality of that same hated rival. Fifteen years had not sufficed to soften the heart of the dark-souled Malay, but had rather impressed it more deeply with the cherished memory of all that he had suffered during that long period.

These dark and vengeful thoughts had often visited the mind of Alompra during his confinement on board the hulk, and they came upon him with redoubled force now that he was at liberty to put them in execution. The fear of being retaken aroused all the dormant energies of his mind, not so much to provide for his personal safety, as to ensure the accomplishment of his cherished scheme of vengeance.

Early on the following morning, he left the lodging-house in Lock's-fields, and proceeded through Bermondsey into Tooley-street; taking that route in order to avoid observation as much as possible. He crossed London-bridge (the one which preceded the present massive structure), and, turning down Thames-street, proceeded towards the docks, as the most likely place to hear of Mr. Hastings. He knew not where that gentleman resided, or even if he were in England or abroad; but, by dint of much perseverance and assiduity in inquiry in the neighbourhood of the docks, he learned that Mr. Hastings had arrived in London a few days before, as the commander of a brig then lying in St Katherine's-docks.

He then went round the docks, narrowly watching the vessel, and elicited that Captain Hastings, as the sailor who gave him the information called him, was not on board the vessel; the sailor did not know where he could be found, but gave the Malay the address of the owners. Alompra then called at the counting-house of the firm of Shipp and Co., at Shadwell, and there learned that Captain Hastings was at the same house at Stratford, in which he was residing at the time of the Malay's trial. Thitherward, therefore, did the vindictive man bend his course, and, having examined the exterior of the house as closely as he could without exciting notice and suspicion, he returned to Shadwell, and lounged about at various public-houses until nightfall. Then he again repaired to Stratford, and, while again watching the house of his intended victim, he was surprised and disappointed to see Mr. Hastings issue from it, and walk rapidly towards town. He was, therefore, compelled to abandon his murderous design for that night at least, and followed Mr. Hastings at a distance, until he lost sight of him in the stream of pedestrians in the Whitechapel-road.

CHAPTER XX.

THE DESERTER.

The young soldier who had deserted from Woolwich at the time the convict Alompra succeeded in effecting his escape, had, in the meantime, reached the home of his childhood in a small village in Essex. Five years before he had left that straw-roofed cottage, sad and dispirited; for want of employment had caused him to enlist in the army, and he left his native village with the gay ribbons in his tattered straw-hat, which denoted that he had bestowed his liberty for bread. Yes, liberty and conscience! for the soldier parts with both when he takes the fatal shilling, and becomes a mere machine in the hands of the oppressors of the order which he quits. The poor fellow could find no employment, for there is always a large reserve of labour, and the competition is eager even for the miserable pittance of six shillings per week; therefore, he became a soldier. Thousands of the British army could tell the same tale. The young recruit soon had reason to regret the fatal step which bound him to do the bidding of every martinet who wore an epaulette; the wearying fatigue of the drill, the domineering of the serjeants, and the confinement in the barracks —less liberty being allowed to soldiers than to apprentice boys—completely disgusted him.

From the moment he became a soldier, he found he had no will of his own; and though his thoughts were free, the expression of them was not—for the soldier must have no ideas or opinions at variance with those of his officers. The British soldier, however, has scarcely the protection which the laws extend to his fellow-subjects, nor is he amenable to the same tribunals or the same modes of punishment. For him there is only the mutiny-bill and the articles of war, the degrading lash, and the shot exercise. Eternal execration for the demon in human shape who invented this body-breaking punishment! It consists in walking in a circle for several hours, and, at every few yards, stooping to pick up a cannon-shot of the largest size, which is carried a certain distance, and then deposited on the ground for a moment, after which it is again lifted, and the fatiguing, monstrous, and useless exercise is repeated.

And then the degrading punishment of the lacerating lash! Why should those to whom is entrusted the honour of our country be subjected to this horrible torture, which the laws will not allow to be inflicted upon the greatest criminal? And yet until lately a man could be flogged to death with impunity, provided he was a soldier. How can honour, rectitude, and virtue be expected from an army which submits to such horrible and degrading punishments?

Complaints are often heard of the licentiousness which prevails in the army, and of which we have lately seen an instance, made memorable by the terrible retribution which overtook the evil-doer; and we know that in Woolwich, in Chatham, and in all places where soldiers are congregated in great numbers, they constitute a social nuisance of the worst degree. This is not less true of the officers than the privates; and, if excuses can be found for the former, how much less culpable are the latter! The immorality which prevails in the army, and which a regiment spreads wherever it is quartered, is chargeable entirely upon government; firstly, from not educating the class from which the army is mainly recruited; and secondly, for the inferior circumstances amid which the soldier is placed, the inevitable tendency of which is to deprave his morals, and brutalise his mind. Why is it that we cannot take ten shops in the streets of Chatham without passing a public-house, or encountering a knot of drunken soldiers? Why is it that the streets of that town, of Woolwich, and of every place where a large military force is constantly maintained, are thronged with unfortunate women? Because the soldier is treated as a machine, and not as a man; because he has not been taught to appreciate intellectual pleasures; because no proportionate encouragement is given to good conduct on the part of the private soldier; because only a certain number in each regiment are allowed to marry; because an immoral example is set them by their officers; and because the soldier's wife must sleep in the same room with the single men of the regiment.

The soul of the Essex labourer revolted against these monstrous evils and iniquities, but he felt that he was powerless, that he was no longer master of his own thoughts, and that the slightest murmur would be severely punished. Workmen may meet to discuss their social and political grievances, and no cognizance is now taken of the sternest language; but such proceedings on the part of soldiers would be considered mutinous, and all who took part in them would be subjected to punishment. How can such an army guard the liberties of the people? The idea is absurd: liberty can only be guarded by those who live under its inestimable blessings. The position of the soldier, therefore, with respect to his condition, and the means of ameliorating it, is a very painful one; he is not only deprived of liberty himself, but he is made the unwilling instrument of perpetuating the political serfdom of others. Every few years the misgovernment of our rulers brings the people and the army into hostile contact. British soldiers, sons and brothers of the people! how do you feel when your officers command you to fire on your brethren of the working-classes? Let our brave soldiers remember that they are constantly liable to be called upon to slaughter their fellow-subjects. Let every man in the army reflect that, in such events, the bullet that he discharges from his musket may pierce the heart of his brother, his father, or his dearest friend. No oath of allegiance can ever annul the sacred ties of humanity, and no allegiance can be greater than that which is due to the people from all who receive the public money. Let these things sink deep into the mind of every British soldier, and let each determine that the next time he is called upon to crimson the soil of England with blood, it shall not be that of the oppressed people.

The discontent of the young soldier reached its climax when he was refused leave of absence to visit a beloved sister, a capricious exercise of the irresponsible authority of his officers, on account of his having rendered himself obnoxious to them by his frequent murmurings. The peremptory and cruel refusal made him resolve upon desertion from the regiment, which he accomplished in the manner already described. But, alas! he found his sister already dead, and his aged parents were compelled to seek refuge in the parish workhouse, after a life of wealth-creating toil. What a paradox for a country which vaunts itself as leading the van of civilization! Those who create the greatest amount of wealth are always those who live in the greatest poverty!

> " The seed they sow another reaps,
> The wealth they get another keeps,
> The robes they weave another wears,
> The arms they forge another bears."

The sorrow-stricken young soldier was traced to his native village, taken into custody, and conducted to Woolwich, where he was tried by a court-martial of his officers, who were at once his accusers and judges, and sentenced to the terrible punishment of three hundred lashes! He received them in the presence of the whole regiment, all his comrades pitying him, and many of them longing for an opportunity to avenge his wrongs. Such scenes as this, the gory triangle and the knotted whip, which, according to the great man-butcher of Waterloo, are absolutely necessary to the maintenance of proper discipline in the army, furnish a startling commentary on the ever-to-be-remembered expression of the same high authority, that "no man need have nice notions about religion who wishes to be a soldier." Certainly, there is no very nice religion in flogging a man to death for returning a blow, nor in strangling three men for stealing a little flour while upon march, and starving. Yet this is the wretch to whom three or four statues have been raised, and whom Queen Victoria hesitates not to receive at her palace, stained as he is with the blood of his own countrymen and fellow-soldiers!

The young soldier's robust constitution enabled him to recover from the effects of the terrible punishment which he had received, but he felt himself degraded and humiliated, as well as injured, and there was no avenue of escape but through the gates of death. He resolved upon suicide, but he could not bear the thought of leaving the tyrant colonel of his regiment to oppress and trample upon others. He watched his opportunity, therefore, and, on a dark and stormy night, shortly after he had been discharged from the infirmary, he encountered him at a little distance from the barracks, and, after telling him his name, and upbraiding the colonel with his cruelty, he plunged his bayonet deep into his heart. Thus retribution speedily overtook the tyrant of the regiment, and his executioner—we will not call him murderer in such a case—fled to London. He had no hope of escape, however, and, indeed, no such intention; he had only fled, that his fate might be in his own hands.

The following night saw him standing within one of the recesses of Waterloo-bridge; he muttered a few hasty ejaculations, and then suddenly mounting the parapet, leaped into the dark and murmuring flood that rolled below. Thus from oppression sprang murder and suicide!

Let us contemplate for a moment the difference between the condition of the British soldier and the French soldier, equal in courage, in heroic achievements, and in the glory which they have acquired. Here the soldier is a mere machine in the hands of the government, without any political rights, or the least freedom of will. In France, he enjoys the franchise, and all the rights of citizenship; here he is subject to the degrading torture of the lash. In France, the abolition of flogging in the army and navy was one of the first decrees of the present government; here promotion is by purchase, and the officers consequently consist of the reprobates of every aristocratic family, while the private soldier has no chance of rising in his profession, however great may be his merit. In France, promotion is by merit; and, from the ranks, the school of Napoleon's marshals.

What, then, is the secret of this contrast—this striking difference between the relative conditions of the English and French soldier? Let us whisper it, and let every soldier in the British army ponder well upon it—FRANCE IS A REPUBLIC!

CHAPTER XXI.

THE VENGEANCE OF ALOMPRA.

FOR several days the Malay skulked about the east-end of London, subsisting by begging, and sleeping in the low lodging-houses about Wapping, but keeping a keen watch on the motions of Mr. Hastings. At length, on the fourth night after his escape from the convict-hulk at Woolwich, he dogged his intended victim from St. Katherine's-docks into the Commercial-road, and from thence to his abode at Stratford. The night was dark and stormy, and suited well his murderous designs; a drizzling rain was falling, and every hour became heavier, and the wind howled and moaned among the chimney-pots in fitful gusts. It was past midnight when Mr. Hastings reached his abode, little thinking that his relentless enemy was on his track; and the vengeful Malay took up a position from which he could watch the house, and where he was sheltered from the driving rain.

Presently he saw a light in the chamber which he had ascertained was occupied by Mr. Hastings, and his dark eyes glistened, and his hand clutched convulsively the Spanish knife which he had purchased to accomplish his sanguinary intentions, as he gazed upon it. Now and then he saw the shadow of his enemy upon the blind, and at length the light was extinguished, and he knew that Mr. Hastings was in bed.

Alompra glided like an evil spirit towards the house, the wind and rain preventing his movements from being heard, and listened until every sound was hushed within the house, and he knew that the inmates were buried in a profound sleep. He waited until the hour of two boomed on the silence of the night from the numerous churches of the eastern part of the metropolis, deadened by the distance and the wind and rain; and then he prepared to put his long meditated vengeance into execution. Quietly springing over the low palisades which skirted the garden, he cautiously approached the house, and with a small crow-bar, which he had fashioned from a piece of rod-iron, proceeded to force the back door.

9

Slowly the door yielded to the force of the instrument, and the Malay effected his entry noiselessly by gradually increasing the power applied to the door; at length he stood within the kitchen, and having closed the back door, he stole with cautious and cat-like steps through the sitting-rooms to the foot of the stairs. Then he stopped a moment to listen, lest his movements should have aroused any of the inmates, but not a sound met his ears, except the monotonous ticking of the clock; and grasping his knife firmly in his right hand, he silently ascended the stairs.

Slowly and silently he opened the door of the chamber occupied by Mr. Hastings, and advanced on tip-toe towards the bed. The room was in darkness, and not a single star shed light on the scene without; but with the light touch of an oriental robber, Alompra ascertained the position of the sleeping man, and but for the darkness a horrid smile might have been seen upon his dark countenance, and a gleam of demoniac triumph in his black and glittering eyes.

He raised the knife above the prostrate body of his unconscious victim, and then swiftly his arm descended, and the weapon was plunged to the haft in the breast of Mr. Hastings. The blood of the unfortunate man spurted hotly on the face of the revengeful Malay, and crimsoned the guilty hand that struck the murderous blow. A low groan escaped the lips of the victim of Alompra's jealousy and revenge, and in a moment life was extinct; the assassin knew that no second blow was needed, and drawing his ensanguined weapon from the breast of the murdered man, he glided towards the door.

His retreating footsteps fell silently on the carpeted stairs, and, quickly gaining the ground-floor, in another moment he had left the house. He threw the knife with which he had committed the murder into a neighbouring garden, trusting that the rain would remove from it every vestige of the crime, and then hastened away in the direction of Mile-end. With the trepidation of conscious guilt he hurried hastily along until he reached that eastern suburb of the metropolis, when he somewhat slackened his pace, fearing that his haste might seem suspicious, should he encounter any of the city watchmen. The clocks of the neighbouring churches were striking three when he reached Whitechapel; and ensconcing himself in the porch of a house, he curled himself up like a dog, and tried to sleep.

But vain was the attempt; sleep fled from the eyelids of the assassin, for the terrors of a guilty conscience were already upon him, and ghastly images flitted before his eyes. As soon as the nearest public-house was open, he entered the tap-room and sat down in the darkest corner in a most unenviable state of mind. He had accomplished the vengeance which he had cherished for fifteen years, and now he was more wretched than ever. Yet he felt no salutary repentance for the awful crime which he had committed, but rather a feeling of disappointment at finding himself as miserable as he had been before.

The early customers of a spirit establishment in such localities as the back-slums of Whitechapel, or the courts and lanes of Wapping, are those who impress us in the most painful degree with the misery and wretchedness engendered by habitual indulgence in ardent spirits. They consist of dirty, blear-eyed men and women, who have so accustomed themselves to alcoholic beverages, that they can do nothing until they have taken their morning dram, because the nervous debility consequent on excessive indulgence in gin, renders necessary the continued use of the pernicious stimulant; besides these, the morning visitors of the tavern are dissipated artizans who have been intoxicated the night before, and eagerly quaff a half-pint of porter to cool their fevered throats, and dirty drabs bearing the outward form of the female sex, and stunted in their growth by premature indulgence in vicious habits. It is these characters, with the pale and yawning countenance of the barman, the nut-shells and bits of orange-peel which strew the floor, and the strong smell of gas which pervades the atmosphere, which makes the bar of a gin-shop in the first hour after it is open in the morning such a different scene to that which it presents at night, when the polished brass and mahogany fittings reflect the glare of the gas-lights, when the bar-maid is smart and smiling, and gay ribbons, artificial flowers, and a touch of rouge, have effected such a wondrous transformation in those females who are neither maids, wives, nor widows.

The Malay had not been long in the tap-room of the Earl of Effingham when he found that he was attracting the half-suspicious looks of three or four men, who had just before emerged from a dirty court in the vicinity of the house, and casting down his eyes with the trepidation of conscious guilt, he discovered several spots of blood on the front of his shirt. He immediately rose, and left the house; and this movement would undoubtedly have caused his detention on suspicion, had the murder which he had committed a few hours before then been known. Hastily turning down the first street that he came to, Alompra hurried towards Wapping; though the hour was still early, that locality was swarming with life, in the shape of sailors, labourers, costermongers, and fellows of very dubious avocations, who were hanging about the early public-houses. The murderer skulked about this neighbourhood the whole of that day, every hour growing more and more wretched, and at nightfall he found himself in the tap-room of the Old Night-house, in Ratcliffe-highway.

"Shocking thing, that affair of the murder down at Stratford," observed a sailor to his companions.

The Malay started.

"A murder! When?" said another.

"Captain Hastings, master of the brig Mary, lying in St. Katherine's-docks, was found in his bed-room this morning stabbed with a knife, and quite dead," returned the sailor.

"How do they know he didn't do it himself?" asked one of the party.

"Because there was no weapon in the room that he could have done it with; and a Spanish knife with blood upon it, was found under a shed in a neighbouring garden," replied the first speaker. "Moreover, the kitchen door was found open, and there were marks of dirty feet on the carpet, but the rain had washed away the foot-prints in the garden."

Alompra broke out in a cold sweat as he listened to this conversation, and hastily rising, he quitted the house, and rushed madly towards East Smithfield, scarcely knowing where he was going, and reckless of the consequences of the suspicion which might attach to such a precipitate flight. Crossing Tower-hill, he struck into Thames-street, and hurried on towards London-bridge, the predecessor of the present one, and a less noble structure than that which now spans what, in a commercial point of view at least, is the most important river in the world.

His olive countenance was haggard and convulsed, his dark eyes gleamed with an unnatural lustre, and every feature bore the impress of despair and unavailing remorse. He reached the middle arch of the old bridge, and the cool breeze that fanned his cheek seemed to bear to his ears the death groan of his unfortunate victim; while shadowy figures flitted around him, and hands which none but himself could see, beckoned him to the murky and silently-flowing river. The night air failed to chase away those dim and spectral hands; he pressed his rigid fingers on his eyes, but he could not shut them out; and with the wildness of delirium gleaming from his dark eyes, he mounted the parapet of the bridge.

At that moment a cry of terror struck upon his ears, seeming to his distempered fancy the wailing of a ghost shut out from Paradise; and with an unearthly yell he threw up his arms, and leaped into the deep and ever-flowing tide.

The lights on the bridge and along the shore, which seemed to dance before his eyes as he fell from the giddy verge into the rippling stream, glittered like the eyes of a thousand demons, and the shadow cast by his descending figure on the water seemed to him like Eblis hastening to seize his prey. He shrieked involuntarily, but the water rushed into his mouth and choked him; his brain became dizzy, a drumming noise seemed to be sounding in his ears; he tried to shriek again, but could not, and then his faculties forsook him, and the horrible sensation of drowning was succeeded by utter unconsciousness.

The cry of alarm which had saluted the conscience-stricken murderer as he leaped from the bridge proceeded from a passenger who had witnessed the suicidal act, but was not near enough to prevent it. He immediately raised an alarm, but the miserable wretch, the victim of his own fiendish passions, came not again to the surface, but floated with the tide down that mighty river whose waters have closed over so many of earth's best and brightest children. He had worked evil, and evil had befallen him; but what a vain expiation was his death! The wrong that men do lives after them; and had he lived and sincerely repented, he might have atoned in some measure for the evil he had done. The past, as Shelly has beautifully said, is death's, the future only is our own; and all remorse is vain, all expiation useless, unless the penitent criminal make atonement to society for the evil he has inflicted on it, and this can only be done by embracing a life of constant self-sacrifice for the good of humanity.

CHAPTER XXII.

COLONEL ELRINGTON.

LOLAH HASTINGS had now passed her fourteenth year, which the poets of India term the age of love, and her faultless form was fast becoming matured into all the loveliness and grace of womanhood. It was at this time, and a few days before the murder of her father, that she was seen by Colonel Elrington, a sexagenarian voluptuary, while walking with the other young ladies in the neighbourhood of the seminary. The colonel was one of those pests of society who, having passed their youth and maturity in sensual pleasures, become jaded and satiated with the vices in which they have steeped themselves, and seek to revive the vigour of past days by stimulating their passions by the seduction of females of extreme youth. He was irresistibly attracted by the graceful form of the lovely daughter of Mr. Hastings, and the beauty and piquancy of her countenance made him long to possess her; and as he was immensely rich, and well skilled in the profligate and libertine arts which had wrecked the hopes of many an opening floweret of beauty, he doubted not of success in his lawless and criminal desires.

The first step was to discover who she was, and with this view he dispatched a note, on reaching his house near Hyde-park-corner, to Mr. Fitzormond, a young man who had been the jackal of his lusts on many previous occasions. Augustus Fitzormond, a name which those who enjoyed the *honour* of his intimate acquaintance knew to be only an assumed one, lived in the New-cut —that is, he had his dwelling there, for how he lived was one of the many mysteries of our modern Babylon; and as the upper part of a house has the advantage of a purer air than that enjoyed by the inmates of the ground-floor apartments, Mr. Augustus Fitzormond occupied the front garret. The avocations of that gentleman were multifarious, and all of them of a sinister nature; we have already hinted at one, that of jackal to the wealthy sensualist Colonel Elrington, and others will be developed in the course of this veritable narrative.

That same evening, in pursuance of an appointment made in the note which the colonel had sent to Mr. Augustus Fitzormond, the worthy pair met at the Blue Posts, a tavern of flash notoriety in the immediate vicinity of the Quadrant, kept at one time by that "glass of fashion and mould of form," Tom Holt. In the parlour, which was ornamented with several portraits of famous pugilists and race-horses, sat a number of visitors, all of them attired in the peculiar style expressed by the words "nobby," "spicy," and "leary." Most of them wore white hats, and many of them had top-boots; some of the latter had a riding-whip in their hand, to show that they kept a horse. Brandy-and-water seemed the liquor most in demand; the atmosphere of the room was redolent of tobacco-smoke, and the conversation turned mainly on the last fight, the next spring-meeting at Epsom, and Jack Somebody's fast-trotting mare, interlarded with oaths and phrases of more originality than elegance, being apparently borrowed from the lexicon of Seven-dials.

Mr. Augustus Fitzormond was about thirty years of age, of pale complexion, but not altogether unhandsome features, and had a profusion of auburn hair curling over the greasy velvet collar of his bottle-green coat; he wore a brown hat a mosaic-gold guard-chain festooned across a velvet waistcoat, the edges of which were much worn; plaid trowsers, and a ring on one finger, of the same material as the showy ornament which hung across his vest. There was a restless expression in the roving glances of his light blue eyes, and there was a nonchalance in his manners and appearance which showed that he was not only on very good terms with himself, but also that he was not destitute of the self-possession which is so necessary an ingredient in the character of the " man about town."

" You received my note, then," observed Colonel Elrington, with evident anxiety.

" Yes ; and morrissed over to the place directly, colonel," returned Augustus.

" Well, how have you succeeded ?" asked the jaded voluptuary, impatiently.

" You shall hear," said his jackal; " but you had better order a bottle of wine, for the dust has made me as thirsty as a fish."

Colonel Elrington called for a bottle of sherry, and Augustus Fitzormond drank three glasses in succession.

" When I had found out the place," said he at length, " I looked about for a pump, and, by watching the gate in the lane which passes the garden of the school, I found one in the shape of a buxom, merry-eyed wench, who is one of the slavies of the establishment. I soon got into conversation with her, and, by a series of skilfully directed questions and observations, elicited all the information which you require. The young lady is in her fifteenth year, and her father is master of a merchant-vessel ; her name is Hastings, and her mother, who was a native of India, died in that country before she was old enough to remember her."

" Ah! I thought she was a half-caste—a love-child, perhaps," observed Colonel Elrington ; and, after a moment's pause, during which Augustus refilled the glasses, he inquired : " Is her father now at sea ?"

" Yes ; but he is expected home every day," replied his jackal.

The libertine colonel mused a few moments on the use to which the information which he had thus acquired could be put, and then placing a five-pound note in the hand of Augustus Fitzormond, he rose from the table, and quitted the tavern.

A few days passed, during which Colonel Elrington had been unable to devise any scheme for getting Lolah Hastings into his power, and the mysterious murder at Stratford became the all-absorbing topic of conversation. The colonel evinced an unusual interest in the matter, and read with avidity the newspaper-details of the crime. The escape of Alompra from Woolwich, and the finding of his corpse in a swamp on the Essex side of the river, coupled with the evidence of the murdered man on the trial of the Malay, seemed positive evidence of the identity of the pretty school-girl with the stolen daughter of Mr. Hastings ; and Colonel Elrington determined to make this shocking event subservient to his own atrocious schemes.

He was endeavouring to devise some means of rendering this information available for his purpose, when he received a visit from his jackal, the respectable Augustus Fitzormond, who had picked up some additional particulars concerning the unfortunate Mr. Hastings.

" Last night," said he, " I was at a house in the city, where I met an acquaintance named Cheekey, who is clerk to an attorney in Lyon's-inn, and we got talking about the Stratford murder. In the course of conversation he informed me that his employer was the legal adviser and intimate friend of the murdered man's brother, who, it appears, is a commission-agent in East-cheap. He said that Captain Hastings had died without a will, and as the marriage with the mother of Miss Hastings was not valid in England—having been performed in Sumatra, according to the rites and ceremonies of that country—the captain's brother would succeed to what property he had left, and that he had heard Mr. Hastings tell his employer that as he had never been on very good terms with his brother, and had a family of his own to provide for, he should intimate to the proprietress of the seminary where Miss Hastings has been placed, that he should not be responsible for the young lady's future expenses."

" Then, as the quarter has just expired, she will be sent from the school destitute," observed the colonel, his grey eyes sparkling with excitement.

" Yes, the schools have just broken up for the summer-vacation," returned Fitzormond ; " so if you go down there to-day, you will doubtless be allowed to bring her away on some pretence."

Colonel Elrington gave Mr. Fitzormond a sovereign for the information with which he had supplied him, and in the evening of the same day, he proceeded in a hackney-coach to the suburban seminary at which Lolah Hastings had passed the last two years of her life. On arriving at the school and expressing a wish to speak with Miss Crotchet, he was ushered into a formal-looking parlour by the bright-eyed domestic from whom Augustus Fitzormond had elicited the first information relative to the lovely orphan. In a few moments the principal of the establishment—a tall, precise-looking person of about forty years of age—entered the apartment, and inquired the purport of his visit, in a cold and formal manner.

"You have a young lady in your establishment of the name of Hastings, ma'am," said the colonel, in that bland tone which he knew so well how to assume on occasions like the present.

"I have, sir," returned Miss Crotchet, stiffly; and she might have added that she intended to turn her out on the following morning, but she was willing to wait until she had ascertained the precise purport of the colonel's visit.

"You are doubtless aware that her only surviving parent has met his death in a shocking manner, within the last few days," continued Colonel Elrington.

Miss Crotchet again replied in the affirmative.

"Does Miss Hastings know that her father is no more?" asked the wily colonel.

"She does," returned the lady; "but her grief was naturally less violent than if she had been brought up under her parents' roof, which I believe was not the case."

"It was not, ma'am," said Colonel Elrington; "and I understand that her paternal uncle, who has succeeded to the property of her unfortunate father, is either unable or unwilling to provide for the young lady's future support."

"Yes," returned Miss Crotchet. "I this morning received a communication from Mr. Hastings, in which he makes an intimation to that effect; and as the quarter expires to-morrow, the poor thing will have no home to go to, should her uncle decline receiving her."

"It was a knowledge of that circumstance, and a feeling of regard for her father's memory, which brought me here," said the colonel. "I knew the late Captain Hastings well—I became acquainted with him in India, while my regiment was stationed in that country; and under the circumstances of the case—feeling for the young lady's position, and having no children of my own —I have determined to take her into my care. You will have no objection, I presume, ma'am, to my taking her to my sister's to spend the vacation with my nieces; and after the vacation she will doubtless return to your establishment."

"Oh, dear, no!" returned Miss Crotchet, with a prim smile, and much pleased with the promising turn which the affair had taken; for not only had she secured her pupil, as she thought, but she already saw in imagination an accession to her establishment from Colonel Elrington's nieces. "If you will excuse me, sir, I will prepare Miss Hastings for the journey."

The colonel bowed, and Miss Crotchet withdrew from the parlour, and hastened to acquaint the pretty Lolah with this unlooked-for change in her prospective circumstances. Lolah's inquiry for her benefactor's name reminded Miss Crotchet that she was herself unacquainted with it; but she concealed her want of tact in not having already learned it, by assuring her pupil that he was an officer of high rank, though she had forgotten his name.

When Lolah was ready for her departure from the seminary, she accompanied Miss Crotchet into the parlour, and glanced anxiously at Colonel Elrington, as if desiring to read the character of her future protector, but immediately cast down her eyes on encountering the ardent gaze of the libertine colonel.

"The very image of her mother!" exclaimed Colonel Elrington, wishing to remove the impression which his rude gaze at the young lady might have created; and then he hastened to reassure her by speaking in a paternal manner of the regard which he felt for the memory of her father, and the gladness with which she would be received by his sister and nieces.

By an indirect inquiry, Miss Crotchet obtained the information that her pupil's benefactor was Colonel Morton, and that he resided at Acton; and then the aged voluptuary, delighted with the success which had thus far attended his vile plotting, handed Lolah Hastings into the vehicle which waited at the gate, and they were driven towards the metropolis.

CHAPTER XXIII.

LOLAH HASTINGS.

THE lamps were lighted in the streets when the vehicle containing Colonel Elrington and the pretty school-girl entered on the west-end of the mighty wilderness of buildings which constitutes London, and the latter had, therefore, a very imperfect idea of the route they were going, and of the locality in which the vehicle finally stopped. The house was of respectable and even genteel appearance; and the door was opened by a smartly-attired female servant. Colonel Elrington handed Lolah from the vehicle, and having paid the driver, they entered together. In the parlour they found two persons sitting—a stout, masculine-looking female about forty years of age, attired in a style of vulgar finery, mingled with pretensions to juvenility, and a man about ten years younger, dressed in a style of shabby gentility which would have been worthy of Mr. Augustus Fitzormond. His complexion was sallow, his whiskers black and exuberant, and the brilliancy of his dark eyes seemed to have waned, from the effects of dissipation and youthful excesses. In his manners there was an air of swagger and coarse nonchalance not very prepossessing; and the impression which his appearance and manners were calculated to make was not improved by the long pipe which he was smoking, and the deep potations in which he indulged from a glass of gin-and-water which stood on the table, with a slice of lemon swimming on the surface of the steaming compound.

To this lady and gentleman Lolah Hastings was introduced by the worthy colonel, who named them to his young charge as Mr. and Mrs. Jones. The gentleman stared rudely at Lolah, who little liked the appearance of those in whose care she was to remain for the present; but Mrs. Jones received her with more courtesy, and rang the bell for the domestic to conduct her to the chamber destined for her, that she might remove her travelling attire. Lolah followed the servant up the stairs to the back attic, the door of which was opened by the domestic, who then stood aside to allow Lolah to enter first; but, no sooner had she done so, than the door was suddenly closed, and she heard the key turn in the lock.

Lolah started, and turned pale, and the first feeling of surprise which had assailed her at this strange act quickly merged into one of deep dismay; for as she glanced timidly around her, she observed that there was no furniture in the room, the floor of which was covered with several thick carpets, laid one over the other; while the walls, to the height of five feet from the floor, were padded in the same manner. The door was covered on the inside with green-baize, and the window was fastened down, and secured against being broken by a wire blind inside, as well as being guarded on the outside by three stout iron bars.

Lolah trembled; she knew not the precise nature of the danger which ménaced her; but if not something terrible, why all these precautions? That a great evil was in store for her she felt assured; for the suspicious appearance of the young man and the masculine female below, the strange conduct of the servant, and the singular precautions taken in that room, were all indicative of evil intentions being entertained against her. The room was situated at the top of the house, the door was locked upon her, the window was strongly secured against the possibility of escaping or giving an alarm, and in that strangely-contrived room not the faintest sound of the most violent struggle could ever pass the walls, not a cry or shriek could possibly be heard beyond them.

But what was the danger which all these precautions foreboded? Was it murder? She shuddered at the bare thought; but a moment's reflection taught her that this was scarcely probable. No one whom she knew could possibly have an interest in her death, and she had no personal enemies likely to take such deadly and determined vengeance. Yet, if not murder, what could be the fate intended for her? what other crime could require for its perpetration such strange precautions for stifling every sound, and guarding against every possibility of discovery? A sudden thought darted like electricity through her dizzy brain. Could she have attracted the notice of some unprincipled sensualist? was she to be made the victim of Colonel Morton? In a moment she recollected the glance which the colonel had bestowed upon her when she first encountered him in the parlour of Miss Crotchet; and, as the diabolical plot of which she was to be made the victim unravelled itself to her bewildered mind, she covered her face with her hands, and burst into a flood of scalding tears.

From this unavailing outburst of anguish at the anticipation of her dishonour, Lolah was aroused by hearing the footsteps of a man ascending the stairs, and her heart palpitated violently as she heard the key again turn in the lock, and saw the baize-covered door open, and give admission to Colonel Elrington. Catching at the slightest hope of escape, as a drowning wretch clings to a straw, she sprang towards the open door; but in another moment it was closed again, locked on the inside, and the key placed in the pocket of the hoary sensualist, who gazed upon her with enraptured eyes.

"Colonel Morton, what does this mean?" exclaimed Lolah, in an excited tone, partly from terror, and partly also from indignation at the treachery of which she was the victim.

"My little timid beauty, what are you afraid of?" returned Colonel Elrington, smiling as he took her hand. "You are alarmed about nothing, my dear; what have you to fear from me?"

"That is what I want to know, sir," said the affrighted girl. "Why was I brought to this strange-looking room, and then made a prisoner?"

"Do not call yourself a prisoner, my pretty Lolah," said the sexagenarian libertine. "I will take you back to the school, or anywhere else you please, upon one condition, and that will not be very difficult to comply with. Just one kiss, Lolah, and I will tell you what it is."

"For shame, sir!" cried Lolah, indignantly, and blushing deeply as the libertine colonel twined his arms about her, and repeatedly kissed her lips and glowing cheeks.

"Why should I be ashamed to acknowledge that I love you, beauteous Lolah, and you to receive the adoration that is due to so much loveliness as yours?" said Colonel Elrington, still holding in his arms the struggling and bashful Lolah.

"Let me go, sir! you have deceived me," exclaimed Lolah, endeavouring to extricate herself from the grasp of the unprincipled libertine.

"I love you, Lolah, and I am very rich," said he; "will you be mine?"

"If you loved me, you would not have brought me here," returned the young girl, still striving to escape.

"I will surround you with every luxury that money can procure, my Lolah," continued Colonel Elrington, hoping to dazzle the girl's imagination, and allure her into a compliance with his desires without having recourse to violence. "Everything that you can wish for shall be yours, if you will only consent to my wishes: a carriage, servants, jewellery, all that you can desire, are now within your grasp. Reflect well before you decide, but decide quickly, for my passion will brook but little delay. Your consent will obtain for you a brilliant position in a world where gold glosses over a thousand failings, while your rejection of my proposal will gain you nothing; for be assured, you will not be permitted to leave this room until I have obtained what I desire."

"What right have you to use me in this manner?" demanded Lolah, in an agitated voice, her indignation striving with her fear.

"Never mind the right, my dear," replied Colonel Elrington; "it is quite sufficient that I have the power, and, be assured, that that will serve me fully as well as the right."

"Oh, pray let me go, sir!" exclaimed the affrighted Lolah, struggling with the aged sensualist, whose licentious hand now invaded the sanctity of her heaving bosom.

"This is folly!" said the colonel, impatiently. "Will you be mine, Lolah, or must I force you to compliance with my wishes?"

"I will not submit to this infamy while I am able to resist!" exclaimed the

lovely girl, reddening with shame and indignation; but, though an old man, Colonel Elrington was tall and muscular, and his vicious excesses had not entirely destroyed the vigour of a frame constitutionally robust.

The young girl's chance of effectual resistance was therefore very slight indeed, especially in a room prepared as that was in which the struggle took place, for the perpetration of such crimes as that contemplated by the miscreant Elrington.

Long but vainly did Lolah Hastings struggle with her persecutor; in vain her resistance—in vain her screams, for not a sound passed beyond the four walls of that chamber of mystery and guilt. With her shining black hair hanging dishevelled on her shoulders, with her clothes torn, and her face and neck suffused with burning blushes, she was thrown upon the matted floor of that strangely-contrived apartment, and the libertine colonel succeeded in the perpetration of his design.

Then he rose, and quitted the room, locking the door behind him, and leaving the victim of his licentious passion overwhelmed with shame and grief. Sit-

10

ting on the matted floor, with her lovely countenance buried in her hands, and the salt tears gushing through her long and taper fingers, she gave full vent to her grief. But after some time she became more tranquil, and, though sighs and sobs still burst from her surcharged bosom, and a tear trembled on the long dark lashes of each lustrous eye, the paroxysm of her grief had subsided, exhausted by the violence of its first outburst. She felt wretched and desolate, for she was now a friendless orphan; and the position in which she suddenly found herself, in the power and at the mercy of a depraved voluptuary, old enough to be her grandfather, made her look fearfully upon the future, which her morbid imagination placed before her. As she became more and more composed, however, she reflected that her present confinement was her greatest misfortune; for if she were but free, she feared not being thrown upon her own resources for subsistence, now that education had increased and refined the accomplishments which had made her so valuable an ally of the Malay juggler, the drunken violinist, and the itinerant Mr. Allen. It was the present, then, which most excited her fears, and filled her mind with vague and terrible apprehensions. Would the colonel visit her again, and repeat the outrage which he had committed upon her? Would that abominable Mrs. Jones, whom she now felt assured was no better than she ought to be, traffic in her shame, and subject her to the licentious brutality of other scoundrels of the same stamp as the colonel? These were the thoughts which now filled her with dread, and caused her cheeks to glow with the recollection of what had occurred.

CHAPTER XXIV.

THE OPIATE.

From this state of dread and suspense, Lolah Hastings was relieved by hearing the footsteps of a female ascending the stairs, and she rose from her sitting position on the floor of the matted chamber just as the servant unlocked and opened the door.

"I will light you to your room now, miss, if you please," said the young woman.

"Oh! pray let me escape from this horrible place!" exclaimed Lolah, in an agitated voice. "I am sure you have the power; and what have I done that I should be treated as a prisoner?"

"It would be more than my place is worth to let you escape, miss," returned the servant.

"How can you be instrumental in such crimes as are perpetrated here?" said Lolah, with an appealing look. "You do not look as if you were a depraved creature like the woman below; then, why will you abet such villany? Aid me to escape, and let us fly together from this den of infamy and crime."

"I dare not!" said the young woman, in a low voice, and heaving a deep sigh as she spoke. "My life is in the hands of that vile woman whom you saw, and depends on my acquiescence and assistance in the atrocities which are perpetrated in this house. But come at once to your room, miss; the worst is over now, and you will be secure from molestation for this night at least."

Lolah sighed, and followed the young woman down the stairs and along a passage to a bed-room on the second floor; here her attendant left her, locked the door on the outside, and went down stairs. Lolah turned instinctively to the window, which was nailed down; but she looked out, and saw that the room was situated at the back of the house, where nothing but the tops of the houses in a neighbouring court were visible amid the darkness of the night. The young girl turned from the sombre prospect with a sigh, and after walking up and down the room a few minutes to calm the perturbation of her mind, she placed the washing-stand and two chairs against the door, as some slight defence against an intrusion in the night, and then prepared to retire to rest.

Midnight had struck from every tower and steeple in this mighty metropolis before she fell asleep, for her mind was so unhinged by what had passed in the last few hours, that the slightest and most casual sound was sufficient to disturb and alarm her. But so exhausted was the outraged girl, both mentally and physically, that when she at length fell into a deep and refreshing slumber, she did not awake until a faint gleam of sunlight was shining into the chamber through the smoke which hangs continually over London. She immediately rose and dressed herself, and was looking out of the window at the blank walls and roofs which formed the only prospect, when the servant entered with coffee and muffins on a tray, which she placed upon a small table.

" Pray, tell me if there is any chance of escape !" said Lolah Hastings, in an imploring tone.

" Do not think of it," replied the young woman, shaking her head. " All your attempts to escape will be useless, and will only lead to greater restraint being put upon you. Your only chance is by being resigned to your fate, or appearing to be so, until you succeed in lulling suspicion, and then watching for an opportunity of escape. This is what I would advise ; for, if you continue obstinate, I will not answer for your life."

" Good heavens ! you frighten me," said Lolah, clasping her hands together. " What should they kill me for ?"

" To get rid of you, if you are obstinate and troublesome," returned the servant ; " for if they allowed you to escape, you know enough to transport every one in the house."

" But if I promise to reveal nothing," observed the wretched Lolah.

" They will not believe you," said the young woman, shaking her head. " Take my advice, miss ; it is your only chance."

The servant then withdrew, locking the door, as on the previous night, and Lolah sat down to the repast with which she had been supplied. She had just concluded, when the door of the chamber again opened, and Mrs. Jones entered.

" Well, have you made a good breakfast, my dear ?" said the harridan, looking smilingly at Lolah. " Ah, you are a sensible girl, I can see, and know how to make the best of what cannot be helped. Well, what is the use of life, if we do not enjoy it ? I hope you and the colonel parted friends, my dear ?"

" He is a villain !" cried Lolah, colouring with indignation ; " and I do not care if I never see him any more."

" Oh, do not be foolish, Miss Hastings," said Mrs. Jones, deprecatingly. " The colonel is a nice kind of man when you come to know him, and he is very rich, so you must look over his not being so young as he might be."

" I hate him !" said Lolah, energetically.

" Come, do not be foolish, my dear," returned the vile harridan. " The colonel is coming to see you this evening, and I expect you will be a good, reasonable girl, and receive him as you ought to do."

Lolah started at this intimation of another visit from the colonel, but made no remark on the subject to Mrs Jones, who shortly afterwards took her departure. The dinner was brought up by the servant, and after the repast two young girls introduced themselves to her, bringing up fruit and a bottle of champagne. They were about twenty years of age, pretty in features, and attractive in figure, and smartly but loosely dressed ; one of them spoke a foreign accent, and the other was an English girl. They entreated Lolah, in a lively tone, to make her miserable life happy, and endeavoured to prevail upon her to take wine with them, but she declined, and received the advances of her visitors with coolness. The profligacy of their manners and conversation disgusted her, and she was not sorry when they took their departure, which they did not do without ridiculing her for what they termed her mock-modesty. With her natural penetration and acuteness, fostered as they had been by the vagabond life she had led with Alompra and Mr. Allen, she had seen through the character of these young girls, and the object of their visit, which was to excite her passions and inflame her imagination by champagne and licentious conversation, and thus prepare her for the visit of Colonel Elrington.

In the evening the colonel came, and found his victim sitting at the window, and gazing listlessly on the roofs of the adjacent houses and the blue smoke that ascended from a chimney. She coloured deeply as the hoary libertine advanced towards her, and attempted to take her hand, which she snatched from him with an indignant gesture.

" Still cold and coy," observed Colonel Elrington, attempting to kiss her, but in another moment she had rose from her seat, and seizing the chair with both hands, she stepped back a pace or two, and raising it in a menacing manner, prepared to defend herself.

The colonel tried to close with her, and deprive her of her means of defence, but, exerting all her strength, Lolah struck the libertine so heavily with the chair, that he staggered backward, and falling on the fender, received a severe cut on the back of his head, from which the blood flowed profusely. Lolah then put down the chair and darted towards the door, hoping to effect her escape; but she had only descended half the stairs when she was met by Mrs. Jones, who had heard the sound of the colonel's fall. The vile harridan immediately seized the terrified girl by both arms, and called lustily for " Bill!"

" What's the row?—what's up now?" inquired Bill; and the young man whom Lolah had seen in the parlour on the evening before, made his appearance on the stairs.

" Just come here, Bill; the hussey has killed the gentleman, I am afraid," returned Mrs. Jones; and, still holding Lolah by the arms, she dragged her back to the bed-room, followed by Bill.

Colonel Elrington had risen from the floor, but was dizzy and nervous from the effects of the blow, and was led down stairs by Bill; while Mrs. Jones reviled Lolah for what she called her ingratitude and obstinacy, and again locked her in her chamber.

" I will tell you what we must do, Bill," said Mrs. Jones to her paramour, for such was the young man whom she addressed thus familiarly; " we must get rid of that girl, or she will be more trouble to us than she is worth; and perhaps get us into a mess some fine day. I will tell you what we will do; we will hocus her, and then take her away and leave her in some bye-place. She does not know where she is, and if she should split there will be no clue to this place; and we shall have her again, of her own accord, in a few weeks, for she is quite destitute; and, if we keep our eyes upon her, we are safe to have her, for after what has passed, I will warrant that she will not lay down and starve for her virtue's sake."

Bill grinned as he nodded acquiescence in the diabolical ingenuity of Mother Jones, and the servant was sent out for three-pennyworth of laudanum. In an hour afterwards, the soporific drug was poured into the glass of beer sent up for Lolah's supper, and but a few minutes elapsed after she had drank it before its effects began to be manifested upon the victim of aristocratic depravity, and she sank insensible upon the carpet. About an hour after this result of the infernal scheme of Mrs. Jones, that respectable personage entered the room, accompanied by the equally respectable Bill, and proceeded to raise the young girl from the floor.

" I am blessed if she isn't dead!" exclaimed Bill, as he looked at her pale countenance, and felt her cold hands and rigid arms.

" Then that settles the matter," returned Mother Jones, in a cool, indifferent tone; " and perhaps it is as well as it is—the dead tell no tales; and we can get a coffin of Mr. Holdfast, and bury her in the vaults at his chapel."

" Why can't we shove her away along with the other stiff'un, and say nothing about it?" said Bill.

" Because we can't tell what may happen, and if anything was to be found out, we should all get lagged for life, and perhaps tucked up," returned the old harridan. " Whereas, if Mr. Holdfast gets paid for his coffin, and a place for it in the vaults, he will ask no questions, and say nothing about it."

Bill then replaced the cold and motionless form of Lolah Hastings on the floor, and the worthy pair withdrew to carry out their plans as speedily as possible.

CHAPTER XXV.

THE MYSTERIES OF THE CHAPEL.

In the house adjoining that of Mrs. Jones, there lived one Habakuk Holdfast, an undertaker, and a very pious man, according to the worldly idea of piety, which is unfortunately so prevalent in this country. He was proprietor of a small chapel in a court near his dwelling, and, as the neighbourhood was a thickly-populated one, being that little-explored district bounded on the north by Holborn, on the east by Chancery-lane, on the south by Fleet-street and the Strand, and on the west by Drury-lane; and, as the pious man's charges and fees were extremely moderate, he drove a very thriving business. As his work was done for the most part by apprentices, and as he calculated on the reversion of the coffins for firewood, he was enabled to offer this economy to the public without any sacrifice of profit; and, as he constantly removed the coffins as the vaults became full, and broke them up for firewood, it promised to be a valuable property for the Holdfasts of many a future generation, since it never became any fuller, though hundreds were interred therein every year. There was another profitable occupation which Mr. Holdfast followed, in connection with the chapel, and that was the disposal of newly-interred bodies to the surgeons; for the time that we now speak of was previous to the passing of Warburton's Anatomy Bill, by which the corpses of paupers were consigned to the scalpel of the anatomist—a fine specimen of the economical and harmonizing tendencies of the government under which we have the pleasure to live.

This profession of Mr. Holdfast's, by which he sought to supply a want which the legislature had not then thought of, and which therefore marks his philanthropy and his veneration for science the more prominently, was a secret to all but those surgical professors with whom this profitable avocation brought him in contact; and the manner in which he supplied himself with fuel was unknown to all but himself, for there was a private communication between the vaults of the chapel and the pious man's cellar, the sacred edifice standing in a court at the rear of his house. It has been said that charity covers a multitude of sins, and so does religion, or rather the semblance of religion; for as Habakuk Holdfast regularly attended divine service at his own chapel three times on each Sabbath, was punctual in the payment of all pecuniary demands, dressed well, and talked evangelically, he was unanimously voted to be a highly respectable man.

Bill Simpson waited upon the pious undertaker, and informed him that a servant of Mrs. Jones, a friendless girl from the country, had died suddenly, and as Mrs. Jones was fearful that she had contracted some contagious disease, she wished her to be buried as speedily as possible. Mr. Holdfast immediately accompanied Bill to the house of his mistress, and, while engaged in measuring the unconscious form of the beautiful Lolah, he recollected that he had received an order for a young female subject from an eminent surgeon at the west-end of the metropolis; and informed Mrs. Jones that he had a cheap coffin, ready-made, which would be just the length, and if she wished it, the interment could take place immediately. This arrangement precisely suited Mrs. Jones and Bill Simpson, and the undertaker was not long in bringing the coffin to their house; the inanimate form of Lolah Hastings was then placed therein, and, the lid having been screwed down, the coffin was taken to the chapel in Mr. Holdfast's light cart. While one of the apprentices of the pious undertaker drove the cart to his master's premises, the others assisted him to place the coffin in the vaults beneath the chapel—not a very agreeable task, in consequence of the horrible effluvium which arose from the human remains packed up in the vaults, in every stage of decomposition.

Having covered over the mouth of this revolting charnel-house, the undertaker quitted the chapel with his apprentices, locked the door, and then returned to his own house. Chuckling over the profit which he hoped to derive from the night's business, for he had received double fees for the interment, in consideration of its having taken place at night, and knew that he would receive a good sum for the subject. Habakuk Holdfast then bent his steps towards the residence of the surgeon who had applied to him for such a one, and whom he had already supplied with the means of pursuing his anatomical studies and inquiries on many previous occasions. If any of our readers should feel surprised at the manner in which such a suspicious affair as the interment of Lolah Hastings had been arranged between Mrs. Jones and the evangelical undertaker, we beg to remind them of the proverb, that "persons who live in glass-houses should not throw stones." The respectable Mr.

Holdfast, even if he had had any suspicions on the subject, was too prudent and discreet a man to hint such a thing to Mrs. Jones, for he asked no questions and made no remarks so long as he got his money—and he had in perspective the twenty pounds for the corpse; moreover, he knew that any information which he might give to the coroner or magistrates touching the matter would not only deprive him of the profits of the night's business, but lead to unpleasant exposures relative to himself.

Arrived at the residence of the surgeon in Bedford-square, a very few words sufficed to put him in possession of the facts of the case, and, as the night was now far advanced, the surgeon's double-seated chaise was got ready, and they proceeded towards the abode of Mr. Holdfast. Leaving the chaise at the door, Mr. Melville and the undertaker entered the house, and the latter, having procured a light and certain tools, led the way to the cellar.

A strong unpleasant odour pervaded that damp and unwholesome place, at one end of which a quantity of old and partially-decayed coffin-boards were piled up, and in a corner were a quantity of human bones heaped pell-mell; these the worthy undertaker was in the habit of selling to the bone-crushers, bone-dust being a very excellent manure for turnips; and thus, through the instrumentality of that pious and enlightened man, the bones of one generation were made to promote the growth of turnips for the consumption of the next.

" What is the age of the subject, Mr. Holdfast ?" inquired the surgeon.

" Fifteen, sir ; and quite a woman in appearance to many girls of that age," replied the undertaker.

" So much the better," responded Mr. Melville, putting his thumb and finger to his olfactory organ. " Faugh ! what a stinking hole."

Habakuk Holdfast had now opened a door communicating with the vaults below the chapel, and it was the pestilential effluvium which escaped from that horrible place which induced the surgeon to make the last observation, and which nearly extinguished the light which the resurrectionising undertaker carried in his hand. It was a strong, sour smell, such as would cause a delicate person to faint, and deprive a strong man of his appetite for two or three days, unless he was accustomed to it. The noxious gas which is evolved from decomposing animal bodies will not support flame, and the resurrectionists were obliged to wait a minute or two before entering the vaults, in order to allow the air from without to mingle with that which had been pent up in that horrid receptacle of putrefaction.

" There will be a bad fever break out in this neighbourhood before long, Holdfast," said the surgeon. " This place is enough to poison the air for a mile round ; and, if it were not for the opportunity it affords me of getting a good subject when I want one, I would take up the question on public grounds, and indict the place as a common nuisance."

" You are very kind, sir—kind as you are candid," observed the undertaker, drily.

They now entered the vaults, if the place merited such an appellation, being merely a space of about six feet in depth, surrounded by the foundation walls of the chapel, and covered by the floor. Coffins of all sizes were packed one upon another on every side of the place, and some of those at bottom, being the most decayed, had fallen to pieces, owing to the weight upon them, and exposed to view the grim and grizzly remains of mortality which they enclosed. Myriads of creeping things and small flies swarmed on the floor, on the coffins, and in all parts of the vaults, the latter penetrating into the chapel, and the former into the undertaker's cellar. In the centre stood the plain, slightly-made coffin of the unfortunate Lolah Hastings, the lid of which Mr. Holdfast proceeded leisurely to remove with a screwdriver, and then the pale countenance and inanimate form of the young girl were exposed to the gaze of the two resurrectionists.

" She has been a beautiful girl," observed Mr. Melville ; " her countenance is as placid as if she were only asleep."

As he spoke, he held up the sack with which he had provided himself for the purpose, and the undertaker proceeded to lift the subject from the coffin, and place it in the sack, the mouth of which he tied up, and then assisted Mr.

Melville to carry it from the vaults, and deposit it underneath the seat of the chaise. The surgeon then gave Mr. Holdfast the stipulated sum, and drove rapidly towards the west-end, while the undertaker closed the front-door of his house, and returned to the vaults.

" A tidy night's work," he muttered to himself, as he descended the cellar stairs, jingling the gold which he had received from Mr. Melville. " What a pity it is I cannot sell them all ! This vault has been the making of me, and will be a valuable property for my son. What a happy thought it was to build a chapel ! I could not have done better if I had built a gin-shop. What an accommodation the vaults are, too, in a crowded neighbourhood like this ; for it keeps taking them in, and never gets any fuller. What a thing it would be if the authorities were to compel me to close the vaults !—why, it would ruin me, and the people would have to go into the country to be buried. But they would never do that, I think ; it would be such a shameful violation of the rights of property, and the government is very sensitive upon that question ; and so they ought to be, for if I were to be deprived of my interest in these vaults, it would be a precedent for depriving the Dean of Westminster of his interest in the brothels of Orchard-street and the Almonry. Ah ! privilege, vested interests, and the rights of property, are great words in England, and I trust they will always be respected !"

While he had been thus soliloquising, Mr. Holdfast was engaged in looking round the vaults, and examining the condition of the coffins ; and when he had ceased speaking, he took up that of Lolah Hastings, and placed it on his shoulder.

" This will do for somebody else, now," said he, as he left the vaults, and closed the door. " It would not be a bad plan to serve them all so ; they could rot as well out of a coffin as in one ; but what would Mr. Melville and my other medical patrons say to it ? No, that will not do ; but there is some consolation in knowing that they will all come in for firewood, some day or another."

Consoling himself with this reflection, Habakuk Holdfast placed the coffin in his shop, and prepared to retire to rest ; and as he looked upon all that he had done that night as a matter of business, and regarded the vaults and their contents as his own, with which he could do as he pleased, he doubtless slept as soundly as if the evening had been spent in the practice of virtue.

CHAPTER XXVI.

THE RESURRECTION.

MR. MELVILLE drove rapidly to his residence in Bedford-square, and on his arrival called his groom to take charge of his horse and chaise, and carried the sack and its contents into the apartment which served him for the scene of his anatomical studies. This was a small room on the ground-floor, having a sky-light in the roof, and a door opening into a small garden, besides another communicating with the passage leading to the front door. Having placed his subject on the dissecting-table, he left the study by the latter door, and locked it after him, deferring until the following day the operation and experiments which he wished to perform, in consequence of the lateness of the hour.

The opiate which Lolah Hastings had taken in the house of Mother Jones had induced a lethargy which the harridan and Bill Simpson had mistaken for death ; and in this state of unconsciousness the unfortunate girl had been, as we have seen, placed in a coffin and afterwards in the vaults of Habakuk Holdfast's chapel, from which she had been brought to the study of Mr. Melville. Contact with the cold marble slab on which she had been laid by the surgeon aided in restoring her to animation : consciousness slowly returned, and she opened her eyes with a shudder, and looked around her. It was already morning, and a faint greyish light came through the skylight in the ceiling, and enabled her to perceive the various objects by which she was surrounded. Two human skeletons, in glass cases, were immediately opposite to her ; various preparations in spirits stood upon a shelf, and several drawings of dissected portions of the human frame were suspended against the wall.

Lolah was fortunately not a timid girl, nor one easily divested of her presence of mind. The strange and ghastly objects which met her gaze, therefore, though they caused an involuntary shudder to agitate her frame, evoked no shriek or cry from her pale lips. She sat upright on the dissecting-table, and tried to compose her mind and concentrate her mental energies upon one point. How she had come there, she knew not; for she remembered nothing from the time of taking supper at the house of Mrs. Jones, and how long a period had since elapsed she had no means of ascertaining. She shivered with cold; and as she again looked around the study and cast her eyes upon various surgical instruments lying upon the dissecting-table, a dim perception of the truth began gradually to steal upon her mind.

She was evidently in the study of some anatomist or surgeon; and she must have been brought there under the impression that she was dead. She had no recollection of having been treated like the victims of Burke and Hare, who, not long before had been executed at Edinburgh; and therefore concluded that an opiate had been given her for the purpose of producing a profound lethargy —in which state she had been brought thither. This impression derived additional weight from the observation of Mother Jones's servant, that the old harridan would not hesitate to murder her if she became troublesome. Whether the surgeon had bought her, for the purpose of dissection, from Mrs. Jones, or an intermediate party, she had no means of knowing; but if the former was the case, the vile harridan must have supposed that the quantity of laudanum administered would be sufficient to cause death. Having arrived at this conviction, she felt rejoiced that she had escaped from the clutches of Mother Jones, even in so horrible a manner, and regarded it as a proof of the good which is sometimes educed from what seems only evil.

Feeling cold—for she had nothing on but her chemise, and the opiate had produced a numbness of the limbs and a languid circulation of the blood—she stepped from the dissecting-table, and looked about for something to wrap round her. A frock or blouse, which Mr. Melville wore when engaged with the scalpel and saw, immediately caught her eye, and she hastened to put it on. In so doing she cast her eyes upon the floor of the study, and shuddered again as they fell upon the sack in which she had been brought from the vaults of Habakuk Holdfast's chapel. She did not wish needlessly to alarm the family and servants of Mr. Melville by making any noise or outcry, and thinking it most probable that the surgeon would enter the study early in the morning, she determined to wait quietly for his coming.

A faint gleam of sunshine presently beamed through the dusty sky-light, and soon afterwards she heard the clocks of the neighbouring churches strike five; another half-hour passed, and then she heard footsteps approaching the study. Lolah trembled, she knew not why, and the colour mounted to her cheeks, as the door was opened, and a young and good-looking man entered the room. It was Mr. Melville. A glance showed him that his subject had disappeared from the dissecting-table, where he had left it the preceding night, and, for a moment, he stood motionless with intense surprise. He put his hand to his brow, as if startled and bewildered, and then glanced uneasily round the apartment. In a moment he beheld the trembling Lolah standing in one corner, and becoming alternately pale with fear, and red with shame.

" Good heaven! how comes this ?" cried the bewildered surgeon, starting violently.

" I do not know how I came here, sir—I do not, indeed," said Lolah, in an earnest tone, and blushing deeply at the singular position in which she found herself.

Mr. Melville was as much perplexed as poor Lolah, and scarcely knew what to say, or how to act.

"How long have you recovered?" said he, at length, approaching the young girl.

" About an hour and a half," replied Lolah, timidly; " but I have no recollection of how I came here, or where I was brought from."

" What is the last thing you can remember ?" asked the surgeon, becoming less embarassed as he began to penetrate the nature of the mysterious case.

"I do not know when it was, sir; but the last thing I can remember doing, is having my supper at a house where I had been trepanned and shamefully treated," replied Lolah.

"Ah! I begin to understand it now," observed Mr. Melville; "but where was the house situated?"

"I do not know, sir," returned the young girl; and then she related as briefly as possible the circumstances connected with her leaving the seminary of Miss Crotchet with the pretended Colonel Morton, and the treatment she had experienced at the house of Mrs. Jones, not forgetting to mention the conversation she had had with the servant at that place, relative to the possibility of escape.

Mr. Melville was extremely puzzled to decide upon the best course to adopt in the strange and perplexing circumstances in which he found himself placed; he had no reason to doubt the young girl's statement, and it was quite evident that foul play had been practised; but a discovery of Lolah's presence in his house, or an inquiry into the black and mysterious circumstances which sur-

11

rounded her story, would compromise himself to such an extent as, in all probability, to be the ruin of his rising reputation and practice. With every desire, therefore, to bring the guilty parties to punishment, he felt himself compelled to let the matter rest; and as Lolah had not the clue which he could obtain from Habakuk Holdfast, he felt that he held the affair in his own hands.

"As you know not the house, nor even the street in which you met with the treatment you have described, I do not see what can be done to punish Mrs. Jones and her odious associate," said the surgeon, after a long pause. "It is useless to attempt to disguise from you the circumstances under which you were brought here, and you must be aware of the injury to my professional interests which would inevitably result from a revelation of them. It is something to have escaped from that vile woman, Jones; and if I procure you some clothes to leave this house in, and make you a present of ten pounds as an indemnification for the unpleasant night you have passed in this room, I do not think you will have much to complain of."

Lolah Hastings perceived that there was much reason in these observations of Mr. Melville, and at once expressed her acquiescence in the proposed arrangement.

The surgeon then left the study, and proceeded to his bed-chamber, where he acquainted his wife with the singular occurrence that had taken place, and the means by which he proposed to avert the danger of an exposure which might be seriously detrimental to his interests. Mrs. Melville approved of what her husband intended to do, and supplied him with certain articles of apparel from her own wardrobe, for the use of Lolah Hastings. With these things the surgeon again proceeded to his study, and, having given them to Lolah, together with ten sovereigns, he unfastened the door leading into the garden, and passed through. The young girl then divested herself of the surgeon's dissecting-frock, and, having attired herself in the clothes which had been placed at her disposal, she quitted the study, and was again in the presence of Mr. Melville. The surgeon complimented her on her improved appearance, and immediately opened a gate which afforded egress into a street near Bedford-square. Wishing her good morning, he hastily closed the gate, and the young girl found herself alone in a part of the metropolis with which she was little acquainted, at six o'clock in the morning.

She felt an inexpressible relief on again finding herself at liberty, and the cool air of morning gave an elasticity to her mind which she had not experienced since her departure from the seminary with Colonel Elrington, and inspired her with a feeling of freedom and self-reliance. Anxious to get away as quickly as possible from a neighbourhood associated in her mind with such strange and terrible reminiscences, she hurried towards Holborn, and turned into Drurylane, which reminded her more of the scenes of her early childhood.

The coffee-houses in the vicinity of Covent-garden are open at an early hour, for the accommodation of those frequenting the market, and in one of these Lolah Hastings sat down to break her fast. She sat some time in the coffee-house, revolving in her mind various plans for her future subsistence; at one moment she thought of seeking out Mr. Allen and his travelling *troupe*, and offering her services again as a dancer; at another she resolved to apply at the minor theatres for a situation in the ballet. The latter plan seemed the most practicable, and was also the most congenial to her mind, after the two years which she had passed in the seminary presided over by Miss Crotchet; and, as a preparatory step, she proposed to engage a lodging in the vicinity of the principal theatres. With this view she asked the waitress if she could recommend her to a lodging in that neighbourhood, and was told that Mrs. Fubbs, in Charles-street, had a room to let, and thitherward the young girl accordingly bent her steps. Mrs. Fubbs, a stout, red-faced woman, with an exceedingly dirty cap, stared rudely at Lolah, and informed her that the room was let; but that, if she liked, she could be accommodated with "the respectable young person that lodged in the two-pair back," by which means she would save a shilling a-week in her rent. The lodger alluded to then made her appearance; and, as Lolah saw nothing discreditable in her manners, she acquiesced in the proposed arrangement; by which the landlady got two lodgers at half-a-crown per week instead of one at three-and-sixpence, which she preferred to letting the room which had been recommended to Lolah by the waitress at the coffee-house, and which was not really let, the landlady well knowing that in such a thickly-populated neighbourhood she would have no difficulty in procuring two lodgers for that also.

CHAPTER XXVII.

SAM SKELTER.

THE reader has seen the effect which the violent death of Mr. Hastings had upon the fortunes and prospects of his daughter, and therefore will not be surprised to learn that it produced a similar change in those of his *protégé*, Sam Skelter. If the brother of his murdered benefactor, the cold, calculating, money-grubbing agent in Eastcheap, cared nothing for his youthful and lovely niece, he was not likely to be more compassionate with regard to the reputed son of the wooden-legged sailor. Sam had been two years at the academy in which he had been placed by the generosity of Mr. Hastings, and he was now fourteen years of age; and, being gifted with application and a good memory, he had acquired enough of the elements of instruction to make his way in the world, when once he was placed in the right direction. But the death of his benefactor disturbed all his plans for the future; and all the aerial castles which he had amused himself in building were blown into air, like the soap-bubbles cast from a pipe by some experimental juvenile.

On the morning preceding the evening on which Lolah Hastings was taken from the seminary by Colonel Elrington, Sam Skelter was called to the desk of the principal of the academy, who had received a similar letter to the one forwarded to Miss Crotchet, and proceeded to acquaint Sam with its contents. In a few days the Midsummer-vacation would commence, and then the boy would again become destitute; he therefore passed the intervening time in endeavouring to form some plan of action by which to save himself from starvation, or the unpleasant alternative of supplying his own wants at the expense of others, which is only legal for monarchs and their ministers. Sam had a good suit of clothes to leave with, but not a penny in his pocket, in consequence of the vacation being so near; and when he left the school, one fine morning in June, he knew not which way to turn in quest of the means of subsistence. He had been unable to form any plan for his future support; for, groping in the sewers was repulsive to him, after two years of the amenities of a boarding-school; and the idea of thieving was more repugnant to his mind than ever.

Yet it was with a light heart that the boy bent his steps towards London— vast, mighty, mysterious London! the grave of many hopes, the strand from which rocks and wrecks serve not to warn the deluded wretches who rush thereon in quest of wealth or fame. Disappointment and ruin serve not to deter others from rushing into the vortex; and though many sink in the hopeless struggle, and a few only achieve a fortune on the ruin of others, yet hope sustains them all, and London continues to be the focus of attraction for the ambitious, the avaricious, the needy, the dissipated, and the criminal. To this city of many mysteries, this mighty refuge of many crimes and many sorrows, Sam Skelter directed his steps, with a heart as light as his purse; and at noon stood on London-bridge, with his little bundle in his hand, gazing at the forest of masts which thronged the river as far as he could see, and the boats and barges which were continually passing in all directions.

He stood on the bridge some time, not knowing what course to adopt, and then turned back towards the city, and wandered about the streets without any aim or purpose. At length he found himself in the neighbourhood of Smithfield cattle-market, and the idea occurred to him that he would apply for advice to his old companion, the solitary of the sewers; for he saw nothing before him but the dire alternatives of starvation or theft. He therefore crossed the market, and plunged into the dark and vice-infested region of West-street, and in a few minutes stood before the dilapidated house in which he had dwelt with the aged mud-lark. It was in a more ruinous state than when he had last been there, and the door was easily opened, being completely dismantled; he closed the door and listened, but no sound reached his ears within the house, and he judged that the old man had either changed his residence, or was absent on a visit to the sewers. He ascended the stairs, which creaked and cracked beneath his feet, and entered the room which the mud-lark formerly occupied.

A ghastly object huddled up in one corner of the apartment caused him to start, and for a moment he felt inclined to fly from the spot; only a feeble light struggled through the rough boards which had been nailed over the broken window, but even that glimmer enabled him to perceive the outline of a human form. He drew nearer, though breathless with surprise and fear, and found that the object which had so startled him on first entering the room was the skeleton of a man wearing the shattered garments of the old mud-lark, huddled up on a heap of filthy rags in one corner! The first emotion of fear having subsided, Sam Skelter opened the closet, and found there the papers spoken of by the old man as containing the narrative of his life, and a few halfpence. The old man had not died of hunger, then, for there were the means of purchasing a substantial meal, and Sam hesitated not a moment to take possession of them for his own use; and the papers he also thrust into the pocket of his jacket. Illness had doubtless overtaken the old man, already enfeebled by old age and vicissitudes, and he had perished miserably for want of assistance.

Sam hurried from the ruined house, and again sought the purer air of the market; entering the tap-room of a public-house, which was filled with butchers, drovers, and horse-dealers of a low grade, he expended his halfpence in bread and cheese and a half-pint of porter, and sat some time to rest himself and listen to the conversation which was going on around him. Refreshed by his meal and an hour's rest, but not much edified by what he had heard, the boy quitted the public-house, and recommenced his purposeless wanderings about the streets. Evening was now drawing on, the gas was lighted, and the shop-windows of Ludgate-hill and Fleet-street looked even more brilliant than by day; for Sam Skelter had entered the former thoroughfare by passing the Old Bailey.

"Now, what shall I do?" the boy thought to himself, as he walked slowly along the Strand. "Shall I break a lamp, pick a pocket, or walk about till morning? But I shall be tired of walking before midnight, and if I sit down on a door-step the police will lock me up for being destitute; if I break a lamp, I shall insure myself board and lodging for a month, but I shall be deprived of my liberty; while, if I pick a pocket, I shall get the means of eating and drinking, and obtaining a lodging; and detection is by no means a matter of course. Still I do not like to thieve if I can help it; and, if I can get over to-night, perhaps I may be able to procure some employment."

This consideration decided him: he neither broke a lamp nor picked a pocket, but walked towards Charing-cross, when he bethought him of the shelter afforded by the dry arches of Waterloo-bridge, where he had passed the night before his meeting with Mr. Hastings two years since, and turned towards Westminster-bridge. Having crossed the bridge, he struck into the Belvidere-road, and pursued his way towards the bridge of refuge—the beautiful structure desecrated by a name replete with no associations save those of misery and bloodshed. He sat down under the bridge, with his back to the arch, and about midnight he fell asleep, with his head resting on his arms, which were folded across his knees. While thus sitting and sleeping, a young girl passed under the arch, accompanied by a well-dressed young man. The girl was tall, and very fair, about nineteen years of age, and evidently belonged to that unfortunate class of females who congregate so numerously in the streets adjacent to the Waterloo-road.

"Poor youth!" said she, casting a look full of compassion upon Sam Skelter; "he does not appear to have been used to that life, if we may judge by his clothing. He looks quite genteel, poor boy!"

The young man made some indifferent observation, and the pair continued their way along the Commercial-road until they reached the bottom of the Cornwall-road, where they turned up as far as John-street. A little distance up that street is a narrow dark passage leading to a court at the back of the street; on the farther side of this court is a high wall, but flanking John-street there are five or six houses, each consisting of only two rooms, one above the other, the whole being occupied by unfortunate girls. The young female who had compassionated Sam Skelter unlocked the door of one of these houses, and admitted herself and her companion; where, for the present, we must leave them.

The cool air from the river awoke Sam Skelter at an early hour, and he arose from his uncomfortabe position, and ascended the steps by the Feathers public-house; he wandered about the Waterloo-road and the adjacent streets until eight o'clock, when, the pangs of hunger again assailing him, he stopped before a baker's shop, and looked wistfully at the rolls and biscuits in the window.

" Are you the youth that I saw sleeping under the bridge last night ?" said a pleasant female voice ; and, looking round, Sam saw the unfortunate girl who had looked on him with compassion the preceding night.

" Very likely, for I did sleep there," rejoined Sam Skelter, with a faint smile.

" Had you no other place to sleep ? no friends ? no money to procure a lodging ?" asked the girl.

" Neither one nor the other," said Sam ; " and yet I left boarding-school only yesterday morning."

" Have you had any breakfast ?" inquired the young girl.

" I have had nothing to eat since yesterday afternoon, and I have no money to buy even a biscuit," replied the youth.

" Well, you shall breakfast with me, if you will," said the girl ; " and then you can tell me how you came to be in this destitute situation."

Sam expressed his gratitude for the girl's kindness, and, when she had purchased a loaf at the baker's, she desired him to accompany her to her dwelling. Her abode was the upper room of the house which we have already described, and there Sam partook of a substantial breakfast ; after which he briefly informed the kind-hearted girl how he had been so suddenly plunged into destitution. She expressed a hope that he would soon be successful in obtaining employment, and that he would breakfast with her every morning until he did, but that he would not visit her afterwards, for fear the acquaintance might compromise him with his employers.

Thus refreshed and encouraged, Sam Skelter left the lodging of the frail Samaritan, and in the course of the morning offered his services as a clerk or messenger at several offices in the city ; but some of those to whom he applied scarcely deigned to look at him, and others were particular as to reference and character, and Sam was unable to satisfy them. Then he applied to several tradesmen for the situation of errand-boy ; but in this he was equally unsuccessful, and at length he began to despair. He was sauntering down Chancery-lane in the afternoon, when he saw a gentleman alight from a horse, and look round as if seeking some one to hold it ; Sam proffered his services, which the gentleman accepted. The latter then entered the office of an eminent solicitor, where he remained some time, and on his return he gave Sam sixpence, and a letter which he wished to be delivered immediately in a contrary direction to that in which he was going. Sam thanked him, and readily undertook the mission, while the gentleman rode off, consoling himself for his generosity with the fact that he should charge the delivery of the letter to his client, as if it had been sent by one of his own clerks.

Sam delivered the letter, and waited for an answer, by which he found that the gentleman was an attorney in Lyon's-inn. At that place the youth again met his employer, to whom he gave the answer, and inquired if there was anything else he could do. The man of law replied in the negative. Sam then ventured to observe that he had been two days seeking for employment, and had been unsuccessful, adding that he had just left boarding-school, and was completely destitute.

" Just left boarding-school, and completely destitute !" repeated the attorney, looking fixedly at Sam. " That is a strange story ; let me see a specimen of your writing."

Sam Skelter obeyed, and wrote his name in a neat commercial style.

" You write a very good hand," observed the attorney. " Go over to Mr. Ashley's chambers, and say you were recommended by me ; he wants a junior clerk, and I think you will exactly suit him."

There was something in the tone in which the attorney uttered the last observation which Sam did not like; but he thanked his patron for the recommendation, and hurried to the chambers of Mr. Ashley, who was a barrister. We shall not at present formally introduce this gentleman to our readers; he will have to figure prominently in a more advanced period of our narrative; and it will be sufficient in this place to simply state that he was shrewd, needy, and avaricious; and hence the expression of his friend, the attorney, that Sam would exactly suit him; for Sam, in his present destitute condition, was delighted to accept Mr. Ashley's offer of permanent employment, at a rate of remuneration barely sufficient to find him in food and lodging. The youth entered upon his employment immediately, and received a trifling advance of money to enable him to exist until his first week's wages became due, from which the trifle thus advanced was to be deducted. He ceased his labours with his fellow-clerks, one of whom recommended him to a decent lodging; and here, for the present, we must leave him.

CHAPTER XXVIII.

CAROLINE ALLEN.

THE young girl who had become the fellow-lodger of Lolah Hastings, was prepossessing in appearance, and agreeable in her manners; and, with the view of cultivating that intimacy without which they could not expect to live very comfortably together, Lolah confided to her the circumstances which had reduced her to her present position, without any reservation or concealment. Her companion was not equally communicative; for she was, in fact, a young woman of exceedingly loose character, and feared to awaken the fears of her fellow-lodger by a too sudden revelation respecting herself. Moreover, she had conceived an unlawful desire to appropriate to her own use the ten sovereigns which Mr. Melville had given Lolah; and this she did in the course of the first night which the young girl passed in her new lodging, by taking them from under the pillow while Lolah was asleep, she having wrapped them in a piece of paper, and placed them there on retiring to rest. She then decamped from the house and the neighbourhood; and, when Lolah awoke on the following morning, she was overwhelmed with grief and amazement at the loss of her money. Missing her companion, she arose immediately, and called Mrs. Fubbs; but the landlady knew not that her lodger had privately left the house in the night, and was as much vexed at the affair as poor Lolah; for she had lost a week's rent by the absconding of her dishonest lodger.

This heartless robbery had again reduced Lolah Hastings to a state of complete penury; but, as bewailing her loss would not recover it, she went out in the hope of encountering her treacherous and dishonest companion, and compelling her to restore the money of which she had been so cruelly plundered. She was walking slowly along the Strand, much depressed in spirits on account of her loss, when she met a countenance which she well remembered, though she had not seen it for two years. It was that of Caroline Allen, the former tight-rope dancer of the strolling company to which Lolah had been attached previous to the meeting with her father in Essex. The recognition was mutual: the two young girls held out their hand, and exchanged a sisterly pressure.

"How strange that we should meet here!" said the fair rope-dancer. "How much you have grown, Lolah. But what are you doing now? I heard of your loss, dear, and was truly sorry on your account."

"Since the dreadful end of my poor father, I have had to endure vicissitudes so strange and terrible, that I shudder even to think of them," returned Lolah, sighing. "You will scarcely believe the tale I have to tell, Caroline—but it is too long to be told now. I believed I had surmounted all my troubles, when, last night, the dishonesty of a fellow-lodger plunged me into new difficulties—I was robbed of every farthing I possessed in the world, and now I am completely destitute; for my father had made no will, it appears, and my uncle refuses to acknowledge me, or to do anything for me."

"I am grieved to hear all this, Lolah," observed Caroline; "and if you will come with me to my lodging, I will hear all your story, and we can consult together what is best to be done. I live over the water, for I have left my father a long while; and I too have had my troubles, I assure you."

"Well, let us compare notes, and see which has suffered most," said Lolah Hastings, assuming a cheerful tone. "I think you will allow that I have endured the most in the shortest time; for in three days and nights, I was trepanned and vilely outraged, then drugged and buried alive, and, finally, taken up again and sold for dissection."

"Horrible!" exclaimed Caroline Allen, shuddering. "Yes, I must admit that your experience of evil has been more terrible than mine; and yet I have suffered much, and I still think my feelings have been more painfully wrung than yours."

"If you have been wounded in your affections, dear Caroline, I will grant your claim," said Lolah Hastings; "but what I endured in those three days might well have turned the brain of any poor girl with weaker nerves than mine."

While they had thus been speaking, the two young girls had crossed Waterloo-bridge, and, turning down a street on the left, had emerged into the Cornwall-road, and entered John-street. Then the ex-tight-rope dancer turned into the passage of which we have spoken in the preceding chapter—for Caroline Allen was the frail girl who had taken such compassion on the destitute condition of Sam Skelter. The apartment to which she now introduced her young friend was small, and meanly furnished; containing only a stump-bedstead, a couple of chairs, a small deal table, a crazy chest of drawers, a strip of carpet, and the usual appertenances of the fire-place. On the mantle were a few ornaments of the most common description, and a piece of broken looking-glass; above them were suspended lithographic portraits of Madame Vestris and Mrs. Honey.

"Now you shall tell me your adventures, and afterwards you shall hear mine," said Caroline Allen, taking off her bonnet and shawl. "You must stop and have some dinner with me, and then we will have a consultation upon your present position and future prospects."

Lolah Hastings then began her narrative, and, after alluding to the happy days she had passed at the school presided over by Miss Crotchet, she related in detail the extraordinary occurrences of the last three days and nights; the manner in which she had been trepanned by Colonel Elrington, the outrage which the hoary sensualist had committed in the den of infamy kept by Mother Jones, the fearful allusions and warnings of the servant, her interment and exhumation, and the scene in the study of Mr. Melville.

Caroline Allen then proceeded to relate to her friend the narrative of her life, since the retirement of Lolah from the itinerant company of her father; which we shall place before the reader in a more connected form than it was told by the fair narrator, prefacing it with a relation of some things which had occurred previous to that period, and which Lolah was already acquainted with.

About three months previous to the meeting of Lolah and her father at the fair in Essex, the strolling *troupe* of Mr. Allen were performing at a village in Kent, where Caroline became acquainted with a handsome Italian, who called himself Count Danzelli, making a tour of pleasure through the south of England. His features were unquestionably handsome, his complexion dark, his eyes brilliant, his hair black and curling, and his whiskers and moustaches not to be surpassed; moreover, he dressed well, and in the extreme of fashion, and his manners were bland and insinuating. He was accompanied by his friend the Honourable Augustus Fitzormond, a young man with whom the reader is already slightly acquainted, and concerning whose avocations and modes of life we have promised more complete revelations than have yet been made—a promise of which we shall not be unmindful. Count Danzelli was an ardent admirer of the fair sex, but inconstant as the butterfly which roves from lily to rose, and from sweet-pea to mignonnette, sipping the sweets of each, but staying long with none. The blue eyes, bewitching countenance, and graceful figure of the blooming Caroline, had attracted his attention as she stood in front of her father's canvas pavilion; and the ease and grace which she displayed upon the tight-rope completed the impression which she had made upon his susceptible heart. It happened that a Sunday intervened between the days of the fair, and it was on this day that an accidental meeting occurred between Caroline Allen and the ardent Italian. The latter was accompanied by Augustus Fitzormond, who, on this occasion, was as well dressed as the count, and displayed a profusion of meretricious jewellery; and the lovely rope-dancer, by the pretty Lolah Hastings. After a little light conversation, and some hesitation on the part of Caroline and her friend, the young ladies accepted the invitation of the gentlemen to take a walk with them, and paired off—Caroline with Count Danzelli, and Lolah with the Honourable Augustus Fitzormond.

It was a beautiful evening, and the walk was a long one; and, before they parted, Caroline Allen was deeply smitten with the handsome Italian, whom she informed of the route which the *troupe* would take on leaving the village, in order to afford the count an opportunity of meeting her again. When she retired to rest, she confided to Lolah the secret of her heart, and questioned her respecting Fitzormond; but the pretty dancing-girl was then too young to receive any lasting impression of the tender passion, and she had merely endured the company of Augustus, in order to allow Caroline that of the Italian. Count Danzelli followed in the route of the strollers, and, in every town and village in which they stopped, he renewed his acquaintance with the fair professor of the tight-rope. Caroline found her heart irrecoverably lost; and the count's passion became stronger at every interview. They met in woodland glade and flowery dell; and Danzelli, perceiving the impression which he had made upon the tender heart of the lovely Caroline, determined to bring the amour to a speedy issue.

It was on a fine starlight night in summer, a few weeks after the meeting of Lolah Hastings and her father, that the blooming Caroline met her lover in a sweet sequestered nook of Hainault-forest. It was on such a night that the enemy of mankind stole into the garden of Eden; and ever has the balmy twilight hour been the most fatal to those daughters of Eve in whose unguarded hearts Love has kindled his sacred flame. They sat together on a mossy bank; the nightingale warbled her pensive melody from the leafy covert of a neighbouring oak, and heaven's glorious canopy of blue, studded with silver stars, was visible through an opening in the umbrageous foliage of the copse. The hour and the opportunity were favourable, and Danzelli was too practised a seducer not to avail himself of it; passion triumphed over prudence in the young girl's beating heart, and she surrendered herself, almost without a struggle, to the embraces of her lover.

The count assured her of his unalterable attachment, and proposed that she should accompany him to London. Caroline consented, and the following morning saw the lovers on their way to the metropolis. Furnished apartments were taken in the neighbourhood of Leicester-square, and a fortnight passed rapidly and delightfully in the soft dalliance of love. Sweet was this long day-dream of bliss to the loving and susceptible heart of Caroline Allen; but the awakening was proportionately terrible. The fifteenth night came, and found Caroline a lonely watcher for her seducer's return. Midnight had tolled from every tower and spire of the mighty city; but Count Danzelli returned not to the arms of his deluded victim. The sun of another day rose and set, and he came not; a second and a third night passed away, and still he was absent. Hope grew fainter and fainter in the heart of the forsaken one, as the hours passed slowly and mournfully along; and when a week had elapsed, and he neither came nor wrote, the dread conviction forced itself irresistibly upon her mind, that she was deserted by him whom she had so fondly loved.

CHAPTER XXIX.

THE VICTIM OF SEDUCTION.

WHEN the conviction that her seducer had forsaken her forced itself slowly and painfully upon the heart of the deceived Caroline, her first step was to remove to a cheaper lodging, consisting of one room only, on the second-floor of a house in Drury-lane. A feeling of pride prevented her from returning to her father after casting off his protection and control; and she thought she

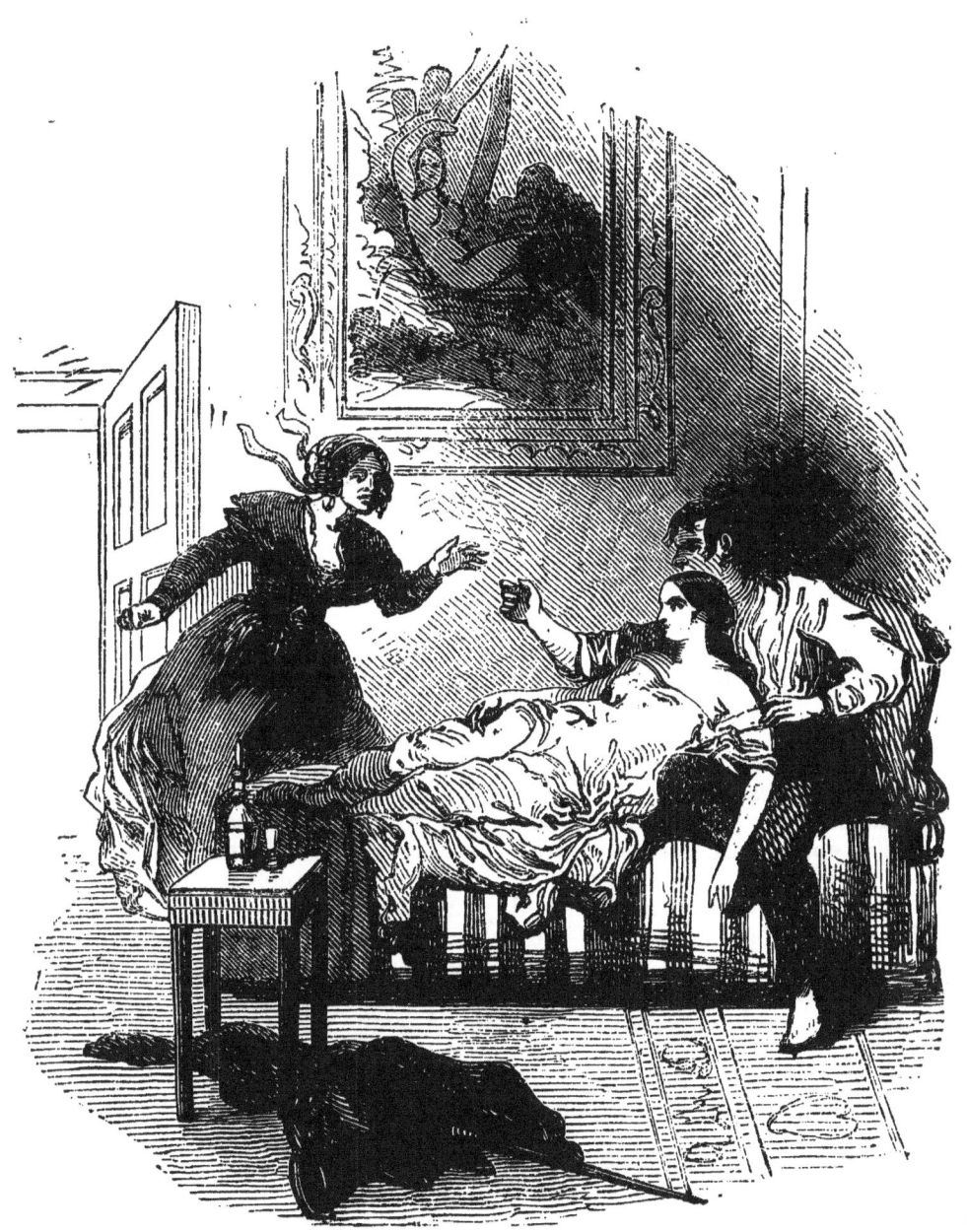

should be enabled to obtain an engagement at Astley's Amphitheatre, or with some itinerant manager frequenting the metropolitan and suburban fairs. Her application at Astley's was unsuccessful; and her little supply of cash became every day smaller, until her last penny was expended, and she owed her land-lady a week's rent. She passed a whole day without food; but on the second day of abstinence, the cravings of nature became insupportable, and she went out and pawned a dress for eighteen-pence. The landlady soon discovered the state of her lodger's finances, and, as a second week's rent was nearly due, she became clamorous. To appease her, Caroline pawned a shawl, and paid the demand upon her.

At length the day came on which she had neither food nor money, or any clothes to pawn, save those upon her back, and she was again indebted to her landlady. She went forth from her cheerless lodging with thoughts of evil in her mind, balancing gloomily the dire alternatives of prostitution or suicide. In this mood she was met by Augustus Fitzormond, who was lounging along the Strand, smoking a cigar.

12

" Oh, Mr. Fitzormond ! can you tell me what has become of Count Dan-zelli ?" exclaimed Caroline, in an imploring tone.

" Theodore Danzelli is now in prison awaiting his trial for fraud committed at cards," replied the young man, after a short pause, during which he regarded Caroline with extreme attention. " I believe I am addressing the lady whom we met at Wingham ?"

Caroline made a graceful inclination, but seemed agitated by the intelligence she had just heard.

" And now Mrs. Danzelli, I presume ?" continued Fitzormond, with unblushing effrontery.

Caroline blushed, cast down her eyes, and made no reply.

" Come, I see how it is, as well as if you had told me yourself," said the impudent Augustus. " That scamp of an Italian has deceived and forsaken you, as he has many others. But never mind him, my dear; the fellow is a regular Don Giovanni; but he is one of the most notorious card-sharps in London, and at last he has got laid by the heels, and I should not wonder if he gets seven years."

" I thought he was an intimate friend of yours," observed Caroline Allen.

" So he was, at one time; but I have cut him," returned Mr. Fitzormond; " and you may as well do the same, for I suppose he has not made you a settlement ?"

" The little money he left me is all gone," said Caroline, disconsolately. " I owe my landlady a week's rent; and all my clothes are pawned, except what I have on."

" A pretty girl like you need not want money long," observed Fitzormond; " and it was foolish to spout your toggery. But what do you think of doing now ?"

" I do not know; drown myself, I think," replied the young girl.

" Nonsense !" exclaimed Augustus, throwing away the end of his cigar. " There are scores of men in London as good as Danzelli, and a blessed deal better—myself, for instance; but you want money for present use. I could see as much in your countenance before you told me so. Now I can give you a letter of recommendation that will procure you a couple of sovereigns before as many hours. If you had not pawned your best clothes, I could have insured you five; but your appearance will show that you are not in a position to refuse anything. Come into this coffee-house, and have some refreshment, while I write the letter."

The face and neck of Caroline Allen had become crimson during this impertinent speech; but she subdued her indignation by reflecting on the helplessness of her position, and followed Fitzormond into the coffee-house. She then partook of the refreshments which the young man called for, and sat in silence, agitated by a variety of contending emotions, while he penned a short note, which he handed to her. She took it up mechanically: it was addressed to " Colonel Elrington, United Service Club-house."

" There is the means of getting a couple of sovereigns, my dear," said Augustus, in a bold, confident tone: " do as you like about using it. But you have not told me where you lodge yet, and perhaps I may call when I am passing, to see how you get on."

Caroline hesitated a moment, and then, informing Fitzormond of the number of the house in Drury-lane at which she lodged, she rose to depart.

The young man left her when they gained the street; and Caroline walked slowly westward, to deliver the note which he had given her. She could not doubt the nature of the contents; but the suggestion of Fitzormond was her only resource, and she had half resolved on that course when she encountered him; for who, with youth, health, and beauty, does not cling to life, amid whatever circumstances it may be passed ? She reached the club-house, and delivered the note; the servant who took it returned, and inquired her address. With a deep blush suffusing her countenance, and some hesitation, she gave the required information, and then returned to her humble lodging in Drury-lane, wondering whether the colonel was young or old. She informed her landlady that she expected a gentleman to visit her—an old friend of her father's—who would doubtless place it in her power to pay the trifle which she owed her.

This intimation was not made without some hesitation and blushing; and then she sat down in her little room, to await the colonel's visit.

Scarcely an hour had elapsed before she heard his footsteps on the stairs—for the jaded voluptuary was eager to meet the new prize which his jackal had discovered; and her cheeks became alternately pale and red, and she trembled with the conscious dread of shame. The interview was a short one; and when the colonel took his departure, Caroline found herself richer by two sovereigns than when he came, but bankrupt in honour.

The poor girl immediately paid the demand of her landlady, and went out to redeem her clothes from the pawnbroker, and purchase various necessaries. As she passed down Drury-lane, she again encountered Mr. Augustus Fitzormond.

" Well, my dear, did I not tell you truly?" said he. " I can see that I did: you are going to redeem your clothes. That is right. I will wait for your return."

Caroline was so abashed by this meeting, and the effrontery of her adviser, that she was unable to reply, but entered the pawnbroker's shop, which she had just reached. When she came out, she found Augustus waiting in the street.

" Come and have a glass of rum-and-water, my dear," said he, drawing her arm within his own; and, crossing the lane, they entered the Cock and Magpie, a tavern which, having been the resort, in former times, of highwaymen and footpads, has now degenerated into a rendezvous for thieves of the lowest grade, and vagabonds of every description.

" Pay for this, my dear," said Augustus, as they sat down in the parlour, and were supplied by the waiter with a glass of the potent fluid which he had mentioned; " I have no small change, and I know you will not mind standing a glass for the recommendation which I gave you; for I can see, by your countenance, that you are a girl of spirit."

Caroline paid for the rum-and-water; and, as a morbid feeling was fast stealing over her mind, she drank eagerly and deeply of the intoxicating beverage. The draught seemed to inspire her with a new being—like the golden elixir of Cornelius Agrippa—and enabled her to surmount the feeling of wretchedness and shame which she had experienced after her interview with Colonel Elrington. The exhilaration of her feelings increased every time that she raised the steaming fluid to her lips, and the glass was replenished again and again. At last she seemed to be conscious that she had imbibed too much: but this conviction always arrives too late; and though she roused herself, and left the house with the intention of returning to her lodging, she was seized with a giddiness on reaching the open air, and would have fallen down in the street, had she not been supported by Fitzormond, who had followed her. The young man then called a hackney-coach, and having handed Caroline in, took his place by her side. She immediately sank into a state of obliviousness, and retained no knowledge of the route taken by the coach.

The vehicle proceeded down Wych-street and Newcastle-street, along the Strand, and over Waterloo-bridge, stopping at a house about half-way down Tower-street, on the right-hand side. Here Augustus Fitzormond and the unconscious Caroline alighted; and when the lost girl awoke on the following morning, she found herself by the side of that impudent and unprincipled character. In a moment the events of the preceding night recurred to her memory, and she felt that she had deviated from virtue beyond the possibility of a return; she had erred from sheer necessity, and her scruples were still unremoved—a faint regret yet lingered in her mind. Fitzormond assured her that she would have been consigned to durance vile by the guardians of the night, had he not taken her under his protection; and his reasoning on the subject of a deviation from chastity was so specious and sophistical, that she had not a word to reply. Byron says—

" There is a tide in the affairs of women,
　Which, taken at the flood, leads—God knows where !
Not all the reveries of Jacob Behmen
　With its strange whirls and eddies can compare."

But this opinion could only have been formed from an imperfect knowledge of the deep and hidden springs of the human heart. Truth lies in the depths, and must not be looked for on the surface. The tide in the affairs of Caroline Allen, which at this time had led her to form a Platonic intimacy with the disreputable Fitzormond, is not to be explained by such superficial reasoning as that contained in the Byronic stanza :

> " In her first passion, woman loves her lover ;
> In all the others, all she loves is love ;
> Which grows a habit she can ne'er get over,
> And fits her loosely, like an easy glove."

We would rather account for the amorous *penchants* of unfortunate women by that necessity of loving which we believe to be an inseparable constituent of the female character. Woman's nature seems to require something to love, to cling to, to depend upon ; and hence those attachments which the noble poet considers as the inexplicable whirls and eddies of the tide of woman's life. In the midst of the grossest moral debasement, this necessity of loving is still found to exist, and is evidenced by those apparently unaccountable attachments to which we have alluded.

Augustus Fitzormond became the "fancy man" of the unfortunate Caroline Allen ; and this connexion continued up to the time of her meeting with Lolah Hastings, as recorded in the preceding chapter. The real name of this profligate young man was James Johnson ; but thinking this name not sufficiently aristocratic, he had abandoned it for the more high-sounding one by which he was known among the sharpers and "swell-mob's men" of the west-end of town. He was familiar with every knavish trick resorted to by "bonnets" and card-sharps ; he knew the secrets of Tattersall's and the mysteries of the prize-ring, and was well known in every resort of the dissipated and the depraved, from Hyde-park-corner to Temple-bar. His former companion, Theodore Danzelli, was a notorious gambler, who, after being kicked out of every gaming-house in Paris, had found his way to London—

> " The needy villain's general home,
> The common sewer of Paris and of Rome."

He was a well-known character in the neighbourhood of Leicester-square, and, though he had been denounced to Caroline Allen by his former friend and accomplice, Fitzormond, there was not a shade of difference in the amount of their moral turpitude.

CHAPTER XXX.

FREDERICK SHIRLEY.

A PAUSE of some minutes followed the conclusion of Caroline's narrative of her seduction, and her initiation into a life of prostitution. Lolah was thinking of what she had heard, and comparing her situation with that of the tight-rope dancer, after her desertion by Danzelli; and the latter was reflecting on the singular coincidence which had consigned them both to the arms of the hoary voluptuary, Colonel Elrington, and on the probable share which Augustus had had in bringing about the ruin of her young friend.

" Well, what do you think of doing, Lolah ?" said Caroline, in an anxious tone.

" What would you advise me to do ?" returned Lolah, after a brief pause.

" I scarcely know what to advise, dear," said Caroline, pensively ; and then she added, in a brisker tone: " I know what I should advise, if Colonel Elrington were a young man instead of an old one."

" Oh, do not mention him, Caroline!—I hate him !" exclaimed Lolah, blushing.

" Well, you have enough to hate him for. I acknowledge," returned Caroline

Allen; "but, seriously, I think you must resign yourself to the necessity of accepting the protection of some one. You have asked my advice, and I will give it candidly: your attempt to obtain an engagement will be fruitless; and even if there were any hopes of success, you have not the means of present subsistence. You will get in arrears with your rent, be compelled to pawn your clothes, just as I was; and, after living in misery and on the verge of starvation for two or three weeks, you will be driven, by the sheer necessity of living, into the only path which is open to the destitute female in this country. You may think I am giving you evil counsel, but I speak from painful experience, and from the observation of two years; and since the course which I have suggested is the only one open to you, I put it to your own good sense, whether it would not be better to enter upon it with the appliances of good clothes and a beautiful countenance, than to wait until poverty has compelled you to pawn the one, and impaired the attraction of the other?"

Sadness gloomed upon the lovely countenance of Lolah Hastings as she listened to these words, the bitter truth of which she could not deny, and upon which she reflected deeply. There was, indeed, too much truth in them—too much for our professions of Christianity—too much for the boasted blessings of the system under which we live. Whence all the abject poverty, the wide-spread misery and vice, with which the country is deluged? Are the people of this generation more immoral than their forefathers? No; for our criminal statistics prove that offences against the person have considerably decreased within the last twenty years; while offences against property have increased very considerably in the same period. What does this prove? That our population is too great to be provided for under the present system of society; for the steam-power of this country alone is capable of producing, in one year, the materials for clothing all the inhabitants of the world for three years; and, while the population is rapidly increasing, employment is decreasing, owing to the increase and improvement of machinery. Here we have the cause of the awful increase of pauperism and crime; the increase of population and the diminution of employment throws every year upon society hundreds of thousands of destitute persons, to fill our workhouses and prisons, and to swell the ranks of female prostitution.

A knock at the door interrupted Lolah's reverie, and Caroline ran down to answer the summons. It was Augustus Fitzormond, making much the same appearance as when we first presented him to our readers.

"Caroline," said he, "I shall have a friend to see me this evening; and, after I have done with him at cards, I shall bring him here."

"Who is it?—any one that I know?" inquired Caroline.

"Frederick Shirley, one of the clerks at Ashley's in Lyon's-inn," returned Augustus. "I know he has got some tin, and we may as well have it as any one else; and he is safe to get sporting his ochre at H's, or that blessed place in Catherine-street, if I do not get him over to my crib in the Cut."

"Very well," said Caroline Allen, "I shall stop at home, then;" and, Augustus having departed, she returned to her room.

She then invited Lolah to spend the evening with her, and, as the young girl felt the need of company in her present sadness and embarrassment, she readily accepted the invitation. After some further conversation on the suggestion of Caroline Allen, that Lolah should seek the protection of some amorous noble or gentleman, Fitzormond to act as the negociator of the delicate affair, the friendless young girl gave a partial consent to the proposition; and it was arranged that she should, for the present, occupy the room below that of the ex-rope-dancer. It was not without considerable repugnance that Lolah Hastings brought her mind to this determination; but she saw that it was her only resource, and the example and counsel of Caroline Allen had materially influenced her decision. We think we hear some rigid moralist, one of those who, because they know nothing of the world, think they know everything, say, as he or she peruses these pages: "Pooh! pooh! why did she not go to service, or get some needlework to do?" We beg to remind those strait-laced persons who, not having charity, are but "as sounding brass or a tinkling cymbal," that there is at all times a large reserve in the female labour-market, both for domestic service and for every branch of work for which the services of females are now called into requisition, and that from this reserve the army of prostitution is mainly recruited. We would also remind them, that this reserve enables employers to offer almost any remuneration they please to those whom they do employ; and that this inadequate remuneration obliges many of those who are so employed, to resort to the streets, in order to eke out a subsistence. Not only is this the case with many of the needle-women of Shoreditch, but it is equally true of the dress-makers of the west-end.

It was about eight o'clock in the evening when Fitzormond and his newly-made acquaintance, Frederick Shirley, sat down in the lodging of the former in the New-cut. There was no appearance of its being the bed-chamber of Augustus, as well as his sitting-room, for his couch was a sofa-bedstead, and the washing-stand had been removed; the room was decently furnished, but the windows were somewhat dim with dust, of which there was also a goodly collection on the mantel; for as the drudge of the household was a dirty, slip-shod girl of twelve years old, and Mr. Augustus Fitzormond was sometimes in arrear with his rent, the apartment received very little cleaning, more especially as that dissipated young man was very seldom at home during the day, and frequently passed the night at the lodging of Caroline Allen. Under the grate lay the fragments of a tobacco-pipe, and, on the mantel, the end of a cigar and a little heap of ashes, a pack of cards and a box of dominoes.

Frederick Shirley was about twenty-five years of age, and, as Fitzormond had stated to Caroline Allen, a clerk in the employ of Mr. Ashley, the barrister in whose service Sam Skelter had lately had the good fortune to be entered. Frederick Shirley was a handsome young fellow, with jetty whiskers and curly hair, and well and fashionably dressed, though rather too much in the "gent" style; for, to the uneasiness of his worthy parents, Frederick was ambitious of the character of a *fast boy*. Aiming at being a water-colour copy of the Chester-fields and Waterfords, he had lately made many acquaintances which did not redound greatly to his credit, and among them Mr. Augustus Fitzormond; with the same ignoble view he had also become a frequenter of H's, the Adelphi-shades, and the more aristocratic resort of Goodered's in Piccadilly, and patron-ised the songs and suppers of the Harp, the Sheridan Knowles, and the Mogul.

Fitzormond drew from his pockets, on entering the apartment, a small bottle and a lemon, and then ringing the bell, he desired the little servant-girl to bring up a jug of hot water and two glasses, and to ask her mistress to lend him some sugar. Having been supplied with these requisites, he and Shirley sat down, and proceeded to concoct two steaming glasses of toddy; having tasted, smacked his lips, and pronounced it "none so dusty," Fitzormond then placed the cards on the table, and proceeded to light a cigar. They played with varying success for nearly three hours; but as the fumes of the liquor mounted to Shirley's brain, he played with less caution, and rose from the table a loser to the amount of ten shillings. Having declared that he should play no longer, Fitzormond proposed an adjournment, and they quitted the house together.

"Come with me, and I will introduce you to the prettiest girl in the neighbour-hood," said Augustus, as they reached the top of the Cornwall-road; and in a few minutes they arrived at the lodging of Caroline Allen.

Augustus introduced his mistress and Frederick Shirley to each other, and the trio proceeded up-stairs, where Fitzormond was somewhat surprised to meet Lolah Hastings; but as he knew not that she was the young lady who had been trepanned by Colonel Elrington, he bowed, and made no remark. Frederick Shirley looked from Caroline to Lolah, as if he was doubtful to which the description belonged, of being "the prettiest girl in the neighbourhood;" but his glance lingered longest upon the dark-eyed Lolah.

Fitzormond lit another cigar, and the fair Caroline, after introducing her young friend, proceeded to prepare the toddy for her visitors. Augustus started at the name of Hastings, and looked hard at Lolah, but could scarcely believe that she had so soon escaped from the vile clutches of Mother Jones. Lolah soon perceived the impression which her charms had made upon the barrister's clerk, and the tell-tale blush which each glance from the dark eyes of Frederick Shirley called to her sunny cheeks, showed that her bosom was agitated by emotions kindred to those which her beauty had excited in the young man. Frederick, on his part, immediately perceived the distinction which existed between the beautiful Lolah and the blue-eyed mistress of his friend, and was assiduous in his attentions to the former. Caroline saw this predilection with secret pleasure, and about midnight called Augustus out of the room, and made him acquainted with Lolah's history, and the conversation they had had in the afternoon. Fitzormond, more unprincipled and selfish than his mistress, was little inclined to acquiesce in the proposition to give up the barrister's clerk to Lolah Hastings; but a little consideration showed him that Shirley's own inclinations were in favour of Caroline's arrangement, and he agreed to further it. During the temporary absence of Augustus and his mistress, Frederick Shirley had succeeded in coming to terms with Lolah Hastings, which was the more easily effected for the impression which his handsome features and elegant manners had made upon the young girl's heart.

> "The cold in clime are cold in blood,"

says Byron; and, as the same argument will apply to the natives of the sunny south, Lolah was of a temperament as warm as the spice-bearing clime of which her maternal progenitor was a native, and in which she herself first saw the light. Frederick Shirley was the first man who had ever caused her a sensation; and the tender feelings which now stole upon her heart, made her resign herself to the course suggested by Caroline Allen with the less regret. She retired to rest in the room below, immediately after the return of Augustus and Caroline, and, in a few minutes, was followed by the enraptured Frederick, leaving Fitzormond in the company of the blue-eyed Caroline.

CHAPTER XXXI.

THE QUARREL AT MOTHER JONES'S.

WE must now return to the house near Shire-lane, where Lolah Hastings was entrapped and violated by Colonel Elrington, and afterwards hocussed by the vile harridan Mother Jones, and consigned to the vaults of Habakuk Holdfast's chapel. Our readers are, doubtless, anxious to learn the secrets of that house of infamy and crime, and to unravel the horrible mysteries involved in the hints and allusions of Bill Simpson and the young woman who was the household drudge of Mother Jones. But the full development of those mysteries must be left to time; and all we can do at present, is to describe what took place one evening a few months after the premature interment of Lolah Hastings, and her almost miraculous escape from the vaults of the chapel.

The servant sat in the kitchen, perusing several letters which lay on the table, and, though an unbidden tear would sometimes fall on them, she appeared to derive a melancholy pleasure from the occupation. Her countenance was sad and pensive, and a sigh often heaved her bosom, which the lines that were there written had once caused to thrill with pleasure, but which now throbbed with the anguish which those reminiscences of the happy past had awakened there. Into the causes of the secret grief which evidently weighed heavily on her soul, and the hidden mystery which bound her body and soul to the abominable service of Mother Jones, we will not now seek to penetrate; for in the apartments above, the storm was already gathering which was soon to burst over that den of infamy, and expose the guilt of which it had been the scene.

In the back parlour, Mother Jones lay asleep on a sofa, emitting most delectable music from her nasal organ, and smelling strongly of the liquid called " cream of the valley," which the old harridan was wont to indulge in to such an extent as to render her oblivious of all that was passing around her, and render it necessary for her to seek her couch. In the front parlour, Bill Simpson was seated on the sofa, without his coat and boots; and the French girl who had visited Lolah Hastings after the outrage perpetrated by Colonel Elrington, was reclining at full length upon the sofa, with her head on the shoulder of Bill Simpson, and one arm around his neck; the young man's right arm was thrown around her waist, and his left hand supported his meerschaum pipe.

The young French girl possessed an attractive and piquant countenance, and a round and supple form of most perfect symmetry; but the pervading expression of every look, tone, and gesture, was that of wantonness and profligacy. In complexion, she was a brunette, but a lively colour glowed upon her sunny cheeks, now heightened by sensual passion and the sparkling champagne which stood upon a table near them. Her dark brown hair was arranged in smooth and shining bands upon her temples, her neck was bare, and the lowness of her silk dress revealed the white and swelling charms of a full and voluptuous bust.

"The old woman has no suspicion at present," observed Bill Simpson, in a low voice; "but when she does pipe us, there will be a blow up; for she is as jealous-disposed an old catamaran as ever I knew. Fortunately, she is as much in my power as I am in hers; and, if it comes to a rumpus, I'll nail her at once, before she has time to blow the gaff."

"You will not kill her, Bill?" observed the girl, in an undertone.

"No, that would not be a safe job for myself," returned Simpson; "but I would fix her in Newgate, as sure as she's alive; and I defy her to put anything upon me, if I keep my own counsel, and do not admit it myself. There is enough against her to hang her. But I am not going to tell you everything: so do not look so curious about it."

"That affair of Miss Hastings and the colonel would be sufficient to transport her," observed the French girl.

"Yes; but you do not know half of that business, nor of several other black jobs that have been done in this house," said Bill Simpson. "That girl in the kitchen knows a little, but not so much as I do. If I knew where the old woman keeps all her tin, I would nail it, and hook it over to France."

"Oh, how delighted I should be to return to Paris!" exclaimed the girl, joyfully.

"I think you and I could carry on a tidy game at the Palais Royal, Elise," observed Simpson, smiling.

At this point in their conversation, the door was opened violently, and Mother Jones burst into the room, her countenance purple with rage, and ready to explode with jealousy and hatred.

"I think you have carried on a tidy game already, Mr. Simpson; and you too, you vile, artful, abandoned hussey!" she exclaimed, in a voice hoarse and almost inarticulate with rage. "So you'll nail all my tin, will you, Mr. Simpson? Hook it over to France with that foreign wretch, eh? I should like to catch you at it, Mr. Simpson. You will blow the gaff, and get me scragged, will you? Mind your own neck, you good-for-nothing, circumventing vagabond!"

"Come, that will do, Mother Jones," said Bill Simpson, who had sprung from the sofa as she entered, apprehending violence from the harridan's excited passions. "You know that you are more in my power than I am in yours; and if I have any more of this chaff, I'll blow the whole concern."

Elise had become pale from terror, and clung to the arm of Bill Simpson, who assumed an air of determined defiance, and advanced towards the door.

"You ungrateful scoundrel! to talk of hanging the best friend you ever had!" exclaimed Mother Jones. "I hate you, and I'll transport you and that girl too. Take her away, before I tear her eyes out!"

"Fetch my coat and hat, Elise," said the young man, preparing to put on his boots.

"She shall not go!" screamed the exasperated and malevolent woman, stamping her foot. "How dare she to come here at all?"

"I will not leave Elise here with you: you would be capable of murdering her," said Bill Simpson. And having pulled on his boots, he opened the street-door, and after whispering a few words to the young French girl—who had already put on her bonnet and shawl, as if desirous of quitting the house as speedily as possible—she took her departure.

"Now, Mrs. Jones, if you will allow me to fetch my hat and coat, I will never darken your doors any more," said Bill Simpson. And quickly ascending the stairs, he put on his coat and hat, and in another minute was again in the presence of the jealous and vindictive Mother Jones.

"You wretch, I'll transport you and that girl, if I get my neck in a halter at the same time!" exclaimed the furious woman; but Simpson heeded her not, and let himself out of the house.

The first impulse of Mother Jones was to follow him, and give him into custody upon certain grave charges in which they had both been implicated, and to denounce Elise as an accomplice; but, as her rage gradually subsided, she feared to leave the house in the charge of the servant; for though she knew the young woman was completely in her power, and dared not betray her, yet guilt is ever cowardly and suspicious, and the vile woman feared and suspected every one about her. Then she trembled at the thought that she might already have been denounced by the reckless Simpson; and, had she possessed sufficient courage to meet death, she would have committed suicide; but this failing her, she proceeded to fortify herself with gin, of which she drank several glasses.

The servant had started from her reverie in the kitchen, on hearing the voices of her mistress and Bill Simpson in altercation, and advancing to the

13

foot of the stairs, she overheard all that was said.   She heard Elise and Simpson quit the house, and in less than an hour afterwards she heard a heavy fall on the floor of the front parlour.   She ran immediately to that apartment, and found Mother Jones lying on the carpet, having rolled off the sofa in a state of helpless intoxication.   The idea of escape instantly shot across her brain, and, almost trembling with mingled hope and fear, she hastily gathered up her clothes into a bundle, threw on her bonnet and shawl, and quitted the house by the front door.

It was about seven o'clock when Bill Simpson and the French girl left the house, and the clocks of the neighbouring churches were striking nine when the former returned and knocked at the door.   The summons was not answered, and he repeated it with no better effect; he then drew a key from his pocket, and opened it himself. Closing the door after him, he entered the front parlour, and there beheld Mother Jones still lying upon the floor; he listened attentively, and the only sound in the house was the loud snoring of the inebriated wretch at his feet.

"Good," muttered he to himself; "the slavey has bolted, and small blame to her. There is nothing to fear from her, because she has too much to answer for herself. How shall I dispose of this old beast? I should like to shove her into one of Holdfast's coffins, and let her get sober in the vaults.   I would take her up to the matted room, and leave her there, where she might scream till she was hoarse, but she is too heavy to carry up-stairs.   It would not be a bad plan to shove her into the cellar, and there she would have company enough when she awoke; but then, if any discovery should be made, I shall be suspected of having murdered her.   I must merge my desire for revenge, in considerations of personal safety, and, leaving the drunken wretch where she is, content myself with the contents of her cash-box."

Having come to this determination, Bill Simpson stooped down and rifled the harridan's pockets of a purse with three sovereigns and some silver in it, and a bunch of keys.   He then went up-stairs, unlocked a drawer in Mother Jones's bed-room, and took therefrom a tin box, which he also opened, and found it to contain bank-notes and gold to the amount of nearly four hundred pounds.   Having possessed himself of this treasure, he descended the stairs, and quitted the house, with the intention of leaving the metropolis at midnight, for the continent.   He was joined by Elise, according to previous appointment, at a public-house near St. Clement's-court, and they immediately proceeded through the city to the London-docks, where they took a passage to Boulogne, in a steamer that was to leave the docks at midnight, arriving at its destination at noon on the following day.   We shall leave them for the present on their way to France, and proceed with our elucidation of the many mysteries which hang about the docks, the wharfs, the bridges, and the ever-flowing current of Old Father Thames.

CHAPTER XXXII.

THE MURDER-HOLE.

It was not until Bill Simpson and his mistress were already on their way to *la belle France*, that Mother Jones, having slept off the fumes of the gin which she had drank after the quarrel, awoke with a cold shudder, and found herself lying on the floor in complete darkness.   She turned over, and wondered how she came there; and, not being able to solve the question with satisfaction, she rose, and groped her way to the bell-rope, which she pulled vigorously.   At that moment the clocks of the neighbouring churches struck two, but no one replied to her summons, and the old harridan sat down on the sofa in a state of most decided mystification; by degrees, however, recollection returned to her, and she became conscious of all that had passed; and, finding that it was now morning, she concluded that the domestic slave had retired to rest, and felt much incensed with her for doing so without assisting her up-stairs.   Impressed with this conviction, she found her way to her bed-room, and, having undressed and got into bed, she soon fell asleep again.

The first thing which caught her attention when she awoke the next morning, was the tin box, which had contained the fruits of many a crime, standing on the drawers, and, starting up in her bed, she perceived, to her consternation, that it was empty, and that the drawer in which it had been deposited by herself, a few days previously, was open. Horrified at this discovery, the harridan got out of bed, and went fuming and fretting to the servant's room, but it was untenanted, and the bed had evidently not been slept in. Returning to her own room, muttering most horrible imprecations, the harridan hastily dressed herself, and, quitting the house, proceeded to the residence of an active officer of the Bow-street establishment, whom she acquainted with the robbery, and the descriptions of the three persons upon whom her suspicions rested: Bill Simpson, Elise, and Susan Walters, the servant. The officer returned with her to the house, and gave his opinion that no burglary had been committed, but, that the property had been carried off by some one in the house, or else that the thieves had been admitted by some one upon the premises.

Mother Jones consoled herself for the heavy loss which she had sustained, and the inconvenience and vexation which had been caused her by the flight of Bill Simpson, the French girl, and the servant, by copious potations of her favourite liquor; and, as she possessed a number of houses of an infamous description in various parts of the metropolis, the enormous rents derived from them assured her against the remotest fear of poverty. But, apart from the jealous passions excited within her by the discovery of Bill Simpson's amour with the French girl, she was alarmed and peplexed by the absconding of Susan Walters. That young woman had been bound to her service by the shackles forged by sin, and she despaired of replacing her by another in whom she could confide as implicitly; moreover, Susan Walters was acquainted with certain dark and hideous crimes of which that house had been the scene, and she feared to bring another servant into the place, lest a discovery should be made which might consign her to an ignominious death.

As she sat brooding over these terrible thoughts, she was startled from her reverie by a loud knock at the door; she rose, and peeped from the window, to see who it might be who required admittance, for the harridan's guilty conscience rendered her fearful and suspicious. She saw a Bow-street officer and the back of a young female, and, immediately concluding that the visit related to the robbery of the preceding night, she hastened to open the door. She had no sooner done so, however, than she started violently, uttered a piercing shriek, and fell on the floor of the passage in a state of insensibility; for her eyes encountered the form of Lolah Hastings, whom she had consigned to a premature grave in the vaults of the chapel. This meeting, so appalling to the conscience-stricken Mother Jones, was thus brought about: Lolah had seen the proceuress on her return home after her application to the Bow-street officer relative to the robbery, and, having watched her until she had become sure of the identity, she followed her to her abode, and then gave information at Bow-street, respecting the manner in which she had been inveigled to the house near Shire-lane, by the pretended Colonel Morton, and the treatment to which she had there been subjected by the colonel and Mother Jones.

" That looks blue against her, anyhow," observed the officer who accompanied Lolah, alluding to the effects of the meeting upon the mind of the proceuress. " I think this is evidence enough of the identity, and I suppose you will be able to tell if this is the right house."

" Oh, yes !" replied Lolah ; " I remember this passage, that door, and the stairs, perfectly."

" I ought to have brought somebody with me, but I'll just shove the ruffles on her, and lock her in this room till we are ready to start," observed the officer ; and, raising the harridan from the floor, he dragged her into the parlour, and laid her upon the sofa.

He then took a pair of handcuffs from his pocket, with which he secured her hands ; and, then leaving her in the room, he locked the door.

" Now lead the way up-stairs, miss," said he ; and Lolah unhesitatingly ascended the stairs, followed by the officer, and led the way, first into the bed-room where she had been confined after her liberation from the matted chamber, and afterwards into that vilely-contrived apartment, the scene of many a crime which had never been brought to light. They then returned to the passage, where the officer advised Lolah to proceed at once to the office in Bow-street, and there await his arrival with the prisoner. When the young girl had left the house, thinking it strange that no one had been found in the house but Mother Jones, the officer descended to the kitchen, and, while looking around him, his attention was drawn to a door secured by a strong iron bar and a huge padlock. Accustomed to regard everything with suspicion, the officer drew nearer to the door, and discovered several dark red stains upon the edge of the door, which looked like the marks of bloody fingers. These gory finger-marks seemed to point unmistakeably to a horrible tragedy, and the officer determined upon a further search in that den of mystery and crime.

He therefore returned to the front parlour, where he found Mother Jones just returning to consciousness; and, having removed the handcuffs, he allowed her to put on her bonnet and cloak, and without saying a word of the disco-very which he had made, he took her at once before the magistrates at Bow-street. The procuress was very pale, and seemed extremely agi-tated; when she was placed at the bar, and she saw Lolah Hastings enter the witness-box, she fixed her eyes upon the young girl as if her presence was a mystery which she could not solve.

Lolah then recapitulated the statement which she had previously made to the officer, which caused the utmost sensation throughout the court; the magistrates were amazed at the extraordinary character of the young girl's evidence, and asked a number of questions with the view of testing its truth. When she professed her ignorance of the name of the surgeon who had pur-chased her for the purpose of anatomization, one of the magistrates shook his head, and whispered his colleague that it resembled the case of Elizabeth Canning. But when the officer who had arrested Mother Jones handed a written paper to the magistrates, informing them of the discovery which he had made in the kitchen, and his suspicions, they looked grave, and, after consulting together, ordered the prisoner to be remanded for a week.

Mother Jones was then removed from the bar, and the officer, accompanied by another, returned to the house where he had effected the capture, and pro-ceeded to force open the door in the kitchen with a powerful crow-bar. The opening of the door disclosed to their view a dark and gloomy cellar, the air of which was damp and fetid, and in which nothing could be seen for the dark-ness. One of the officers then lighted a candle, but scarce had its glimmering light fell upon the damp walls and floor of the cellar, than he started back, and gave utterance to a cry of horror.

On the floor of the cellar, within a few feet of the door, lay two skeletons, another against the opposite wall, and a fourth in the farthest and darkest corner of that horrible hole! The officers stood gazing upon the dreadful spectacle as if petrified with horror; and several minutes elapsed before their nerves were sufficiently restrung to enable them to make a more minute survey. Of the two skeletons nearest to the door one was lying across the other, and these two seemed to have been deposited there at a later period than the others, for the integuments were still soft; the undermost appeared to be that of an old man, for patches of grey hair still adhered to the skull, and the fragments of clothing which remained were those of the male sex. The other was evidently that of a female, as was evidenced by the long, black hair which hung from the scalp, and by such parts of the victim's clothing which had not been carried away by the rats. The skeleton which lay near the opposite wall appeared to have been there for a much longer period of time than the others, for nought remained but the white bones; and the sex was in this case a matter of conjec-ture, though apparently the remains were those of a woman or a youth. The fourth tenant of this horrible murder-hole was the skeleton of a child, and evidently of very tender age, for the remains were more cartilaginous than osseous, and the bones of the legs were slightly bent, as in those of a newly-born infant.

One of the officers remained in possession of the house, and the other returned to Bow-street, and made a report to the magistrates of what had been discovered. The account was heard by the persons in the court with a shudder of horror; the news spread in a short time all over the metropolis, and created everywhere the utmost excitement; an immense mob assembled before the house which appeared to have been the scene of so many fearful tragedies, and the exertions of a large body of constables were scarcely sufficient to restrain the throng from violence. As night came on the crowd gradually dispersed, and on the following day an inquest was held on the remains, but adjourned for want of evidence.

Search was made throughout the metropolis for Bill Simpson and Susan Walters, but every attempt to find them was fruitless, and when Mother Jones was brought up for re-examination there was no more evidence than at first. The procuress was committed for trial, however, for being accessory to the outrage perpetrated upon Lolah Hastings by Colonel Elrington, as that was the only offence which could be proved against her; and such was the popular indignation which the horrible discoveries at her late residence had excited, that she had to be guarded to and from the police-court by a large body of constables, in order to prevent the mob from inflicting summary vengeance upon her.

At the adjourned inquest upon the human remains found in the cellar, no fresh evidence being adduced, a verdict was returned which would not prevent a new inquiry in the event of anything occurring to throw additional light upon the horrible and mysterious affair. Mother Jones had great hopes of being acquitted of the crime laid to her charge, for she was determined to maintain strict silence herself, and flattered herself that the unsupported evidence of her victim would fall to the ground. But when the trial came on, the testimony of Lolah Hastings was corroborated in a material point by Miss Crotchet; and, though Susan Walters, Habakuk Holdfast, and Mr. Melville, all kept in the background, each for important reasons upon which the crafty procuress knew how to calculate, yet the testimony of her victim could not be shaken, and received so much circumstantial support from the evidence of Mrs. Fubbs and Caroline Allen, that the guilty woman was sentenced to transportation for seven years.

The result of the trial was most gratifying to the public in general, and more especially to those who, with every wish to punish the vile Mrs. Jones, were compelled to withhold their evidence from considerations of personal safety or reputation, and even Augustus Fitzormond shared in the general feeling. The appalling discovery of the skeletons in the cellar of Mrs. Jones's house continued to be involved in as much mystery as ever, and came to be regarded by the public as the evidence of one of those inexplicable atrocities which, like the murders of Eliza Grimwood and Eliza Davis, seem to be fated to remain in obscurity for ever.

CHAPTER XXXIII

THE ORPHANS.

WE have now arrived at a point in our narrative when the development of those mysteries of which we have yet raised only a corner of the veil, requires a wider scope; for Sam Skelter and Lolah Hastings are now fairly launched upon the troubled stream of life, and new scenes and new characters now claim our attention. We have been absent too long from the shores of Old Father Thames, but the due elucidation of the mysteries which belong to his rippling waters and sedgy banks required that we should dive into the holes and nooks of the mighty city through which his murmuring waters flow unceasingly; and the progress of our story requires that we should now change the scene to that part of his course where his silver waters gush over their pebbly bed, and pursue their devious way through the vales of Gloucestershire.

" My dear boy, and you, my dear little girl, this early trial which seems to break your young hearts, is but one of those dispensations which happen every day, and which Providence sends to chasten the heart, and subdue it to humility and resignation. It is a sad loss for you, Ellen, but we must all die, you know; and, if you have lost a father, I have also lost a brother. Well, all flesh is grass, as the best book of all tells us; which springs up and flourishes to-day, and to-morrow is cast into the oven."

The speaker was Mr. Ashley, the barrister who had some time before taken Sam Skelter into his employment as a clerk, and whom we must now introduce to our readers more at length: he was rather more than forty years of age, and habitually wore a suit of black, on account of the additional gravity and respectability which that sombre colour bestows upon the wearer. A suit of black, even when worn and faded, seldom fails to attach an appearance of gentility to the individual who wears it; it is also the colour usually worn by the clerical and learned professions, and on this principle Mr. Ashley always wore black. He was rather tall, sallow in countenance, and dressed with the most elaborate care, though as plainly as possible; it being the chief point of his "making up"—to use a theatrical term—to impress his friends and clients with large ideas of his piety, morality, and conscientiousness. We think we see the reader smile at the idea of a lawyer's conscience; we have seen attornies undertake a hopeless case for the sake of the fees, and barristers accept money for causes which they never intended to plead, and we have an idea that such proceedings, though customary in the profession, are not honest; but we will leave the conscience of Mr. Ashley to develop itself in the progress of our narrative.

While enunciating, slowly and with an oily smoothness of tone, the pious commonplaces which we have placed upon record, Mr. Ashley stood with his back to the fire, and his hands supporting the tails of his coat. His hair, which was of a reddish hue, was cut close behind, and carefully brushed up in front, in order to show as much as possible of his somewhat low and receding forehead. His eyes were large and grey, and had the faculty, convenient for a lawyer, of never looking any one in the face; while speaking, the eyes of Mr. Ashley were always either bent in seeming humility upon the carpet, or raised in pious resignation to the ceiling.

Mrs. Ashley, the wife of this exemplary man, was about the age of her husband, and what is generally termed a fine woman, which appears to us a synonyme for coarseness and elephantine proportions. She was tall, stout, and of masculine appearance and manners, and had a ruddiness of countenance, for which she was mainly indebted to the frequent use of a certain potent spirit from the distillery of Sir Felix Booth. Such are the usual characteristics which constitute a *fine* woman, as seen through the glass of fashionable opinion by the genteel mob of society, who appear to derive their notion of female beauty from the "fat, fair, and forty" qualifications of the bloated debauchee George IV., rather than from the ideal imaginings of a Byron, a Titian, or a Canova.

The pious reflections of Mr. Ashley were addressed to a youth about fifteen years of age, and a little girl who could not have much exceeded ten years. The youth was tall and finely proportioned; if he had not precisely the grace of the Apollo Belvidere, he possessed the supple and athletic mould of the Farnese Hercules. His dark hair curled on his ample forehead, and his eyes, though dim with tears, beamed with candour and intelligence; his features were undeniably handsome, and a physiognomist might have detected in the expression of his eyes and mouth a resolute and daring spirit. He sat on the sofa, with one hand supporting his head, and the other locked in that of his sister, the little girl already mentioned.

The eyes of the little girl were red with weeping, but even her tears could not dim their peerless lustre, nor efface the loveliness of her expressive countenance. Her black and glossy ringlets fell in rich profusion on her alabaster shoulders, and on a complexion of exquisite fairness dwelt a bloom that might have rivalled that of the peach, and a colour that would have tested a painter's skill, so rich yet delicate its hue. Her features were small and regular, and the outline of her sweetly-innocent countenance might have served for a model for the choicest productions of the sculptors of ancient Greece, in the palmiest days of the divine art. She was yet too young for a correct conception to be formed of what symmetry her figure might be when fully developed into the ripeness of womanhood; but it was slight and supple, and there was an infantile grace in her movements, and an elasticity in her step, which promised greatly for the attractiveness of her form when a few more years had passed over her head.

" I am glad to see you begin to view your loss with that resignation to the will of an inscrutable Providence, which is the greatest ornament of the Christian character," said Mr. Ashley, as little Ellen ceased weeping, and looked affectionately at her brother, whose hand she held in her own, as if he were the only friend that remained to her in the wide world. " It is true that you have lost your father—a kind and too indulgent father, but I shall endeavour to supply his place towards you, and your aunt will be more than a mother to you."

" It is a sad loss for them, poor things !" observed Mrs. Ashley, in a manner the patronising tone of which deprived it of the compassion which her words seemed to imply.

" Alas, for the mutability of human affairs !" exclaimed her husband, casting his eyes up to the ceiling ; and then, seating himself at the table, he applied himself to the wine. " We are here to-day and gone to-morrow, as one may say. Take a glass of wine, nephew. We know not what the lapse of a single day may bring forth. To-day we are here, rich and sparkling as this wine," continued the barrister, raising the glass, and looking at it with the manner of a connossieur, " and to-morrow where are we ?—in the silent grave !" and he quaffed the sparkling sherry as he spoke, as a practical illustration of the truth of his remark.

Mr. Ashley was the younger brother of the late Sir Norman Ashley, and the youth and girl were the orphan children of the deceased gentleman. On the death of their grandfather, the mansion and park of Oakwood-hall, with extensive landed property in the neighbourhood, descended to Sir Norman Ashley, the father of the orphans, in virtue of the law of primogeniture, the estates being a royal grant to the first baronet of the family. Being unable to alienate the landed property from the title, Sir Norman's father had bequeathed the bulk of his funded property to his second son, Edward, who had been educated for the legal profession ; but the money thus acquired by Mr. Ashley was not so considerable in amount as to enable him to lay aside the study of Blackstone and Chitty, and he had accordingly continued to dwell among the dust and cobwebs of Lyon's-inn, only making a brief sojourn at Brighton or Cheltenham every summer, as a change of air for Mrs. Ashley and their son, who was about the same age as his cousin Norman.

Sir Norman Ashley was a man of most exemplary character—conservative in politics, yet ever anxious for the welfare and comfort of his poorer tenantry ; attached to the ancient institutions of the country, yet no bigot ; and hospitable and generous, yet not lavish or extravagant, and frugal without being parsimonious. His probity was undoubted ; and in the matter of those minor morals which contribute so much to the refinement of society, he was exact without being austere. He had married a woman whose singular beauty was excelled only by her goodness of heart and amiability of manners ; and though only the daughter of his father's steward, she was better fitted by nature for the adornment of a throne than many of those who fill the high places of western Europe, and are distinguished only by their vices. Their union had been blessed with two children, a son and a daughter ; and to bring them up as virtuous, intelligent, and useful members of society, had been the constant solicitude of Sir Norman and his amiable lady. But Lady Ashley had been dead some years before the opening of our tale ; and the entire care of the children devolved upon Sir Norman, who was thinking of sending his son to Eton, to complete his education, when illness overtook him, and he died.

Mr. Ashley was of a character and disposition the very reverse of his brother —which may be partly accounted for by the nature of his studies and the profession which he had chosen, and partly by the asperity and bitterness of feeling naturally induced by contrasting his position in society with that of his elder brother, whom an unjust law had placed in so much more elevated a rank than himself. It is morally impossible that a man should pass his life, from boyhood to mature age, in the chicanery of the law, without imperceptibly gathering much of the turpitude by which its practice is distinguished : as well might a man expect to walk through mud without soiling his boots. When it is remembered that the late solicitor-general, the eminent but not very conscientious Sir William Follet, often took fees for causes to which he never afterwards gave any attention,* it is not surprising that—in finding precedents for injustice and dishonesty, in torturing acts of parliament so as to screen from punishment the swindler and the sharper, in aiding dishonest guardians to rob the orphan, and in endeavouring to give the colouring of an honourable transaction to knavery and fraud—Edward Ashley insensibly contracted much of the moral filth through which he was compelled to wade.

Nor is there much to excite surprise in the circumstance that the barrister conceived himself injured by the law which compelled him thus to prey upon society, while his elder brother enjoyed wealth and influence without the necessity of labour, or the corroding cares and anxieties of business. The law of primogeniture and entail is a legal monstrosity which deserves the reprobation of all honest and honourable men. Its first effect is to make the eldest son a luxurious idler, and to leave his brothers to prey upon society as professors of the chicanery of the law, or the horrid and unholy business of war; and its second effect is to place the land in the hands of a few pampered idlers, who may oppress and eject their tenants, starve the peasantry, and swindle their creditors, but are prevented by the law of entail from disposing of their estates, either by sale, gift, or bequeathment.

Upon learning the serious illness of Sir Norman Ashley, the man of law hurried down to Oakwood-hall, and arrived at the stately mansion of his brother just in time to behold him expire. Norman and little Ellen were naturally inconsolable for the loss of so good a father, and, the intercourse between the baronet and the barrister not having been marked by a very fraternal feeling, owing to the dissension-breeding circumstances to which we have alluded, they looked with shyness and distrust upon the lawyer and his lady. The instinctive feelings of a child rarely fail to form a correct estimate of the characters and dispositions of those with whom they are brought in contact; and little Ellen felt a dislike towards her uncle and aunt the moment she found herself under their care and control, and even Norman experienced an antipathy for which he could scarcely account, as if the sententious gravity and austerity of Mr. Ashley, and the stately and patronising manners of his aunt, were a restraint upon his warm and generous feelings.

CHAPTER XXXIV.

THE WILL.

" What a beautiful place this is, to be sure," observed Mrs. Ashley to her husband, as they sat at supper after Norman and Ellen had retired to their respective chambers for the night. " I wish it was ours."

" It might be," returned the barrister, in a tone of semi-abstraction, as he sat gazing between the bright bars of the grate, as if plunged in a profound reverie.

" How ?" exclaimed his wife, looking eagerly towards him; " the estates are entailed, and Norman must have them. True, he might die—and then they would come to you; but he is a strong, healthy youth, and that is a contingency not to be calculated upon."

" I was not calculating upon it," returned Mr. Ashley; " but still I say that there is a chance of Oakwood becoming ours."

Mrs. Ashley looked at her husband for a moment in silence, and then began slowly stirring the sugar from the bottom of her glass of diluted cognac, as if seeking the solution of the barrister's meaning in the same manner as the superstitious inquirers into the secrets of futurity do—by inspecting the grounds of coffee.

" What do you mean, Ashley ?" inquired the lady, with a puzzled expression of countenance.

" My brother married a girl of humble parentage," said the barrister, turning from the fire to his impatient lady, and speaking in a slow and measured tone—

---

* " So often did they occur, that solicitors and clients, in the agony of disaster and defeat, were in the habit of saying that Sir William often took briefs when he must have known that he could not attend in court; and as barristers never return their fees, the suitor sometimes found that he lost his money and missed his advocate at a moment when he could badly spare either."—*Times*.

"indeed, her father was steward to my father; and this marriage was so displeasing to my father, that, though he would not mark his displeasure by disinheriting Norman, on account of his being the eldest-born, yet he left the bulk of his funded property to me. Now, if it can be proved that no legal contract of marriage was ever entered into between Norman and the late Lady Ashley, and that she was in reality living in a state of concubinage with him, you must be aware that this boy and girl will have no claim but upon our charity as Christians, and as the near relatives of their father."

"But have you any reasons for supposing that such really was the case?" asked Mrs. Ashley, doubtfully.

"Between you and me, I have not," replied her husband; "but, as a lawyer, I have a right to doubt everything until it is proved by competent witnesses. When a large property is at stake, and depends upon the proving of a marriage, so many years ago, between a wealthy baronet and a girl of obscure birth, a lawyer who has such a direct interest as I have in proving that such a marriage never did take place, has a right to assume that such an

14

unequal and ill-assorted union was not probable, until the contrary can be satisfactorily proved. I must have some communication with the vestry-clerk, and ascertain whether such a marriage was ever performed, and whether there were any witnesses, and who such witnesses were."

" And suppose it should turn out that Sir Norman was married properly to the mother of these children?" said Mrs. Ashley.

" In that case, my dear, we must be guided by circumstances," returned the barrister; " and you know that, even if the ceremony did take place, it may be made very difficult of proof. Now, that is the beauty of the law, whether civil or criminal: a man may be falsely accused of murder, and a general opinion may exist in favour of his innocence; but unless he can prove it, he must be hung. So it is with this marriage: no one may have the slightest moral doubt of the ceremony having been performed; but unless the register and the witnesses can be produced in court, there is no evidence of the fact, and nothing in the world can prevent my stepping into possession of the baronetcy and estates."

" But you have not seen the will yet," observed Mrs. Ashley; " and how will it be if the property is bequeathed, by will, to Norman and his sister? for even if illegitimate, they can inherit under their father's will, if they are properly described."

" True; spoken like a lawyer!" returned the barrister, jocosely; for he was in a pleasant mood, on account of the splendid perspective he was planning for himself. " But you forget, my dear, that the law of entail—the same law which prevented my father from leaving the estates to me instead of Norman— would prevent Norman from bequeathing them to any one but the presumptive heir to the baronetcy; and if this supposed marriage can be proved never to have taken place, of course I, as the brother, must inherit the whole, to the total exclusion of young Norman."

" But Norman would succeed to the funded property, if willed to him; and that must be considerable," observed Mrs. Ashley.

" Then the will must be suppressed, and my brother supposed to have died intestate," exclaimed her husband, hastily swallowing a glass of brandy-and-water, to drown the last faint remonstrances of his seared and hardened conscience. " The funded property must be considerable, though I do not know the amount; and the whole shall very soon be mine."

" Well, be careful, and do not run yourself into trouble!" said his wife, who had a great horror, not of the crime, but of the consequences of detection.

" I must act quickly, or suspicion may be excited on the part of the children's maternal relatives," said Mr. Ashley; " but you may be certain I shall act with all the caution consistent with speed. It is not so much caution that is required, as that kind of tact which no one in the profession possesses in a greater degree than myself. I hope so to arrange my schemes as to have an unpleasant surprise for Norman after the funeral."

" Did your brother's marriage take place in Thame, or at Cirencester?" asked Mrs. Ashley.

" Neither, my dear," replied her husband, " but at a little village in Berkshire, in the neighbourhood of Eton; and there I will be to-morrow-night."

" But if you succeed so far as to suppress the evidence of the marriage, we shall lose the funded property, if the will is in the hands of your brother's solicitor," suggested Mrs. Ashley.

" Make yourself easy on that score," said the barrister; " for the will is in the house—though Norman went off before he could tell me where it was deposited—and the children are under my guardianship. But I had better see after the will at once, and secure it." And Mr. Ashley took one of the candles off the table, and left the room, to search after the will of his deceased brother, whose orphan children he was about to rob of their just inheritance by so cunningly-contrived a plot.

Having reached the chamber of the dead, in which he understood, by his brother's gestures and motions, when the power of articulation was denied him by the breath-stopping pressure of Death's icy hand, that the will was deposited, he gently opened and reclosed the door, and commenced his search. For some time he searched in vain; desk and box were opened, and their contents turned out, but still the much-coveted prize eluded his search. At length, in his vexation at not being able to discover the document, he closed a writing-desk with considerable violence, and immediately heard a clicking sound within; he eagerly opened the desk again, and found, to his inexpressible joy, that the force with which he had closed it had caused the spring of a secret drawer to give way, and the drawer to start about an inch out. With joyful eagerness he opened the secret drawer thus discovered, and there lay the document of which he was in search. He clutched it in his grasp, and hurried from the room to peruse it, and proceed, according to its tenor, in his nefarious schemes.

Mr. Ashley returned to the drawing-room with the will in his possession, and immediately proceeded to read it aloud to his worthy co-partner in iniquity. The document set forth that all the unentailed landed property was bequeathed to Norman Ashley, his lawful successor in the baronetcy and the estates which appertained thereto; that his daughter Ellen should receive five thousand pounds on the day she became of age, or in case she married before she attained her legal majority, on the day of her marriage, provided that such marriage received the approbation of her guardian; that a like sum was bequeathed to his brother, Edward Ashley, whom he appointed sole executor and guardian over his children; and that the residue of his funded property should be inherited by his son, to assist him in the improvement of the estates.

"You see, my dear," said Mr. Ashley to his lady, "that our course is clear: we must suppress this will, then take the necessary steps to render the proving of the legitimacy of the children a matter of difficulty, if not impossibility, and everything becomes ours. If we make it appear that my brother died intestate, and that the children are illegitimate, I am the next heir, and plain Mr. Ashley, the barrister, will become Sir Edward Ashley, a baronet, and one of the largest landed proprietors in the county of Gloucestershire."

Mrs. Ashley rubbed her hands complacently at the golden visions of rank and importance which her husband's words conjured up, and the barrister felt himself an inch taller under the influence of his day-dreams of ambition.

"Shall we reside here, dear, and send Edward to college?" asked Mrs. Ashley.

"Certainly, we shall reside upon our estates, at least during the summer," returned her husband, "and in the winter, when the country ceases to be agreeable, and all the world is in town, we will go to London or Bath. As to sending Edward to college, I have thought nothing of it, and should soon have taken him from school to place him at the desk, and bring him up to my own profession; but with our altering prospects we may alter our intentions with regard to Edward. The heir to a baronetcy and such extensive property should receive a different education to the son of a briefless barrister; and though, as our only son, Edward will not require the divinity, and Greek, and mathematics of a university education, yet it will look tonish and aristocratic to send him to Eton with others with whom he will associate in after-life."

"Eton is less aristocratic than the universities, I think," observed Mrs. Ashley. "I think we ought to send him either to Oxford or Cambridge."

"Well, Oxford by all means," returned the barrister; "Cambridge may produce the greatest number of men eminent in mathematical and scientific knowledge, but we do not want Edward to be a lecturer on geology or chemistry; and Oxford is far more conservative and aristocratic. It is more ancient, more exclusive, and every way fitter for the *alma mater* of our Edward."

"And what is to be done with Norman and Ellen?" inquired the lady.

"Why, when Norman finds that he is dependent upon us for everything, he will be glad to accept any employment that I may propose for him," said the exemplary lawyer; "I shall apprentice him to the master of some collier or coasting-vessel, and then we shall be rid of him."

"And what shall we do with Ellen?" asked Mrs. Ashley.

"Well, I was thinking of sending her down to some factory in Lancashire; but perhaps it will look better to put her apprentice to a dress-maker or milliner, or to learn waistcoat-making, or tambour-work," returned the barrister. "What would you propose, my dear?"

" Well, dear, I was thinking that it would be advisable to seclude them as much as possible," said the lady; " and Norman will be sufficiently out of the way in a dirty collier, but Ellen will be too much exposed to the chance of meeting those who might urge her to enforce her supposed claims, if we place her in the metropolis ; and, as you do not like the idea of sending her to the cotton-factories in Lancashire, I think we could not do better than place her with some cottage people in Buckinghamshire, to learn lace-making. The manufacture of lace by hand is still followed in some parts of that county, and Ellen is too young to be taken as an apprentice by a dress-maker or milliner."

" Well, your idea is not a bad one," observed Mr. Ashley, who had listened attentively to the remarks of his wife and coincided with her upon the policy of that seclusion from the world which she recommended. He thought it not improbable that his injured nephew and niece might cherish the idea that they had been wronged, and that, if thrown among the active and fermenting minds of a large town, they might be induced to make some attempt to prove the legitimacy of their birth, and the right of Norman to the title and estates of his deceased father.

" I will now secure the will," resumed the crafty and knavish lawyer, rising from the table; " and to-morrow I will ride over to the village where Norman was married, and have some talk with the clerk. I dare say he is some poor devil of a petty tradesman, and easily to be managed when his own interest is concerned."

Mr. Ashley then deposited the will of the late baronet in an ebony cabinet which stood upon the table, and carefully locked it.

" I cannot forget," said he, resuming his seat, " that I had a natural claim upon a portion of this property before these children were born; I consider that, as the natural law of right, my father's possessions should have been equally divided between Norman and myself. That is the least of which I have been deprived by the working of the laws of primogeniture and entail; but I have every reason to believe that, could my father have consulted his own wishes and inclinations in the matter, Norman and I would have changed positions at his death, and I should have been the proprietor of Oakwood instead of him."

In this manner Edward Ashley sought to palliate to his own heart the monstrous injustice he was about to commit; forgetting that, arbitrary and unjust as was the operation of the laws which he denounced, he only desired their abolition that his father might have been enabled to commit an equal injustice, by bequeathing the whole of the property to him, to the prejudice of his elder brother. This is a species of self-deception which is too common; we often find men very indignant at an injustice by which they suffer themselves, but propose to them the removal of a greater injustice, by the continuance of which they are pecuniarily benefited, and they will vehemently protest against it, however injurious its continuance may be to others. Thus they expose the selfishness of the motives by which they are actuated, and their opposition to injustice, which before appeared virtuous and pure, turns out to be nothing higher than the grovelling love of self.

CHAPTER XXXV.

PETER TOMKINS.

On the banks of the silver Thames, and not far from the town of Eton, in Berkshire, is a village, the name of which it is not necessary to reveal, as after this and the ensuing chapter we shall have no occasion to refer to it again in the course of our veritable narrative. The church is a small unpretending edifice, built partly of stone and partly of flint, as is the case with many little churches in remote districts in the south of England; the masses of dark ivy that trailed over it, gave it a venerable and picturesque appearance; and, being of considerable antiquity, the grave-yard is full of tombs. Some of these, erected over the vaults of the families of the neighbouring gentry, have large yew-trees shading them with their sombre foliage, and increasing the gloom of the landscape, which was already sufficiently gloomy with the mists and clouds of a dull November day.

It was the morning after the occurrence at Oakwood-hall, related in the preceding chapters, and the grave-digger of the little village was busily turning up the earth near the gate of the church-yard. He was a half-witted fellow, with a grotesque expression of countenance, and about fifty years of age; he wore a very bad hat, napless and shapeless, and the crown partially knocked out, a goatskin waistcoat and red plush breeches, the cast-off encasements of some livery-servant. He was smoking a very short and very black pipe, in order to qualify the dampness of the humid air, and was standing knee-deep in a grave, from which he was throwing out the earth with right good will. There was something about the old man's features which left the spectator in doubt whether Toby Brown was so utterly destitute of sense as he was said to be; and not a few persons in the village affirmed that Toby was more knave than fool; but at any rate he was commonly supposed to be a silly, half-witted fellow, who had just sense enough to prevent his knocking his head against a post, if he encountered one, and no more.

" Well, Toby," said a rustic, looking over the low wall which bounded the church-yard, " whose grave are you digging now, man ?"

" Only a poor body's, Davie," replied Toby Brown, looking up from his work with as serious a look as he could assume.

" Your trade's been dull lately, bain't it ?" inquired the countryman.

Toby shook his head dolefully, and made a very wry face. Since old Dr. Thingumy died, and the overseers had the black ditch covered up as used to run along the back of them 'ere cottages agin the George, I arn't been able to earn salt to my porridge," said the grave-digger. " How am I to live, Davie, if other people won't die ? That's what I want to know. If there was only a good fever now and then, or the choleric morbus, I might rub on; but, what with old Thingumy, the quack, dying, and their sani—what do they call it ?—insanity improvements, my business is going to the dogs. Ah! I wish that blessed disease as is playing the old Harry among the cows and sheep would get among Christians."

" You are a deep old file, and no mistake," said the rustic; " them as buys you for a fool, Toby, will' get preciously sucked in with their bargain ;" and, having delivered this complimentary opinion of Toby Brown, the man walked away.

He had not gone far, however, before the grave-digger called him back, and then resting on his spade, with his grey eyes twinkling in a curious manner, he said :

" I've heard as how parliament voted no end of money to the planters in the West Indies, as compensation, I think they called it, for losing the sarvices of the niggers, when 'em was made free. Now, don't you think it likely as how the overseers might be made to compensate me for my loss of business through the arching over of the black ditch ?"

The man gave a loud guffaw as the only answer to this shrewd question, and then again walked away, while Toby Brown resumed his work, and began singing in a drawling, monotonous voice, interlarding his story with occasional reflections of his own :

> " Two grave-worms in a church-yard met,
>   So runneth my roundelay—
> A fat grave-worm a lean one met,
>   And unto him did say :
> ' Thou reptile starved, what dost thou here,
>   Encroaching on my prey—
> I that fatten on squire and peer,
>   And thou on pauper's clay ?' "

" Well, if the squire is my superior because he lives on venison and turtle, and drinks wine, and I am obleeged to put up with a crust of bread and cheese, and a drink of small beer, why, the gentles as will feed on the squire when he dies must be superior to them as will creep about me."

> " ' On the rich flesh of dukes I feed,
>   Or heart of a parson or squire;
>   But thou in poor man's grave did breed,
>   So back to thy kindred mire.'
>   ' Ho, ho!' quoth his brother, 'it seems
>   That hearts of peers and kings
>   Engender some most absurd dreams
>   Of titles—worthless things!'

"Can you inform me where the clerk of this parish resides?" said Mr. Ashley, who rode up at that moment.

"Ay, master," returned Toby; "he lives in that little white cottage near the George, and a nice living he makes of it: he receives a crown for digging a grave, and gives me a shilling to dig it for him."

"Thank you," responded the barrister, with a smile at this insight into the worldly character of the man he had come to seek; and he rode towards the white cottage, while the grave-digger proceeded with his labour and his song.

> " ' Democrat rude, and poacher vile!'
>   Replied the proud-fed thing;
>   ' Thou'rt not fit guest in the coffin'd pile
>   Of the family vault to cling.
>   Away above to the changeful earth;
>   Leave me to skulls and bones,
>   With the decay which gave me birth,
>   My spirit kindred owns.' "

Mr. Ashley proceeded towards the cottage indicated by Toby Brown, and in a few minutes found himself in the presence of no less important a functionary than Mr. Peter Tomkins, parish-clerk and sexton. The worthy official was a little, bustling, rosy-gilled biped, with a bald head, twinkling grey eyes, and inclined to corpulence; he was dressed with great care, in a suit of black—on account of his connexion with the church—white cravat, and the front of his shirt elaborately frilled. He was a bachelor; and the arrangement of his little parlour evinced a love of order not unmingled with that striving after display which is the invariable accompaniment of the worldly ambition of little minds. His manners were bland and oily to an oppressive degree, and though servile and cringing to the vicar and churchwardens, and the gentry with whom he was casually brought in contact, he was haughty and pompous in his intercourse with the poor. His great failings were avarice and ambition—not a laudable and elevated ambition, a desire to emulate deeds of virtuous nobility and moral greatness, but the miserable ambition of a despicable mind, a craving after the false distinctions of rank, an insatiable desire of amassing gold, that he might become the lion of the mob, the golden calf of their insensate worship. These vices begot another—selfishness; and his very action was stamped with their dark impress, the end which he constantly had in view being his own aggrandisement.

"Your name is Tomkins, sir," began the barrister, taking the seat indicated by the polite clerk.

"Yes, sir—parish-clerk and sexton, at your service, sir," replied Tomkins, obsequiously.

"May I ask if you filled that responsible office twenty years ago, Mr. Tomkins?" inquired the barrister, the allusion to the responsibility of his office being a sop to the clerk's ideas of the importance of his functions—the shrewd lawyer having read his character at a glance.

"Twenty years ago," repeated Mr. Tomkins, with an air of reflection; "that would be about the year 1812, the year of the burning of Moscow—yes, sir, I had the honour to fill the joint offices of parish-clerk and sexton as far back as that eventful year."

"Then you can inform me whether a marriage was solelmnized in your church, in that year, between Norman Ashley and Ellen Grant," said Mr. Ashley.

Mr. Tomkins appeared to consider a moment, and then taking down a book like a ledger, from a book-case, he turned over the leaves with careful attention.

"I make entries in this book of all births, marriages, and deaths, to save the trouble of a reference to the register which is kept at the church," said he. "Here is the year 1812—yes, sir, I did assist, in July of that year, in the solemnization of a marriage between the parties whom you named. They were married by license, and the witnesses were William Grant and Mary Grant—if I remember rightly, the bride's father and sister."

"Very likely," responded Mr. Ashley, in a musing tone. "Do you know, Mr. Tomkins, that I would give a considerable sum if that entry had never been made."

"I am very sorry, sir, if it should be detrimental to your interests," returned Tomkins, in a bland tone.

"If the proof of that marriage could be rendered impossible, I would give a thousand pounds," exclaimed Mr. Ashley, looking steadfastly at the clerk.

"Would you indeed, sir?" said the latter. "I hope you do not suppose, sir, that I am capable of doing such an act; if you intended your observation as a test of my integrity, I assure you, sir, that Peter Tomkins would scorn to take a bribe."

Mr. Tomkins coloured as he thus declared himself cased in the armour of integrity, and he spoke in a pompous manner, and with an assumption of offended dignity.

"Pardon me, Mr. Tomkins," said the barrister, in a deprecating tone, "I meant not to wound your nice sense of honour, nor do I think so meanly of you as to suppose you capable of accepting a bribe. I know that there are men who would not hesitate to cut a leaf out a register for the sake of a thousand pounds, but I do not confound you with them, Mr. Tomkins. It is a considerable sum, and easily earned; and if I were to offer it for the performance of such a service, a less scrupulously-honest person than yourself would, doubtless, hesitate but a few minutes before agreeing to earn it. But of course it would be of no use to offer you double the money."

Mr. Tomkins listened attentively to the artful observations of the barrister, and coloured slightly towards their conclusion, doubtless from excessive modesty at the encomiums of Mr. Ashley on his strict integrity.

"Two thousand pounds!" ejaculated Tomkins, drawing his breath with a long inspiration. "Hem—that is a large sum; and will you give it, sir ——"

"For a leaf from the register and its duplicate in that book," replied Mr. Ashley; and, as he spoke, he took out his pocket-book, and spread twenty Bank of England notes of a hundred pounds each on the table before the greedy eyes of the wavering clerk. "There; let me have the abstracted documents as speedily as possible, and they are yours."

"Really, sir, it is a large sum; but I am afraid to earn it," stammered Tomkins.

"Very well, Mr. Tomkins," said the barrister; "it would be a little fortune for you, I should think; but if you are too squeamish to earn it, why——" And, without finishing the sentence, Mr. Ashley began gathering up the bank-notes.

"Stay, sir!" cried the avaricious clerk, seizing his arm; "it would be a pity not to let them remain where they are. Two thousand pounds are scarcely a fortune; but they may be the foundation of one. I accept the offer, sir."

"And when shall I have the leaf from the register?" asked Mr. Ashley, relinquishing the notes.

"Come here to-night at twelve," said the clerk; "for I have no excuse to go to the church, and if a discovery should ever ensue, it might be injurious to me if I were seen going there. I must go secretly, after the villagers have all gone to rest."

"I will be punctual; and beware of trifling with me," said the barrister. "Give me the leaf from that book now; it will be security for the completion of our agreement."

Peter Tomkins cut out the leaf containing the entry of the marriage, from the book which he had produced, and handed it to the barrister.

"You must oblige me with your name, sir, that I may have some security also," said he, his voice slightly trembling.

"Mr. Ashley, brother of the late Sir Norman Ashley of Oakwood-hall, near Cirencester, in Gloucestershire," returned the barrister, in a haughty tone.

The clerk bowed, and Mr. Ashley withdrew, determining to ride to Eton and there pass the intervening time until the hour when he was to meet Peter Tomkins, and receive the much-coveted document.

<hr>

CHAPTER XXXVI.

THE STOLEN REGISTER.

PETER TOMKINS hurried back to his little parlour, after bowing Mr. Ashley to the door, and hastily gathering up the bank-notes, he placed them in a cash-box which stood on the table, and which never had held so large a sum before.

Then he walked up and down the room, and mused upon what he had done and had yet to do, and the advantages which might accrue to himself from the possession of the money which he had received as the price of his infamous compliance with the nefarious schemes of Mr. Ashley.

"Two thousand pounds!" said he; "and so easily earned! Now I seem on the verge of attaining the summit of my ambition. I shall be a rich man; for this sum, judiciously invested, will be the nucleus of a large fortune. Shall I invest it in English or foreign securities?—in houses, or in railway shares? The Spanish and South American bonds may give the highest interest; but I doubt if they are so safe as consuls or exchequer-bills. Would so much interest be paid on those funds, if it were not to tempt persons to invest therein, and blind them to the risk of losing by a sudden revolution? No, I will invest my two thousand pounds in houses; for the interest on money sunk in land or buildings is greater than can be got in the funds. If I buy houses—which I may do for less than half what they cost—I may get twenty per cent. interest, whereas government-securities only return three or three and a half per cent., and private securities seldom more than five per cent. The chance of their standing empty is not very great in a large town; and if I buy little houses, which pay a larger proportionate rent than large ones, I can collect the rents weekly, and hazard no losses by defaulters. The insurance will be but a trifling drawback, and will more than recompense me for any accident by fire. Yes, I will invest my two thousand pounds in the purchase of small houses in the suburbs of the metropolis, or wherever I can secure large returns for a small outlay. It will buy twenty-five old tenements at eighty pounds each, which will let for twenty pounds each per annum; that will be an income of five hundred per annum, whereas in government-securities at three per cent., I should only get sixty pounds a year. I shall gradually accumulate a large fortune; for, as I keep investing my annual income in profitable investments, I shall become richer and richer every year. I shall be a landed proprietor, a fundholder, and—God knows what! I shall be dubbed, Esquire—Peter Tomkins, esquire!" And the clerk stopped before the fire, and surveyed himself in the mirror suspended over the mantel, with much complacency. "And then who knows what I may become? for wealth is the road to distinction and preferment. I may be mayor of Oxford, and have my portrait hung in the town-hall—Mr. Mayor! Or, why should I not be member for Reading, or even for the county? Peter Tomkins, esquire, M.P.—that sounds well."

Puffed up with his fancied importance, and the aerial castle-building in which he was thus indulging, Tomkins paraded his little parlour for some time; and when evening came, he put the key of the church-doors in his pocket, with a bull's-eye lantern and some lucifers, and betook himself to the parlour of the "George," there to pass the intervening hours until midnight.

"Good evening, Mr. Tomkins," said a dapper little man, the draper of the village; "we were having a little chat about haunted houses, ghosts, and supernatural appearances."

"Bless me, what an inviting subject!" exclaimed Peter Tomkins, smiling. "Waiter! bring me a glass of brandy-and-water. Well, gentlemen, what conclusion have you arrived at upon this interesting subject?"

"Why, we can scarcely be said to have arrived at anything more than a general conclusion that such things have been known; but to account for them we have made no attempt," returned the draper.

"There is scarcely a village in the country but has its haunted house," said an elderly man, of grave and respectable appearance. "I have known or heard of a great many. I once knew a remarkable haunted house in Edinburgh, there is another at Newcastle, and I have heard of more than one in London. The story of the Cock-lane ghost, which Dr. Johnson implicitly believed, is well known; and there is a mansion in the neighbourhood of Croydon which is said to be haunted. I allude to Beddington-house, the ancient residence of the Carew family. In the same town is another supposed haunted house, which was formerly an inn; and it is alleged that, about a century ago, several travellers and hawkers, who lodged in the house, were never seen afterwards.

15

They are supposed to have been murdered by the people of the inn, and to haunt the scene of the crime. Large old houses, from the length of the beams and joists, are apt to give, and at times to crack and split, so as to cause an alarming noise, and excite the imagination to fancy most horrible sounds; even the bricks in the chimnies may get loose, and, rolling down into an empty room, would disturb and alarm a timid or superstitious person. If we only took the trouble to inquire into the causes of sights and sounds apparently supernatural, instead of taking for granted whatever designing or weak-minded men choose to foist upon us, we should discover that they all proceed from natural causes. I once knew a gentleman who was disturbed every night, soon after he retired to rest, by a sound like the tap of a drumstick on a drum. It occurred so regularly that, though far from being timid or superstitious, it had an unpleasant effect upon his nerves. He closely examined the furniture and wainscotting of his room, and made every attempt to investigate the cause of the singular noise, but found nothing to account for it. He removed into another room, but still the sound followed him; it had no reference to the time of his going to rest, but was always heard a few minutes after he was in bed."

"Bless me, how singular!" observed Mr. Tomkins.

"Yes, it was singular," continued the narrator; "and yet the cause was natural and simple. In the gentleman's room was a wardrobe, which had been removed when he changed his apartment, and which he always opened and closed again when undressing. The doors of the wardrobe were very tight, and this caused them to force themselves partly open with a dull, drumming sound, a few minutes after they were closed."

"The cause was very simple, and yet the effect was sufficiently alarming to disturb the nerves of a strong-minded man," observed a young man.

"I once heard a singular account of an old house in Hertfordshire, which was said to be haunted," said the old gentleman who had related the previous case. "In the stillness of evening, and during the quietness of night, sounds were heard to emanate from this old mansion, which seemed like the music of the Æolian harp; but, instead of being pleasing, it terrified all who heard it, on account of its supposed supernatural origin. No one could ever be induced to live in it; and even to enter it was considered a daring exploit. Many years was this mansion known to be thus distinguished, and by no one could the mystery be cleared up or detected; for as no one could be induced to remain all night in the place, there was little opportunity of finding out the cause. Many parties used to be made up to visit this remarkable house; but the visitors invariably scampered off at the slightest noise. As usual in such cases, rumour and imagination added much to what was really known; and strange tales got about of ghosts having been seen at the windows, and shrieks and groans having been heard whenever there was a violent storm. Most likely the house would have remained in its mystery and desolation till this day, had it not been for a circumstance as singular as the house itself."

"Indeed! and what was that, sir?" asked Mr. Tomkins.

"I will tell you, sir," continued the old gentleman, sipping his brandy-and-water. "A young officer, deeply enamoured of a young lady living in the neighbourhood of the haunted mansion, was rallied by the lively girl upon his courage; and, in order to display it, was incited to pass a night under the roof of the haunted house. He provided himself with some ham and bread, a bottle of wine, some cigars, and a brace of loaded pistols, and was accompanied by a large Newfoundland dog. His servant assisted him to open the door about eight o'clock in the evening, and then left him. He lit a cigar, and began walking from room to room. It was a fine summer evening, calm and warm, with scarce a breath of air stirring; and nothing was heard for some hours calculated to excite any alarm. But towards midnight, dark clouds gathered all round, and the wind began to howl and moan through the deserted apartments; then was heard the strange murmuring sound which had so often alarmed the passers-by. The officer felt rather nervous, and dropped his cigar, and even the dog seemed alarmed; but recovering his resolution, the young officer took his lamp in his left hand, and a pistol in his right, and sallied forth to search the house. He closely examined the lower part of the house first, but found nothing of a suspicious character; still he heard the strange, half-musical murmuring sounds, but so interrupted by sudden gusts of wind, that he could not ascertain the precise spot from whence they proceeded. Sometimes they grew more loud, then sunk to a solemn murmur; sometimes they seemed to emanate from one part of the house, sometimes from another."

" How very remarkable !" observed Mr. Tomkins.

" Satisfied that himself and his faithful dog were the only living beings on the premises, he proceeded to sound the partitions and wainscotting of the rooms and closets, but failed to make any discovery of false and sliding panels. But at length he discovered the remains of an old organ, which appears to have been the sole cause of the mysterious noises which had made the old mansion the dread of the neighbours for so many years. It is supposed that the musical sounds were caused by the wind whistling among the broken pipes of the old organ, and thus the mystery of the haunted house was effectually cleared up."

Mr. Tomkins laid down his pipe at the conclusion of this remarkable narrative, finished his brandy-and-water, and left the warm and cheerful parlour, wishing his friends " good night." He buttoned up his coat as he made his exit from the inn, and walked briskly towards the church; for a cold north wind was blowing, and he felt his teeth chattering like a pair of castanets.

He looked about him as he entered the churchyard; but no one was in sight, and the darkness of the night favouring his criminal intentions, he quickly unlocked the side door, and entered the sacred edifice. Striking a lucifer on the stone floor of the church, he lighted his lamp, and, carefully shading it, proceeded to the vestry-room. Taking the parish-register from the place where it was usually kept, he looked for the entry which was required, and having found it, he detached it from the book with his pen-knife, so neatly, that the abstraction could not be detected without a very close examination.

He then replaced the register, and hastened to quit the church. When he had locked the church-door, he concealed the lantern about him, and hastened towards his residence. He encountered no one in his way, and had scarcely reached his cottage when Mr. Ashley again knocked at the door. Tomkins had desired his housekeeper not to sit up for him; so he opened the door himself, and placed the stolen register in the hands of the barrister.

Mr. Ashley smiled as he received the document, partly in his self-gratulation at the success which had attended his schemes thus far, and partly at the pale countenance and trembling hand of Peter Tomkins. The clerk had experienced a nervous tremor on putting the key into the lock of the church-door; and this feeling he had not yet succeeded in repressing. He was heartily glad when the stolen document was out of his possession; and he experienced a great relief when he heard the distant clatter of hoofs, which announced that Mr. Ashley was far from the spot.

Peter Tomkins then returned to his little parlour, unlocked the cash-box, and again feasted his eyes on the two thousand pounds which had been the price of his conscience. The legend of Faustus is no fiction: we see men, daily, sell their souls for a less price than the Prince of Darkness paid the student of Wittenburg; even at so mean a rate as a glass of ardent spirits will men surrender their souls to evil; and gold, titles, worldly fame, are the baits which allure thousands to destruction. Then, when they toss in the agonies of remorse, and feel the hell within their hearts consuming them, they call in vain for a drop of water from the springs of life to cool the burning thirst which parches up their being, and quench the fires of conscience which their evil deeds have kindled.

CHAPTER XXXVII.

THE FUNERAL.

WE must leave the progress of Mr. Peter Tomkins to develop itself in future portions of our narrative, and follow the career of those who have to figure more prominently in these pages, and who more require our notice at this stage of our history.

The day came for the funeral of the late Sir Norman Ashley; and the grief of the orphans was renewed when they saw all that remained of their parent deposited in the family vault at Cirencester, and reflected how much they were alone in the world; for there was no sympathy between their fresh warm feelings, gushing spontaneously from their hearts, and the hollow and corroded heart of their guardian. The being who has no thoughts and feelings in common with those about him, is as much alone in the throng as a stork on the decaying wall of some grey old abbey—ay, more alone; for in solitude he has the sweet companionship of his own thoughts.

The mourning party returned to the hall, the barrister and his wife wearing the outward semblance of grief, little Ellen in tears, and her brother endeavouring to console her, though his own brow was shaded with sorrow. There is an amount of hypocrisy in our mourning for the dead which must be intolerable to all whose minds are superior to the cant of convention. And yet how many of these wear the badge of hypocrisy which their souls abhor, merely in deference to the usages of society, so much are we the slaves of custom! We have too little iron in our composition; we bend like the willow when we should emulate the oak, and bow to every passing wind of custom when we should dare even its lightnings. Shall we play the hypocrite because custom requires us to do so? and what hypocrisy can be greater than the wearing the weeds and sables of mourning by the spendthrift heir who rejoices at the death of his niggard father, or the widow whom the relentless hand of death has freed from the weary curse of a drunken, idle, unloving husband?

"I have a painful task to perform in making you acquainted with circumstances of which you are doubtless unaware," said Mr. Ashley, addressing his nephew and niece after the funeral. "It appears that my lamented brother was never legally united in the holy bonds of matrimony to your mother. This is a fact with which I was not acquainted until the day before yesterday——"

"I will not believe it!" exclaimed Norman, vehemently, while his indignation caused the colour to mount instantly to his cheeks and forehead.

"How, sir! would you charge me with uttering a falsehood?" said his uncle, sternly.

"No, uncle; but you have been imposed upon," returned Norman: "I feel convinced that you have."

"I have been to the church where my brother and your mother are said to have been married, and I have ascertained, beyond the remotest possibility of a doubt, that no marriage ever took place between them," continued Mr. Ashley. And then he observed, in a milder tone: "I can forgive your hasty exclamation, Norman, which was prompted only by your filial affection, and your devotion to the memory of your mother. Both you and Ellen are therefore illegitimate, and must henceforth pass by the name of Grant. Unfortunately for you, my brother has left no will, and dying intestate, the whole of his property descends to me as the heir-at-law. Thus situated, you can inherit nothing, and have nothing to depend upon but my kindness to keep you from the parish-workhouse. But it would ill become me to stand by in selfishness, and see my brother's children dependent upon the bounty of strangers, or the cold charity of the parish-guardians; I shall therefore place you and your sister in positions whereby you may obtain an honest and honourable subsistence: further than this you can scarcely expect me to do. It is for you to say, Norman, what avocation would best suit your inclinations. Would you like to go to sea?"

"No, uncle," returned Norman Ashley, struggling to keep down his rising pride and indignation. "I should like the sea; but Ellen would then have no friend to sympathise with her sorrows and trials when I am far away."

"You need not make long voyages, you know. Suppose you try a collier, or a coasting-vessel?" observed Mr. Ashley.

"No, uncle; the work is too hard and dirty for one who has been educated like a gentleman," returned Norman, colouring.

"You are hard to please, for one who has his bread to earn by his labour," observed his uncle, with some asperity in his tone.

"Be a fisherman, Norman, and catch mackarel and sprats in the sea," said Ellen, in a soft, silvery voice.

"Well, choose for yourself, sir," said the barrister.

"Ellen has chosen for me," said Norman, moodily. "All kinds of labour are alike to me, as I have never been used to any, and if I must earn my bread by drudgery, I will be a fisherman."

"Very well," said his uncle. "I will provide you with a suitable outfit, and apprentice you to one of the Barking or Gravesend fishermen. I have no doubt you will be an honour to the profession you have chosen;" and he darted a malicious glance at his nephew, who sat with folded arms and moody brow by the side of his sister.

"And what would Ellen like to be?" said Mrs. Ashley, in a condescending tone.

"Oh, anything, aunt, that I can get my bread by, and not be dependent upon you," exclaimed the little girl, drying her tearful eyes, and shaking the glossy ringlets from her alabaster forehead with an air of proud independence.

"I am glad to perceive that you know how to bend to your altered situation, Ellen," returned her aunt, biting her lips, and speaking with forced composure. "I have made arrangements with some honest people in Buckinghamshire, to receive you as an apprentice to the pretty art of making lace; and when you have learned it you will be enabled to obtain an independent livelihood by your own industry."

"Thank you, aunt," said Ellen, calmly and even proudly, though her little heart was well-nigh bursting at the thought of the sudden change in her present and future prospects.

"It is settled, then," observed Mr. Ashley. "Norman is to be a fisherman, and Ellen a lace-worker."

Mr. Ashley accordingly wrote instructions to Frederick Shirley to proceed to Gravesend and make the necessary arrangements for apprenticing his nephew to one of the fishermen of that place. In a few days he received an answer to the effect that the preliminaries had been arranged satisfactorily; whereupon he desired Norman and Ellen to prepare for their change of situation immediately.

On the following day, Mr. Ashley left Gloucestershire for London, accompanied by his nephew and niece; and, though their youthful spirits were raised by the prospect of a long journey in a carriage, their exuberance was checked by the reflection that they were leaving for ever the home of their childhood. It was a fine, frosty morning in the beginning of December, when the carriage rolled away from the portals of Oakwood-hall, down the long, gravelled avenue, and through the ornamental iron gates into the high road.

Norman Ashley looked back at the hall, on the front of which hung the escutcheon of the family, and sighed involuntarily; and tears stood in the dark eyes of the lovely Ellen as the carriage rolled past each well-known spot, which she believed she then looked upon for the last time.

"See, Ellen," said her brother, striving to divert her attention from her mournful reflections, "that spring is the source of the mighty Thames, the most important river in the world, though far from being the largest."

As he spoke he pointed through the trees, now denuded of their foliage by the winds of autumn, to a spring of water which welled forth from a bank overhung with the branches of a dwarf oak and a clump of holly-trees, the dark green leaves of which were now enlivened by clusters of its bright red berries. This spot is called Thames-head, and is situate a few miles from Cirencester, and within sight of Oakwood-hall; from thence flows a rivulet called Thame, which name the stream retains until its junction with the river Isis, when the united waters receive the name of Thames, or, as it was called by the Roman invaders of this country, Thamesis, the latter name being compounded from Thame and Isis, the former having its source in Gloucestershire, and the latter in Oxfordshire.

Cirencester was soon left far behind, and now the carriage was whirled over the smooth plains of Oxfordshire, over the beautiful grass lands of Berkshire —for they had now crossed both the Thame and the Isis in their journey towards the metropolis—and in the afternoon they reached Wallingford, just above which the two streams unite, and form the lordly Thames, justly eulogized by Sir John Denham as—

> " Though deep yet clear, though gentle yet not dull ;
> Strong without rage, without o'erflowing, full."

Norman and his sister found themselves insensibly drawn from their reflections on their recent and irreparable loss, and the sad reality to which they had suddenly been awakened, and their conversation gradually became more animated as new scenes continually arose on either hand ; and the youth amused his sister by telling her tales from English history, pertaining to the objects of interest which they passed in their journey, such as Eton-college, Windsor-castle, and Magna Charta island.   He drew her attention to the ford at Walton, where the Romans crossed the Thames on their first invasion ; to the brown foliage of the New-forest, looking misty in the distance, where Richard of Normandy was gored by a deer, and where Rufus was accidentally slain by an arrow shot from the bow of Walter Tyrell ; to the ancient towers and park of Windsor, the scene of the courtship of the tyrant Henry and the beautiful and unfortunate Anne Boleyn ; to the palace of Hampton-court, a monument of ecclesiastical pride, and once the prison of a king who dared to trample on the liberties of his people ; and the groves of Richmond, in whose seclusion the third Edward passed the close of his life, soothed by the caresses of the lovely Alice Pierce, and forgetting in her arms the distresses of his subjects.

Then the carriage rattled over Kew-bridge, and in a short time the suspension-bridge at Hammersmith drew forth Ellen's wonder and admiration ; now they drew near Knightsbridge, and in a few minutes the carriage stopped in Sloane-street, Chelsea, where was situate the dwelling of Mr. Ashley.   Here Norman and his sister remained until the following morning, when the youth bade Ellen a long farewell, and, leaving her in tears, accompanied his uncle in a cab to the east-end of the metropolis.

Leaving the cab, on reaching Gracechurch-street, Mr. Ashley and his nephew turned down Eastcheap, and proceeded on foot towards Tower-hill.   At an outfitting-warehouse in Postern-row, the barrister purchased for Norman a blue pea-jacket, one of those oilskin-hats which sailors term sou'-westers, and half-a-dozen blue shirts.   These were tied up in a handkerchief, and then they returned over Tower-hill, Norman carrying the bundle containing his meagre outfit, and, turning into Thames-street, a few minutes' walk brought them to the St. Katherine's Steam-wharf.

" Norman," said the barrister, giving the youth a sovereign, which he reluctantly drew from his purse, " here is a sovereign ; take care of it, and you will some day be a rich man, with the additional gratification of knowing that you have become so by your own industry and perseverance.   You will proceed to Gravesend by the first boat, and, on the arrival of the steamer at that town, inquire for Mr. Shrimp, the fisherman ; any one will tell you where to find him, for he is the most respectable man of his profession in Gravesend."

" Thank you, uncle," returned Norman ; " if I cannot be a gentleman, I will lower my ambition to that of being the best fisherman on the river."

He spoke with more cheerfulness than heretofore, owing to the exhilaration of a drive through the mighty metropolis, and the change of scene so new and strange to him.   He even shook hands with his uncle, and having walked over the gangway to the deck of the steamer, was soon absorbed in the contemplation of the moving panorama around him.

Mr. Ashley hired a cab to convey him to Chelsea, where he dined, and again proceeded in a cab to the Bell Sauvage inn, Ludgate-hill, accompanied by his lovely niece.   Here he took the Aylesbury coach, and late that night Ellen and her uncle reached the village where the people resided with whom she was to be placed, in order to acquire the art of making lace.   Leaving Ellen at the cottage which was to be her future home, Mr. Ashley slept at an inn in the nearest town, and on the following morning returned to London by the Aylesbury coach.

CHAPTER XXXVIII.

THE YOUNG FISHERMAN.

GLORY to steam! Honour to the shades of Fulton and Watt! The white and misty vapour flowing from the funnel of a steamer seems to me the flag of the future; and every stroke of the piston sounds to me like the death-knell of the old world. Yes! steam is the great revolutionist, the mighty innovator evolved by science to be the deliverer of the human race from the thraldom of poverty and ill-requited toil—the saviour-power which shall soon redeem the suffering millions from their present virtual serfdom, and rescue the children of labour from the Moloch of capital? Mighty steam! we have heard men curse thee in their misery, when they saw thy stupendous power supplanting themselves and their families in factory and mill; not discerning in their anguish the benefits to be derived from the right application of the enormous power which thou placest at their disposal. But when the toiling millions obtain leisure for mental improvement, and see thy giant power performing all the drudgery of life, not as their tyrant, but their servant, they will exclaim, in gladness of heart, "O steam! thou art our saviour!" Even now, the uttermost parts of the world are brought together by the application of its power to the purposes of navigation; and as the bands of brotherhood are drawn closer, national prejudices are fading away, and the nations are awakening to the truth and beauty of the principle, that "all men are brethren."

While Norman Ashley gazed in wonder and delight at the forest of masts which rose from the rippling bosom of the Thames, the clanking of the machinery announced that the vessel was in motion, the paddles rapidly revolved, and the vessel shot into the stream. Vessels of all descriptions and all nations were moored in the pool, and the navigation being thus rendered intricate, the progress of the steamer was slow, and afforded time for the youth to look about him.

An Indiaman was getting under weigh, boats and lighters were crossing the stream in every direction, and steamers were continually passing up and down; but after passing Greenwich the river became more clear, and the steamer shot a-head, lashing the water on either side, and leaving in her wake a furrowed line of foam. The river became broader and broader, the channel being sometimes nearer to the flat coast of Essex, and sometimes approaching the shore of the rich and fertile county of Kent. Then the rustic church and chalk-pits of Northfleet arose on the right, and then the town and pier of Gravesend, with its windmill-crowned hill.

"Ease her! stop her!" were the sounds which speedily followed each other, being passed by the call-boy, from the captain on the paddle-box, to the engineer below; the machinery stopped, the paddles ceased to revolve, and the vessel was made fast to the town-pier. Norman Ashley went ashore with his little bundle, and inquired of several persons the residence of Mr. Shrimp, the fisherman, but found to his surprise that no one was acquainted with the whereabouts of that eminent personage. He walked slowly up the High-street for a short distance, and then inquired again of a man wearing a fur cap and a coarse pilot-coat which completely shrouded his form.

"I dare say it's old Sam Shrimp," returned the man, removing a very short and very black pipe from his mouth. "Go up that street on the right, and you'll find him somewhere about the end of it, if he's at home."

With this somewhat vague direction, young Ashley turned up West-street, towards the end of which he again made inquiries at a little dirty shop, the window-board of which was covered with shrimps and periwinkles, and succeeded in eliciting the information, that the object of his search lived a little further up. The dingy-looking shop, built of wood, the narrow street, the mire which covered even the foot-pavement, and the fishy odour with which the atmosphere was loaded, were not calculated to inspire Norman Ashley with much liking for the life he was about to adopt. The disagreeable sights and smells by which he was surrounded caused his heart to sink; but he kept up his spirits as well as he could, and assumed a cheerfulness which he was far from feeling.

At length he found the residence of the fisherman, and tapped at the door with a feeling of disgust which he could scarcely repress; for it was small, and built of wood; and, when the door was opened by a girl about sixteen years of age, the room exhaled a disagreeable odour of salt-water, fish, and tobacco-smoke. The floor was sanded, and the furniture was meagre and of a rude description; two or three coloured prints of shipping and marine views adorned the walls, in common black frames, and a few shells lay on the mantel, and a piece of sea-weed, which served for a barometer. A good fire burned in the grate, however, and a large black cat lay basking in the agreeable warmth.

On one side of the fire sat the fisherman, and on the other his wife, a decent-looking woman, somewhat past the middle age; the fisherman was a bluff, weatherbeaten old fellow, of near sixty years of age, dressed in a heavy blue pea-jacket, blue shirt, and trowsers of thick, coarse blue cloth. His hair was grey, and there was an appearance of good-humour in his countenance which immediately prepossessed the youth in his favour; he was smoking a short black pipe, and repairing the meshes of a net which lay on the floor.

The fisherman's daughter, the girl who had admitted Norman, was a comely lass, with light-brown hair and sparkling blue eyes, which darted mischief and vivacity with every glance; her complexion was fair and clear, her figure good, and, though not exactly pretty, there was something in her bright, laughing eyes, and the expression of her mouth, which seemed formed for smiles and coquettish pouting, which was exceedingly attractive.

"My name is Ashley, the apprentice whom I believe you expected from London," said Norman on entering, by way of introducing himself.

"Oh, ah—all right; sit down, lad," said the old fisherman, eyeing the youth with some surprise. "But you don't look as if natur' intended you for a fisherman—you are too genteel-looking."

Norman coloured slightly, and tried to smile; but it was almost a failure, and he laid his bundle on the table, and took a seat. Nancy Shrimp, the fisherman's blue-eyed daughter, looked at the handsome youth with considerable satisfaction, until Norman's dark optics turned involuntarily towards her, when she turned away her head, and looked earnestly between the bars of the grate.

"You won't go out in the boat before to-morrow, my lad," said Sam Shrimp, "so you can take a look about the town, if you like."

Norman rose at this intimation, and was glad of an opportunity of escaping into the street; he hastened from the neighbourhood of Shrimp's dwelling, the oldest and dirtiest part of Gravesend, and walked up the ascent of Bath-street, towards the New-road. A few minutes' walking took him into a rural part of the country; and, though the day was cold and hazy, he was more comfortable than he would have been had he remained in the fisherman's cottage. When he returned in the evening, having dined at an eating-house, he found the family circle increased by the fisherman's sons, two stout, fresh-coloured young men, of the respective ages of nineteen and twenty-one. They stared at Norman, exchanged a significant smile, and, without speaking a word, continued to make fearful inroads upon the bread and butter.

"We are going to the Compasses," said the eldest of these amphibia, after tea. "Wilt come with us, young man?"

"You had better stay here," interposed their mother; "and, if you like to smoke, you can have a pipe with Shrimp."

Norman accordingly declined, and the brothers went out; while Nancy Shrimp bestowed an approving smile on her father's apprentice, and proceeded to fill him a pipe from the old man's pouch with her own fair hands.

Norman had never attempted to smoke before, and he coloured slightly as he received the pipe from Nancy, and proceeded to light it at the paper which she held herself for that purpose. After a few puffs, he felt himself constrained to lay down the pipe; but, finding the effects of the dense cloud exhaled by the old fisherman nearly as bad, he resumed it in a short time, and succeeded in smoking it out. Having been reminded that he would have to rise early in the morning, he expressed a wish to retire to rest about nine o'clock, upon which Nancy lighted a candle for him, and directed him to his chamber, a double-

bedded room, the other bed being occupied by Sam and Ned, the amphibious bipeds who were slaking their clay at the Compasses in Bath-street.

Long before daylight on the following morning, Norman Ashley was roused from his slumber by the voice of the old fisherman, who placed a lantern on the floor of his room, and desired him to be quick. He dressed himself between sleeping and waking, buttoning his pea-jacket closely round him, and knocking his "sou'-wester" firmly on his head, and then accompanied Shrimp to the shore, where Sam and Ned were already busy with the boat and their nets. It was a bitter cold morning, and a thick haze overhung the river. The three fishermen were puffing vigorously at their blackened dudeens, by way of qualifying the humidity of the atmosphere; and the tide was slowly running out with a sullen murmur, as the waves broke over the mud and shingle on the shelving banks of the river.

Norman felt his teeth chattering with the cold, and, when the boat got into the stream, the cold increased, and seemed to pierce his bones. As they sailed down the river, a dull red streak appeared on the eastern horizon, which

16

gradually became broader and brighter until the haze cleared away, and the rippling waves of Old Father Thames were glowing like those of the fabled Phlegethon. The sun rose like a ball of heated metal above the broad bosom of the estuary which opens into the North Sea, and then the cold was partially mitigated by his watery beams.

Neither his avocations nor his companions were calculated to imbue young Ashley with much liking for his new mode of life; and, when he returned home with Shrimp and his sons, discontent was sinking deep into his heart. He strove, however, to conceal his feelings on the subject from the fisherman and his family, and the smiles and good-humoured sallies of the lively Nancy gradually restored him to cheerfulness.

At the end of a week, however, he wrote to his uncle, and begged to change the occupation of fishing for the situation of junior clerk in Mr. Ashley's office; but the answer was a peremptory refusal: he had chosen his lot, and he must abide by his own decision. His discontent increased, and at length he was only prevented from leaving the fisherman by the want of money to support himself until he could procure some employment in London, or friends to recommend him or interest themselves in his behalf. He had commenced a life to which he was wholly unaccustomed, in an inclement season; and the disgust which his avocation produced was increased by the idea, that he had been wronged by his uncle, which constantly rankled in his breast, and became stronger every day. The discontent which was inspired by his situation might have been surmounted, could the youth have divested himself of the idea that he had been wronged, and that he was doomed to toil and drudgery, while others were enjoying that which of right belonged to him. This it was which mainly contributed to make him discontented with his situation, and rendered him careless and indifferent as to the satisfaction he gave to the old fisherman.

His growing discontent and the example of the fisherman's sons led him to spend first one, and afterwards two or three nights in every week at the "Compasses," or at the "Fishermen's Arms," in the High-street; houses which are mainly frequented by fishermen, pilots, and others connected with the river. As summer came on, and the morning air grew less cold and piercing, his occupation became less intolerable, and he would, doubtless, have surmounted his repugnance to it, but for the sense of wrong which rankled like a barbed arrow in his heart.

Nancy Shrimp had conceived a partiality to the handsome youth as soon as she saw him, and strove on all occasions to win his regard, and to console him, by various little kindnesses, for the discomfort of his situation. On his part, Norman Ashley felt grateful to the young girl for her attentions to his comfort, and felt springing up in his heart the germs of a feeling which time might have ripened into love. But young Ashley knew not the nature of his feelings towards her, and though he often escorted her to Windmill-hill, or along the river to Northfleet or Chalk, in the fine Sabbath evenings of the summer, yet love had never entered into his thoughts, and not a word had been spoken upon the subject. The summer passed away, and the yellow leaves of autumn succeeded the flowers and the fruits; dreary winter once more covered the earth with his mantle of snow, but no alteration had taken place in the feelings or prospects of Norman Ashley.

CHAPTER XXXIX.

SUSAN WALTERS.

WE must now return to Lolah Hastings, who had been under the protection of Frederick Shirley since her first introduction to him, and had become much attached to him, and no symptons of cooling had yet appeared in his conduct towards his young and beautiful mistress. She was passing over Waterloo-bridge one fine morning in the summer of 1830, about twelve months after her fearful series of adventures in the house of Mother Jones, the vaults of Habakuk Holdfast's chapel, and the study of Mr. Melville, when she met a young female whose countenance seemed familiar to her. She looked again, and perceived that the person was regarding her with equal attention.

" Are you not the young person who lived at Mrs. Jones's?" inquired Lolah, beginning to feel positive that she was not mistaken in her supposition.

" Hush !" exclaimed Susan Walters, for it was really her whom Lolah had encountered. " Do you wish to transport me?   I am that person, and you are Miss Hastings."

" Yes ; but I have no desire to harm you, Susan," replied Lolah. " Mrs. Jones has been rightly punished, and I wish Colonel Morton could have been discovered, and sentenced to the same fate."

" He would have been hung, no doubt," said the young woman. " You look well, Miss Hastings ; I hope you are now comfortable and happy."

" I have nothing to complain of, Susan," returned Lolah, smiling; " but come to my lodgings, and tell me how you escaped from the power of that odious Mrs. Jones."

Frederick Shirley had removed his mistress from the court in John-street, Cornwall-road, to two rooms on the first floor of a house in Roupell-street, in the same locality. She was returning home when she met Susan Walters on the bridge ; and thither the young woman accompanied her, at Lolah's invitation, and proceeded to explain the causes of the thraldom in which she had been held by Mother Jones, and which had prevented her from appearing to give evidence against her on the trial.

" You have rightly guessed that the full horrors of that den of infamy and crime were not unknown to me," said Susan Walters, in reply to an observation from Lolah Hastings. " The seven years which I passed in that house were marked by more intolerable mental anguish than was ever experienced in the same period by a prisoner in the dungeons of the Bastille, an exile in the wilds of Siberia, or a slave in the mines of Peru. Sin was the cause ; and the sins of others were made the punishment of my own. Seven years ago, I was taken from St. Giles's workhouse, a friendless orphan of sixteen, and became the servant of Mrs. Jones. I knew not then, nor for some time afterwards, the precise nature of her means of living ; for the house was only used for such cases as that of which you became the victim. But I was destined soon to learn, in my own person, the abominable traffic from which Mother Jones had amassed a considerable fortune.

" I slept in one of the attics ; the other was the terrible matted chamber ; and though it was always kept locked, I had not the most remote suspicion of the purposes to which it was applied. Mrs. Jones behaved tolerably well to me—better, indeed, than many would have done—and allowed me more liberty than is enjoyed by servants in general. She had her reasons for this, as the sequel will show. I became acquainted with a soldier, a private in the Guards ; and one evening Mrs. Jones observed me conversing with him, he having accompanied me home after a walk in St. James's-park. She then gave me permission to receive his visits at the house ; and of this permission the guardsman frequently availed himself. Simpson made himself particularly agreeable to the soldier, and once invited him into the parlour to take a glass of gin-and-water and smoke a cigar with him. I have no doubt that it was at this time that the mode of my ruin was arranged between Simpson and my deceitful lover ; for the next time he came to see me, Mrs. Jones called me up, and gave me some rum, in order, as she said, that Edward and I might make ourselves comfortable. I mixed a glass of rum-and-water, which the soldier tasted, and complained that it was not sweet enough. I rose to get the sugar, and while my back was turned, I heard a sound as if the soldier was stirring the liquor ; and I have no doubt that, in accordance with the diabolical prompting of Bill Simpson, he took the opportunity to pour into the glass a small quantity of laudanum. I resumed my seat, and drank some of the liquor, after adding some more sugar, and in a few moments I came over very drowsy, upon which my companion urged me to drink again, saying that it would rouse me. I did so, and immediately fell into a state of complete unconsciousness, from which I did not recover until the next morning, when I found myself in bed, and in the arms of the deceitful Edward. I wept, and reproached him ; but he laughed at my regrets and fears, and asserted that all that had taken place had been with my own free will. His manners, and the mode in which he had taken advantage of me, proved to me, ignorant of vice as I then was, that Mrs. Jones must have been accessory to my ruin; and I felt so enraged at my lover's conduct, that I determined to have no further intimacy with him.

" But it was not in my nature, weak and credulous as I was, long to resist the importunities of one whom I had once loved; and at the end of a few weeks, I not only forgave him, but freely yielded to the gratification of his passion. At this time I discovered the real character of Mrs. Jones, which I was led to suspect from what had happened to myself, and these suspicions were confirmed by the evident familiarity of her and Simpson, and some observations which fell from the soldier. After my intercourse with the guardsman had continued two or three months, I found myself in a situation to become a mother, and confided my condition to my seducer. He told me I must do the best I could; and I never saw him afterwards. This discovery, and my lover's desertion of me at that time, weighed heavily upon my mind; and the secret grief that oppressed me was, doubtless, injurious to the innocent evidence of my dishonour.

" At length the dreaded time arrived when I was to give birth to the offspring of sin and shame, and as I had striven to conceal my situation from Mrs. Jones, I was overwhelmed with fear lest a discovery should take place at the moment most to be dreaded. I have wondered since how it was that I lost not my senses under so terrible a trial; and really the fortitude and presence of mind of young women, in such cases, under certain circumstances, is most extraordinary. The hapless offspring of my amour with the soldier cried once, and then its little heart ceased to beat; it was dead, and, suffering horribly in mind and body, I carried it into the kitchen for the purpose of concealment. The cellar in which such an appalling discovery was made by the Bow-street officers, when they apprehended Mother Jones, had always been secured as it was then found, but I had seen a key in the parlour closet, which I thought belonged to it. I possessed myself of this key, and with some trouble succeeded in unlocking the door of the cellar; holding the light in one hand, and carrying the dead infant with the other, I entered the gloomy hole, but scarce had I advanced a step when I perceived, to my horror and amazement, a human skeleton lying upon the floor of the cellar. I screamed aloud, and, dropping both the child and the candle, I rushed breathless with terror from the accursed spot.

" Another light, another person was in the kitchen; it was Mrs. Jones: she had discovered my secret, had penetrated my motives, and followed me down the stairs. She was somewhat pale, and yet there was an expression of infernal triumph upon her countenance. Weak and exhausted as I already was, I was now so overpowered with terror, that I fell upon the floor, and fainted. When I recovered I was in bed, having been carried up, as Mother Jones afterwards informed me, by Bill Simpson. In this infirm state, both of mind and body, Mother Jones reduced me to the most abject submission, by threatening to have me hanged for the murder of my babe, if I ever betrayed the grim secret of the cellar, or in any way disobey her commands. I was very ill for two or three weeks after the terrible occurrences of that night, the horrors of which will never be effaced from my mind.

" Six years have elapsed since that fearful night, but I have formed no other attachment, nor did Mother Jones ever seek to coerce me into a life of infamy, as I at first feared she would; she had me completely in her power, and that was the point to which she wished to bring me. During that period, I became fully initiated in the mystery of that chamber with the matted floor and walls; and many were the unsuspecting creatures that I ushered into it, only to leave it polluted and ruined. The victims were mostly young girls inveigled from boarding-schools or from comfortable homes, and sometimes servants and workwomen, or apprentices—those, in fact, whom their wealthy destroyers could not obtain in any other way. Some resigned themselves to their fate, and became the mistresses of those whom their unfortunate beauty had attracted; and some bore imprisonment and repeated brutalities before they yielded, some to fear and shame, others to the allurements held out by Elise and the other girls whom Mother Jones would introduce to them for that purpose. Then they were sent to the houses of ill-fame which that vile woman possessed in various parts of the metropolis. The skeleton which I saw in the cellar was, doubtless, that of some wretched girl, who, for her firmness in withstanding iniquity, was disposed of as you were supposed to have been; and most fortunate was it for you that you were placed in that horrible hole, instead of being consigned to the vaults of the chapel.

"The old man whose skeleton was found in the cellar met a retributive death at the hands of his intended victim, the young woman whose skeleton was found lying across his own. I remember well the night of that awful tragedy. Several hours had passed since the old gentleman had entered the matted chamber, and Mother Jones, who at first had been very jocular about it, at length began to be alarmed; and, on going up-stairs, found the old man weltering in his blood, and his intended victim in a state of insensibility. A penknife lay upon the thickly-carpeted floor, with which the desperate girl had committed the dreadful deed; Mother Jones screamed; and, on Bill Simpson rushing up-stairs, he found that the wretched old man was quite dead. He immediately procured a sack, into which he thrust the lifeless body of, the miserable libertine, and dragged it down to the cellar, where it was flung in; and the marks observed upon the door were the prints of the bloody fingers of Bill Simpson.

"The wretched murderess, more to be pitied than her victim, remained more than a week in the scene of her crime, stained with the blood which her desperate hand had shed in defence of her honour; but how she was disposed of I know not, more than that she was carried down stairs by Bill Simpson, and thrown into the cellar. Whether she died of fright or grief, or was drugged to death with laudanum, I cannot say: I only know that Simpson or Mother Jones visited her every day until she was brought out a corpse. I have now told you all that I know of the mysteries connected with the human remains discovered in Mrs. Jones's cellar, and explained the causes which enabled that detestable woman to hold me in a bondage at which my soul revolted. I effected my escape while she was lying upon the floor in a state of beastly intoxication, after a quarrel with Bill Simpson, whom she had detected in an intrigue with the French girl, Elise; and since then I have been living in the service of a benevolent lady at the west-end of the town; to whom, knowing the goodness of her heart, I ventured to make known my sad and terrible story."

CHAPTER XL.

THE STORY OF ELISE.

SUSAN WALTERS was compelled to take her departure immediately after she had concluded the recital of her misfortunes, and the terrible scenes that had been enacted in the house of Mother Jones; but, before she reached her home, she encountered another person, whom she had met in that house of mystery and crime. This was Elise, the young Frenchwoman, whose amour with Bill Simpson had led to the disturbance at Mother Jones's, which had facilitated the escape of Susan Walters from the horrible thraldom in which she had been held by the procuress. Simpson and Elise had returned from Paris a few days before, and the latter was walking along the Strand, when she was met by Susan. The recognition was mutual; and, after a little amicable conversation, Elise accepted the invitation of Susan Walters to take tea with her. Elise was naturally a kind-hearted and good-tempered young woman, as was evidenced by her retaining much of those amiable qualities amid the scenes of sensual profligacy by which she had been surrounded from girlhood; and, taking into consideration those facts in her history to which we are now alluding, it is more surprising that she became not wholly depraved, than that she should have fallen so low as the reader has already found her.

Over the friendly cup which "cheers but ne'er inebriates," Elise related to Susan Walters the narrative of her life, which the latter repaid by a like confidence; and, as the story of the young Frenchwoman affords a striking illustration of the evils arising from the Roman Catholic institutions of the confessional and the convent, its introduction here will require no apology.*

* In order, if it be necessary, to show that we have not exaggerated the abuses of the convent

" My father," said Elise, " was a shopkeeper in the market-place of Louviers, and so rigid was he in the due observance of all the rites and ceremonies of the Catholic church, and in inculcating on the ductile minds of his children the strictest veneration for its doctrines and priesthood, that I became so imbued with religious veneration and aspirations after the perfection of holiness, that I earnestly besought my parents to allow me to enter the convent of Ursuline nuns, in my native town. I was then very young, and, having passed through my novitiate without seeing anything in the discipline of the convent to turn my mind from its aspirations after a life of devotion and holiness, I received the veil, and became a nun. But no sooner had I pronounced the irrevocable vows, than I began, by degrees, to be assailed by doubts and fears, and to tremble lest I should have mistaken the path which leads to hell, for that which I had been led to suppose would conduct me to heaven. My fears and suspicions were first excited by certain questions put to me by the monk who came to the convent to receive the confessions of the nuns, and which were of such a nature as to suffuse my cheeks with blushes, and render it impossible for me to reply immediately. Father Ambrose increased my confusion, by attributing it to a consciousness of guilt, in respect of those things whereof he questioned me ; and I was so overwhelmed with shame, and so agitated by the questions of the confessor, that I was unable to rebut his insinuations. Conscious of my innocence, for my life had hitherto been pure and irreproachable, I retired to my cell, and began to pray fervently to the Virgin ; but the behaviour of Father Ambrose had so disturbed the peaceful equanimity of my mind, that I was unable to pray with my usual devotion and singleness of heart, and I was agitated by feelings and thoughts such as I had never experienced before.

" The discourse of Father Ambrose, on the ensuing sabbath, was on the danger attending ignorance of sin, which he treated in a sophistical and ambiguous manner ; saying that we could not be firmly grounded in holiness, unless we had withstood sin ; and, if we had never been exposed to sinful influences, we could not be assured of our ability to resist them. When I had returned to my cell, I reflected much on what I had heard in the chapel, and reviewed my past life to judge of the temptations to sin which I had ever experienced, and looked searchingly into my heart to test its ability to resist sinful influences. The next time I went to the confessional, Father Ambrose pursued the arguments of his discourse, and urged the necessity of involuntarily exposing ourselves to temptations, as the surest test of holiness and divine grace. I ventured to express my dissent from his views ; but he told me I knew nothing about it, and that my scruples were a proof of presumption and self-glorification, adding that there was no merit in virtue that had never stood the test of temptation. These remarks troubled me very much ; for they made me doubtful of my own strength, and fearful lest the germs of sinfulness should exist in a dormant state in my nature, waiting only for their development for those exterior circumstances which serve to fan our nascent passions into a flame.

" Father Ambrose strenuously urged these views of sin and holiness whenever he saw me, and said that to avoid temptation was a sign of weakness, and only those who had triumphantly withstood sinful influences could be truly considered irreproachable. I was so bewildered by these doctrines, that I knew not what to think, and the confessor seeing the state of doubt and confusion in which my mind was wavering, redoubled his endeavours to bend me to his evil purposes. He assumed a parental tone, represented in vivid colours the danger in which I stood from my ignorance of my ability to resist temptation, and expatiated on the happiness and peace of mind I should derive from the knowledge that I had passed through the ordeal of temptation, and become the refined gold from the crucible of the artizan. He urged me, with all the infernal sophistry and dangerous eloquence which he so largely possessed, to expose myself to this ordeal,

---

and the confessional, we beg to refer the reader to *Lasteyrie's History of Auricular Confession,* a translation of which has recently been published. The reader will there find the narrative of a nun of Louviers, which not only describes similar scenes to those disclosed by Elise, but contains revelations of so revolting a nature, that it is utterly impossible even to allude to them in the following story. The lewdness which existed in the English convents, suppressed at the Reformation, was as nothing to that which prevailed among the nuns of Louviers; and we shudder at the depravity which too often exists under the cowl of a monk.

assuring me that I need apprehend no danger from himself, as every passion and desire had long since been crucified within him, on the cross of mortification and self-denial. I trembled as if I stood on the brink of some terrible danger, and yet I was like a bird subjected to the fabled influence of the serpent, for the sophisty of the monk rendered me powerless to resist what the inward but almost stifled monitor told me was wrong. He proceeded to render his doctrines practical by a gradual series of the most unwarrantable freedoms, which crimsoned my burning cheeks with shame, and overwhelmed me with modest confusion. It was not until it was too late that I perceived the full danger of the ordeal to which I had tacitly consented, for I was completely in the power of that execrable monk; to retreat would be converted into an acknowledgment and a proof of moral weakness, and to stay was to fall into the snare that he had so artfully spread for me. Alas! retreat was no longer possible, and my virtue became a sacrifice to the confessor's sensuality.

"The wily monk, having succeeded in his vile purpose, endeavoured to gloss over our natural frailty with his usual sophistry, saying, that though marriage was forbidden to those who had taken the monastic vows, yet, as faith was sufficient to insure grace and salvation, those who had dedicated themselves to the service of God were not compelled to deny themselves the pleasures of the flesh, being assured of salvation through faith and divine grace. These assurances did not entirely console me for my deviation from the straight path of virtue, for I felt humiliated in my own eyes by my fall; and the sophistry of Father Ambrose lost its influence when I returned to the privacy and solitude of my cell. Under the impression that the wily monk had deluded me for the gratification of his own passions, I made application to the abbess of the convent to be allowed the visits of another confessor, but this request was peremptorily refused. I was thus left entirely under the dangerous control and guidance of Father Ambrose, who required me at each confession to yield myself to his embraces, for which he gave me absolution, and for which I experienced less repugnance on every occasion. In fact, an entire change seemed to have come over my nature; my confessor had roused my dormant passions, and they soon became ungovernable, merging every consideration of religious duty in sensual gratification. I had never felt the influence of love before entering the convent, and for Father Ambrose I often experienced a feeling of disgust amounting almost to abhorrence, yet I unreservedly abandoned myself to his caresses, for he was necessary to the gratification of the fierce passions which he had excited within me.

"The discipline of the convent prevented any confidential conversation between the nuns, but there can be no doubt, from the scenes which I witnessed after my seduction, that all the younger nuns had become, as I had, the victims of the confessor's sophistry and sensuality. He frequently required us to receive the sacrament of the Lord's supper with our clothes unfastened, and stripped down to the waist, so that our bosoms were exposed to his licentious gaze; and on one occasion, when a nun refused to comply with this command, he made the others unfasten her clothes, and when the abashed young woman endeavoured to cover her bosom with her hands, they were snatched away by the abbess. He also preached the strange and demoralising doctrine, which I have since heard was a revival of an old heresy, that to be worthy of heaven we must become as our first parents were before the fall, and being free from sin must also be devoid of shame; which he alleged was only attendant upon a state of sin, and those who were regenerate by faith ought not to experience it. Hence he commanded us to appear naked in his presence, and in that of each other, and there were many who did not scruple to obey the suggestions of the confessor's sensual mind. In the passages of the convent, and in the garden, which was screened from the observation of those without by a very high wall, might be seen the deluded nuns in complete nudity, as Eve appeared in the garden of Eden; and all this profligacy was veiled under the mask of religion! The abbess was a mere tool in the hands of Father Ambrose, who was a man of wealthy and powerful connexions, and would undoubtedly have risen high in the church had he taken priest's orders, instead of assuming the cowl of the monk, which he preferred for the opportunities it gave him of corrupting the minds of the nuns whom he confessed, and making them the victims of his inordinate desires. Thus the convent became his harem, and most of the nuns abandoned themselves, without scruple or reserve, to every suggestion of his depraved mind. Human nature is the same in every condition, and a nun is only a weak woman, despite her vows; the elopements of the Spanish and Portugese nuns with the soldiers of Napoleon, and the immorality that has been detected so frequently in the convents of Italy and Germany, prove the truth of this assertion, if any proof is required; and the greater the pressure upon our natural instincts, the greater will be the reaction. Priests and legislators can never destroy the instincts which nature has implanted within us, and an enlightened wisdom would seek only so to direct them as to secure the greatest amount of happiness for all.

CHAPTER XLI.

MORE REVELATIONS.

" The abominable wickedness of Father Ambrose at length received a check; such wholesale and rampant profligacy among women vowed to purity and holiness, was sure to cause a reaction. One of the nuns, she who had protested against the shameless scene in the chapel, and whose modesty had often been rebuked by the confessor, and ridiculed by the abbess and the most abandoned of the sisterhood, at length became so disgusted with the conduct of Father Ambrose and many of the nuns, that she found means to forward a complaint of the irregularities existing in the convent, to the superior of the monastery to which the libertine monk belonged. Had there been any similarity in the characters of Father Ambrose and his superior, this complaint would have produced no results, but the latter was just such an ascetic as Scott's grand master of the Templars, Lucas de Beaumanoir. Father Ambrose never appeared again at the convent of the Holy Heart, but this was not a sufficient remedy for the immorality which he had introduced; some of the nuns were penitent, and confessed themselves devoutly to their new confessor, but others of stronger passions and desires had become weary of a conventual life, and longed to escape from its discipline and restraint. Among these was myself; I had violated my vows, at the instigation of one whose duty it was to have guided me in the path of holiness; I had thrown off all the restraints of female modesty and the decencies of society, and my whole nature had become changed by the profligacy with which the libertinism of Father Ambrose had imbued it. The removal of my seducer at an earlier period, when I stood wavering on the moral rubicon, I should have hailed with pleasure; and I had even solicited the favour of being confessed by another at that time, but my application had been disregarded; and now the change filled me with discontent, so complete was the change that had come over me.

" I demanded to be released from my vows, since a violation of them had been sanctioned by my confessor; but all I could obtain was liberty to enter another convent. This did not correspond with my views and wishes: it was a change of life which I desired to realize, rather than a mere change of scene. I addressed a complaint to the bishop of the diocese, stating the gross immorality which had resulted from the seduction of the nuns by Father Ambrose, and declaring my intention to make the whole affair public, through the liberal journals, if I were not released from my vows. After some delay, a commission of priests was appointed to inquire into the truth of my allegations, which were found to be correct; and, in order to avert the scandal which their publication would have brought upon the church in general, 1 and the nun who had procured the removal of Father Ambrose were allowed to leave the convent, with liberty to go wheresoever we pleased. This was all that I required; and, without going near any of my relations in Louviers, I proceeded to Paris by the diligence at once.

" I had no very definite idea of what I was going to do in Paris; but I certainly had no intention of becoming a candidate for the prize of virtue. Having exchanged my monastic garb for more becoming attire, I took a very humble lodging in a street near the Palais Royal; for I knew that I should

soon be destitute of pecuniary resources, unless I could obtain a wealthy lover. After some deliberation, I had my name inscribed on the police-register, and on the evening of the same day, I commenced the promenade of the Palais Royal, which abounds in gaming-houses, taverns, music-rooms, cigar-divans, and other places frequented by the gay and dissipated. I soon succeeded in attracting the attention of a young officer, whom I accompanied to a house of a certain description; and so much was he captivated, that he remained with me until the following morning, and then made me an offer of protection, which I readily accepted. For three months, I led a life of pleasure and gaiety in his society; but at the end of that time he received orders to join his regiment at Melun, and declined taking me with him. I had, therefore, to seek another lover, and in less than a week had succeeded in fascinating an elderly gentleman whom I met one evening at the theatre. To him succeeded a student of the Ecole de Medicine, and when he had become weary of me, or found himself unable any longer to support me, I lured within the meshes of my attractions a gay young English nobleman.

17·

In this manner had passed about two years from the time when I left the convent at Louviers, and after the return to England of my last lover, I again became a regular promenader of the piazzas of the Palais Royal. One evening I met with my old confessor, Father Ambrose; he was in plain clothes, and at first I was doubtful of the identity, but when I got a full view of his countenance my doubts were all removed. I spoke to him, and found that he had taken priest's orders, and was the curate of a small village in Normandy, where he also officiated as parish schoolmaster. At first he behaved rather coolly to me, but eventually accompanied me to my lodgings, where he stayed with me until the following day. Dropping one evening into the roulette-room at Frascati's, which is much frequented by gay ladies, I made an acquaintance with a young Englishman of pleasing exterior and elegant manners, who became so captivated with me, that he entreated me to accompany him to London, which I did in about a week after our first meeting. He took apartments for me in the neighbourhood of Bayswater; but, as I had anticipated, his passion was too ardent to be permanent, and in a few months he first neglected and then deserted me. On finding myself forsaken, I removed to lodgings at the west-end of the metropolis, and shortly afterwards became acquainted with Simpson, though not, at that time, with his precise situation with regard to Mother Brown. In a French newspaper, which I took up at a coffee-house about this time, I found tidings of Father Ambrose, who, having been detected in an equivocal situation with a female scholar, had been dragged through the village by a number of peasants, pumped upon, and afterwards scourged with nettles in an unmerciful manner. The perusal of this account caused me a laugh, partly at the nature of the punishment awarded to the amorous priest, and partly with gratified malice, for he richly deserved it.

"A long illness, at this time, so absorbed all my resources, that, on my recovery, I became an inmate of what is termed a dress-house, belonging to Mother Brown; and, as it is from the class of dress-lodgers that the French houses are mainly supplied, I soon found my way into one of those infamous places, which also belonged to Mrs. Brown. These houses exist only at the west-end of London, and are patronised only by the aristocracy; they are frequented almost entirely by old gentlemen, worn-out voluptuaries like Colonel Elrington, and mere youths whom wealth and influence have procured commissions in the army at sixteen years of age—aristocratic juveniles with too great a supply of pocket-money, and corrupted by older profligates in the schools of Westminster and Harrow. The females who inhabit these houses are mostly natives of France and Belgium; but since they have become more common, many English girls have been initiated into the shameless scenes which are enacted in them, and which are only exceeded in grossness by some of those which I witnessed in the convent of Louviers. A high sense of modesty is by no means incompatible with a life of degradation, for a pure soul may often reside in a polluted body; but with the females of this class, of all others the most degraded, the sense of shame is utterly lost, and they abandon themselves to the grossest immorality. It was for this reason that Mother Brown sometimes sent for us to overcome the scruples of some poor girl who had been lured to her den, and whom she intended to force into a life of infamy.

"Bill Simpson had become much attached to me, and often wished me to leave Mrs. Brown's house for some other, so that he might be able to visit me more frequently, and without the fear of our intimacy becoming known to that vile old harridan. But I was somewhat in Mother Brown's power—though not so terribly as you were, Susan—not having been able to free myself from the fatal trammels of debt which hangs continually about the neck of the unfortunate female who once becomes a dress-lodger. The fracas between Simpson and Mother Brown, which resulted from my last visit to that abominable den, settled the question at once, and Simpson and I went over to Paris. Simpson is a knowing card-sharp, and he made enough at the gaming-hells in the Palais Royal to keep us both in ease and pleasure, until our return to England a few days since."

To this narrative of the ex-nun of Louviers we have little to add; it speaks for itself as to the evils inseparable from monastic institutions and auricular confession, and it must be remembered that the latter is an evil not confined to convents, and which exposes even private families of every grade in society to the dark and insidious influence of such profligate wretches as the confessor Ambrose. The whole subject is a painful one; but shall we suffer evil to exist unnoticed, and to spread its hideous ramifications throughout the whole framework of society, for fear of shocking the sensitive by its exposure? Let us choose the least of two evils; to unmask an abuse is the first step to its removal. Above all, it should be remembered, that it is society, and not nature, which forms such moral monstrosities as the monk Ambrose; nature makes only bright-eyed children, pure-hearted and simple-minded, and it is the vicious institutions of society which transform man into the criminal, Hyperion into a satyr. This is a truth which science well illustrates by analogy; for the germ of the lowest vegetation is capable of development as a fungus, an alga, or a lichen, according to the external conditions of heat, light, and moisture, amid which it is cast; producing fungi upon decomposed organic remains, lichens upon earth or stones, and algæ where water is the medium in which the germ is developed. So it is with human nature, morally as well as physically; the same elements of character exist in all, and whether the germs of good shall be developed, perverted, or crushed out, is entirely dependent on the external circumstances amid which the being is reared.

CHAPTER XLII.

THE THREE GAMBLERS.

In the back parlour of a public-house in the neighbourhood of Leicester-square, dimly lighted by a dusty skylight, three dissipated-looking young men were seated over a solitary and half-emptied glass of gin and water. They were our old acquaintances, Augustus Fitzormond, Bill Simpson, and Frederick Shirley, all of them having changed for the worst in their personal appearance, since their first introduction to the reader. Fitzormond was decidedly the shabbiest of the trio, for Shirley had contrived to preserve the externals of respectability, and a run of ill-luck had had less effect on the pockets of Bill Simpson than on those of his present allies, his visit to the French capital having produced him a better supply of cash, as Elise had intimated to Susan Walters. But though the barrister's clerk had been enabled to maintain the respectability of appearance which had characterised him previous to his acquaintance with the worthies in whose company we now find him, the paleness of his handsome countenance, the sunken appearance of his dark eyes, and a certain nervousness of manner, told an unmistakeable tale of reckless dissipation and late hours. Through his connection with Lolah Hastings, and his intimacy with such men as Simpson and Fitzormond, he had been discarded by his friends, had become involved in pecuniary difficulties, and, to complete his embarrassment, had been that morning discharged from his situation for his culpable neglect of his duties and his employer's interest. Fitzormond and Simpson were in no better circumstances than himself, and the three dissipated young men had met that morning to talk over their present position, and devise some plan for the future.

" It is easy to say what might be done," observed Bill Simpson, in reply to a remark of Augustus Fitzormond; " but without funds we can do nothing. Our first consideration must be how to raise the wind, and when we have got the mopusses we can make a move on a larger scale. If I had the blunt, I would go over to Paris again; that is the place for business, my boy. Talk of the Quadrant, why it's nothing to the Palais Royal. There is always a supply of green coves to be picked up there, canary-birds, as the French call them; foreigners come to London for a living, but they flock to Paris in pursuit of pleasure. Everything in our line is there systemised; the theatres are supported by the government, the hells are regularly licensed, and the flag-hoppers, the *filles de joie*, are all registered at the bureau of the prefect of police, and under the surveillance and protection of the state."

" I should like to visit Paris," observed the barrister's clerk. " I think Frascati's must be a finer place than Crockford's."

" The chief difference that I observed was the presence of females in the roulette-room, and that mysterious-looking apartment at the back, with sofas all round it, and dimly lighted by one lamp of ground glass suspended from the centre of the ceiling," returned Simpson.

" But without money, as you just now observed, we can do nothing," said Augustus Fitzormond. " For my own part, I have just enough to pay for another glass, and that is all. If I could only raise a sovereign to start with, I would make the tour of the provinces, and do a little business at fairs and races."

" Cannot we manage to get hold of that young swell that Simpson caught flying at billiards the other night?" suggested Shirley.

" Ah, a good thought! Who is he, Gus?" said Bill Simpson.

" The very ticket!" exclaimed Fitzormond, slapping his hand on the table. " A young lord with plenty of tin, and spirit enough to spend it. Lord Clanrobert—that's the cove—thinks he has got learning enough for a lord, and has left college at sixteen years of age, and in five years he will step into a splendid fortune."

" He looks more than sixteen," observed Frederick Shirley.

" Yes, because he is tall, and cultivates his moustaches," returned Fitzormond; but I have the Red Book by rote, and I know him to be no more than I have stated. The late Lord Clanrobert died when the present one was a mere child, and, having plenty of money and a taste for pleasure, his guardians have enough to do to prevent him from kicking over the traces."

" But how is he to be got at?" inquired Simpson.

" That is the difficulty," observed Fitzormond, in an embarrassed tone. " I never met him till the other night, and I don't know his haunts or his companions."

" Then I don't see what can be done," returned Bill Simpson; " I suppose we must wait upon the chapter of accidents, and see what will turn up in a day or two."

" Well, let us separate, and meet again in the evening," suggested Fitzormond; " during the day, game may be started worth running down, and at eight o'clock to-night we will meet at the crib in Catherine-street."

The three sharpers then rose from the table, Augustus casting a melancholy glance at the empty glass; and, having left the house, they separated, and went in different directions.

It was past eight o'clock in the evening when Bill Simpson sauntered down Catherine-street, and entered a house on the left-hand side, which had been selected for the meeting with his unprincipled associates. It is so customary, in London, for vice to put on the semblance of virtuous respectability, that a cigar-shop is often the vestibule to a gaming-house, and what appears to be a fashionable milliner's is frequently a house of ill-fame. The house where Simpson had appointed to meet Shirley and Fitzormond was ostensibly a coffee-house, and those acquainted with the mysteries of the locality in question will doubtless recognise the house to which we allude. Gaming is there carried on in a dark dingy room at the back, and many a *pigeon* has been there plucked to the last feather, the house being the habitual resort of card-sharpers, gentry of the dog-fighting fraternity, and those degraded samples of humanity known as " fancy men," such as Augustus Fitzormond. Gaming, however, is not the only vice which finds favour in the eyes of the proprietor of this den; it is also a house of accommodation for the visitors and their female associates, nothing which can be made a source of profit appearing to be objectionable to those who grow rich upon the vices of their fellow-creatures.

Bill Simpson entered with the air of one thoroughly initiated in the mysteries of the place, and sat down in the apartment behind the coffee-room, where a youth of about sixteen years of age was playing at dominoes with a dissipated-looking young man, whose clothes were in the last degree of seediness. The youth seemed old beyond his years, and his opponent seemed to have discovered the fact that his anticipated victim was not so easy to pluck as he had expected. Standing near the table was a young woman, flauntingly dressed, and having a gipsey-like appearance both in her countenance and the style of her dress; her complexion was very dark, her eyes brilliant and roving, and long gold ear-drops glittered through the bands of shining black hair which descended from the temples upon each embrowned cheek. Bill Simpson had scarcely taken a seat when Frederick Shirley entered hastily, and whispered a communication of an important nature.

"Fitzormond has picked up Lord Clanrobert, and has got him in tow at Jem Burn's," said he; then observing the youth who was playing at dominoes, he said: "What, Sam Skelter!"

"Yes, it's me, Mr. Shirley," returned the youth. "Will you take anything? This game will soon be over, and then I will play you, if you have no objection."

The ex-clerk declined both Sam Skelter's invitations, and quitted the coffee-house, followed by Bill Simpson. Making the best of their way to Crown-court, they found Augustus Fitzormond and Lord Clanrobert smoking their cigars in the parlour of the tavern referred to by Frederick Shirley, over a bottle of wine. The young noble, who, it will be remembered, was in reality the son of the wooden-legged sailor of Ratcliffe-highway, was a tall, handsome-looking youth, whom circumstances had thrown, at this early age, into the vortex of dissipation, to which the bent of his education and training had inclined him. The sons of the aristocracy are never so trained and educated as to become useful members of society; they never aspire to utility, and, if they did, such laudable aspirations would be damped and checked by parents and tutors, as if their tendency was vicious and mischievous. Lord Clanrobert was an exception to the general rule; becoming, while yet a child, an hereditary legislator and a peer of the realm, with splendid pecuniary resources in the perspective, when he should have attained his majority, he considered application to his collegiate studies as beneath the dignity of one who had nought to consult but his own pleasure, and learning was cast aside as worthy only of the sons of poor clergymen aspiring to a professor's chair. We gather not grapes from thorns, nor figs from thistles; the educational system of our universities and public schools is vicious, and it produces few but vicious characters. Lord Clanrobert already longed to be his own master entirely, and to cast off the restraint which his guardians were compelled, to a certain extent, to place upon his restless and haughty spirit.

"Well met, Simpson, my boy," said Augustus Fitzormond, as his colleagues entered the room. "His lordship has now an opportunity of obtaining his revenge. What say you, my lord?"

"Oh, I cannot play billiards to-night," returned the youth. "I have no objection to a game at cards, though. You know some of those places about the Quadrant, I suppose?"

"We can play without going to a common gaming-house," observed Simpson. "My apartments are not far from here, and there we shall be quite comfortable."

"Agreed," said Lord Clanrobert, rising, and throwing the end of his cigar under the grate.

"You and Fitzormond will join us, I suppose?" observed Simpson, turning to Shirley.

"Certainly," returned the discarded clerk; and he and Simpson led the way together.

"Simpson has one of the finest women in London," observed Augustus Fitzormond to the young noble, as they quitted the house. "You will see her, and you will be enraptured with her."

"Is she accessible?" inquired Lord Clanrobert, in a whisper.

"Hush! Simpson will hear us," returned the wily Fitzormond; and, having thus raised the hopes and anticipations of the youthful peer to the highest pitch, he forbore to say any more upon the subject.

CHAPTER XLIII.

LORD CLANROBERT.

HAVING arrived at the lodgings of Mr. Simpson, the young nobleman was introduced by that gentleman to his mistress, whose beauty and manners were well calculated to make an impression upon a youth of such susceptibility as

Lord Clanrobert. Elise was well dressed, and in a style which displayed the symmetry of her form to the greatest advantage ; while her dark eyes sparkled with animation, and all the witchery of her charms was exerted to enslave the heart which they had caught within their silken meshes. Simpson placed a pack of cards and some cigars upon the table, and the little drabby servant of the house was sent out for some brandy, and desired to bring up glasses and hot water. The attention of Lord Clanrobert was abstracted from the game, which immediately commenced, by the thrilling glances and soft smiles of the wanton Elise ; and, even if this had not been the case, he would have no chance of success with such unprincipled gamesters as his present associates. In a few hours, he had lost a considerable sum, Fitzormond being nominally a loser also, in order to prevent suspicion of foul play ; and the latter, having protested he would play no longer, he and Shirley rose from the table.

" Are you really going ?" observed Simpson.

" It is growing late ; and I must be in the city early to-morrow, returned Frederick Shirley.

Fitzormond and the barrister's clerk took their leaves of Lord Clanrobert and the charming Elise, and were about to depart, when Bill Simpson pretended to have some private communication to make to them ; and the trio of gamblers left the room together, leaving the young nobleman in the seductive society of the wanton Frenchwoman. A few moments elapsed, and Lord Clanrobert began to feel slightly embarrassed ; he drew forth his gold repeater, and glanced at the hour.

" You are not going yet, my lord ?" said Elise, in her softest and most winning tone.

" The moment Simpson returns, I must leave," rejoined the young lord. " It is just upon midnight."

" Will you not take another cigar until Simpson's return ?" observed the young Frenchwoman.

Lord Clanrobert hesitated a moment before lighting the fragrant weed, and his mind wavered between doubt and hope as to the real character of the fascinating Elise. During the desultory conversation which followed, the youth insensibly drew his chair nearer to that of Elise, who perceived the impression she had created, and resolved to profit by it ; her manner became imperceptibly more tender, her voice was soft and low, and a voluptuous languor was visible in her dark lustrous eyes.

" Simpson will not return to-night," said she, glancing in a peculiar manner at her companion, as the clock struck one ; " he must have gone somewhere with Shirley and Fitzormond."

" How can he neglect so much loveliness !" observed Lord Clanrobert.

" Flatterer !" exclaimed Elise, smiling. " I do not regret his absence, I can assure you, since it has afforded me the pleasure of your lordship's company."

" A truce to compliments !" cried the impassioned youth. " Tell me seriously that I am not indifferent to you, and you will make me happy."

" If that assurance will render you happy, my lord," returned Elise, " you need not wait longer for your hoped-for happiness. We fulfil our relative positions to each other, by contributing to each other's happiness and pleasure."

" You shall be my tutoress in this philosophy," said Lord Clanrobert, smiling, and again shifting his chair nearer to that of the young Frenchwoman. " It must be even more pleasant than that which the old Grecian learned from the lips of Aspasia. If we had but such teachers of philosophy as you at Eton, what adepts we should all become !"

" Is it agreed that I should be your lordship's tutoress ?" asked Elise, turning all the seductive influence of her bright dark eyes upon the youth's impassioned countenance.

" By all means : I am impatient for the first lesson," returned Lord Clanrobert.

" At this hour of the night—or, rather, morning ?" said the young Frenchwoman, laughing.

" It is the hour of love, as it is of philosophic contemplation ; and the present opportunity is one which may not every day occur," rejoined the young noble, reading encouragement in the brilliant eyes of Elise.

" You plead so well, as to make me doubt whether you require my teaching," observed the French girl, laughing.

" Then I will be your tutor, according to the rules of Ovid," said Lord Clanrobert; and drawing close to the ex-nun of Louviers, he passed his arm round her waist, and pressed his lips upon her warm dark cheek.

The manner in which Elise received these freedoms convinced the youth of her character; and drawing his purse from his pocket, he thrust it into her bosom, while he again and repeatedly kissed her. The French girl knew for what purpose Simpson had left the young noble in her company; and, as it was now drawing near two o'clock in the morning, she rose from her chair, and taking up the candle, glanced invitingly at Lord Clanrobert, as she moved towards her chamber. The youth needed not a more explicit invitation; and while Bill Simpson reposed at a neighbouring tavern, his mistress and Lord Clanrobert lay folded in each other's arms.

We will now return to Sam Skelter, whom we left at the coffee-house in Catherine-street, which he quitted shortly after the departure of Frederick Shirley and Bill Simpson, and returned to his humble lodging in the salubrious locality of Clare-market. He had now been in the service of Mr. Ashley nearly two years, and was a tall, good-looking youth, with a peculiar *don't care-ish* expression of countenance, which agreed well with his free and easy manners, and a latent love of mischief which betrayed itself on every favourable occasion. He seemed to have a peculiar genius for practical joking, and, if he sometimes overstepped the strict boundaries of morality, it was more the ebullition of exuberant spirits than the evidence of a vicious inclination. He had never once revisited the purlieus of Wapping and Shadwell in quest of his reputed father, for the wooden-legged sailor had often told him that he was not his progenitor, and the manner in which they had parted left Sam no inclination to renew the acquaintance. The example of Frederick Shirley had not been without its influence upon young Skelter; for we scarcely need to remind the reader that, whether for good or for evil, example has greater inuflence over the minds of youth than precept and admonition, however frequently repeated. The man in whose company Shirley had seen him at the coffee-house in Catherine-street was one of the habitual visitors to the place, with whom Sam Skelter had casually become acquainted; but the youth was cognizant of his associate's true character, and would have scorned to acknowledge him as a friend. It was this which constituted the point in his character upon which hopes might be rested for the future; for, though not always acting either wisely or well, he had a correct perception of what he ought to do.

The same might perhaps be said of Frederick Shirley, but in him this perception was obscured by vanity, the pervading weakness of his character. He had not iron enough in his composition always to do right; he succumbed to opinion, to the opinion of those more reckless and profligate than himself, and had not moral strength sufficient to withstand the temptation to do wrong if his associates declared that it was right. His extravagant and profligate career had enstranged him from his relations, and the neglect of his duties, which was the consequence of that profligacy, had caused his dismissal by Mr. Ashley, as before mtioned. Then he became the habitual companion of those who had first led him into evil courses, and may be said to have taken a degree in the college of chicanery and fraud. The ex-clerk could not fail to see his position, and to know that he stood on the brink of a moral Rubicon, but he knew not how to retrace his steps. At this crisis his father came to his aid; on the morning after he had assisted Simpson and Fitzormond to victimize Lord Clanrobert, he received a letter from his father, informing him that if he would renounce, at once and for ever, all his vicious associates, and resolve to lead a more creditable life, a situation was ready for him at a rural station on the London and Birmingham railway, where he would be removed from the temptations and contaminating influences of the metropolis, and be enabled to retrieve his reputation.

The perusal of this letter excited the most serious and salutary reflections in the mind of Frederick Shirley, but a principle of honour, which in itself was admirable, caused him to hesitate before accepting his father's offer. His connection with Lolah Hastings had existed some time, and the attachment had become stronger on either side; yet he well knew that the young girl would come under his father's category of "vicious associates," and the principle of honour which dictated his hesitation. He handed his father's letter to his mistress without making any comment, and waited in silence for her observations.

Lolah laid down the letter with an air of embarrassment, after perusing it attentively, and for a few moments neither spoke; she felt a strong regard for Frederick Shirley, but she had never closed her eyes to the precarious nature of her position, and had never expected that their connection would be permanent.

"Would you advise me to accept my father's offer, Lolah?" inquired the ex-clerk, in a hesitating manner.

"Certainly, Frederick," she replied. "You cannot do better than take your father's advice."

"But the conditions, Lolah?" said he, with an air of embarrassment.

"Our separation is the implied condition of your father's offer," said the young girl, in a tremulous tone; "but do not let me stand in the way of your welfare and advancement."

"Noble girl!" murmured Frederick Shirley. "I shall leave you with regret, but I feel that it is the condition of my salvation."

They parted. Lolah shed a few tears when he had gone, but it was a change which she had always been prepared for, and had been expecting since the discharge of her lover from the office of Mr. Ashley. She strove to forget him, and through the instrumentality of the jackal, Fitzormond, who was informed of her position by Caroline Allen, she, in a few days afterwards, received and accepted an offer of protection from the Earl of Glenvale, an elderly nobleman, who had been for some years separated from his wife, and who gave Lolah a very handsome allowance.

CHAPTER XLIV.

ELLEN ASHLEY.

LET us now glance at the condition of poor little Ellen, the orphan daughter of Sir Norman Ashley, whose situation in the cottage of the peasant whose wife was to teach her the art of lace-making, was far from being an enviable one. The coarse manners of these poor and uneducated, though honest and well-meaning people, and the tedious and monotonous process of making lace by hand, could not but be repulsive to a child reared in the lap of luxury, and removed suddenly from the midst of all the refinements and elegancies of life, to all that poverty exhibits of ignorance, vulgarity, and repugnant toil. Not only was she made to work early and late in the manufacture of lace, but also to nurse the woman's child, and to assist in the household drudgery, like a veritable parish apprentice. Poor Ellen often sighed over her hard lot, often bedewed her pillow with her tears, and wept herself to sleep. Twelve months passed away, during which Ellen never saw her uncle or her aunt, nor received any intelligence of her brother; another year passed in like manner, and Ellen Ashley was now twelve years of age.

For several months Ellen had contemplated a flight from the peasant's cottage, her dwelling, but not her home, and had resolved to put her scheme into execution on the attainment of her twelfth year. That time had now arrived; and, without any other preparation for a journey of which she knew not the distance or the definite aim, than a consciousness of innocence and rectitude and confidence in herself, she left the village. It was a bright morning in early summer, when she left the cottage of the lace-makers, and rambled away she scarce knew whither; bees were humming from flower to flower, the gauze-winged butterflies were chasing each other along the flowery banks, and unseen minstrels warbled from every hedge and tree. Ellen left the village behind her; and as she increased her distance from the cottage, her spirits seemed gradually to recover the buoyancy and elasticity of earlier and happier days. She wandered through the meadows, the greenery of whose carpet of Nature's spreading was spangled with the yellow buttercups; and then the cool shade afforded by the spreading trees of a large wood tempted her to thread the narrow and

devious path that wound through it. The sunlight came subdued and softened
through the interlacing branches of the oak and the crab, from the verdant foliage
of which came clear and melodious notes of the goldfinch and the linnet; and
the ceaseless hum of summer insects seemed to fill the air with unseen music,
which a poetical imagination might have fancied the melody of the fairies.
But science has banished those tiny bright-winged creatures from all their old-
accustomed haunts, and the places that once knew them know them no more;
though, in remote parts of the rural districts, the elfin rings are still pointed out
on the grass, where the tiny people were wont to dance under the light of the
silver moon.

Ellen threaded the devious path through the wood, and emerged from its
shade into the flowery meadows on the other side, from whence the eye commanded an extensive and varied prospect, embracing woods, meadows, corn-
fields, and farm-houses, and in the distance the river Thames gliding through
the fertile plain, like a silver thread over a carpet of green velvet. Little Ellen
gazed a moment on the smiling landscape, and listened to the merriment of the

18

haymakers, and then continued her way. The last load of hay was leaving the field, and the labourers were shouting joyously, as if they had a direct interest in the success of their operations, a participation in the profits of the crop which their labour had produced; but they worked not for themselves—theirs was the labour, but the produce helped to enrich one who toiled not, but amassed wealth from the ill-requited labour of others. Unhappy labourers of England! when will ye learn to realize the text which says, in language not to be mistaken, " The labourer shall be the first partaker of the fruits thereof?" Take a lesson from the bees, the insect community which has solved instinctively the social problem of the organization of labour, the solution of which has yet to be worked out by the labourers of this and other countries; the glossy-winged denizens of the hive work for themselves, each for the whole, and the whole for each, the true formula of industrial association.

If Ellen Ashley had been asked where she was going, and how she intended to live, she would have been much puzzled to reply; but she had a vague idea of meeting with her brother, though for two years she had not seen him, or had any communication with him, the reason of which will appear hereafter. As evening came on, she began to feel both hungry and fatigued; and when darkness began to gather over the earth, she became impressed, for the first time, with a conviction of the difficulty and danger of the adventure upon which she was entering. She knew not whither she had wandered, and she began to comprehend the necessity of obtaining rest and shelter for the night; but she was fearful of being taken back to the cottage of the lace-maker, and this deterred her from applying for shelter at any of the farm-houses which she passed in her way. At length it became very dark, and poor Ellen crept into a cart which stood under a shed near a farm-house, and stretching her weary limbs on the straw which lay on the bottom of the cart, she fell into a profound sleep, in spite of the cravings of hunger and the strangeness of her situation.

When she awoke the sun was shining brightly, and hearing some rough voices in the farm-yard, she trembled lest she should be discovered, and suspected of some felonious design. But the voices were gradually lost in the distance as the men quitted the yard, and then she crept out of the cart, and stole timidly into the high road. She much wished to beg a cup of milk and a piece of bread of the farmer's wife, but she was afraid of being compelled to give an account of herself, and therefore went on her way. As she walked slowly along the road, she strove to reconcile herself to the humiliation of asking charity; but the idea of begging was repugnant to her mind, and, after much reflection, she determined upon trying to obtain a few pence by the exercise of her vocal abilities—that being the only mode of honourable subsistence which at the moment suggested itself to her mind. About noon, therefore, when she reached the next village, she placed herself in the centre of the street, and, after a pause of modest embarrassment, she sang the following stanzas in a soft and melodious voice:

" Oh! breathe not the names of the dead,
    Who responded to liberty's call,
For their country combatted, bled,
    And deemed it an honour to fall:
Oh, no! leave the patriot band
    To the silence and shade of the grave;
For tyranny hangs o'er the land,
    Like a pall o'er the true and the brave.

But when tyranny's knell shall ring out,
    And earth from its fetters upspring,
We will echo their names with a shout,
    And make it through palaces ring;
Then shall statues and monuments tell
    The names and the deeds of the brave,
And over the spot where they fell,
    The banner of liberty wave.''

Two or three halfpence were thrown into the road as Ellen concluded her song, which she picked up with a blush at the near alliance which her auditors appeared to think existed between her vocation and that of the mendicant, and then moved a little further up the street. Here she repeated her song, the only one she could think of at the time; and, having been rewarded with a few more pence, she went into a baker's shop, where she purchased a penny loaf, and begged a mug of water, by which she was considerably refreshed. When she had got out of the village, she went into a field, and sat down on the grass to rest herself; after which she took off her shoes and stockings, and having laved her tired feet in the clear stream which ran through the meadow, she put them on again, and continued her journey.

At the next village she repeated the patriotic melody which she had sung before; and, as the period of which we are now writing was during the reform agitation of 1832, the sentiments of the song found a response in every honest heart, and the pretty songstress obtained a largesse sufficient to pay for her lodging and her supper, at a little alehouse which she had reached late in the evening. She sang for her breakfast in the morning, and in the evening of that day, having gathered a few halfpence in a village which she had passed through in the afternoon, she sat down on a stile, and looked over the green meadows, through which the silver Thames meandered, in which the speckled trout were leaping in the fading twilight. While she thus sat she heard the noise of wheels coming slowly along the dusty road, and looking round, saw a cavalcade approaching, which appeared to be some travelling exhibition on its way to some country fair. The foremost vehicle was one of those perambulatory residences used by the proprietors of such exhibitions both as a house and a means of conveyance; the horse was led by a stout red-faced man in a velveteen jacket, and wearing a white hat; and behind the travelling abode of the proprietor came one of the caravans used by the keepers of itinerant menageries to contain their animals, and also to transport them from one place to another. By the side walked a young fellow in a brown smock frock, who appeared to be in the habit of sleeping with the horses, or perhaps under the caravan, if one might judge from the hay which clung to his bushy hair; a fierce-looking dog followed at his heels, and the cavalcade was closed by a platform on wheels, such as is used for the exterior stage of itinerant theatres and exhibitions, on which were packed the poles, canvass, lamps, and other properties used in the erection and decoration of the pavilion.

While Ellen was gazing with wonder and curiosity at this cavalcade, the red-faced man in the white hat looked earnestly at her for a moment, and then stopping his horse, the other vehicles coming to a stand at the same time, he walked up to her slowly, with his hands thrust to the bottoms of his pockets. At the same moment the door of the travelling abode, which was painted a bright yellow, was suddenly opened, and a gipsey-looking female countenance appeared, which, from the black velvet bonnet which surmounted it, seemed to belong to the proprietor's wife.

CHAPTER XLV.

THE SHOWMAN.

" Didn't I see you singing in the village yonder?" inquired the red-faced man, looking attentively at Ellen.

" Yes, sir," replied the young lace-maker, in a tremulous voice.

" You don't look as though you were accustomed to it, nayther," observed the man.

" Indeed, I am not, sir," returned Ellen.

" I thought as much," said the proprietor of the caravan; "and I dare say you would prefer riding along with my missus, to vagabondizing about the country by yourself. We are going to exhibit at the next village, and if you like to go with us, I will put you in a better way of living than singing ballads."

Ellen hesitated; there was an expression of good humour in the countenance of the red-faced man, which seemed to assure her that she might repose confidence in his promises, and yet she liked not to accept his offer, lest it should be no improvement upon her situation at the lace-maker's.

" What say you, my dear," said the man ; " will you travel with us, or shall we leave you on the road ? If you don't like our life, you can leave us at the next village, you know, and you will have had a lift for nothing."

" Besides seeing the hexibition," observed the woman, who was attentively regarding Ellen from the door of her perambulatory dwelling.

" I will go as far as the village with you," said the young lace-maker, rising from the stile ; " but I cannot promise to stay with you, until I know what you want me to do."

" Oh, there ain't much to do, my dear," returned the red-faced proprietor of the exhibition ; " so jump up, and my missus will tell you all what we want you to do."

The man assisted Ellen Ashley into the vehicle, where she was graciously received by the gipsey-looking woman in the black velvet bonnet, who invited her to take a cup of tea with her, an offer of which Ellen availed herself with joy. The cavalcade was again got into motion, and moved slowly on towards the village ; just as it started, a low sullen roar proceeded from the second caravan, which startled poor Ellen, and caused her to turn a glance of timid inquiry towards her companion.

" Don't be alarmed, my dear," said the lady in the velvet bonnet; "it is only the lion, who has been disturbed by the jolting of the caravan.

" The lion, ma'am !" exclaimed Ellen, with mingled fear and surprise.

" Yes, child," returned her companion ; and then setting down her cup, and spreading out her hands in an oratorical manner, she added : " This is an hex- ibition of the wonderful works of natur, and the power of man over the brute creation ; you will see the great Numidian lion, the royal Bengal tiger, and the spotted leopard from the Cape of Good Hope, all living in harmony together, and performing the most wonderful acts in obedience to the word of command. Also, the astonishing performances of that wonderful little girl, the Lion Queen, whose surprising power over the wild beasts of the forest is acknowledged, by all who have witnessed it, to be unsurpassed by any similar display ever ex- hibited before. That's you, my dear—you are to be the Lion Queen."

" Me, ma'am !—what shall I have to do?" exclaimed Ellen, in surprise.

" You will enter the cage of the wild beasts, and sit on the lion's back," replied the woman, coolly ; " but you need not be alarmed, my dear, for the creatures are quite tame, and the master will stand by, you know. We had a young girl as used to perform with the hanimals, and they was quite attached to her, but she took a fever somehow, and died five weeks ago, and we hasn't been able to replace her since. But you will do ad-mi-rably, and the beasts won't hurt you a bit, 'cause they are used to all that sort of thing."

In spite of the assurances of the proprietor's "missus," Ellen could not avoid feeling some degree of timidity at the idea of entering the cage containing the lion, tiger, and leopard, even though protected by the presence of the red-faced man in the velveteen coat. She made no objection, however, and the cavalcade proceeded along the dusty road to the village where it was intended to exhibit, previous to erecting the pavilion at another place a few miles distant, where a fair was to be held in a few days afterwards.

On arriving at their destination, the vehicles were drawn up on the little green, the stage facing the road, and the caravan containing the animals further back, with a space between them for the erection of seats for the spectators. A crowd of children gathered around, full of wonder and curiosity, and several gaping rustics stood about the green, endeavouring to peep through the canvass which covered the space between the stage and the caravan, and to read the bills pasted on the sides of the caravan, which set forth the wonderful character of the performances to be witnessed within. But it was not the intention of the proprietor to exhibit before the following evening, and on the next morning Ellen Ashley was introduced to the animals for a preliminary rehearsal. The side of the cage which faced the spectators was moveable, there being on the inside a strong grating of iron rods, before which hung a curtain of green baize. Ellen was dressed in a short-skirted frock of spangled muslin, with a gilt tiara on her head, the costume in which she was to appear in public being given her for the rehearsal, that the animals might become accustomed to her ap- pearance.

Taking a short whip in his hand, loaded at the end with lead, the red-faced man cautiously opened a door in the end of the cage, and glided in ; a low growl was heard, which made Ellen tremble, followed by the dull heavy tread of the animals as they paced round their cage. The door was then again opened, and the red-faced man held out his hand to assist Ellen to enter the cage, while he extended the whip to the animals, who were grouped together at the farther end. Ellen trembled as she entered the cage, but the wild beasts made no attempt to molest her, and the presence of the proprietor seemed to assure her of safety.

"Don't be afraid of 'em," said the latter; "they are as docile as so many cats. Come here, sir !"

This was addressed to the lion, a noble animal of the black-maned variety, who immediately approached him, and crouched down at his feet. He then desired Ellen to sit down, and rest her head on the lion's shaggy mane, but it was only after repeated assurances as to the animal's docility that she could be prevailed upon to do so. She obeyed at last, with fear and trembling, but the quiet forbearance of the lion inspired her with more confidence than the assurance of its master. She felt considerably relieved, however, when the red-faced man told her to rise; and the lion having risen at the same time, she was next desired to sit upon his back, and was borne round the cage by the noble and docile beast. She was next required to test the docility of the tiger and the leopard in the same manner, but quitted the cage, followed by the man in the white hat, who went backward with his eyes fixed on the animals whose natural ferocity he had so far succeeded in subduing.

In the evening steps were placed in the front of the platform, and the large paintings, which represented the nature of the exhibition within, were unrolled to the admiring eyes of the gaping rustics, who gazed with wonder on the lions, tigers, and leopards there represented in every imaginable attitude. The red-faced man then began vigorously beating a large drum, while his wife planted herself near the entrance to receive money, and Ellen Ashley beat time with her pretty feet, and attracted the admiration of all the youthful peasants. As soon as the canvass pavilion was filled with spectators, the red-faced man and Ellen Ashley left the platform, and disappeared behind the curtain of green-baize which was drawn in front of the caravan containing the animals.

Presently a bell tinkled, the curtain drew up, and the showman appeared in the midst of the wild beasts—the lion crouching at his feet, the tiger standing up, with his paws on the man's breast, and the leopard seated on his shoulders. When the applause of the spectators had subsided, the tiger and leopard dropped to the floor of their cage, and the showman proceeded to display their docility by making them leap through hoops and over his whip, after which he opened the lion's jaws, and put his head between them. Then Ellen Ashley entered the cage, not without trepidation, notwithstanding the rehearsal of the morning, and, after bowing to the spectators, laid down with the lion, resting her head upon his mane. Then rising slowly from her recumbent position, the lion rose in obedience to a motion of the showman's whip, and Ellen seated herself on his back, and rode round the cage, amid the enthusiastic applause of the spectators. The bell tinkled again, the curtain fell, and Ellen was glad to escape from a situation that was not entirely free from danger.

On the following morning the canvass pavilion was taken down, and the establishment was removed to the village where the fair was to be held in a few days, and which was situated in the vicinity of Eton—the party having crossed the Thames in their route, and entered Berkshire. Ellen knew that her cousin Edward, who was now about seventeen years of age, was receiving his education at Eton-college, and the reflections which the contrast between her past and present prospects and position excited in her mind, rendered her for the time dissatisfied and unhappy. On the evening before the first day of the fair, she strolled into the fields, and sitting on a stile which commanded a view of the more distant towers of Windsor Castle, the lines of Gray immediately recurred to her memory:

" Ye distant spires, ye antique towers,
    That crown the watery glade,

> Where grateful Science still adores
> 	Her Henry's holy shade ;
> And ye that, from the stately brow
> Of Windsor's heights, the expanse below
> 	Of grove, of lawn, of mead survey,
> Whose turf, whose shade, whose flowers among,
> Wanders the hoary Thames along
> 	His silver-winding way."

As she repeated the last line, she heard footsteps approaching the spot where she sat ; and her cousin Edward passed, accompanied by another of the collegians : he stared rudely at Ellen, and walked on without deigning to appear to recognise her. Ellen was not sorry that he had chosen this conduct ; for there was a proud independence in her heart that would have rebelled against the condescension by which his manner would have probably been marked had he spoken, and which would have been more humiliating to the orphan-girl than his cold neglect of their near relationship.

CHAPTER XLVI.

THE PROPHECY.

ELLEN ASHLEY saw her cousin no more during the time that the exhibition remained in the neighbourhood of Eton ; she knew that her uncle would thus become acquainted with her singular mode of life, but she did not anticipate that he would institute any search after her, with the view of compelling her to return to the servitude and monotonous toil of the lace-maker's cottage. She became daily more familiar with the animals, and evinced less timidity in her performance with them ; while the lion, in particular, became as much attached to her as a favourite dog to its mistress. In this manner she roved about the counties of Berks, Oxon, and Bucks, during the delightful summer months ; and then passing from town to town, and from village to village, in the western part of Surrey, the exhibition at length arrived at Wandsworth, on the eve of the annual fair. While the red-faced man and his assistant were erecting the canvass pavilion for the exhibition of the following day, Ellen Ashley quitted the town, and walked a little distance along the banks of the Wandle, a tributary stream which has its source near Croydon, and, after serving several mills and factories during its course, at this point swells the mighty waters of Old Father Thames.

The twilight was beginning to fade into darkness when Ellen left the footpath by the side of the river, on which were several boats and barges, and turned into the fields which intervene between the town and the furze-covered breadth of Wandsworth-common. She had not got far, stopping now and then to pick some pretty wild-flower, or to listen to the vesper hymn of the soaring lark, when two young men leaped over the stile, and walked hastily across the meadows. They were well dressed, and were conversing in hurried tones, though their manner and looks betrayed a deep and earnest excitement.

" You have calculated the time, you say ? Well, the result ?" exclaimed one of the young men, eagerly.

" Exactly twenty minutes and five seconds after nine," replied the other, solemnly.

" My own calculation, exactly, except the seconds !" cried the first speaker, with a start ; while his companion clasped his hands in an excited manner. " And at that moment the earth will be exactly at that point in its orbit which the comet will cross in its fiery path."

" What a strange and terrible coincidence !" said the other, shuddering. " Contact is inevitable ; and how awful the reflection that, in a single moment, our planet may become a wreck, and every living soul be hurried into eternity !"

" The man's strange eloquence moved me when first I heard him," observed his companion. " His long white hair, flowing wildly upon his shoulders, the light in his keen orbs, and his fervid and impassioned oratory, make him appear like a prophet of the olden time, speaking from the inspiration of the Eternal. For more than fifteen years he has travelled from place to place, preaching everywhere that the last day was approaching, and exhorting all to penitence and self-denial. Several years ago, he prophesied that the earth would be destroyed at the passing of Beila's comet over our planet's orbit, and now we are within an hour of the awful moment."

"How close the air is," observed the other, speaking in a husky voice, and glancing uneasily across the meadows.

"It feels hot and oppressive as the breath of a furnace," returned the first speaker. "Look at the sky, too; see the purple and copperish hues that pervade it; it has quite a metallic appearance; and even the birds have ceased to sing, as if they had a presentiment of the approaching destruction."

"See that crowd upon the common!" exclaimed the other young man, in an excited tone. "So numerous, and yet so silent, as if impressed with awe! Hark, some one is addressing them—'tis the Prophet!—'tis Robert Ashdowne! Let us hear him."

Ellen Ashley had not heard the latter part of their conversation, but, having followed them through the meadows, she saw them run towards the common, and then beheld a large concourse of people of all classes, who appeared to be listening with eager attention to the address of a venerable old man, with long white hair, who was elevated on a temporary rostrum on the edge of the gorsy common. The two young men ran forward to hear the discourse of the Mad Parson; and Ellen also drew near the assemblage, attracted by the rhapsodic manner of the preacher.

"Use well the last brief moments of grace that yet remain to the unrepentant, for an hour hence will be too late," said he, in a tone of fervour and solemnity, which was, undoubtedly, sincere, however erroneous his views and misdirected his zeal. "Even while I now speak, the fiery harbinger of destruction is rapidly nearing our globe, and the awful moment of contact is at hand; the eternal sun has set for the last time upon our planet, and, to all who dwell thereon, time will soon have merged into eternity. What an awful reflection to those who have not yet repented of their sins, and thus made themselves meet to enter the pale of grace! Consider that, before the next half-hour shall have passed away, the comet, which you may all have seen glowing athwart the sky, will have come in actual contact with this green and fertile earth, upon which we have our being; and the dreaded concussion will cause mountains to split in twain, the earth to yawn and gape, the sea to forsake its bed, and the volcanoes to belch forth fiery ruin upon the desolate earth."

"Shall not a remnant be saved? Shall the righteous perish even as the ungodly?" asked a young man near the preacher, whose pale face and trembling voice bespoke his fears.

"Not one!" replied the Prophet, solemnly. "None shall survive in mortal form, but heaven's lightnings and the pealing thunder shall usher all to judgment; and then the sheep to the right hand, and the goats to the left."

While he was yet speaking, the hour of nine struck from the clock of Wandsworth church, and every countenance in the throng was pale with fear; even those who had disregarded the prophecy of the Mad Parson, and ridiculed the fears of their awe-stricken companions, could not repress the vague terrors that stole imperceptibly upon them, in spite of their avowed incredulity.

"Repent! repent! for you have heard the sound of the church-clock for the last time!" cried the Prophet. "In twenty minutes all will be over, and the solid globe will be whirled through the boundless fields of space a blazing wreck!"

At this terrific announcement, the two young men, who had crossed the meadows before Ellen Ashley, looked at each other, as they noticed the extraordinary coincidence which was manifest in the calculations made by three different persons in separate places, as to the precise time when the comet, which had been for several days visible, would cross the orbit of the earth in its course.

"The sign has been hung out night after night in the heavens, the book of Jehovah's own writing, so plain that all may read, and yet how few there are that are truly penitent!" continued the Mad Parson. "Was not this day foretold by the apostle as coming upon the world like a thief in the night, when the mountains shall be thrown down, and the rocks shall be melted with fervent heat? What means this solemn stillness of nature, but the lull before the coming storm? and what is this oppressive atmosphere, but the prelude of the fiery ruin which will speedily overwhelm the globe? Woe to those who have not repented of their iniquities! woe to the oppressor of the fatherless and the widow! woe to those who have grown rich upon the sufferings of the poor!"

As the preacher uttered these denunciations, the sky, which had been growing more and more overcast since he commenced his discourse, became ominously dark with the metallic hues observed by the young men who had calculated the period of the comet's transit over the earth's orbit; and just as he uttered the last words, a low and distant peal of thunder rattled along the horizon. Many a cheek grew pale at this herald of elementary wrath; and some of the most timid fell on their knees in anticipation of the awful moment.

"God speaks in thunder!" said the Prophet, in an impressive tone. "Let us kneel down and await in prayer the final accomplishment of his will."

At that moment a vivid flash of lightning streamed from the murky clouds, followed by a burst of thunder, so loud that the earth seemed to quiver as if the circumambient atmosphere was violently agitated. The females who were present screamed, and the whole assemblage fell upon their knees; the lightning making their pale countenances as ghastly as those of the dead. Impelled less by the prophecy of the Mad Parson than by apprehension of being overtaken by the coming storm, Ellen Ashley sped across the meadows towards Wandsworth; and the two young men who had preceded her to the common took out their watches to note the time. It wanted but five minutes to the time which the Mad Parson's prediction and their own calculations had fixed as the exact moment when the earth would be destroyed by coming in forcible contact with the comet.

Again the electric fluid flashed from the black and threatening clouds, followed by a peal of thunder like the booming of heavy ordnance; and as the affrighted wretches on the common stole a timid glance around, a red flame shot up in the distance, waving about like the forked tongues of a legion of fiery dragons. The awe and terror inspired by the fearful prophecy of the Mad Parson had now reached its height; and all who heard the pealing artillery of heaven, and saw the lightning and the distant blaze, believed that their last moment had arrived, and that the globe was already in the throes of dissolution. Some threw themselves prostrate on the ground, some raised their hands to the threatening sky and prayed aloud; several women fainted, and Robert Ashdowne believed that his prophecy was on the point of fulfilment.

The red glare in the distance continued to increase in extent and brilliancy, until it illuminated the whole horizon in that direction with its lurid glow; and the lightning still continued to stream from the murky clouds, and the thunder to roar as if earth and heaven were about to meet. Robert Ashdowne prayed fervently; and all the assemblage remained on their knees, expecting every moment would be their last. Presently several heavy drops of rain fell; and in a few moments a deluge of water descended from the overladen clouds, wetting every one present to the skin. Still they remained on their knees—still the lightning flashed and the thunder rolled, and still the flames arose in the distance like a fiery curtain.

At length the elementary warfare ceased, and one of the young men who had calculated the time of the comet's transit looked again at his watch: it was half-past nine; and with a feeling of reawakened hope, he showed it to his companion. The latter started: a faint flush, as of new life, appeared in his pale cheeks; and he drew from his pocket a clasped note-book. Hastily turning over the leaves, he came to one covered with figures, which he conned with keen attention. After a few minutes' earnest study of his astronomical calculations, he seemed to have made some discovery; for he rose from the ground, and after gazing a moment at the distant fire, which was now considerably diminished, he drew a long breath, and wiped the perspiration from his pale

brow. He had made an error of a month in his calculations; for though the comet had really crossed the earth's orbit at the time given in his table, our globe was not due at the same point until a month later.*

He immediately communicated his discovery to his companion, who was for a moment astounded at the error into which both had fallen in their calculations; but when he was convinced that they really had committed the same mistake, he took to his heels, followed by his fellow votary of science. This movement caused many of the trembling and dripping audience to look about them, and finding that the brilliant flame had subsided into a dull red glow, they ventured to rise; others followed their example, and the panic having gradually subsided, the crowd rapidly dispersed for shelter from the pouring rain, the mad parson

* In 1832, Beila's comet passed through the earth's path about a month before the arrival of our planet at the same point. In the opinion of many eminent astronomers, if the earth had been a month earlier at that point, or the comet a month later in crossing it, the two bodies would have come in contact, in which case they suppose that the earth would instantly have been rendered unfit for the existence of the human family.

having already disappeared from the spot which had just before been the scene of so strange an exhibition of religious fervour.

CHAPTER XLVII.

THE ACCIDENT.

As Ellen Ashley sped across the meadows towards Wandsworth, to seek the shelter of the caravan in the fair from the coming storm, two vivid flashes of lightning gleamed from the dark clouds that were piled overhead, followed by peals of the loudest thunder she had ever heard, and then she beheld the red flame rising into the air amid the darkness which overspread the earth, which had so stricken the panic-stricken spectators on the common. Though not imbued with the feelings of those whom she had left behind, most of whom had heard the warnings and exhortations of the mad parson on previous occasions, she became frightened by the electric flashes and the peals of thunder which succeeded them, and gazed with mingled curiosity and alarm at the red glow which hung over that part of the town in which the fair is held.

Flash succeeded flash as Ellen ran quickly along, the thunder rolled incessantly, and before she reached the town the rain poured down in torrents; but she perceived that the flame arose from the quarter of the fair in which the establishment with which she was connected was situated, and a presentiment of evil crossed her mind; she ran swiftly towards it, and arrived at the spot drenched through all her clothes by the pouring rain. She found the town in a state of excitement and consternation, and the reports which were repeated in accents of alarm, informed her that the pavilion of the red-faced showman had been fired by lightning, and that the wild beasts had effected their escape. In the neighbourhood of the fair the affrighted people were running wildly in all directions, tumbling over each other in their eagerness to escape from the scene of danger, and parents were inquiring anxiously for their children. The electric fluid had struck the caravan containing the trained animals, and also the proprietor, who was standing in the canvass pavilion, and fell dead instantaneously; the caravan immediately broke into a blaze, and the roarings of the terrified animals were fearful to hear. The showman's assistant hastened to extinguish the flames, but the bystanders were afraid to approach the caravan, and the flames spreading rapidly, he was seized with a sudden panic, and fled. The police hastened to the spot, and, impressed with the danger which might attend the escape of the animals, endeavoured to extinguish the flames, while some of the bystanders ran for the fire-engine; but before it arrived, the affrighted animals, maddened by the appearance of the flames, dashed themselves against the side of their cage, which being partly consumed gave way, and, with a terrific roar, the three animals sprang out.

Then commenced a scene of the wildest confusion; the groups of people scattered about the fair fled in all directions, and the women and children ran screaming into the nearest houses. The liberated lion bounded through the affrighted people without attempting to injure any one, and then walked gravely through the streets, the inhabitants hastily closing their doors, and the children running hither and thither for safety. The leopard darted up a bye-street, and made for the fields; and the tiger rushed at once into a shop, the door of which was open, and laid down under the counter, as if under the influence of an absorbing terror.

Scarcely had Ellen Ashley been informed of the cause of the conflagration, and the alarm which prevailed around the fair, than the lion was seen walking leisurely up the street, and the bystanders fled precipitately, or took refuge in the houses. Ellen was startled for a moment by the appearance of the lion, but the pacific manner in which the noble animal walked up the street, and the influence which she was accustomed to exercise over him, emboldened her to attempt his capture. She waited quietly for the approach of the formidable quadruped, and when he came near her, she called him; the lion recognised the voice of the courageous girl, and came towards her, holding down his head, and wagging his tail like an attached dog. The people gazed at her from their windows in wonder and admiration, though they trembled for her safety, until they saw her seize the lion's shaggy mane, and lead him along the street. Ellen feared to conduct him back to the fire to look for the showman and his assistant, and she knew not where to lodge her formidable charge for present security. At this juncture, two policemen came up, and, seeing how quietly the lion was following his lovely conductress, they recommended her to cage him for the present in some outhouse, and with their assistance the animal was safely housed in the coach-house of a neighbouring inn.

Ellen then made inquiries respecting the tiger and the leopard, and went to the house where the former had taken refuge, to the great dismay of the occupants, who had secured the inner door, and retreated up-stairs. The shop-door having been closed, the tiger was to a certain extent secured, and Ellen was afraid to venture into the shop; she therefore proceeded to the pavilion, which was totally destroyed, together with the platform and the caravan which had contained the animals. The wife of the proprietor was inconsolable for the loss of her husband and the destruction of their property, and the driver of the caravans, panic-stricken by the accident, had not yet returned to the scene of the conflagration. The caravan in which the exhibitors lived had been saved by drawing it away, and the fire had now partially burned itself out. Ellen repaired again to the house in which the tiger had been entrapped, and which was surrounded by a great number of people, some of whom were recommending that the animal should be shot.

This, however, was no easy matter, for the tiger was crouched under the counter, and could not be seen; at last it was proposed that a hole should be made in the wall, through which a gun might be discharged until he was killed. This advice was no sooner given than acted upon; a hole was made below the shop-window, and an adventurous butcher stepped forward with a fowling-piece to despatch the animal. Having peeped through the hole, he reported that the tiger was lying down, with his ears laid down, as if frightened; he then thrust the muzzle through the orifice, and fired.

A low, savage growl, a fearful crash of glass, and the infuriated tiger dashed through the window into the midst of the throng of people who had congregated in the street. The butcher was, for a moment, electrified—for the tiger had leaped over him—but quickly recovering his presence of mind, he reloaded his gun, and started off in pursuit. The crowd made way for the enraged animal, no one caring to dispute precedence with so formidable an adversary, and the tiger bounded along the street. A gentleman on horseback at that moment turned the corner of a bye-street, and before he could check his horse's speed, the tiger sprang furiously at them, and fastened his white teeth in the steed's throat, while he lacerated his chest with his powerful talons.

The rider threw himself from the saddle, and sought safety in flight; and the horse reared up and plunged violently in his endeavours to shake off his savage assailant. The butcher fired a second time at the tiger, and the ball struck him on the hind-leg; he did not loose his hold on the throat of the bleeding and terrified horse, and, owing to their struggle, it was impossible to take an aim. Several shots were now fired from the neighbouring windows, and both the horse and the tiger were wounded by these discharges; the butcher continued to load and fire, and at length lodged a ball in the tiger's neck. The latter immediately abandoned the vanquished and prostrate steed, and couched for a spring at his armed assailant, but a gush of blood came from his mouth, and he fell down; the butcher then advanced a few paces, and terminated his existence by shooting him through the head.

A well-armed party then started in pursuit of the leopard, which had dashed up a bye-street immediately he had leaped from the burning caravan, and had escaped into the fields. The rain had entirely ceased, but the night was quite dark, so that after a long and fruitless search the chase was given up until the next morning, when the hunters started off as soon as the sun had risen. After a search of nearly three hours they found foot-prints in some wet clay, which, from their size and form, could only be those of the leopard, but they could only be traced for a short distance. They were sufficient, however, to indicate the direction in which the leopard had gone, and while crossing a field in the neighbourhood of Battersea, they were startled by a low, sullen growl, proceeding from the ditch, which was wide and deep, and overgrown with brambles. This induced some of the party to fall to the rear, and the more courageous hunters, who remained foremost, to look keenly through the bushes, which were agitated in a manner which showed that the leopard was crawling along the ditch under cover of the brambles. One of the party then fired at random into the ditch, to drive the animal into the open field, but the shot had not that effect; a deep, wrathful growl was heard, and, thinking that the leopard had been wounded, the party drew nearer to the spot where he lay crouching in the bushes.

"There he is!" said the butcher, preparing to fire. "I can just see his head through the brambles, and his eyes gleam like a cat's in a dark cellar."

" He had scarcely spoken when the leopard darted suddenly from the ditch, and fastening on his shoulder, dragged him to the ground. The butcher attempted to grasp the infuriated beast by the throat, but, failing in this, he drew a large knife, which opened with a spring, and aimed furious blows at the animal's head. The rest of the party were afraid to fire, for fear of wounding their companion, so rapidly did the leopard and his human opponent change places in their fearful struggle. Though severely lacerated by the animal's claws, the butcher defended himself with such vigour and resolution, that the leopard became exhausted from loss of blood, the knife of the desperate man having inflicted frightful wounds about the animal's throat and head, and at length he decided the conflict by getting the leopard undermost, and plunging the weapon into his heart.

The butcher rose from the ground covered with blood, and so much injured that he had to be carried home on a hurdle by his companions; none of his wounds were serious, however, his vigorous resistance having prevented the leopard from using his teeth; and though the effusion of blood was considerable, he soon recovered from the effects of the deadly struggle.

CHAPTER XLVIII.

THE WANDERER.

ELLEN'S vocation as a performer with the trained animals was now gone, and the following day found her a wanderer on the road to London, with no other means of subsistence than that afforded by the exercise of her vocal abilities in the streets and tap-rooms of the metropolis. Onward she went, through the suburb of Vauxhall and through Lambeth, in the old dungeons of whose archiepiscopal palace the Lollards were imprisoned for that which bigots call heresy—the iron rings and staples in the massive walls still remaining in grim mockery of the wisdom and mercy of our ancestors—through the narrow streets of Stangate, and, passing the foot of Westminster-bridge, along the wharves and stairs of Bankside. Despite her destitute condition, she gazed with pleasure on the sunny river, from whose broad expanse came a fresh breeze, mitigating the heat of a July sun, while its pleasant coolness was apparently enhanced by the gentle dashing of the wavelets against the floating timber, and against the boats and barges moored off the various wharves. Steamers were passing up and down the river, their decks crowded with passengers clad in their holiday attire, and bound on a trip of pleasure to Richmond or Greenwich; and barges and lighters were impelled lazily along, their owners resting on their oars to wipe the perspiration from their heated brows, and gaze after the passing steamers as they glided up and down.

Ellen stopped once or twice and essayed her vocal powers in the narrow streets which lie on either side of the Southwark-bridge-road, but her melody was unheeded; and the public-houses were almost deserted, for it was afternoon, and the mechanics, artizans and labourers of the district were at their employment, and those who had none were grouped at the corners of the streets in sullen or listless apathy, or were vainly going the round of the employers in their various branches of industry, seeking leave to toil, that they might no longer be dependent upon their fellow-workmen, or the cold charity of the relieving officer.

She crossed London-bridge; and glancing up at the tall Monument which commemorates that terrible fire which destroyed the houses which formerly stood upon that bridge, and nearly all the city besides, she wandered mechanically into Upper Thames-street, and thence into Earl-street, blocked up as usual with the black waggons engaged in conveying coal from the numerous wharves along the shore of Blackfriars. On reaching the unsightly structure which spans the river at this point, and is named after the monastery which formerly stood in its vicinity, the girl turned towards Fleet-street, and traversed that crowded thoroughfare to its termination at Temple-bar.

Evening was now drawing on, and the young wanderer began to feel fatigued as well as hungry; she stopped to look at the windows of the pastry-cooks' shops, the ham and beef warehouses, and the eating-houses; but the savoury edibles there displayed only sharpened her appetite; and she walked slowly on along the Strand, wondering if any of the ladies and well-dressed men who passed her would give her a penny, if they knew how hungry she was. She turned out of the Strand into the streets which formerly constituted the sanctuary of Whitefriars, the refuge of criminals flying from justice, and debtors who sought to avoid the sheriff, and where stood the palace of Savoy, which was sacked by the insurgents in the famous insurrection of Wat Tyler. Here stood, at a later date, the palace-like residence of the profligate Duke of Buckingham, the companion of the equally-profligate Charles II., and the mansions of many others of the chief nobility, whose gardens extended to the noble river, and whose sites are now known only by the streets which still bear their names.

She entered the tap-room of a tavern near the river-side, which was filled with coal-heavers, porters, and carters; and here she sang a song, which was rewarded with a few halfpence; and she was about to commence another song, when she was seized in a rude manner by one of her auditors, and, breaking from him, ran into the street. Fearing that her half-drunken admirer might follow her, she hurried away from the neighbourhood, and, in a few minutes, found herself in Parliament-street. She walked past the government-offices at Whitehall, formerly the palace of a king, and afterwards the place of his execution, and, passing through the frowning portal of the Horse-guards, she entered St. James's-park. She had purchased some bread and cheese before leaving the precincts of Whitefriars, and, sitting down on one of the seats, under the shade of the spreading trees, she took it from her pocket, and proceeded to appease her hunger.

There were many people walking about the park for recreation and pleasure: decent mechanics, who had brought their children to inhale a breath of purer air than could be enjoyed in the purlieus of St. Giles or the pestiferous region behind the venerable abbey of Westminster, ladies hanging on the arms of military officers, nursemaids with their young charges, and deluded girls listening to the false vows of private soldiers in the Life-guards or the Blues. Among the loungers were two young men, well but plainly dressed, whose quiet, unobtrusive manners formed a pleasing contrast to the flippancy and swagger which characterised the behaviour of the moustached officers. They both wore their shirt-collars turned over their black-silk neckerchiefs, showing that they agreed with Byron, Shelley, Klopstock, and the chief genii of this and other countries, in their repudiation of the stiff semi-military cravat; and there was an air of intellectual nobility in their high, expansive foreheads, which declared them to be men of cultivated minds and refined tastes. Lavater would have announced them at once as artists or poets; and the conjecture would have been correct: they were young professors of the sister arts of painting and sculpture.

"What a beautiful countenance!" said one of them to the other, as they observed Ellen Ashley seated on the bench. "What a face for a St. Cecilia! Note her figure, too; she is symmetry herself!"

"She is, indeed!" returned the other, pausing a moment to look at the object of their joint admiration. "What a study she would be for my Ariadne!"

Ellen had heard the last words of the admiring sculptor; and, as she looked up with a slight blush at the encomiums passed upon her loveliness, she looked more beautiful than before. The two young men continued their walk and their discussion on the relative merits of Raphael and Titian; and the fading twilight admonished Ellen that she was destitute of the means of procuring a lodging for the night. She rose from the bench upon which she was sitting, and, after walking a short distance, irresolute as to what course to adopt, she perceived a gentleman approaching, wearing a long dark cloak. By his cloak and his moustaches, joined to a certain martial bearing and gait, Ellen judged him to be an officer of the household troops, and resolved to ask charity, which she did, in a modest and timid manner, stating to him the complete destitution of her situation.

"Alas! my child, you implore charity of one as poor as yourself," exclaimed the cloaked individual, with a foreign accent. "Behold these rags!" and, unfolding his cloak, he disclosed a tattered military suit, and a pair of green trousers in the same condition. "Do I look as if I possessed aught to bestow in charity?" he continued, with something of bitterness in his tone. "But I can show you a better lodging than you will be likely to find in the streets. Come with me. Fear nothing from me," he continued, seeing that Ellen hesitated to follow him. "I received this wound in defending a young girl, like you, from the brutality of a Russian soldier, when Warsaw was given up to the hirelings of Nicholas, and the land of my birth was blotted from the map of European nations."

The stranger opened his tattered coat, and showed a deep scar upon his breast. Ellen concluded, from his remarks, that he was a Polish refugee, and she followed him in silence to the trees near the palace, where she found a number of other unfortunates sitting and lying upon the ground.

"Here I have bivouacked all the summer," said the Pole; "but I have done so before, in front of the enemy, on the banks of the Vistula; and you are not so used to it. Take the corner of my cloak to wrap yourself in."

Ellen availed herself of the offer, for which she thanked the houseless patriot; and, feeling the presence of others, many of them females, as a protection against insult or outrage, she laid down to sleep beneath one of the spreading trees. At that moment, a burst of music came from the neighbouring palace, where William IV. that evening entertained his ministers and the foreign plenipotentiaries, forming a strange contrast to the destitution that huddled beneath the trees for shelter, and a striking commentary upon the blessings which our monarchical constitution bestows upon those who have the supreme happiness to dwell beneath its shadow.

"Hark!" said the Polish refugee; "in yonder banqetting-hall, Lieven, and Bulow, and Esterhazy sit at the table of the King of England, as the representatives of the powers who have destroyed my native country; and yet ministers talk of their sympathies for Poland! Ay, they will remonstrate, and protest, and negociate; but will words, spoken or written, restore my country to her place among the nations? Napoleon would have expressed his sympathy with a pen of steel, and in characters of blood; but the policy of the present is peace: peace, though the people perish for lack of food—peace, while a nation's blood is wrung from her vitals by a despot's grasp!"

He spoke with bitterness, and with the flush of indignation upon his dark countenance; then he recollected that his listeners were harmless outcasts, knowing little of what he spoke, and he laid down beneath the tree, and was soon asleep.

CHAPTER XLIX.

GRAVESEND.

Young Ashley had now been more than twelvemonths in the employment of Sam Shrimp, and in all that time he had had no communication with his sister; and, though he had written to his uncle concerning her welfare, he could obtain no satisfactory information respecting her situation. Spring came again, with its sunshine and flowers and green leaves, and Norman felt more discontented than ever with his situation in life, and more than ever resolved to emancipate himself on the earliest opportunity.

One Saturday evening he entered the parlour of the "Compasses," in Bath-street, which was filled with sailors, fishermen, and women of the town, all talking loudly, smoking, and drinking. There were also one or two peripatetic vendors of oranges and chesnuts, an old pilot with spiral curls of grey hair, and a young fellow who was drinking rum-and-water with some sailors, and appeared to be assiduously endeavouring to insinuate himself into the confidence of the open-hearted fellows. He wore a low-crowned oilskin hat, auburn curls of the cork-screw kind, made with a heated tobacco-pipe, blue jacket, striped shirt, and loose white duck trowsers. He had large blue eyes, and a countenance very much freckled, and interlarded his conversation, of which he appeared to possess an inexhaustible fund, with nautical phrases and allusions, to induce a belief in the minds of his auditors that he had followed the profession of the sea from his childhood. But in reality he was one of those cormorants who prey upon the proverbial generosity and simplicity of our merchant-seamen—a character often to be met with about Wapping, and known by the generic term of "alongshore sailors." These land-sharks are a species of amphibious mags-men, whose qualifications consist of a stock of nautical phrases, soon picked up in the company of sailors, the ability to dance a naval hornpipe and sing a nautical song, and a glib fluency of discourse and insinuating address. These qualifications were possessed in abundance by the fellow whom we have here introduced to the reader, and by their aid he managed to live in idleness and dissipation; but, being in danger of an arrest for robbing a sailor at a disreputable house in Old Gravel-lane, he judged it prudent to decamp from that neighbourhood, and take a trip to Gravesend for the benefit of his health.

Sitting at the same table was a girl, about eighteen years of age, with a narrow band of velvet across her forehead, no bonnet, a row of large coral beads round her neck, and a large shawl enveloping her body, but thrown off the shoulders, and the corsage of her dress so low as to display no small proportion of her maturely-developed bust—a style of costume which is now considered immodest, though it was fashionable a century and a half ago, modesty appearing to the worshippers of convention as a thing dependent on time and place, and not as a fixed principle of conduct. Her dark hair, smooth and shining, was arranged in plain bands, coming down upon the brown cheeks of the young girl; her dark hazel eyes roved wantonly from one to another of the sailors, and her figure was short, and more famed for plumpness than symmetry.

"I thought Ned Shrimp was here," said Norman Ashley, glancing round the room, and speaking to a young fisherman whom he knew.

"He's up at the Fisherman's Arms," returned the man, exhaling a huge cloud of tobacco-smoke.

"Won't you sit down, young man? there is plenty of room," said the syren just described, leering at the handsome youth, and making room for him by her side.

All young Ashley's bashfulness, if ever he had any, had long worn off by association with the mixed society which necessarily forms the company even of taverns which aspire to be thought respectable; so he accepted the syren's invitation to sit by her side, and called for a glass of rum and water.

"Will you have a cigar, Ashley?" said a young man dressed as a sailor, whom he was slightly acquainted with; and he accepted the proffered luxury, the other holding out to him a dozen to select from, which he took from the pocket of his blue jacket, where he seemed to carry them loose.

Norman Ashley raised the steaming liquor to his lips, and having drank, passed the glass along the table to the frail young woman; he then lit his Havannah, and enveloped himself in a cloud of fragrant smoke.

"Do you know that young man?" the girl whispered to Norman, alluding to the man who had given him the cigar.

"Slightly; who is he?" rejoined the young fisherman.

"His name is Corbet—he is a smuggler," replied the girl, in the same mysterious whisper as before.

"Well, lads," said the land-shark, "let's splice the mainbrace, and drink a fair cruise to the bark *Astrea*. That reminds me," he continued, setting down the glass, "that the first voyage I ever made was in a bit of a coaster called the *Astrea;* she used to run between London and Whitby, and I'll tell you a circumstance that took place on that very voyage. We were lying in Yarmouth-roads, bound for the London-river, and it was just daybreak in the morning, when the skipper comes on deck, and sees a light collier coming from the nor'ard, spanking along with all her canvass spread. She was bearing right down upon us, and our skipper sings out: ' Hard a-port! or you will be over us!' but the words were hardly out of his mouth, before the collier runs into us, and damages our starn. The skipper began to storm and swear, and the master of the collier pops his head over the side, and says, drily: ' Eh, mon, ye're sae smaal, I couldna see ye.' Our skipper takes a swear, and then he sings out to Captain Graham, who was lying next to us in the Roads: ' Did you see that?' ' Nay,' says he, 'what was it?' The skipper told him what had happened, and he sings out: ' Where is he? I'll run after him, and make him pay for it.' Wasn't that a good'un, though?"

" The idea of running after a light collier!" exclaimed one of the sailors, with a loud laugh. " Come, drink, lad."

" I think I've had the pleasure of seeing your face before, young man," said a thick-set, sandy-whiskered sailor, in a straw hat, blue woollen shirt, and tarry canvass trousers, who advanced from the further end of the room, and placing his hands on the table at which the group we have described were sitting, looked steadfastly in the face of the pretended sailor.

" Well, and where was it?" said the other, rising, and hitching up his trousers; " was it out at the Cape, or going round the Horn?"

" Neither," replied the sailor, with an expression of ineffable scorn; and then he asked in a stern, significant tone: " Do you remember the fire at Fenning's-wharf?"

" What if I do?" demanded the shark, evidently discomposed by this question.

" Why, you are the man who robbed me of my watch," returned the sailor, sternly; " you picked my pocket while I was looking at the fire; and that is the way you get your living, you damned lubberly shark!"

" On hearing this denunciation, the pretended sailor sidled towards the door, and slunk out of the room, while the accuser addressed the group upon whom he had been preying like a leech.

" That fellow is nothing but a land-shark," said he; " and no more a sailor than that wench is. He robbed me of a silver watch, and though it could not be found, and I couldn't swear that I saw him take it, yet the Thames magistrates committed him for three months for not giving a good account of himself. He lives by sponging upon sailors, and robbing 'em; and I could see he was sneaking into your acquaintance, or I should not have interfered with him."

Norman Ashley had fallen into a moody reverie, from which this incident aroused him, and he called for another glass of the potent liquor.

" Will you have another cigar, Ashley?" said he whom Norman's frail companion had called Corbet, again holding out a handful of prime regalias.

Ashley accepted the proffered gift; and when this had been duly converted into smoke and white ashes, and the glass was again empty, the young girl whispered: " Come with me to my lodgings, and we will have a glass there; they will be shutting up here presently."

Norman rose, and accompanied the girl from the room; he was far from being intoxicated, but, to borrow a word from the silken vocabulary of high life, he was *excited*, and hence he accompanied the young girl, without hesitation, to a house in Pump-court. No light shone from the windows of this abode, and the door was opened by an old man, in obedience to a tap from the fingers of the young woman. He was a short, grey-headed, hard-featured man, between fifty and sixty years of age; and the candle which he carried displayed the smoky walls and dirty floor of the passage.

The girl did not speak, but led the way into the back room, a meanly-furnished apartment, with bare, discoloured walls, and containing only a deal table and four ricketty chairs, though a cheerful fire was burning in the grate.

" Leave the light, and bring us a quartern of rum," said the young woman to the old man, while throwing off her shawl, and placing the kettle over the

fire. " Bring me a glass and a spoon, Mr. Sanders, and a piece of sugar," she continued; and then she held out her hand to Norman, and said, quietly: " Give me some money."

Norman placed a shilling in the girl's hand, with which she paid for the rum, which the old man soon returned with; and, having again left the room, she mixed a glass of rum and water, hot and strong, and handed it to Norman, after tasting it herself.

" There!" said she, " that is real Jamaica, and never paid a farthing of duty—it's all the sweeter for that."

" I should like one of Corbett's cigars, upon the same principle," said Norman, smiling as he took the glass from the hand of his frail companion, and raised it to his lips.

" You can have one," returned the girl; and, opening the door, she called to the old man to bring a cigar, which she paid for out of the change which she had received when she gave Sanders the money for the rum.

The girl seated herself close to young Ashley, who passed his arm round her
20

waist—a position which he had not assumed many minutes, when the door again opened, and in walked Corbett and a fair blue-eyed girl, whom he had encountered on leaving the " Compasses."

"You seem to be enjoying yourselves," said he, smiling; and, having ordered a quartern of rum, he sat down on the opposite side of the fire, and the young girl seated herself by his side, after removing her bonnet and shawl.

"Ought I not to enjoy myself?" said Norman, who was now verging on intoxication. "Shall I not allow myself the pleasures of a gentleman, when I was born to be one, though I am now but a humble fisherman?"

"Ay, ay!" exclaimed Corbett, with some surprise. "Well, I always thought you were above your condition; and a fine, bold, high-spirited young fellow like you cannot be expected to take very kindly to hard work, when he knows he ought to be enjoying himself, if he had his rights."

"That's it," said young Ashley, striking his hand on the table. "Why should I drudge and slave while another enjoys my property, and keeps me out of it? It is an injustice which I will not any longer submit to, and, the first opportunity that offers, I will emancipate myself."

"Bravo!" cried Corbett, holding out his hand to the youth; "tip us your fin; damme, you are a game cock, and no mistake. Meet me to-morrow night at the " Duncan," and I'll put you in the way of accomplishing what you desire."

Norman Ashley grasped the proffered hand of the smuggler, and promised to keep the appointment. Corbett and his companion then left the room, and Ashley emptied his glass; after which he leaned on the table, resting his forehead on his arms, and, overcome by the fumes of the liquor he had drank, he fell fast asleep. The girl endeavoured in vain to rouse him, for he had drank and smoked more than he had ever done before; and, after several ineffectual attempts, she untied his handkerchief, unbuttoned his shirt-collar, and left him asleep in the chair.

CHAPTER L.

THE FISHERMAN'S DAUGHTER.

IT was early in the morning when Norman Ashley awoke from his unquiet slumber, and the first beams of the rising sun were faintly struggling through the dirty windows of the infamous house in Pump-court. He had slept off the immediate effects of the previous night's debauch, but his head ached, and his hands shook with a nervous tremour; he shivered with cold, too, and pressed his hands upon his heated and feverish brow, in an endeavour to recall to his mind the occurrences of the past night. By degrees every event rushed upon the tablet of his mind, from the hidden cells of memory, and he recollected all that had occurred at the " Compasses," his coming to the house where he found himself with a female, and his subsequent conversation and appointment with Corbett.

While he thus sat, with his elbows on the table, and his hands supporting his aching head, the girl in whose company he had left the tavern in Bath-street, on the preceding night, entered the room, and wished him "good morning."

"Ain't you cold?" said she. "Why, you look like a hunted devil! Do come up to my room, and have a wash."

" I shall feel all the better for it," returned the youth, colouring; "for my head aches confoundedly:" and he followed the girl up the dirty stairs to her bed-room. It was small and meanly furnished, containing a French bedstead, a strip of old carpet, a three-legged chair, a piece of looking-glass over the mantel, and a washing-stand, with a blue bason, and a white jug with the handle knocked off.

Having performed his ablutions, Norman Ashley went down stairs, and despite the endeavours of the syren to detain him, he quitted the house, and walked towards the adjacent village of Northfleet. The cool air from the river fanned his fevered brow, and reinvigorated his frame; and as he walked fast, the chilliness which had benumbed his limbs, through sitting up all night at the house in Pump-court, soon gave way to a healthy glow.

The broad river lay rippling and sparkling in the first beams of morning, and on the opposite coast was Tilbury-fort, while on his left were the Clifton-baths, the Rosherville-gardens, and beyond these the village and church of Northfleet. But not a sound yet broke the stillness of early morning, save the rushing of the tide on the mud and shingle of the banks of Old Father Thames, and the young man continued his walk through the village and along the London-road.

The church clock was striking six when he turned the corner of Bath-street, and proceeded with slow and hesitating steps towards the residence of Sam Shrimp. Just as he reached the house, he encountered the fisherman's sons, who were coming out.

"Well, young fellow, where have you been all night?" said the elder amphibia.

"I was at the 'Compasses' last night, where were you?" returned Norman, evading Sam's question.

"Oh, at the 'Fisherman's Arms,' but we got in about twelve or one o'clock, and you havn't been home at all, have you?" said the fisherman. "Well, the old man don't know what time we came in, and so you can say you came home with us. You go in, and if Nance comes down before we get back, say we are gone to the public to get half a pint of beer."

Under existing circumstances, Norman Ashley thought this encounter most fortunate, for it saved him the unpleasantness of giving an account of himself to the old fisherman.

"Bless me! you are up early," observed Nancy Shrimp, as she entered the room; "I suppose your boiler was hot, Master Ashley."

"Why, it is past six o'clock, Nancy," returned the youth, smiling; "and that is not an unseasonable hour for a fisherman, though it is Sunday morning."

"But what time did you come home last night?" inquired Nancy, with a meaning glance; but at that moment her brothers returned, and Norman was saved the necessity of a reply.

During the morning, Nancy Shrimp was reserved and depressed, as if something had occurred to vex or grieve her; and she went to church in the afternoon without speaking a word to Ashley, whom she would sometimes ask to accompany her. Young Ashley could not fail to observe her unusual reserve and her poutiness towards himself, and in the evening he asked her to take a walk with him; for as vague thoughts of leaving the old fisherman were floating through his brain, he did not wish to leave in enmity or coolness with the kind-hearted Nancy.

The young girl hesitated a moment, and then put on her straw bonnet and her new shawl, without speaking; Norman offered her his arm as they left the house, which she accepted, and they walked silently and thoughtfully towards High-street.

"What is the matter, Nancy?" said Norman, as they turned up Windmill-street. "You seem vexed and displeased; have I offended you?"

"You are master of your own actions, Mr. Ashley, and I have no right to interfere with you," returned Nancy, in a tone which evidently showed that she was wavering between her tenderness and her pride.

"You are offended with me for stopping out so late last night," observed Norman, in a hesitating manner.

"You were out all night, Norman, and it's no use to deny it!" exclaimed Nancy; "but I am a fool to be so vexed about it, it is nothing to me; but I am sure you could not have been in very good company."

Norman was silent; he could not deny the charge of absence, and he could see, through the affected indifference of Nancy, that her vexation proceeded from love for him—an idea which till that moment had never entered his mind.

"Nancy," said he, after a pause, "will you forgive me if I promise never to offend in the same manner again?"

The heart of the fisherman's daughter was too full for her to speak without sobbing, for her pride could sustain her no longer; and, being in a much frequented street, she strove to conceal her emotion, and could only press the youth's arm in token of her forgiveness.

They passed the Tivoli-gardens, and Nancy having now recovered the command of her feelings, they sat down on a rustic seat on the hill, in front of the

Belle-vue tavern. Cockney children were running about in the exuberance of their joy, feeling like young birds escaped from their cage to the freedom and fresh air of the woods and fields; and well-dressed visitors were walking about or sitting on the benches, some looking through a telescope at the distant coast of Essex, and others discussing the various refreshments and exhalirating fluids provided by the host of the Belle-vue tavern.

Norman looked at the tearful eyes of Nancy Shrimp, and read there the confirmation of his suspicions as to the state of the young girl's heart, which might have still remained a secret to him but for the emotions she had displayed that evening, when she conceived herself injured and slighted by his visit to Pump-court, of which she had been informed the night before by a young female of her acquaintance. Norman had never experienced any other feeling than that of friendship for the fisherman's daughter, and perhaps her own feelings were scarcely known to herself until the occasion which called them forth. There was something flattering to the heart of the youth, in the preference of a young girl older than himself, and he was pleased too that he had found some one to love him and take an interest in his career; but this newly-awakened feeling was not strong enough to induce him to lay aside his views with reference to leaving the service of Old Shrimp, and seeking his fortune in the wide world.

"You have forgiven me, Nancy?" said Norman Ashley, taking her hand in his own, and looking into the clear depths of her bright blue eyes.

"Yes, Norman," replied the young girl; "I could not refuse forgiveness to one whose friendship is so necessary to my happiness!" and as she thus spoke, a deeper colour tinted her cheek, as if she thought she had said too much.

"Let us walk in the fields," said young Ashley, rising; "we shall be less observed, and can converse more at our ease."

Nancy rose, and having been assisted over the stile near the windmill, by the youth, they walked down the fields on the southern side of the hill.

"I will now explain to you the cause of my absence from home last night," said Norman.

"I do not require it, Norman," said Nancy, mildly.

"But the explanation is necessary for my own sake," returned the youth; "for you may have heard more than the truth, for that you have heard something is evident. I went, then, to the 'Compasses,' expecting to meet your brothers there, but they were not there, and I remained drinking with a man named Corbett, until twelve o'clock, when Corbett invited me to his lodgings, where we had some more drink, and this being more than I am accustomed to, I became rather fresh, and Corbett prevailed on me to stay all night at his lodgings."

"But Hannah Wood says she saw you go up Pump-court with a young woman!" said Nancy, in a hesitating tone.

"Oh, that is false!" exclaimed Ashley, colouring; "your friend must have been mistaken."

"Well, let us forget it, Norman," said the young girl, pressing the arm upon which she leaned against her heart.

"You know how I am situated, I dare say, Nancy," said Norman, after a pause; "and you know that my uncle, who apprenticed me to your father, is a gentleman of large property."

"Yes, the person who came to my father, your uncle's clerk, I believe, told us all about you," returned Nancy.

"He told your father, I suppose, that I was an illegitimate son of the late Sir Norman Ashley," said the youth, with a spice of bitterness in his tone.

The fisherman's daughter replied in the affirmative.

"I do not believe it!" exclaimed Norman. "It was a vile fabrication of my uncle's, and I am determined to assert my claim to the title and property of which I firmly believe I have been cheated."

"Then if you succeed you will be a baronet, and very rich?" observed Nancy, with renewed apprehensions.

"Yes, for my father was one of the largest landowners in Gloucestershire," returned Norman; "but you do not seem pleased with the prospect of my being a rich gentleman, Nancy."

"I am pleased for your sake," said the young girl, mournfully; "but I am afraid—— I know you will think me selfish, and I am a foolish girl to think anything about it."

" What is it that you are afraid of, Nancy ?" inquired Norman, tenderly.

" Nothing," replied Nancy, almost sobbing.

" You love me, Nancy, and you fear that were I to acquire rank and wealth, I should be too proud to associate with a fisherman's daughter," exclaimed Norman, looking keenly at his companion.

Nancy blushed deeply, and, turning her eyes to the ground, made no reply.

" You wrong me, Nancy, if you think that, were I successful in asserting my claims, I should become proud and disdainful," continued the youth. " If I crave rank and wealth, it is because they are my right ; and were I a king, the girl whom I love should share my throne, even if she was but the daughter of a humble fisherman."

" Forget what I have said to you, Norman," said Nancy, with deep feeling. " I have been weak and foolish, but I shall try and forget it all. Let us take our proper stations ; you as the heir to a title and estates, me as the daughter of a fisherman."

" But I am not, and never may be, what I aspire to," observed Norman Ashley.

" But you will forget me in striving after your rights, and why should you think of me ?" sobbed Nancy Shrimp, turning away her head to conceal her tears. " But my foolish heart will rebel, and I cannot help it—it will break if I do not tell you ; and though you may despise me for my weakness, I love you, Norman Ashley, and never can forget you."

This burst of feeling was more than Norman had expected, but he wiped from Nancy's cheeks the tears that gemmed them like drops of dew upon a ripe peach, and said :

" If there is one female for whom I entertain more regard than for others, it is yourself, Nancy ; but love is a feeling which I have yet scarcely experienced, and though I have never spoken of love to you, I love no other."

This assurance appeared to convey a degree of consolation to the heart of Nancy Shrimp, and she murmured :

" You do not despise me, then ?"

" No—why should I ?" responded Norman, taking her hand. " Come, let us seal our friendship with a kiss, and date from this evening a new phasis of our lives."

The blushing Nancy offered no resistance to his caresses, and her long-pent-up love having at length found vent in confession, she returned the kiss which Norman pressed upon her lips. Now that her heart had been lightened of its secret, her blue eyes again sparkled with vivacity, and her usual gaiety returned. Norman was not so deep in love as she was, but he strove to soothe her warm feelings towards him, and Nancy was never so happy in her life as on that evening."

CHAPTER LI.

THE SMUGGLERS.

As Norman Ashley and the fisherman's daughter entered the town by Pleasant-row, having come through Northfleet to prolong a walk so agreeable to the latter in particular, the moon was silvering the waves of Old Father Thames, and by her light a small vessel was seen lying near the shore, between the village of Northfleet and the town-pier. Norman took no notice of it at the time, and having accompanied Nancy to her parents' abode, he pleaded an appointment as the reason for not entering with her.

" You are going to leave us, Norman," said Nancy, in a quivering voice.

" I have no present intention of doing so, Nancy," returned the youth ; " but you must be prepared at any time to hear that I am gone. I am determined to assert my claims to the property I have been unjustly deprived of, and I may find it necessary to leave Gravesend suddenly."

" You will not leave to-night," said Nancy, looking at him tenderly.

" Understand me, Nancy," said he : " I am going to meet Corbett, the man I was with last night ; he knows my situation and my claims, and has a plan to propose to me connected with them.   If that plan should require me to leave to-night, you must not be surprised, though I have no reason at present to suppose that my departure will be so sudden."

" Well, good-bye, dear Norman," said the young girl.

" Good-bye, Nancy," returned Ashley, pressing her hand, and then they parted—the youth proceeding towards the " Admiral Duncan," a public-house in Pleasant-row, a row of wooden houses abutting on the road leading from Bath-street, towards Northfleet.

Entering the parlour, where a number of fishermen and sailors were assembled drinking and smoking, together with several smartly-attired young women, he glanced quickly round the apartment, and perceived Corbett sitting in a corner. He nodded in a friendly manner to young Ashley, who took a seat near him, and was soon engaged in the combustion of a mild cigar, which Corbett placed before him.

They sat till near eleven o'clock, by which time the fumes of the rum and water were beginning to mount into Norman's brain, and the subject which they had met to discuss had not yet been broached.

" Come, drink that up," said Corbett, rising from the table, " and then we will have a walk ; it is a fine moonlight evening."

Ashley finished the glass, and quitted the house with his new acquaintance, who led the way towards the town-pier.

" Petrel, ahoy !" sang out Corbett, hailing the vessel which lay at a short distance up the river.   " Come on board my vessel, and have a glass of grog and another cigar," said he to the young fisherman.

A boat put off from the vessel's side, and in a few minutes was alongside the pier.

" Come, jump in, Ashley," exclaimed Corbett ; and the youth having dropped into the boat, he followed, and taking an oar, for only one man was in the boat, they pulled towards the bark.   It was a small lugger-rigged vessel, but of lighter build than such vessels usually are, and though in appearance nothing more than a Dutch smack, yet her hold, when homeward-bound, would be found to contain brandy, hollands, tobacco, and cigars, rather than turbot and plaice ; in fact, the Petrel was as tight a little bark as ever deceived a custom-house galley, or gave the slip to a revenue-cutter.

Norman Ashley followed Corbett aboard the vessel, and into the little cabin, where they sat down, and the master of the Petrel, as Norman's companion had declared himself to be, placed on the table two steaming tumblers of hollands and water.

" Is this your vessel, Mr. Corbett ?" said young Ashley.

" Yes, we are bound for Flushing ; would you like a cruise in her ?" returned his companion.

" I should like it better than the monotonous drudgery of fishing," said young Ashley, in a musing tone.

" Well, when you declared to me your determination of leaving Old Shrimp, I thought of offering you a berth," returned Corbett.   " I am short-handed at present, and if you like to try my service, you shall have the full wages of an able-bodied seaman ; while, except in heavy weather, I shall only want you to act as my clerk."

" The berth will just suit me," exclaimed Norman, pleased with his new prospects ; " when do you sail ?"

" We shall be dropping-down in half an hour, so make up your mind," returned Corbett.

" I have already," exclaimed Norman. " Captain Corbett, I await your orders."

" Well, finish your cigar," returned Corbett, smiling.

Norman Ashley could hear overhead the various sounds that announced that the lugger was getting under-weigh, and when the hour of twelve, sounding from the town-clock, was borne by the night breeze to their ears, Corbett showed him his berth, and went on deck.   A short thick-set man, about fifty years of age, was steering, and a boy was pacing the deck humming a tune. Corbett took the helm, and the old man went below, and another took his place, to whom Corbett gave some directions, and then retired to his hammock. Gravesend was now concealed from view by the winding of the river, and the moon was slowly sinking behind the blue and distant hills of Kent, which became gradually more dim and indistinct, until nothing was visible beyond the rippling bosom of the broad river, but a dusky line which marked the coast on either hand.

Norman Ashley had now broken the indenture which bound him to Old Shrimp, and shaped out a course for himself which he thought more consonant to his views and inclinations. He would now have greater freedom of action than his piscatory avocations allowed him, and being better paid, he would be enabled to take some steps towards defeating what he believed to be the nefarious projects of his uncle. These reflections occurred to him as he threw off his clothes, and lay down in his narrow berth aboard the lugger; but he soon fell asleep, and slumbered soundly until six o'clock the next morning.

When he went on deck the sun was gilding the broad estuary of the Nore with his beams, and the vessel was gliding over the billows like the bird from which she derived her name. Corbett was already on deck, who introduced Norman to the crew, consisting of two men and a boy, and then invited him to take coffee with him in the cabin.

On reaching Flushing, a port much frequented by contraband traders, a cargo of brandy and hollands was got on board the lugger, which again put to sea, and was steered towards the Nore. It was evening when the vessel passed Gravesend, and Ashley cast a long look at the town from the deck of the lugger, and thought of Nancy Shrimp. His feelings in reference to that young girl were difficult of analysis, even to himself; there was a certain attractiveness in Nancy's arch looks and coquettish manners; long and familiar intercourse had inspired him with friendly feelings towards her, and her recent avowal of preference for him was flattering to his vanity, and yet he could scarcely be said to love her, and it is certain that he did not regard her with that ardent affection which the fisherman's daughter had conceived for him. Nevertheless, there was an evident charm in the attachment of Nancy Shrimp, for the youth sighed as he thought of her; her remembered words stole softly to his mind, and he inwardly determined to see her on the earliest opportunity.

The shadows of night were now stealing over the river, enveloping the banks in a light haze, and the bark floated slowly upon the rippling tide, following the sinuosities of the channel, which lies in some parts of the river nearer to the verdant shores of Kent, and in others to the marshy coast of Essex.

" It is a fine night for our purpose," observed Corbett to Norman Ashley, as they stood together upon the deck of the lugger. " There is a bit of a moon, but the clouds keep skimming athwart it, and we shall be able to run our cargo ashore, without the fear of observation and detection."

. By the time the lugger reached Long-reach, the night was dark as they could desire, and the breeze bore to their ears the sound of the clock of Barking church striking the hour of eleven as they brought up at Horseshoe-corner, a point of low marshy land, lying between Long-reach and Barking-creek, and so called from its peculiar shape.

The beams of the argent moon silvered the upper edges of the dark clouds which glided across her disk, but the black and gathering masses of vapour allowed but a partial illumination of the river and the shore, which, unless for a moment, at intervals, when the moonlight broke through the darkness, remained wrapt in gloom and obscurity. Silence reigned around, a silence broken only by the rippling of the tide, as it broke against the lugger's side, or murmured along the shingle, and the rustling of the night-wind among the tall rushes which grew along the banks of the river.

" Now, my hearties," said Corbett, addressing the crew, " lower the boat, and get the cargo out of her as quick as you can."

The boat was lowered, and one of the crew entered it, and received the kegs of brandy and hollands from the other man and the boy, while Corbett kept a sharp look-out to see if any of the custom-house smacks or Thames-police boats were on the alert to prevent the delivery of the cargo, of which Norman kept an account as the kegs were passed over the side. All this was done as noiselessly as possible; and when the boat was too heavily laden to carry any more, the smuggler who had charge of her pushed off from the lugger, and, dipping his oars noiselessly into he water, he pulled towards the flat marshy beach of Horseshoe-corner.

Slowly and silently the heavily-laden boat was run into a small indentation in the shingle-covered shore, where it was concealed from observation by the tall rushes, and where the landing could be effected without any fear of detection. At that moment the stealthy tread of men's feet, and the dull trampling and splashing of horses' hoofs, were heard coming over the extensive marsh in a direction which would bring them to the little creek where the lugger's boat was then lying. As soon as these sounds met the listening ears of the wary smuggler, he put his fingers to his mouth, and gave a long low whistle, which the approaching party replied to by a very good imitation of the cry of an owl.

The allies of James Corbett presently appeared through the rushes, and proceeded to load their carts with the kegs of spirits brought from the lugger. They were stout active young men in the garb of agricultural labourers, and apparently well acquainted with the business in which they were engaged. The carts having been loaded were driven away, and the boat returned to the lugger, having made several trips, during the transfer of the cargo, to the carts for inland conveyance. The remainder of the cargo was concealed among the rushes along the swampy shore of Horseshoe-corner, in order to be fetched by the carts on the following night, and then the lugger stood over to the opposite coast.

CHAPTER LII.

THE CAPTURE AT THE NORE.

In a few days the lugger sailed again for Flushing, to take in a cargo of tobacco and spirits, there being no duty on the former article in Holland, and the latter being the manufacture of the country. The heavy duties imposed by the British tariff upon tobacco, being 3s. 2d. per pound upon the unmanufactured leaf, and 9s. 6d. per pound when manufactured into cigars, act as a strong temptation to import it without paying the duty, besides leading to extensive adulteration of that article. In no other article is smuggling carried on to such an extent as in tobacco, and various calculations have been made as to the quantity so imported, some going so far as to assert that three-fourths of the whole quantity imported into this country is brought in by contraband traders. Scarcely a single steamer arrives from Rotterdam, or any other Dutch port, without bringing a larger or smaller quantity of tobacco or cigars, which are privately imported by the sailors and engineers, and often secreted in such a manner as to defy the strictest search of the Custom-house officers. Even when a seizure is effected by those functionaries, it is almost impossible to discover the smugglers; and the loss is so trifling, when compared with the profit on successful ventures, that we believe the most stringent laws would be inefficient to suppress the traffic. The fact that the common tobacco is often sold wholesale at an advance of only 2d. above the duty, and never more than 4d., is a proof of the extent to which the contraband trade in that article is carried on; and an idea of the profits realized by smugglers may be formed from the fact, that a cigar of foreign manufacture, which in England costs 3d., may be purchased in Holland for a farthing.

The lugger sailed with a fair wind from Flushing, the chief centre of the contraband trade, and had reached the broad estuary of the Nore, when she was seen and suspected by the commander of a revenue-cutter, which was watching for their arrival. The evening twilight was fading away when Corbett perceived the Nore-light on the left, and at the same time he descried the cutter, and mentioned the circumstance to Norman Ashley, who was with him on the deck.

"We will give them a run for it," said he; "and if they gain upon us too fast, we must sacrifice a portion of the cargo to save the rest."

He then ordered all the vessel's canvass to be spread to the breeze, in order

to attain a degree of speed equal to that of the cutter, which was adapted for quicker sailing, especially as she carried nothing but her guns and stores, though she had less sail aloft than the lugger, the latter being a three-masted vessel, while cutters have only one mast, being rigged similar to sloops, though usually of lighter construction.

The contraband trader rushed rapidly over the dark billows of the Nore, which foamed and tumbled as if they delighted in the freedom of their resistless run down the German Ocean, and the additional canvass caused her to bound forward like a thing endued with life, and participating in the feelings of those who trod her deck. The moon was now rising above the flat and distant coast of Essex, which the vapours of night concealed from their view, and the leaping waves reflected her silvery light, and sparkled as they rolled one over the other, or were cast aside from the bows of the lugger, as the gallant vessel flew onward before the pursuing cutter.

"They are gaining upon us, Ashley," said James Corbett, looking back. "We must lighten the vessel of her cargo. Heave the hollands overboard, my

21

lads ; we shall have enough on board then to pay for the voyage. Bear-a-hand there, Ashley ; I would sooner throw the stuff into the Thames than let the custom-house sharks overhaul it."

Norman Ashley and the two seamen who composed the crew of the lugger then set to work getting the kegs of hollands out of the hold, and throwing them over the side into the river. Corbett went to the wheel, and under his guidance the little bark bounded swiftly over the waves, becoming each moment lighter as the kegs were cast overboard, and drifted away to leeward. The unlading was a work not quickly effected by three men, and the cutter continued to gain upon the lugger, being at this time near enough to see the smugglers lightening their vessel by throwing the kegs of spirits into the Thames.

Onward flew the lugger, her white sails filled with the night-breeze ; onward came the pursuing cutter, and, as the moon rose higher and illuminated the broad river with her pearly light, the chase became of an exciting and animated nature. One after another the casks were thrown into the river, and the lugger, lightened of a portion of her lading, bounded with increased celerity over the foam-tipped billows, until her masts bent before the pressure of the breeze upon her ample canvass ; still the cutter gained gradually upon the flying bark of the smugglers.

A bright flash, a puff of smoke from the side of the revenue-cutter, and the report of a gun boomed across the moonlit river ; the shot struck the heaving billows a hundred yards from the lugger's stern, and, after skimming from wave to wave for a short distance, plunged below the surface and disappeared.

"That is only throwing away good iron," observed James Corbett ; "but the next may be better directed. What a fool I was not to have the swivel-gun that old Vandersplyk recommended me ! one well-directed shot might cut away their mast, and cripple them effectually."

"Shall we load the muskets, sir ?" inquired Norman, entering into the excitement of the chase with all the ardour and enthusiasm of youth.

"Yes, lad ; and bring me my pistols out of the cabin," returned Corbett. They shall not rob us without some resistance ; and I may as well be transported for manslaughter, as ruined by the confiscation of the vessel and cargo, and an exorbitant fine. Get out the cutlasses, and lay them ready to repel boarders."

Bang went another gun from the cutter, and this time the shot struck the jib-boom of the lugger ; the shattered fragments fell clattering on the deck, and the mizen-trysail fluttered in the wind.

"That is a good deal too near to be pleasant, Mr. Corbett," observed Norman Ashley. "If they strike the wheel, they will bring us to, whether we will or no."

"We must try the effect of a musket-shot as soon as they come nearer," said the smuggler captain. "Hand me a musket, Ashley, and take the wheel for a moment."

Norman did as he was directed ; the smuggler took the piece, and proceeded to take a steady aim at the cutter's deck.

"Hard down, Ashley," said he ; and, the lugger being steadily poised for for a moment, he pulled the trigger.

He was not near enough to perceive, by the uncertain light of the moon, the effect of his shot, but the cutter came skimming rapidly over the waves, and in a few moments another gun was fired at the retreating lugger. It was aimed at the rigging in order to prevent the escape of the smugglers, and the shot carried away the foremast, which fell upon the deck with a crash, bringing with it the spars and rigging. The sailing powers of the lugger were so much crippled by this disaster, that the cutter quickly ran down upon her, and the smugglers were driven to the necessity of either submitting or defending their property to the last extremity. Corbett knew not the effect of his shot, and this strengthened his determination to resist the boarding of his vessel by the men of the preventive-service.

He therefore ordered his men to fire in a volley upon the cutter, as it bore down upon their own vessel, and this time they saw one of the crew fall backward, as if mortally wounded. The volley was returned from the revenue-cutter, which came alongside a few moments afterwards; one of the smugglers was wounded by the discharge, and, the bowsprit of the cutter coming across the lugger, became entangled in her mizen-rigging. The crew of the cutter leaped on the deck of the contraband trader, and for a few minutes the clash of steel mingled discordantly with the furious oaths and imprecations of the combatants.

The smugglers, however, were far outnumbered by the crew of the revenue-cutter, and, after a short but desperate encounter, the whole of them were disarmed and handcuffed together. Corbett and another of the smugglers were wounded in the struggle, but neither of them mortally; and, the prisoners being transferred to the cutter, some of the preventive-service men were sent on board the lugger to navigate her up to the Custom-house wharf. Two or three of the cutter's crew were wounded, but no lives had been sacrificed; and this was a circumstance in the smugglers' favour, when their trial came on at the Old Bailey. On reaching London, which they did not do until the following morning, the prisoners were given into the custody of the Thames-police, and lodged in the station-house until they could be taken before the magistrates who preside over the criminal jurisdiction of the river.

CHAPTER LIII.

THE RIVER-PIRATES.

THE smugglers had not long to wait in the station-house before they were taken before the Thames magistrates, and, after a long examination, the whole party were committed to take their trial at the next Old Bailey sessions. Norman Ashley wrote to his uncle, begging his assistance in obtaining counsel to defend him on his trial, but the wily and selfish barrister thought this a good chance of getting rid of his nephew, and resolved to abandon him to his fate, earnestly hoping that he might be transported. The prisoners lay in Newgate until the sessions; and there being many extenuating circumstances in Ashley's case, as compared with the other prisoners, the sentence upon him was imprisonment for three months; while Corbett and the other two were sentenced to twelve months' imprisonment, and Corbett, as the principal offender, to be fined one hundred pounds, in addition to the confiscation of the lugger and her cargo, by the Custom-house authorities, and to be further imprisoned until the fine was paid.

Three weary months were passed by Norman Ashley in the gloom and solitude of a prison, during which time he received two or three letters from Nancy Shrimp, expressive of the affectionate and tender sympathy of the warm-hearted girl for the youth's misfortune, and these were the only manifestations of interest in his situation which he received from the world without. These epistles he duly answered; but his letters breathed not the warmth, the tenderness, the entire devotion, which seemed to inspire every line of those penned by the fair hand of the fisherman's daughter; they were rather the communications of an attached friend, and the language was that which might be addressed by a brother to a beloved sister. Nancy could not fail to perceive these indications of the difference between the feelings which glowed within her own bosom, and those which actuated him in whom she hoped to find a lover; and though she could not conceal from herself how much her heart was wounded by the contest, her pride gradually revolted against the thought that her love was bestowed upon one who did not appreciate the warm and tender heart that was entirely his own.

At length the period of Ashley's imprisonment expired, and he again stood on the pavement of London's busy streets—again breathed the free air, which for three months had only reached him over high walls—again felt the warm sunbeams on his countenance, and heard the merry sounds which greet the ear in a populous and commercial city. He lingered a moment near the prison, to think of some plan for the future: but this was not easily done; he had no hope of assistance from his uncle, old Shrimp might refuse to receive him again after having absconded from his service, and James Corbett was still a prisoner. Nancy Shrimp had in her last letter called his attention to the necessity of deciding what he would do before he left the prison, but he had not been able to do so satisfactorily, and he was still as irresolute as ever.

He stood at the corner of a street, perplexed and hesitating, and with a cloud upon his clear and open brow, when he heard himself addressed by his name, and looked round in some surprise. The speaker was a youth a year or two older than himself, wearing a ragged blue jacket and tarry trousers, the primitive colour of which had been white. Norman immediately recognised the youth as a recent fellow-prisoner, who had been liberated that morning on the completion of the term of imprisonment to which he had been sentenced, for stealing a coil of rope from the deck of a brig lying in the river.

"Well, Ashley, what do you mean to do now?" was the question asked of the youth by this aquatic depredator, whose name was Slingsby, though he was familiarly known by his associates as Shark, except when they wished to show him particular respect, and called him Shark Slingsby.

"I was just asking myself the same question," returned Norman, with a faint smile.

"And got no answer," said Shark, quickly.

Ashley was silent, and almost resolved to return to Gravesend, and fulfil his indentures with Sam Shrimp.

"Don't stop here—come down east, and let us have a pint of beer together," continued Shark Slingsby.

Norman Ashley hesitated a moment, and then followed his late fellow-prisoner through the crowded streets of the city; they stopped not until they reached Limehouse, when Shark Slingsby entered a beer-shop called "The Bald Stag," and Norman followed him. The house was a notorious resort of river-pirates, and all the lawless characters of every description who lived in the neighbourhood; and the principal of these, the parlour customers, formed a sort of confederacy, keeping up a communication with others of the thieving fraternity at Rotherhithe, Deptford, and Greenwich, as well as in the eastern parts of the city suburbs. In the tap-room, into which Shark conducted Norman Ashley, several men were stated, some wearing blue jackets like sailors, and others in striped "slops," like those worn by railway-excavators; and this costume was adopted by the frequenters of "The Bald Stag," for the more convenient concealment of small articles which might be stolen from the vessels and lighters in the river, or off the wharfs.

The plans of robbery pursued by these people are various: sometimes two will go in company, with a light-cart, and when they see property exposed at the doors of warehouses, or in carts or vans which are left unguarded for a moment, during the operation of loading or unloading, the cart is stopped, one of the thieves jumps out, and transfers a firkin of butter, a box of candles, or whatever the property may consist of, to the vehicle of his confederate, which is immediately driven off. Others are labourers employed about the docks, who become connected with the thieving fraternity through a congeniality of habits, and are useful to the latter in giving information to them respecting ships which are left unguarded. The amphibious magsmen, or pretended sailors, form a third class of river-thieves, but the habits and mode of operations of this class have been already described.

The Thames-pirates form another and numerous division of this lawless confederacy, and these confine their operations entirely to the river, and principally to those parts of it lying between Gravesend and London-bridge, though they will sometimes go as low as the Nore, and as high as Vauxhall. The class of Thames-pirates is sub-divided into several grades, of which the lowest are the less honest of the *mud-larks*, amphibious men and boys who have already been slightly described; these watch for an opportunity to plunder the barges, or to pick up any article that may be lost overboard from vessels in the river, or cast ashore by the tide. The next grade of river-thieves prowl about the wharves and docks, and carry off anything they can lay their hands on, if it be left for a moment unguarded; they sometimes pretend to be porters and dock-labourers, and in this manner extend their nefarious operations to the decks of vessels moored off the wharves, and if interrogated as to their business, reply that they have come aboard the wrong ship, and inquire where such a vessel is lying. The next gradation brings us to the real pirates, usually men who have belonged to the naval or merchant-service, and who possess a large boat, or sometimes a lighter ; these are generally manned by two or three men, who board vessels that are left unguarded, or guarded only by a man or boy, and plunder them of the cargo, and any articles of value they can find.

Shark Slingsby called for a pot of beer and some bread and cheese, and, when the latter had been disposed of, for pipes and tobacco ; the latter was smuggled, a circumstance of which Ashley was informed in a low voice by his new acquaintance.

"Well, what have you made up your mind to?" inquired Shark, as he exhaled the first puff of smoke from his short pipe.

"I was thinking of going down to Gravesend, and resuming my old employment of fishing," replied Norman Ashley, in a musing tone.

"Well, every one to their liking, but there are many more pleasant ways of living on the river than that," observed Shark.

"As what, for instance ?" said Norman, looking at his companion.

"Smuggling, if you like," returned Shark, smiling.

"You are right," said young Ashley, after a pause ; "but, to carry on the contraband trade in a systematic manner, one wants a ship and comrades."

"Would you not like to be a rover?—to carry the black flag at the masthead, and roam over the ocean at your pleasure ?" said the wily Slingsby.

"Yes, I think piracy is as justifiable in an individual as war in the nation," exclaimed Norman, with sudden energy.

"Just my opinion," observed Shark ; "and if a crew of forty or fifty men have a right to carry on piracy on the sea, which governments justify in war-time by issuing letters-of-marque to the masters of privateers, why not four or five upon the Thames ?—why not," he added, in a lower tone, " why not you and I ?"

"Norman started slightly, but the words of his companion sank deep into his mind, and made an evident impression upon him.

"Vessels lying in the river, or moored at the wharves, are often left unguarded at night, or guarded only by one man, or perhaps a boy," continued Shark. " What would be easier than for us two to board them in the night, overpower the solitary seaman or cabin-boy, and take what we like?—it is nothing but privateering on a small scale ; and I can hire a boat that will serve our purpose capitally, until we can set one up for ourselves. What say you, Ashley ?"

The deep sophistry of Shark Slingsby's arguments was not readily perceivable ; if his premises were right, and wars of conquest be justifiable, then his conclusion was right also, however startling such an opinion may be to those who have been taught to admire the glories of successful war. But his premise was false, and his conclusion necessarily false also ; an abstract truth the full force of which was not seen by Norman Ashley at that moment. He was thus induced to fall into his companion's plans, and when they left the beer-shop, he accompanied Shark to the residence of the person of whom he proposed to hire the boat ; remarking, that a row down the river would do them both good after their confinement between the four walls of a prison.

CHAPTER LIV.

THE NIGHT-CHASE.

On leaving the beer-shop at Limehouse, Norman Ashley and Shark walked up to Wapping, and there hailed a waterman to take them over to the Surrey-side of the river ; they were put on shore near the eastern extremity of Rotherhithe-wall, and a few minutes' walk took them from thence to Duckett's-wharf, as was indicated by a cracked and dried-up board, which appeared to have been last painted many years since. A small wooden counting-house stood in the yard, which corresponded in outward appearance with the board which indicated the name of the owner ; and behind the counting-house were two or three dirty trucks, with their poles erect in the air. A small boat was moored to the wharf, but there were no visible signs of business about the place, which had altogether a deserted and mournful appearance, strangely at variance with the animated aspect of the river and the bustle of the neighbouring street.

"Master Duckett!" said Shark Slingsby, as he first tapped at the door of the counting-house, and then opening it, thrust in his head, and said a few words which Norman did not hear.

An old man then made his appearance, a little grey-headed fellow, as withered and shrivelled as everything else appeared about the wharf; sallow in countenance and meanly attired, yet with an air of sharpness and shrewdness, acquired by the experience of half a century in every species of knavery.

"Yes, you can have the boat, my lad," said the old man, glancing keenly at Norman Ashley while addressing himself to Shark, apparently in answer to an inquiry to that effect made by him.

"If we pick up anything of consequence, we will bring it here, and leave it with you," returned Shark; "but if it should be only a bit of old rope or metal, or some such trifle, we shall moor the boat to the wharf, and take the swag to the marine-store shop."

Old Duckett was one of the numerous agents in connection with the Limehouse confederation of river-thieves, and his wharf was used by them for landing the goods stolen from the shipping in the river. He had a warehouse where stolen property was stored until it could be disposed of, and the trucks were let out for the removal of stolen and contraband goods; he also let out boats on hire to the inferior grade of river-pirates, and acted as their agent in disposing of the proceeds of their robberies. He also kept a horse and a spring-cart for the removal of large quantities of goods, or to convey them quickly to a distance, and for this purpose he kept a man to drive the cart, and mind the wharf in his absence.

Shark Slingsby dropped into the boat, and, being followed by young Ashley, they took up the oars, and casting off her moorings, pulled away from the shore. Evening was coming on when they crossed the river from Wapping; and as they dropped slowly down the Pool, a deeper gloom settled upon the water, and the tall warehouses on either side were scarcely distinguishable from the darkness which shrouded them. A forest of masts marked the sky with black lines on their left, and a number of colliers and small vessels lay along the Surrey shore, while many other ships of different nations were anchored in the middle of the Pool, some singly, and others in twos or threes, with their sails flapping idly against the mast.

Shark Slingsby regarded these vessels with a keen eye as he and Norman pulled slowly down the river, and observed to his companion that they should find some of them unguarded, or feebly so, but that they must look out sharp to see that none of the Thames-police boats were watching them. They rowed down the river nearly as far as Greenwich; and when they perceived the huge black hull of the Dreadnought hospital-ship floating like some sleeping monster of the deep upon its rippling surface, they turned up the Pool again. It was now quite dark; but here and there a light glimmered along the banks, and the distant lamps on London-bridge shone like an arch of glittering stars. The grey walls of the Tower looked more frowningly than ever upon the silent river; and here and there a church-tower or spire rose above the confused mass of buildings, blended together by the general darkness.

"This must be the one," said Shark, in a low voice, indicating, by a rapid gesture, a small schooner whose low, sharp hull, and high, raking masts, had attracted his notice as they rowed down the river. "I saw one of the crew fasten down the hatchway, and put off in a boat as we went down; and most probably he is at this moment in the height of enjoyment at the Mariner's-saloon or the Pavilion-theatre."

The boat was rowed alongside of the schooner, and in a few moments Shark and Ashley were aboard; the former carrying a small crowbar which he had taken from the bottom of the boat. By means of this instrument, the hatch was forcibly raised; and the bold intruders descended the companion-ladder, and entered the cabin, after wrenching open the door. There they found a case of mathematical instruments, a few bottles of wine, and a musket which, upon examination, proved to be loaded. Consigning the bottles and the case of instruments to their pockets, they then proceeded to the hold; but, when they had with much difficulty forced up the lower hatchway, they found that the cargo consisted of wine in pipes, and consequently could not be removed. They were therefore obliged to content themselves with what they had got; and with these they proceeded to leave the ship.

"Hark! what was that?" said Shark, as they were descending the schooner's side to their boat "I thought I heard the splash of oars."

"I heard nothing," returned Norman, listening.

"I must have fancied it," rejoined his companion, stepping into the boat, and taking up the oars; for nothing was now to be heard but the dashing of the water against the schooner's side.

They had scarcely got an oar's-length from the vessel, however, when both Norman and Shark distinctly heard the splash of oars, apparently a little higher up the river; and looking anxiously around them, they saw a boat, with several men in it, glide from the shadow of a large brig, and make towards them.

"The Thames-police, by all that's unfortunate!" exclaimed Shark Slingsby: "pull away, Ashley. We cannot land at Duckett's, or they will pipe the whole concern. We must row down the Pool, and run the boat ashore below the Isle of Dogs."

"Boat ahoy!" was shouted from the pursuing boat; but the pirates paid no attention to the hail, and pulled vigorously down the river.

This was deemed a confirmation of the strong suspicions entertained by the police, of the character of Shark and Ashley; and a chase commenced which promised to be of long continuance; for the boat from Duckett's was lighter than the Thames-police boat, and they had the start of their pursuers, with the tide in their favour. The night was dark; and they were leaving behind them the light of the myriads of lamps reflected upon the sky above the sleeping city, which enabled them to mark their course by the most prominent objects along the banks of the river.

The tall spire of Limehouse-church was quickly passed, rising above the forest of masts which denoted the position of the docks; and shortly afterwards the mast-house at Blackwall rose dark and ill-defined against the sombre sky. The perspiration dropped from their heated foreheads as they pulled down the silent river; and they now discovered that their pursuers were gradually gaining upon them. They bent to their oars with redoubled vigour, until the little boat seemed to fly over the rippling waves; but still their pursuers hung closely on their stern.

The Isle of Dogs was now passed, and Greenwich-college rose on their right, standing out in dim relief from the background of darkness which hung over land and river; and then a brief consultation was held concerning the most favourable spot for landing and effecting their escape. Norman Ashley proposed the marshes near Woolwich for that purpose; but Shark dissented, and insisted upon landing on the Essex shore, as he had at first proposed. Norman ceded the point; and the boat was pulled to the northern side of the river, to select an eligible place to run the boat ashore. This manœuvre was perceived by their pursuers, who made the most strenuous endeavours to get between them and the land, and thus prevent their escape.

"Curse them! this will stop them," exclaimed Shark. And catching up the musket which they had brought from the schooner, he cocked it hastily, and pointed it at the pursuing boat.

"Back! or I'll fire!" said he, in a determined tone; but the police did not heed the threat, and came rapidly down upon them.

The pirate's finger lingered a moment on the trigger, and then he pulled it: there was a flash amid the darkness, a loud report, and then a cry of pain from one of the police.

"They would have it," muttered Shark, as he laid down the musket; and again resuming the oars, the boat sped quickly towards the low, marshy coast of Essex.

The attention of the police was drawn from the flying pirates to their wounded comrade; and the boat was run ashore in a little creek where it was almost concealed by the tall rushes which grew along the flat and marshy shore.

"We cannot stop to pull the boat ashore," said Shark Slingsby, as he leaped among the rushes; "old Duckett must be the loser of that. Bring the musket, though."

Ashley caught up the musket, and followed his companion; and in another moment both had disappeared in the swamp, leaving the boat aground in the creek.

CHAPTER LV.

THE VILLAGE ROUNDHOUSE.

The spot at which Norman Ashley and the pirate had landed was a solitary part of the swampy shore of Galleon's-reach, frequented only by men who sometimes went ashore to cut osier-twigs for the use of basket-makers. Running with hasty strides over the marshy ground, the osiers and tall reeds and rushes bending on either side as they rushed onward, they were soon beyond the observation of any one on the river or along the shore; and then they stopped to listen. They heard the murmur of voices, the distant splash of oars, which seemed gradually to recede, and the faint sound of the outrunning tide rolling over the shingle as the dark waters of Old Father Thames ebbed slowly towards the broad bosom of the German Ocean. It was clear that their pursuers, finding that they had escaped on shore, and in consideration of their wounded comrade, had abandoned the pursuit, and were returning up the stream. They therefore slackened their pace, and struck into a narrow path—or rather beaten track—which appeared to lead from the shore to a hamlet at a little distance from the marsh which extends along the Essex-side of the river.

They passed through the hamlet, which seemed to consist of a few farmhouses and cottages scattered at intervals along the road, not a light being visible, as if all the inhabitants were fast asleep; and after passing a small triangular-shaped green, they came to a wider and more beaten road, at the corner of which was a direction-post. The night was too dark for them to perceive the names of the places to which it referred, until Shark mounted upon the shoulders of Norman Ashley, and was thus enabled to perceive that the road led in one direction to Barking, and in the other to London. They took the latter, Ashley still carrying the musket, and the bottles of wine and the case of mathematical instruments being stowed away in their pockets; and after walking to some distance, they came to the outskirts of a considerable village. First they passed a small public-house with a horse-trough in front, then a row of cottages; the village church peeped out from amidst a clump of ancient elms, and then they entered the long, straggling street of the village. All was dark and silent; and when they had passed the pound for strayed cattle, and the village gaol, or roundhouse, as it was locally termed—close to which was the stocks, formerly the terror of rustic evil-doers, but now almost obsolete—they again found themselves between high, green hedges.

As yet they had not encountered a single human being, but shortly after passing the last of the houses in the village, they heard the sound of a horse's feet advancing toward them, and soon discovered that it was the mounted patrol. Ashley walked close to the hedge, that the musket which he carried might not be perceived, but the patrol checked his horse, and threw the light of his bull's-eye lantern full upon them.

"Where are you going to, my lads?" said he, slowly, while he keenly scrutinised their appearance.

"To London," replied Shark.

"Where did you get that musket?" said the patrol to Ashley.

"Brought it from aboard ship, to shoot in the marshes," returned Norman.

"You choose a dark night for your sport," said the patrol, in a suspicious tone. "Do you both belong to the same ship?"

"Yes," replied Shark, at a venture.

"What have you got in your pockets?—any game?" asked the patrol; and dismounting from his horse, he proceeded very coolly to search his pockets, holding his arm in such a manner that he was unable to use the musket, even if he had been disposed to do so.

The case of instruments and a bottle of wine were drawn from Norman's pockets; and when the officer had examined the former, he transferred them to his own.

"These are so pretty, that I must keep them," said he; "and I very much doubt whether they were honestly come by. You brought a good supply of wine with you," he continued, as he drew another bottle from Norman's pockets, and two more from Shark Slingsby's. "All full, too. Well, I will not trouble you to carry them back to London; and I must have this piece, too, or you will be doing some one an injury with it."

The patrol took possession of all the stolen property, while the two young pirates stood in moody silence, meditating whether it would be better to stand their ground, or to attempt an escape by flight. Presently, however, a policeman came up on foot, and into his custody Shark and Ashley were given by the patrol, with orders to convey them to the cage, upon suspicion of having become possessed of the property taken from them in an unlawful manner. Shark protested against this proceeding, and endeavoured to persuade the

22

policeman that the property was his own; but the officer gave no credence to his assertions, and locked up both the pirates in the village roundhouse.

This was a small, detached building of brick, with a tiled roof, and a door of stout oak, thickly studded with large-headed nails; in the door was a small grating of iron, to admit air, there being no window; and on the floor was a quantity of straw. It was the place in which thieves and vagrants were confined, previous to being taken before the justices for examination, and was as uncomfortable as all places are which are intended for receptacles of the destitute, or such as have incurred the suspicion of crime or the displeasure of the ruling powers.

"What do you think of this, Ashley?" said Shark Slingsby, when the sound of the policeman's retiring footsteps had ceased.

"That it is all up with us, if we stop here," returned Ashley, calmly.

"Just my opinion," rejoined Shark, casting his eyes up to the roof of the cage, which was not ceiled.

"Then we have only to consider the means of getting out," observed Norman.

"That is it," said his fellow-prisoner. "Do you see those tiles?"

"My own idea, the moment I entered," replied Ashley. "But let us rest a little while, and in the meantime the policeman will have returned to have a look at us, to assure himself of our safety, and, when he has again got beyond sight of the place, we will be off."

Norman and his companion laid down upon the straw to rest themselves; and after the lapse of nearly an hour, the policeman approached the roundhouse, threw the glare of his lantern through the grating in the door, and, having seen that his prisoners were apparently asleep upon the straw, he retired again. When they could no longer hear the sound of his receding footsteps, the pirates rose from their straw, and, one mounting upon the shoulder of the other, proceeded to remove the tiles, so as to make an aperture in the roof sufficiently large to admit of their passing through it. Norman went first, and having looked cautiously around, and listened without hearing any sound of advancing footsteps, he laid down upon the roof, and, setting his knees firmly against the tiles, exerted all his strength to draw up his companion. Having with much difficulty succeeded in lifting him sufficiently high to enable him to raise himself by clutching the rafters, Norman sat for a moment on the tiles, to recover breath after his exertion, and to wipe the perspiration from his heated forehead, and then he and his companion dropped to the ground.

The darkness of night was now giving way to the grey light of early morning, and the song-birds were calling to each other from their leafy covert. The fugitives ran a little distance, and then betook themselves to the fields, hurrying along under cover of the hedges. Having travelled some distance, they found the fields bounded by the high road, and were able to perceive, by the misty light of morning, that the road ran in one direction to Romford, and the other towards London. Quitting the fields, they took the latter direction, and walked rapidly along the high road. The daylight increased as they went forward, and they soon began to be overtaken by loads of hay and straw going up to Whitechapel-market, and by pedestrians whose business called them into the metropolis, and whose poverty compelled them to walk thither. Then they found the houses more numerous, but as yet they consisted principally of cottages; then shops began to be mingled with the cottages; and then they crossed the venerable bridge of Bow, erected in the reign of Henry I., and since removed to make way for a more modern structure, and entered the suburban village of Stratford.

Then they turned off from the main Essex road, and passing through Poplar, proceeded towards Limehouse. The early coffee-houses were just opening, and here and there the public-houses gave signs of the same activity. Labourers were going to their work; and now and then a cart rattled over the uneven pavement.

"What shall we do now?" said Norman Ashley to his companion, as they walked along Ratcliffe-highway, which began to present the appearance we have before described.

"We must raise the wind somehow, and then look out for a crib to lay up in," returned Shark. " Come along with me, and I warrant we find something to get breakfast with."

Norman followed his companion, and they entered St. Katherine's-docks. Before they had been many minutes on the quay, Shark walked boldly on board a brig, the deck of which was crowded with men and bales of goods, and, taking up a coil of new rope, he threw it on his shoulder, and coolly walked over the gangway with it. Norman was astounded at the ease with which the robbery was effected, and he hurried after his companion, who walked quickly, but without any appearance of suspicious haste, towards the dock gates. The rope was disposed of at the nearest marine-store shop, without any questions being asked, and with the proceeds they obtained an excellent breakfast, and then made amends to themselves for their want of sleep the preceding night, by adjourning to a lodging-house in Gravel-lane until the afternoon.

CHAPTER LVI.

GREENWICH PARK.

NORMAN ASHLEY awoke before his companion, and the dirty ceiling and walls of the miserable lodging induced a train of reflection upon his present position ; the sophistry by which he had been led to enter upon a career of piracy was too thin to gloss over the robbery committed by his companion in St. Katherine's-docks ; and the young fisherman and smuggler cast about for fresh arguments to justify its commission.

" If the government had not robbed James Corbett of his ship," thought he, " I should not have been led by destitution to fall into the projects of Shark Slingsby ; if I rob in return, it is only fair retaliation, and the government, as the aggressor, must bear the responsibility, and answer for it to the nation. Some people will say that we were the aggressors ; but until it can be proved that right can be made wrong by act of parliament, I shall maintain that the confiscation of Corbett's property was a flagrant and cruel robbery on the part of the government. Some poet says : ' Those who allow oppression share the crime ;' and if men of property support a government which maintains itself by coercion and plunder, they must expect to be paid in their own coin, as the shipowner was, who lost his coil of rope yesterday."

Thus soliloquising, Norman rose from the wretched flock-bed on which he had been lying, and, leaving his companion asleep, strolled towards the nearest pawnbroker's shop, and pledged a handsome silver watch, given him some years since by his father, in order to maintain himself until a more successful expedition than that of the preceding night should furnish him with a supply of money.

He stood a few moments outside the pawnbroker's shop, and debated in his mind whether he should return to the lodging-house where he had left Shark Slingsby. He decided in the negative ; and, entering a tavern in Ratcliffe-highway, remained there until a late hour in the evening. The following day was Sunday, and in the afternoon he walked up to London-bridge, and went on board one of the small steamboats, which ply between there and Greenwich, the deck of which was already laden with passengers, principally young men and women, eager to escape from the close streets and courts of the metropolis into the pure air, the sunshine, and the shade of the green trees. The pale weaver, who all the week had plied the shuttle in the smoke and darkness of Spitalfields—the shoemaker, who had bent over his last for six days—the dressmaker's apprentice or assistant, who had seen the night succeed the day without any cessation of her monotonous employment—the shopman and the clerk, and all the slaves of capital, rush out on the sabbath to the green and pleasant places around the overgrown city ; and as they sit in the shade of stately trees, listen to the harmony of the blackbird and the thrush, and, shutting out from their minds the thoughts of the past week's drudgery and confinement, as well as that of the week which is to come, revel in imagination in the groves of Arcadia, their hearts expand towards all creation, and, in the silent worship expressed in their serene and joy-beaming eyes, God is glorified more than in the act-of-parliament thanksgivings offered on the first day of the week, by those who serve Mammon during the following six.

Greenwich-park may be justly regarded as one of the lungs of the metropolis, and it has been for many years a favourite resort of the humble citizens of Cockaigne. There resounds the merry laugh, as the young men and maidens run joyously down the hill, or chase each other over the greensward; there, in the warm evenings of summer, they amuse themselves with a cosy game of "kiss in the ring;" and there many an acquaintance is made—many an engagement formed, which speedily terminates in disappointment, perchance in shame.

Norman Ashley sought the park as soon as he had partaken of some refreshment, and walked about to observe the groups who were seated on the grass, or sauntering in the shade of the tall and venerable trees. Naturally high-spirited, fond of adventure, and possessed of that elasticity of mind which no misfortune could wholly destroy, the youth thought less of the peril from which he had escaped the morning before, and the mischances which might attend his future depredations upon the river, than of the bright eyes—black, blue, and hazel—that occasionally met his own with a sly and wanton glance, or were cast down in modest confusion upon the green turf, and the ringlets of shining black, or sunny auburn, or silky light-brown, that peeped couquettishly beneath the corners of modish bonnets.

Among those who most attracted the youth's attention, were two elegantly-dressed young females, the elder of whom was tall and fair; while, as if to enhance the loveliness of each by contrast, her companion was of extremely dark complexion, with soft black eyes and glossy ringlets of the same jetty hue. Their light shawls being thrown off their shoulders on account of the heat, allowed the youth's eyes to linger with admiration upon their faultless figures; and a stray glance from the dark eyes of the younger lady inspired him with feelings and desires stronger and deeper than any he had before experienced, and caused him to follow the beautiful strangers, in the hope of catching another glimpse of the countenance which had exercised such magical influence upon his mind and heart.

"What a handsome young man!" said Lolah Hastings to her friend and companion, Caroline Allen; for they were the two females by whose loveliness Norman Ashley had been so enchanted.

"Which?" said Caroline Allen, glancing around her.

"He whom we just passed—a sailor, apparently, by his blue jacket and cap," returned Lolah, stealing another look at Norman over her companion's shoulder. "He is following us, I declare; just observe his curly hair and his quick, dark eyes!"

"Well, he is certainly not a bad-looking young man," observed Caroline Allen, when she had obtained a better view of the young fisherman's countenance.

"Not bad looking! he is decidedly handsome—quite a love of a man!" exclaimed Lolah Hastings. "If any one could tempt me to forget Frederick Shirley, or be untrue to the Earl of Glenvale, it would be that handsome young sailor."

"You judge entirely by appearance, Lolah," observed Caroline.

"The countenance is usually an index to the mind, I think," said Lolah, speaking more seriously than she had done before; "and it evidently must be the countenance which makes the first impression upon those who seem irresistibly drawn to each other upon their first interview, and appear to read each other's character as well as if they had known each other all their lives."

Norman Ashley longed for an opportunity to introduce himself to the houri who had enchanted him; but none offered, and he wandered about the park, still keeping Lolah and her companion in sight, until he saw them leave its shade and verdure for the town, and walk towards the pier. He followed them on board the steamboat, hoping to find occasion to address the object of the sudden passion which had inflamed him, during the short voyage to London-bridge; but no opportunity occurred, without appearing obtrusive, until the arrival of the vessel at the Old-shades Pier, when he eagerly hastened to hand them along the gangway. The ladies thanked him for the attention, and, when he would have bowed and gone on his way, Lolah asked him, in her sweet and silvery voice, to enhance the obligation by procuring a cab for them.

The young smuggler offered the ladies his arm, and having escorted them up the steps leading from Thames-street to the level of the bridge, he called a cab for them. As he took the hand of Lolah Hastings to assist her into the vehicle, a thrill of pleasure pervaded his veins, and seemed to communicate itself to those of the lovely brunette; for the rich colour in her cheeks became heightened as she thanked him, and their eyes explained to each other the secret of the emotion which held them in its magic chain. The circumstance also served to make him acquainted with the address of his inamorata, which he gave from her to the driver of the vehicle; and bowing to Lolah and Caroline as the driver gathered up the reins, he stood gazing after the cab until it turned into King William-street.

Then he turned his footsteps to where the Monument rears its flame-tipped head to perpetuate a falsehood engendered by prejudice and bigotry, and walked slowly down Eastcheap, thinking of the beauteous being who had enchained his heart. Her rounded and symmetrical form, of which a Canova or a Thorwaldsen might have been proud for a model, the small hand that had for a moment trembled within his own, the silvery tones of that voice which still seemed vibrating in his ears, the raven curls that waved on either side of that brunette countenance, and the soft and tender expression of her dark, lustrous eyes, altogether formed a theme which he felt he could dwell upon for ever. Every thought that he had ever indulged respecting Nancy Shrimp faded from his mind before the transcendent loveliness of her whose name was yet unknown to him; and he longed to meet her again, that he might have an opportunity of unfolding to her his own sentiments and feelings.

On the part of the lovely object of his sudden passion, neither the railing of Caroline Allen, nor the position in which she stood with the Earl of Glenvale, prevented her from dwelling on the handsome countenance and manners—so far above his social station—of the young fisherman, as they were driven to her lodgings, and even after she had retired to rest. The Earl of Glenvale, her protector, had gone to the moors of Scotland to enjoy the sport of grouse-shooting, a few days previously; and as he was not expected to return to the metropolis for a month or six weeks, Lolah felt herself more free than if she lived in daily expectation of a visit from a man whom she did not love, and scarcely, even, esteemed. She could not conceal from her own heart the fact that she felt an interest in the handsome young sailor whom she had met at Greenwich; and she hoped that circumstances would again place her in his way, as on the former occasion.

CHAPTER LVII.

THE INDIA TRADER.

NORMAN ASHLEY was walking along Shadwell when he encountered Shark Slingsby, who accosted him with: " Halloa! where have you been to?"

" I have just returned from Greenwich," replied Norman.

" I began to be afraid you had been nabbed," said Shark. " Come down to the Bald Stag, and, if you have not been frightened by the adventure of Friday night, I will let you into an affair that promises to be easy and profitable."

" I am with you, then," said Norman; " and I only wish we could get a bit of a smack, and then we could do our business in a more systematic manner."

Having reached the beershop at Limehouse which formed the head-quarters of the river-thieves, Norman and Shark entered the parlour, and setting down in the most secluded corner, called for some refreshments, with which they were immediately supplied.

" There is a fine Indiaman aground near Galleon's-reach, where we were the other night," said Shark, as he lit his pipe. " She came in contact with a large brig that was getting down the river this morning, and was so much damaged that the captain had her run aground to save her from sinking. It will take all day to-morrow to stop her leaks and get her afloat, and I much doubt whether it will be done before Tuesday, and then she will probably be towed into dock by a steam-tug. In the meantime she lays there with only the second mate on board to take care of her cargo, which is reported to be very valuable. Now, if we wait till to-morrow night, we shall have to run the chance of her repairs being completed before that time, and it will, therefore, be best to do the job at once."

" We must have a good boat to make it worth our while," observed Ashley; " and it will be no good, I expect, to try the old fellow over at Rotherhithe, after losing his boat the other night."

" I know a bloak as will lend us a lighter," returned Shark, "and everything else that we may have occasion for. He lives down by Irongate-wharf, and we may as well go to him at once."

Having drank the liquor which they had ordered on entering, Ashley and Shark left the beershop, and proceeded to the place mentioned by the latter; and near the waterside they found the warehouse of a dealer in marine-stores, who was the party alluded to by the pirate. It was now growing dark, and in the low and dirty lanes near the river a fog was slowly creeping up, rendering the grey walls of the Tower indistinctly visible on the right. Shark tapped at the door of the marine-store dealer's domicile, and, in a few minutes, it was opened by an old man who might have passed for the prototype of the celebrated Dirty Dick. The warehouse was filled with a miscellaneous collection of old materials, such as coils of rope, pieces of copper and copper nails, such as are used for the bottoms of ships, lead stripped from the roofs of empty houses, heaps of old iron, and other articles of a similar description, purchased by the proprietor from the mudlarks who made that part of the river the scene of their operations.

Norman Ashley remained outside the warehouse while his companion explained the affair of the Indiaman to the marine-store dealer, who was a notorious receiver of stolen goods from the Thames-pirates, as well as from those who confined their depredations to the land. He rented a small wharf at the bottom of the narrow miry lane, and possessed a lighter, which he was in the habit of lending to those pirates who needed it for their predatory pursuits. Apparently, Shark had little difficulty in obtaining the loan of the lighter, for in a few minutes he emerged from the warehouse, accompanied by the old man, and was followed by his companion to the wharf.

It was a little, narrow, ruinous-looking place; the adjacent buildings seemed tottering to the fall, some of them describing an angle of thirty degrees with the river, and fit only for the habitation of rats. A lighter was moored off the wharf, and there was sufficient light for them to perceive that the tide was just about to turn downward. Norman and his companion stepped into the lighter, cast off her moorings, and, taking up the oars, pushed her from the wharf, and pulled out into the wide and rushing stream.

It was a dark, uncomfortable night; a fog hung over the river, and penetrated up the lanes and yards on either side, the distant lights twinkling feebly through the moist vapour, and a drizzling rain fell to increase the obscurity and unpleasantness of the night. The shipping lay motionless on the water, and, being the night of the Sabbath, no sound of pauls as the anchor is slowly raised from the muddy bottom of the Thames, no creaking of blocks as the yards are braced in tacking about the Pool, no hearty " Yo-heave-ho!" as the sailors spread the canvass to the breeze that is to waft them from the shores of their native land, gave animation to the silently-flowing river.

The lighter dropped slowly down with the tide, caution being necessary in the Pool, as well on account of the fog which prevailed, as the necessity of avoiding observation. They passed Limehouse, the masts of the shipping in the docks being unperceived through the fog which shrouded them; they passed Blackwall, from whose shores the humanising tendencies of modern society has long since banished the mouldering gibbets and blanched skeletons of pirates and mutineers pendent therefrom, as unnecessary adjuncts to social reformation; they passed that low strip of land called the Isle of Dogs, where tradition asserts that the murder of a blind minstrel was discovered by the fidelity of his dog, who would not quit the spot where the ruthless assassin had buried the body of his victim; and then the lighter of the pirates dropped slowly down along the low marshy coast of Essex, until it reached the stranded Indiaman at Galleon's-reach.

"Steady!" said Shark, in a whisper; "take these;" and he took from the pockets of a pilot coat, which he had purchased since the robbery in Saint Katherine's-docks, two pairs of pistols, one pair of which he gave to his companion.

The lighter was then suffered to float down the stream with the falling tide, and when she came alongside of the vessel, Norman dropped a rope's-end over the side of the lighter, so that the touch could scarcely have been felt aboard the Indiaman. No light was visible on board the vessel, whose spritsail-yard had been carried away in her collision with the brig; her flying-jib, jib, and staysails were hauled down, and her lower and topsails, royals and skysails, closely furled upon their respective yards. The pirates knew that the fog, which seemed to be increasing, would shroud them from the observation of any passing boat or steamer, and boldly prepared to ascend the side of the grounded vessel.

They gained the deck of the Indiaman, and moved quickly towards the hatchway, when they suddenly heard a movement below; a light flashed up from between decks, and then the shadow of a man fell upon the companion-ladder, and a rough voice exclaimed: "Who is there?"

"Silence!" cried Norman Ashley, in an authoritative tone, and he proceeded to descend the companion, followed by Shark.

"Pirates, by heaven!" exclaimed the mate, who appeared at the foot of the companion, with a drawn cutlass in his hand.

Ashley and Shark presented a pistol in each hand at the sailor's head, and he drew back, and lowered the point of his weapon.

"What do you want?" said he, hesitating between his duty to the owners of the vessel, and his fear of resisting two men provided with fire-arms.

"Drop that cutlass!" exclaimed Norman, levelling a pistol at the mate's head.

The man hesitated a moment, and then dropping the cutlass on the deck, rushed towards the open door of the cabin; but Norman, foreseeing his intention, sprang forward, and struck him down with the butt-end of the pistol. He then put his pistols in the pockets of his pea-jacket, and, kneeling on the prostrate seaman, held him down while Shark tied his legs together with a piece of strong cord, and, making a running noose at the other end, passed it over his head in such a manner that if he attempted to stand upright he would tighten the noose, and perhaps strangle himself.

Norman picked up the cutlass; and, leaving the sailor on the deck, with the blood flowing profusely from his wounded forehead, he and Shark entered the cabin, where they found a brace of loaded pistols, which explained the movement of the mate when he dropped the cutlass. Some of the lightest and most valuable portions of the cargo had been brought out of the hold before the seamen left the vessel, and was between the decks; these consisted of India muslin, silk handkerchiefs, and rich Cashmere shawls, several bales of which were got into the lighter as expeditiously as possible. Having plundered the vessel of as much of these goods as could be conveniently stowed away in the lighter, the two pirates revisited the cabin, and added to their spoils the mate's pistols, a valuable chronometer, a telescope, and a few fancy articles of oriental workmanship.

Coming on the deck of the Indiaman for the last time, the pirates fastened down the hatchway, and, returning to their lighter, pushed off from the vessel. The tide was still running out, and, as the lighter was now deeply laden, their progress was necessarily slower even than before; the fog, too, had greatly increased, and, by the time they had reached the Pool, it was so thick that they were in constant danger of running foul of the numerous vessels which render the navigation of that part of the Thames so intricate even by daylight, and in clear weather. But, though the fog was so dense, the darkness was gradually yielding to the first faint light of morning, and, by the time they reached Irongate-wharf, there was twilight enough for them to perceive the wharf of the old maine-store dealer, and to moor the lighter at the place from which they had taken it the preceding night.

CHAPTER LVIII.

THE OLD HOUSE AT WAPPING.

HAVING safely moored the lighter off the wharf, Norman and Shark went to the house of the dealer in marine-stores, and knocked at the door. The little dirty old man put his head out of the window, and, seeing who the applicants for admission were, hurried on his clothes, and hastened to the door. A few words made him acquainted with the success of the enterprise, and the old man followed the pirates to the wharf, and superintended the removal of the plunder to his warehouse, where the whole was snugly stowed away. He then gave them a sovereign each, and promised to meet them in the evening, at the " Bald Stag," after he had ascertained the value of the property stolen from the stranded Indiaman, and give them the remainder of the money which might be due to them.

The two river-pirates accordingly went down to the beer-shop at Limehouse, and remained there until the evening, when the old marine-store dealer came down, and, having beckoned them from the tap-room, led the way into a private room up-stairs. Having been supplied with glasses of grog, he secured the door against the chance of an interruption, and then took a canvass bag from his pocket and proceeded to count upon the table a number of sovereigns.

" Now," said he, when Ashley and his companion had transferred the money to their own pockets, " you had better be out of the way for a little while, till this affair has blown over ; for information of the robbery has been given to the police, with a particular description of both of you, and there will be a warm search made after you. I was afraid you would be taken here, for this house is sure to be visited, and you had better be off at once."

Norman and Shark did not wait for a repetition of this advice, but hastened to quit the house, and immediately dived into the darkest and dirtiest courts and lanes in that region of dirt and depravity, with the view of avoiding, as much as possible, the observation of the police.

" There is a crib in Wapping where we can lay snug for a month, if necessary," said Shark Slingsby, as they walked rapidly along. " It is a beer-shop, like the place we have just left, and the landlord is an old smuggler, and awake to every move that was ever made on the river or alongshore. It is a very old house, and used formerly to be much used by smugglers, and in war-time by sailors who had deserted from the navy, or who wished to avoid the press-gang. It is a queer place, I can tell you, and some of the arrangements of that house will surprise you."

Slingsby then described some of the curious arrangements to which he alluded, which we need not repeat here, and thus the time was beguiled until they reached the house in question. It was an old-fashioned-looking house, situated in the lowest part of Wapping ; and, as the public drinking-rooms were in the rear of the premises, it was apparently a quieter house than most of its class in that neighbourood. The dash of the tide against the wharves and stairs could be heard close at hand, and mingled with the creaking of masts and cordage, and the sighing of the night-breeze among the rigging of the vessels in the river.

" This is the crib," observed Shark, as they entered the house ; and, pausing in front of a narrow bar, a stout man, still jolly-looking, though advanced in years, came out of a small room beyond, smoking a long pipe with a bowl of proportionate dimensions.

" Well, my lad," said he, addressing Shark, but glancing keenly at Norman Ashley.

" Anybody in the cave ?" inquired the pirate, in a semi-whisper.

" Only Mark Grayson and the girls," replied the landlord, in the same subdued tone of voice. " Is it that little affair down at Galleon's-reach that you want to hide for ?"

" You have guessed it, Master Boltrope," returned Shark ; and, as the landlord opened the hatch-door leading into the bar, the river-pirates passed through, and were conducted into the room behind.

Boltrope opened the door of what appeared to be a portable cupboard, stand-ing in one corner of the apartment, and, touching a spring, the shelves and sides disappeared into the wall, and disclosed another door, which, being opened, revealed a dark flight of stone stairs.   Boltrope took up the candle; and, having allowed Ashley and Shark to pass through, he closed both the doors, and preceded them down the stairs.   They had not descended far when they heard voices and laughter at some distance underground, and, having reached the bottom of the stairs, and traversed a narrow subterranean passage, they per-ceived a glimmering light before them, which increased as they advanced, until they reached a doorway, and entered a subterranean chamber of moderate dimensions.

It was excavated in the earth, and formed a cool and pleasant retreat in summer, while in winter the temperature could be raised to the desired degree of warmth by means of a stove, the pipe of which communicated with the chimney above.   There was a table in the centre, and a form on each side of the table, on which were seated an athletic black-whiskered young man, in the garb of a sailor, and two young females; one of these was a fair girl about sixteen years of age, and the other was five or six years older, with darker hair, and a less pleasing countenance. Three stump bedsteads stood on one side of the apartment, with very narrow spaces between them, so that whenever the number of those who sought shelter in the Cave, as it was called, exceeded four, they had to sleep three together; for the two females lived constantly in that confined, unwholesome atmosphere, and devoted themselves to the river-pirates and others whom circumstances might induce to become temporary inhabitants of the subterranean.

The customary salutations passed between Boltrope and Mark Grayson; and, when the former withdrew, the young fellow in seaman's attire nodded familiarly to Shark Slingsby, and stared at his companion.

"How are you, Mark? Tip us your fin," said the river-pirate, shaking hands with Grayson. "This young man is a very particular friend of mine, and, as we have both mixed up in the same business, and the waterside was 'most too warm for us, we have come to share the hospitality of the Cave."

Ashley and his companion sat down, and received a keen examination from the eyes of the two females. Shark Slingsby then proceeded to give Grayson an account of their adventure at Galleon's-reach; and, as the females soon discovered from this narration, that the pockets of the new-comers were well lined with gold, began to show the most marked attention to them, in order to insinuate themselves into their favour.

"How do you get anything you want in this place?" inquired Norman Ashley, looking around him.

"Allow me to show you, young man," said the younger female, rising. "You see this knob?" she continued, directing the youth's attention to a rusty knob near the stove. "That communicates with a wire which passes with the stove-pipe through the roof of the cave, and rings a bell in the little room behind the bar. Now observe this wooden spout: it communicates with the same room, and the refreshments required are passed through the spout, and the money returned in the same manner.

"But how does the landlord know what to send down?" inquired Norman.

"By a code of private signals communicated by means of the wire, which also rings the bell," replied the young girl. "You see the figures marked on the brass plate on which the knob slides? Well, the knob is pulled down, which rings the bell, and, being then adjusted to the number which represents the refreshment required, it indicates the same on a corresponding plate in the room above."

"Well, since you understand the telegraph so well, oblige me by ordering a half-pint of rum and half-a-dozen cigars," said Norman Ashley. "I suppose you have water here, and I see you have glasses and the means of getting a light."

The young girl gave the telegraphic order for the articles mentioned by Norman, and the other female proceeded to wash the glasses. The rum and cigars having been sent down the spout, the money was sent up in the same manner, and the whole party proceeded to test the merits of the grog. A fresh supply had soon to be obtained from above, and, as he became exhilarated by this indulgence and the novelty of the situation, Norman Ashley found himself every moment growing more familiar with the fair-haired girl who had explained to him the mysteries of the telegraphic communication between the Cave and the apartments above. This familiarity became so complete about midnight, that when the party retired to rest, he and the blue-eyed nymph of the subterranean agreed to occupy the same bed; and in this singular retreat we shall, for the present, leave him, while we glance at another character who has been longer before our readers.

CHAPTER LIX.

THE SOLITARY OF THE SEWERS.

Our readers will remember that when Sam Skelter accompanied the old mud-lark to his miserable habitation in West-street, the latter had made the observation that he had not always been in circumstances of such utter destitution, and had directed the youth's attention to a roll of paper, which he said contained the narrative of his misfortunes. They will also remember that when Sam revisited the ruined house near Smithfield, and found the remains of the wretched outcast lying upon a heap of musty straw, he had taken away with him the roll of paper referred to. The manuscript was laid aside by him at his lodging upon entering the service of Mr. Ashley, and it was not until some time afterwards that the youth, in turning over the contents of his box, had his attention again called to it; and, as he had nothing to engage his mind at the moment, and a deficiency of cash compelled him to spend the evening at his lodging, he sat down to peruse it. The narrative appeared to have been written at different periods, and some of the paper was yellow with age, and the writing rendered almost illegible by the dampness of the situation in which it had lain in the wretched tenement in West-street. Some portions, indeed, could not be deciphered on this account, and others had been gnawed by the rats who frequented the crazy building and the sewer below; what was sufficiently legible to be read ran as follows:

" Why have I determined to write my life? Why do I seek to record the misfortunes that have befallen me, when I know that the chances are ten to one against these pages being ever read by any eye save my own? Because the thoughts that oppress me must have a vent, or they will sear my brain, which thus seeks to relieve itself of the pent-up misery beneath which it seems almost to reel. It is just possible, too, that these pages may fall into the hands of some one who will publish them to the world, and thus society will be benefitted, and trade be shown its deformity as in a mirror. For I am one of those thousands whom the car of the modern Juggernaut every year crushes, and it shall be my task to unfold the mysteries of the shop and the counting-house, and to reveal the turpitude with which the competitive system of production and distribution is rife, but the frightful extent of which is only known to those engaged in it.

" My father was at one time a partner in a manufacturing firm in the West Riding of Yorkshire, which at one time did an extensive business; but, owing to a long period of commercial stagnation, and the failure of a firm in America which was largely indebted to them, they became bankrupt, the partnership was dissolved, and my father was never able to retrieve his losses, or to recover the position he had held. He became a travelling agent for another house in the same branch; and, as I was his only son, he contrived to give me a respectable education. I began the world as a draper's assistant, and in this capacity I remained a few years in my native town, and then obtained a situation at the west-end of the metropolis. Here I had ample opportunities of observing the daily frauds, the chicanery and deception that are practised under the guise of trade, from the wealthy manufacturer down to the common huckster. Probity is expected from the shopman, while a dishonest system is at work around him; he must victimise the customers for his employer's profit, but he must not abstract a penny of those profits for his own benefit, not even to save a wife or child from death. Embezzlement is only another term for the practises of the counter: the employer trades; the servant, who may be rendered dishonest by example, embezzles. Yet what sacrifices men make to maintain this vicious system! what ruinous sacrifices of health, of moral principle, and of time that should be employed for intellectual improvements, are made by draper's assistants! Between fashion on the one hand, and excessive competition on the other, their best hours are wasted, rendered worse than useless to themselves and to society.

" My health began to suffer from the confinement within doors for so many hours, which makes the employment the Moloch worship of civilization, and I longed to escape from it. I had also become acquainted with a young female who was similarly situated, and whose loveliness and amiable manners had made a deep impression upon my heart. She was a milliner's assistant, and worked for a fashionable house in the neighbourhood of Regent-street. Poor girl! her lot was as miserable as my own. She worked hard for fifteen or sixteen hours per day, and was sometimes at work for as long a period as thirty-six hours, when work had to be finished by a certain time, that the Countess of

Somebody might attend that scene of fashion and frivolity, the royal drawing-rooms. The roses began to fade from Fanny's cheeks; but what cared Madame Crevecœur, or her lady patronesses? For the credit of the sex, I would fain believe that the latter sanction the atrocious system from mere want of thought; but no such excuse can be found for the employers, whom I always regard with horror and loathing, as ogresses living upon the unfortunates who sell to them their labour. The vampire is no creature of the imagination, as the work-rooms of the dress-makers and milliners of the west-end, with their groups of pale and languid victims, can amply testify.

"I gave up my situation, married my beloved Fanny, and, with a little money which I had become possessed of at the death of my father, I took a small shop in a country town, and commenced business on my own account as a haberdasher and hosier. My new position was scarcely more enviable than that which I had quitted. I was harassed by new cares and fresh responsi-bilities. The travelling-agents of wholesale houses gather about a young tradesman in a small way of business, like flies upon a carcase. I was assailed on one side by these, and on the other by hawkers, who sold the commoner sort of articles at a lower price than that which I was charged by the wholesale dealers; for it is an incontrovertible fact, that the latter supply hawkers at a lower rate than shopkeepers, who have to contend with this additional competi-tion, with the disadvantage of having to pay taxes, parochial rates, gas, and insurance, besides the risk of bad debts. I will mention a few instances of the manner in which wholesale tradesmen in the metropolis do not scruple to act towards their humbler brethren, for the sake of gain. A commercial traveller called upon me with samples of new goods; I declined to give him an order, but he made a note of my address, and in a few days I received a large quantity of the articles of which he had shown me samples. His employers were deter-mined to do business at all risks; but as I had not ordered the goods, and was not in want of them, I sent them back. Had I kept them, I should probably have been called upon to pay for them at a time when I might not have been able to meet the demand. On another occasion, the agent of a wholesale house in the city, to whom I had declined giving an order, from an opinion that the articles he showed me would not meet with a ready sale, agreed to leave me a small quantity, to be returned, if not sold when he called again. Three months passed, and the collecting-clerk of the firm called on me with the bill of the goods with which I had been credited; I informed him of the terms on which I had taken the goods, five-sixths of which remained unsold, but he refused to take the remainder back, and demanded payment for the whole. I was power-less; I had no legal remedy against this flagrant robbery, and I paid the money.

"When I commenced business I paid ready money for all the goods which I purchased, by which I gained fifteen per cent., and sometimes more; but as I had to give credit to many of my customers, I was forced to take credit of the wholesale dealers. This they are always eager to give; for when once a trades-man gets upon their books, he is to a certain extent in their power: they can charge him more for inferior goods than they would for good articles if he were entirely independent of them, and even compel him to take quantities of goods of them which he does not require. Many a young man has been brought into the Insolvent Debtors' Court by these nefarious means. I strove by the strictest economy to conduct my business without getting into debt; but as my shop was getting scanty of goods, I was induced to give a large order to a wholesale dealer near Cheapside, agreeing to pay ready money for half, and for the other half in six months. I paid for the one half when I gave the order, and the whole of the goods were to be forwarded on the following day; but a fortnight elapsed before I received them, during which time I was greatly in need of both money and goods. A month afterwards this man became bankrupt, and I had to borrow the money to pay the assignees the amount of the liability which I had been induced to incur.* I had been in business about three years, struggling against the most adverse circumstances,

---

* Many of our readers can doubtless testify to the sad truths contained in this exposure of our commercial and industrial system, the instances adduced having come within the experience of the author.

and getting every year deeper in debt, when the failure of a wholesale trader in London involved me in the same ruin. I became insolvent, was six months in prison, and was then discharged under the act for the relief of men in my then unfortunate position.

"I went into business again, and had less difficulty in obtaining credit than I had anticipated. Manufacturers have always a large amount of stock in their warehouses which, in times of commercial depression, they are glad to get rid of on any terms; and the wholesale dealers, who act as middle-men between the manufacturers and the retail traders, will give credit to a man who has been thrice a bankrupt, rather than keep their goods in the warehouse, and their shopmen idle behind the counter. This time I opened a shop in a small country town where I had no opposition to contend with, and for a few years I got on very well, and began to hope that I should succeed in establishing myself. But at length another shop in the same line was opened nearly opposite my own, and the proprietor began selling at reduced prices, and using every other means of supplanting me. He advertised, he gave away thousands of hand-bills, he enlarged the shop, and he fitted it up with plate-glass windows, mahogany counters, and a profusion of gilding and other ornamental work. I began immediately to perceive that my customers were deserting me: the gentry went to the larger and the handsomer shop, and the poor to the one where they could purchase the cheapest articles. I knew that I could not oppose my rival by fair and honourable dealing, and in a few months I gave up the attempt, and closed my shop; and very soon afterwards my opponent absconded deeply in debt, both to the tradesmen of the town and to the wholesale dealers in the metropolis.

"I removed my stock to another shop, and tried again; in vain—competition was keen in every locality, and business had become a scramble for the means of subsistence. I strove hard, I economised every shilling, but it was all in vain; the more I struggled the poorer I became. My wife had borne me two children, but both died in early childhood; for they were poor, sickly things, as might be expected from parents in whom the springs of life had been withered by long hours of toil and confinement in the work-room and behind the counter. I sank lower and lower, and my customers became fewer and fewer in proportion as my want of money or credit prevented me from keeping a sufficient stock in trade; at last my goods and furniture were seized by the landlord for arrears of rent, and I removed with my wife to London. We took a humble lodging, and I endeavoured to obtain employment as a commercial traveller. After enduring much poverty, I succeeded; but I had become careless and indifferent alike to praise or censure, and my misfortunes had driven me to habits of intemperance. My wife died, worn down to the grave by care and trouble; and then I became still more reckless and intemperate, until I lost my situation. I had managed to preserve something of the externals of respectability until this; but now I sank lower and lower, until I hated myself, and looked almost with loathing on all whom I saw engaged in the insane scramble in which I had been ruined. This frame of mind grew upon me until at length I resolved to retire from the world, and forsake the haunts of business for the subterranean ways below the city."

Several pages followed, but were almost illegible; and what could be deciphered was written in an incoherent style, as if misery had affected the brain of the hapless wretch who had written them.

CHAPTER LX.

THE FLOWER-GIRL AND THE SCULPTOR.

LEON COPLEY, that pale young man with the long hair, intellectual countenance, and shirt-collar turned down, who had admired the loveliness of poor Ellen Ashley, in St. James's-park, quitted his lodgings near Soho-square, a neighbourhood much frequented by those connected with the fine arts, and walked with a pensive air towards St. Martin's-lane. It was not alone meditation, nor too close application to the divine art of sculpture, which had produced the paleness that dwelt upon the young artist's countenance; the germs of pulmonary consumption were implanted within his constitution—that fatal disease had marked him for its own. Hence the brilliance of his dark eyes, the evanescent tinge of bright carnation that sometimes would mount to his usually pallid cheeks; that delusive symptom which appears a prognostic of returning health, while it only marks the progress of decay, and those fits of melancholy succeeding periods of enthusiasm and gaiety which make up the existence of the consumptive patient.

The young sculptor turned into Long-acre, and, passing down Bow-street, entered the area of Covent-garden market, a spot which he often visited to look at the flowers and fruits there displayed for sale, and to indulge the reflections which they excited in his poetic mind. Gazing on those beautiful flowers and those luscious fruits, unheeding the busy throng that passed and repassed in the market, his imagination revelled in the gardens and conservatories of Italy, or conjured up visions of " those old tales Arabian, those old Arabian Nights." His imagination, dilating as he gazed, would then seek to give a personal identity to inanimate objects; and he would compare in his mind the choice flowers in bright red pots—the cuphea with its delicate scarlet blossoms, or the fuchsia with its gracefully pendent blossoms of crimson and violet—to the trained and impassioned beauties of some eastern harem; and the rose or camellia, which adorned the button-hole of a gallant until it began to droop, and was then cast away, and trampled upon by careless passengers, until it mingled with the mire of the street, to the hapless victims of seduction, lured from their homes, and consigned to the streets when the destroyer had become satiated with their charms.

Leon Copley walked slowly through the market, stopping every moment to observe some beautiful flower or fruit, or perchance to catch a passing glance of some countenance of surpassing loveliness; for he was a lover of his art, and, therefore, of beauty throughout all nature's works; and, as he quitted the warm and fragrant atmosphere of the market, he again encountered Ellen Ashley. Slightly pale, and neatly dressed, though in a style of extreme poverty, the serenity of her countenance showed that adversity had not affected her disposition, or her morals, any more than it had impaired her loveliness. There was the same radiance in her soft, dark eyes, the same air of purity upon her alabaster forehead, the same mixture of dignity with grace in all her movements, as when first we introduced her to our readers. But she was now verging upon womanhood; she had grown taller, and the white and swelling bosom, which a little faded handkerchief thrown over her shoulders only partially concealed, marked the progress she had made from childhood to maturity. She stood on the edge of the footpath, holding in her hands a few bunches of moss-roses, which she offered for sale to the passers by.

Leon recognised the beautiful girl whom he had seen in the park, and paused an instant to gaze upon her speaking countenance; and she, catching the eyes of the young sculptor bent with artistic admiration upon her, hastened to offer him her roses, of which she had that morning sold but one bunch.

" Buy a moss rose, sir?" said Ellen, raising her fine dark eyes to his, while a modest blush gave a livelier carnation to her cheek at the evident admiration with which the young sculptor regarded her.

" Give me the prettiest bud," said Leon Copley, in his usual pensive tone; and Ellen's hand trembled, she knew not why, as she selected the best bud in her little stock of floral beauties, and received sixpence in exchange.

" If it were not for the fear of offending you by the proposition, I could offer you a pleasanter and more remunerative occupation than this," observed the young sculptor, surveying the symmetrical form of the young girl with increasing admiration.

" As what, sir?" said Ellen, in a hesitating manner; for her gains as a flower-girl were small and precarious.

" I am a sculptor," replied Leon Copley; " and without intending the least flattery, such a countenance and figure as yours would be an acquisition to me as a study."

Ellen blushed at the compliment as much as at the sculptor's proposition, and for a moment she made no reply.

" What remuneration do you give for such a singular service?" she inquired, at length.

" It depends upon the beauty and symmetry of the model, and the extent of the service rendered; but to you the terms would be liberal," replied the sculptor. " But if you will accompany me to my study, which is not far from here, I will explain more fully the nature of the service which would be required of you."

Ellen Ashley followed Leon to the house in which he lodged, and into the apartment which he used as a study and workroom, which was lighted from the ceiling, and filled with blocks of white marble, plaster casts from the antique, unfinished busts and small figures, and various instruments of the sculptor's art. There was a bust of Byron, another of the Earl of Chatham, a beautiful Venus, covered over with yellow canvass, an unfinished nymph, and numerous casts in plaster of Diana, Andromeda, Apollo, and the Graces.

" This is the most beautiful work of art that my chisel has yet produced," said Leon Copley, raising the canvass which covered the marble Venus. " I am now engaged upon this nymph, but I have not yet found a model of such perfect symmetry as I could desire. This unfinished nymph and the perfect Venus will give you an idea of the nature of the work, and what is required from a model. As we have a difficulty in obtaining good subjects for study, we pay liberally for them ; and I shall be happy to offer you a sum equal to what is received by the best models in the metropolis."

The sum which he then named so far exceeded Ellen's expectations, that it banished the scruples which she at first experienced ; and she hesitated no longer to accept the service which he proposed to her. Her correct understanding, and the purity of her mind, enabled her to distinguish between that modesty which is the safeguard of virtue, and that spurious feeling which is often confounded with it, and which is called into action by very opposite causes. The blush which mantles on the cheeks of modesty is called there by the instinctive consciousness of insulted purity ; that which glows upon those of shame arises from the train of impure thoughts upon which the insult falls, from sympathy rather than from abhorrence. The one is a natural sentiment, the other is only its counterfeit.

" If agreeable to you, I will retouch the left arm and shoulder of the nymph at once," said the young sculptor, taking up his mallet and chisel.

Ellen laid down her flowers, took off her bonnet and the handkerchief which she wore over her shoulders, and having denuded her left shoulder, placed herself in the position in which the sculptor intended to represent the nymph. The graceful slope of her dimpled shoulder, and the round white arm, enabled Leon to give to his statue the perfect symmetry of the antique remains of Grecian art, from which he had formed his ideal. While he alternately studied the contours of Ellen's arm and shoulder, and strove to transfer their beauty to the marble which seemed to spring into life under his hands, his manners were reserved and respectful, as if he were absorbed in his pleasing labour, or was fearful of offending her delicacy, even by a complimentary allusion.

At length the lovely flower-girl quitted the studio of the young sculptor, and, after breaking her fast (which she had not done until then), she returned to Covent-garden to sell her rosebuds. When night came, she returned not to the shelter of the trees in St. James's-park, beneath whose friendly shade she had passed many a night since her arrival in the metropolis, but took a humble lodging in the house of an honest workman, where she would be neither offended nor contaminated by the immoral examples which abound in the low lodging-houses.

On the following morning, she presented herself at the studio of Leon Copley, and again submitted her alabaster shoulders for his study ; and as one day followed another, and the sculptor's work progressed, she began to feel an interest in the marble which his artistic skill and genius seemed to endue with life. As Leon proceeded with his work, his lovely model had to bare her bosom, that he might impart its charms to the marble nymph ; and as he gazed upon the white and heaving breasts of that beautiful young girl—scarcely a woman, and yet no longer a child—he may be excused if he lingered over his task, and gazed upon the matchless charms of that speaking countenance, that swan-like neck, those graceful shoulders, and that plump and snowy breast, until his admiration deepened into love, and his worship of ideal beauty merged in a passionate attachment for the lovely young creature who had realised his visions.

CHAPTER LXI.

ST. JAMES'S-PARK.

IT was a fine evening about a month after her visit to Greenwich-park, where she had first beheld Norman Ashley, that Lolah Hastings encountered him again in St. James's-park. She was walking alone on the margin of the ornamental water; for the earl never appeared with her in public, and she had no acquaintance save Caroline Allen. She had stopped to look at the aquatic birds sailing majestically over the unruffled surface of the water, or darting under the drooping branches of the trees in pursuit of insects; and, on turning round to continue her walk, her eyes encountered those of the young smuggler. She had thought of him several times since the occasion of their last meeting; and though a month had passed without her seeing him again, and consequently the impression made upon her heart was beginning to be obliterated, yet she had not forgotten him, and a thrill of pleasure pervaded her bosom, and was reflected from her soft, dark eyes and on her cheeks, where the flush of joy tinged the clear olive with a richer hue, on thus encountering him again.

" You have not forgotten me, I see," said Norman Ashley, as he took, and gently pressed, the hand which Lolah extended to him.

The young girl was far from being displeased with the familiar manner in which Norman addressed her. There are distances which those who love are glad to see leaped over: the etiquette of the world is only for worldlings.

" The evening was so fine that I could not avoid the temptation to a walk; but I was just returning home," observed Lolah.

Upon this intimation Norman begged to be allowed to conduct her home, and Lolah having unhesitatingly taken his arm, they walked towards the steps leading to that architectural disgrace, the York column, from which we hope, ere long, the figure of the royal duke will be removed and replaced by the statue of liberty. Lolah thought nothing of her companion's nautical dress, for his air and manners were those of a gentleman, and she concluded him to be a mate of some merchant-vessel. She knew that the Earl of Glenvale was out of town; and hence she was under no apprehension of his discovering that she had walked from the park with the young smuggler. The morality of her conduct with reference to the earl she never thought of: she was deceiving him, undoubtedly; but we question whether nineteen in twenty of our fair readers, under the same circumstances, would not have acted in precisely the same manner. Nothing was said during their walk from the park to the residence of Lolah Hastings, which could reveal to Norman the state of her heart with regard to him, or render necessary an acknowledgment of it by the advances of her companion; but on reaching her residence she paused.

" You must leave me here," she said, in a soft, low tone.

" When may I hope to have the pleasure of seeing you again?" Norman inquired, taking her hand, and holding it in his own.

" I do not know—I often walk in the park—but at present we scarcely know each other," returned Lolah, in a hesitating manner.

" My name is Norman Ashley, and I am a sailor," said the youth, quickly. And then he added, with a smile: " It seems to me as if we had been acquainted from our childhood, rather than that this was only our second meeting. Do you think it probable you will be in the park at this time to-morrow evening?"

" Well, I will be there," returned Lolah, after a moment's hesitation. And then they parted, and the delighted Norman returned to his lodgings at Wapping, thinking of every word that had passed between them during their walk from the park.

On the following evening he revisited the park at the same hour as he had before met her, and had the gratification of beholding Lolah walking under the trees opposite the Admiralty, as if anxiously waiting for his appearance. The

[Lolah Hastings.]

young girl extended her hand to him as he advanced to meet her, and the tell-tale blush, that tinged with "celestial rosy red, love's proper hue," the clear olive of her cheek, showed that a mutual passion had prompted them to this appointment

"You are more than punctual," said Norman Ashley, pressing the small, white hand that Lolah held out to him with the fervour of an enraptured lover; and then, drawing her arm within his own, they walked towards the ornamental water, margined with shrubs and trees, and enlivened with one little fountain, which only increases the contrast between the park and the gardens of the Tuileries.

"I need not tell you," said Norman, when they had walked a little distance, "what were the motives which induced me to seek this interview. From the first moment that I beheld you at Greenwich, a month ago, your image has never been absent from my mind—it has been present even in my dreams. You may judge, then, of my delight when I met you here last evening, and received your promise to meet me again to-night. That promise implied—so I

24

flattered myself—that I was not indifferent to you, and gave me hopes of acquiring your undivided love."

Norman paused; he had expressed with sincerity the sentiments and hopes that animated him, and he waited for his lovely companion's reply.

"I feel honoured by this declaration of your esteem, which I believe to be sincere and honourable," returned Lolah, after a short pause, and speaking in a low, harmonious tone, which caused Norman to imbibe, with rapture, every word she uttered. "I am no coquette, and I have no desire to affect the prude; I will therefore frankly acknowledge that I should not have consented to meet you this evening if you had been indifferent to me. I know not why I should conceal my sentiments, or hesitate to admit the reciprocity of feeling which exists between us."

"Your charming frankness, dear girl, has confirmed my hopes," said Norman Ashley, pressing her arm, and gazing with tenderness, mingled with admiration, upon the lovely countenance of Lolah Hastings, to which the slightly heightened colour which her avowal of preference had called there gave an additional charm. I told you last night that I was a sailor, as you may perceive by my dress, but it is time that I should give you my entire confidence. I was reared and educated as the only son of Sir Norman Ashley of Oakwood-hall, in Gloucestershire; but, on my father's death, a few years ago, a claim to the property was set up by my uncle, on the ground that no legal marriage had taken place between my parents. I am therefore obliged to obtain my subsistence by labour, though by birth and education a gentleman. And now, my dear girl, tell me if there exists any impediment to the consummation of our mutual happiness?"

"I am so situated that I scarcely know how to explain my position to you, without incurring your contempt," said Lolah Hastings, after a pause of more than a minute, and looking down to veil her blushing countenance from the observation of her companion. "I have been very unfortunate," she continued, in a sweetly pensive tone; "and misfortune in woman is too often visited with reprobation rather than with the pity which it surely deserves."

"Am I to infer that you have been seduced?" he asked, in a low voice.

"Not seduced, but vilely and brutally outraged by one whom the world calls a gentleman," replied Lolah, blushing deeply, and speaking in a tone of mingled bitterness and indignation.

"I hope, my dear girl, you do not think so meanly of me, as to suppose that the occurrence of such a misfortune could tend to diminish my affection for you," said Norman Ashley.

"Your generous sentiments indicate a noble mind," returned Lolah; "but I have not yet told you all, and when you know it perhaps your good opinion of me will cease. Honour demands that I should make the revelation, and yet I can scarcely summon courage to do it."

For a few minutes both were silent, for Norman felt oppressed by the anticipation of the revelation which the beautiful girl, who hung on his arm, was about to make.

"I throw myself upon your honour, Norman," said Lolah, raising her dark eyes to the youth's countenance for a moment. "You might have been induced, with the characteristic generosity of your profession to make me your wife, but I should despise myself if I deceived you, and should justly incur the suspicion of having deceived you to a greater extent than the truth. I have no relations or friends to care for me; and, after my first misfortune, poverty, rather than inclination, induced me to accept an offer of protection."

"And you are now in the keeping of some wealthy man?" said Norman Ashley, with assumed equanimity. "Have I guessed aright?"

"You have," returned Lolah, avoiding the keen glance of her companion. "I see that you despise me already. Let us forget that we ever knew each other;" and the young girl withdrew her hand from her lover's arm.

"I do not despise you, and to forget you is not within the power of will," said Norman, in a deprecatory tone, as he seized her hand and pressed it.

Within the boundaries of St. James's-park there are some shady, sequestered walks, with which some of our readers are probably acquainted; and down one of these walks Norman and the lovely dancing-girl had now turned, in order to be beyond the hearing and observation of the idlers who thronged the margin of the lake.

" You expressed a hope to acquire my undivided love—will you accept it now?" said Lolah, raising her head, and turning the full witchery of her lovely countenance upon her companion. "I have spoken frankly and candidly, as free from coquetry as from the affectation of prudery, because I would not wholly forfeit your esteem. Had we met before I formed the connection which I have with the person to whom I alluded, I feel that I should have stood in a different position."

" Your undivided love were indeed a prize," said Norman Ashley, as he gazed admiringly upon her expressive countenance. " Your candour has secured you the continuance of my esteem, and no circumstances could ever diminish the ardent passion with which you have inspired me. You need not ask me to accept your love, but should bestow it as a boon which you know will be received with rapture."

" Then it is yours, dear Norman, wholly and unreservedly," exclaimed Lolah; and, as the youth had thrown his arm around her waist while speaking, he drew her closer to him at this avowal, and their lips met for the first time.

Lolah then informed her lover, as briefly as possible, that she was under the protection of the Earl of Glenvale, who was at that time in the country, and that, after the conversation which had passed between them, she should not deem her conduct honourable towards the earl, if she did not immediately renounce his protection and control. Norman admired the young girl's candour and nice sense of honour, and promised to meet her again on the following evening at her residence, to which she no longer hesitated to admit him, intending to write to the Earl of Glenvale on the ensuing morning. After a little more conversation, Lolah Hastings and her lover separated, and returned to their respective abodes, at opposite ends of the metropolis.

CHAPTER LXII.

THE EARL'S MISTRESS AND HER LOVER.

On the morning after Lolah's second meeting with Norman Ashley, in St. James's-park, she wrote to the Earl of Glenvale, informing him of her intention to withdraw herself from his protection; and this she did without a single doubt or fear for the future, so implicit was her reliance upon the honour of Norman Ashley, and so intense the passion with which he had inspired her. Her heart was naturally susceptible to the influence of the tender passion, and her nature as warm as the sunny clime in which she had commenced her existence; the accomplishments she had acquired at the seminary, and the refining influences of that period of her life, had cultivated her understanding, and added the graces of intellect to the charms of her transcendent loveliness, but they had failed to counteract the tendencies of a childhood of vagabondage. Her intellect had been expanded, and her manners refined by the amenities of education, but her moral sentiments had undergone no change; her early years had been passed amid the contaminating influences of lodging-houses, taverns, fairs, and races, in contributing to the gratification of the idle and depraved, who usually formed the majority of the admiring spectators who followed her with eager eyes through the movements of those wanton dances which the Malay had taught her. What effect the deteriorating influence of these circumstances may have had upon her future career, under other conditions than those to which she was suddenly exposed by the murder of her father, it is of course impossible to say. In all the dawning beauty of precocious womanhood, she found herself suddenly plunged into destitution, surrounded by the contagion of example, and with no guide save the impulses of an untrained mind, and the counsels of the frail but kind-hearted Caroline Allen. Necessity and inclination alike impelled her to the course which she adopted upon her introduction to Frederick Shirley; and, after her abandonment by him, the former motive alone induced her to accept the protection of the Earl of Glenvale.

She had now met with one to whom she felt herself irresistibly attracted, even more than she had been towards the handsome barrister's clerk; and when she had posted the letter to the earl, she felt as if she were already free from the shackles of a degrading connection—degrading, because she loved not the earl, and only endured his caresses because dependent upon him for subsistence. She therefore received Norman Ashley, when he visited her in the evening, with an exhilaration of spirits which evinced the serenity of her mind, and immediately acquainted him with what she had done.

" Then the intimacy is at an end, and we will think no more of it than if it had never existed," said Norman, looking fondly at the beautiful girl, who, dressed in a style of elegance which displayed to the greatest advantage the admirable proportions of her matchless figure, sat before him on the sofa.

" You are determined to excel my candour by your generosity," observed Lolah Hastings; " and it would be doubting your affection for me to entertain the most lingering idea that you will think less worthily of me on account of the intimacy which I have severed for your sake."

" I have no right to scold you for what may have occurred before we were acquainted, dearest," returned Norman; " and the charming candour you have displayed in unfolding to me the past, the flattering confidence you have evinced in my regard, and your reliance upon my honour, have raised you extremely in my estimation."

" I am a quick judge of character," observed Lolah, smiling. " Moreover, there is a freemasonry in love which renders those destined for each other as familiar on their first or second meeting as if they had been acquainted from their childhood."

" Animal magnetism," said the youth, with a smile.

" Well, really there is no other means of accounting for thousands of alliances, but the theory of the attraction of kindred affinities," continued Lolah Hastings. " Alliances, right-handed and left-handed, orthodox and Platonic, take place every day, in which neither party can assign the slightest cause for their mutual attachment; and, though a mystery even to themselves, they live comfortably and happily. They have been acquainted with numbers of persons of greater beauty or more brilliant intellect, but no preference is evinced until they meet with one in whose physical constitution we may reasonably suppose there exists an affinity to their own, since to that person they are irresistibly drawn, as if by the influence of the magnet."

" You do not ascribe all marriages to this mysterious influence, I presume?" said Norman, in an inquiring tone.

" Oh, no!" replied Lolah, " far from it; of course, I except all those disgraceful marriages of convenience, which, not being in accordance with the laws which nature has devised for human happiness, inevitably result in discord, misery, and scandal."

" I am inclined to think that there is much truth in your observations, my dear girl," said Norman Ashley; " and I hope that the freemasonry which enabled you to form so flattering an estimate of my character will be a guarantee for our future happiness; for I suppose that the freemasonry of love can only be understood by those lovers whom nature has destined for each other."

" Certainly not," responded Lolah, with a smile and a slight blush; " for others possess not the attraction which nature has given us for our guidance in this matter, which so intimately concerns the happiness of both sexes. But, to speak of ourselves, dearest Norman, could you not give up the sea, or only make very short voyages?"

" Oh, I go with a continental steamer, and, consequently, I am as often in London as at Boulogne," replied Norman, with some confusion, which however was not observed by Lolah.

" I am glad of that," returned the beautiful girl, looking fondly at her lover. " I must give up these apartments, and remove to the Surrey-side of the river, for the rent is high here, and I hope we do not need all this display to make us happy."

" Assuredly not, dearest," said Norman. " With your love, I shall need no other accessory to happiness."

" Do you think you can always love me as you do now?" inquired Lolah, laying her small, white hand on her lover's arm, and looking into his eyes as though she would read his inmost soul.

" Can you doubt me, dearest?" said Norman, in a tone of gentle reproach ; and, folding the young girl in his arms, he drew her close to him, and imprinted a kiss upon her ruby lips.

" I do not doubt you, dear Norman," replied Lolah, returning the kiss. " Let us confide in each other, and be happy."

" When shall you leave here, dearest?" asked her lover.

" As soon as you please ; but when do you leave London again?" returned Lolah.

" To-morrow at noon," replied Norman ; " and, if it be agreeable, you might remove from here during my absence."

" It shall be as you wish," responded the young girl ; " and I will leave my address with the people here."

The lovers sat some time, occupied by their endearments and their arrangements for the future, and then Norman rose to depart ; but they lingered many a minute at the door of the apartment before they could prevail upon themselves to part, looking love into each other's eyes, and exchanging many of those blissful gages of affection, the invention of which Coleridge ascribes to Cupid.

In the course of the following day, Lolah Hastings removed to other apartments in the York-road, a wide street of private houses, extending from the Westminster-road to the Waterloo-road ; and on the third evening from her last interview with Norman Ashley, he came to the house, eager to again behold the beautiful girl whose charms and attractive manners had bound him as if with a magic spell. As soon as she had admitted him, and closed the door of the apartment, Norman caught her in his arms, and impressed a score of kisses on her ruby lips, her glowing cheeks, and her alabaster brow.

" My dearest Lolah," said he, " every minute has seemed an hour since we parted. How delighted I am to behold you again !"

" And I, dear Norman," responded the young girl, tenderly. " I came here on the day after we parted, and I have almost counted the minutes since."

" Now that we have met again, I hope there will exist no necessity for our parting again until I have again to leave London," observed Norman, sitting down on the sofa, and drawing Lolah on his knee.

" I represented myself to the people here as a married woman, and I have taken your name, dear Norman," responded the blushing Lolah, hiding her face upon her lover's bosom, against which her heart beat with a wild tumult, which she sought not to repress.

" You have anticipated my own wishes, dear Lolah," said Norman Ashley ; " and I shall study to make your existence as happy as possible, for I feel as if my whole future happiness depended upon my attention to yours."

Again the lips of the lovers met, and Lolah Hastings shrank not from those caresses, which added fuel to the ardent fire that burned in the bosom of each ; murmured expressions of tenderness succeeded to conversation, and while the young girl lay folded in her lover's arms, the candles remained unsnuffed, and the supper stood untasted on the table. The magic influence that bound them in its thrall was aided by the waning light of the unsnuffed candles, which at length flickered in their sockets, and then went out. The effluvia emitted by the extinguished candles dissipated the charm that had held the lovers in its rosy bonds, and Lolah rose from the sofa, and lifted up the blind at the window, allowing the moonlight to stream into the apartment for a moment, and then lowering the blind again.

" It is beautifully moonlight, dear—come," said she, in a low, soft tone, as she placed her small, white hand on Norman's shoulder.

The youth needed no second summons ; and, rising from the sofa, was led by the beautiful girl into the adjoining room, where the clear moonlight without, throwing a narrow line of silvery radiance between the drawn curtains, fell upon the white drapery and counterpane of the young girl's bed.

CHAPTER LXIII.

LORD CLANROBERT AND ELLEN ASHLEY.

THE marble nymph, the product of Leon Copley's genius and artistic skill, was at length complete, and if the young sculptor looked upon it with the eyes of one devoted to his art, the admiration of his beautiful model was no less enthusiastic and sincere. It was a moment of pride to Leon Copley, when, after having given the finishing touches to the statue in Ellen's absence, he removed the yellow canvass which he had thrown over it to protect it from the dust, when she came the next morning to know if he again required her services, and exhibited to her admiring eyes the finished sculpture. The young sculptor scarce knew which to admire most, the marble statue or the living model; like Pygmalion of old, he might have fallen in love with the creation of his own genius, so artistically beautiful was the conception, and so perfect the chiselling; but, standing by was the living and breathing reality, the beautiful original of that sublime work of art. Here was the classic head, but there the spiral curls of glossy and silken hair of ebon blackness; here the eyes were perfectly chiselled, but destitute of lustre or expression; there the dark lustrous orbs rayed forth the love and the intelligence of the soul within; here the neck and bosom were admirably sculptured after all the symmetry and grace of the model, but there the azure veins were shown upon the soft transparent skin, and the close-fitting dress of dark merino showed the gentle heaving of the young maiden's bosom.

"It is very beautiful!" said Ellen, looking with admiration upon the marble nymph.

"It is beautiful, because it is the counterpart of yourself, Ellen," observed the sculptor. Then, observing the heightened colour which his compliment called up on the young girl's countenance, he added: "You have no reason to blush, Ellen, for I am sure you are as good as you are beautiful. Since you have attended here, I have closely watched your actions, I have inquired concerning you, and the result has proved to me the truth of Plato's maxim, that the fairest body ever incloses the purest soul. I would disdain to flatter, Ellen, and I only make these observations to convince you that I have appreciated your worth.

"You are very good, sir," returned Ellen; and after an embarrassing pause of a minute or more, she added: "Now the nymph is finished, I suppose you will not require me any more?"

"Not for a day or two," replied the sculptor. "Look in again in about three days."

Leon Copley opened the door of his studio for his beautiful model, who wished him "good morning," and returned to her lodging. The remuneration which she received from the young sculptor had enabled her to abandon her former avocation of vending flowers; and the abundant leisure which her new employment afforded her, she spent in visiting the National Gallery, and the gallery of antiquities in the British Museum, having imbibed, in the sculptor's studio, a taste for the contemplation of works of art, which she was thus enabled to cheaply gratify. Her evenings she usually passed in the occupation of needle-work, sitting at the open window of her little chamber, which a long box of mignonette filled with its delightful fragrance, and listening to the carolling of her landlady's sky-lark, whose cage hung out at the door below, from which, standing on his little bit of turf and fluttering his wings, the poor feathered prisoner could just behold the blue sky in which he longed to soar, and leave the noisy, smoky city for the green fields so far beyond. When not engaged with needle-work, Ellen would stroll into St. James's-park, and watch the motions of the aquatic birds, diving and splashing in the ornamental water, or the fountain near the palace, which, though not to be compared with those of Paris or Rome, diffuses an agreeable coolness in the warm evenings of summer.

Ellen was returning from a walk in the park on the evening of the day on which she had been complimented, by the sculptor, on her beauty and the rectitude and purity of her conduct, and having lingered in the park later than was her wont, she was walking hurriedly along in the direction of her humble lodging, when she was met in a court, near St. Martin's-lane, by a fashionably-dressed youth, who appeared to be slightly inebriated, but sufficiently sober to preserve the control of his actions. He stared rudely at Ellen as she came up, and when she strove to avoid him, by removing to the other side of the narrow court, he caught her rudely round the waist, and asked her what she was afraid of.

"Let me go, sir, or I will call the police," exclaimed Ellen, indignantly, though half frightened by the rude violence of the inebriated young man.

"You are a sweet little girl—quite a little divinity," said the latter, clasping her round the waist, and endeavouring to kiss her.

"Police!—help!" cried Ellen, struggling in vain against the licentious violence of the aristocratic ruffian.

"Oh, the police are all down the areas, and in the larders, and they will not interfere with a gentleman's pleasures," exclaimed Lord Clanrobert, for he was the libertine by whom the pretty Ellen had been assailed; and so it appeared, for none came, and the insulted young maiden again screamed aloud.

Just as Lord Clanrobert had succeeded in pressing his lips upon those of the blushing and affrighted Ellen, a quick, firm step sounded behind them, and the young nobleman received so severe a blow on the ear, that he loosened his hold of the trembling girl, and staggered against the wall. He had better have effected his escape at once, but champagne had rendered him valiant; and, clenching his hands, he rushed upon Ellen's deliverer; but he was received with a blow which caused him to measure his length upon the dirty pavement of the court.

"My dear brother!" exclaimed Ellen, in accents of mingled joy and surprise, for in her brave rescuer she immediately recognised her brother Norman.

"Ellen!" ejaculated Norman, in surprise, and, taking his sister's hand, he kissed her with fraternal tenderness. "Come away, and leave this drunken fellow to get up as he can. Where have you been, dear sister, since we parted four years ago?"

Ellen straightened her bonnet, which the rude violence of Lord Clanrobert had discomposed, and taking her brother's arm, related, as they walked onward, the vicissitudes which she had encountered since her clandestine departure from the lace-maker's cottage in Buckinghamshire. By the time she had concluded her narrative, they had reached the house in which she lodged, which the young girl invited her brother to enter, that she might hear from him what had befallen him in the time which had elapsed since they had seen each other.

Norman related as much of his adventures as he could impart to his sister without wounding her sensitive mind by the knowledge of his recent criminal exploits in company with Shark Slingsby, and merely informed her of his leaving the service of the old fisherman, and his connection with the contraband traders. Then they parted, and Norman proceeded towards Westminster-bridge, having been on his way to the York-road when he encountered his sister, in time to rescue her from the licentiousness of Lord Clanrobert.

That profligate young man, when he had raised himself from the pavement, brushed the dirt off his coat; and, having been rendered sober by the blow dealt him by Norman Ashley, he adopted the better part of valour, and sauntered from the spot, endeavouring to devise some tale to account to his gay companions for his dirty plight. Having found his way into Long-acre, he turned down Bow-street, and crossing Covent-garden, was soon in the beauty-haunted locality of Brydges-street. He was now in the centre of those resorts of dissipation and illicit pleasure frequented by the aristocracy, and the contemptible *snobs* who imitate them; before him were that temple of profligacy known as H's, the Elysium, the Albert, and the Sheridan Knowles; a half turn brought the Harp within scope of his vision; and, could his gaze have pierced the market, he might have seen the Garrick's Head. The wine-rooms are seldom filled until after midnight, when the theatres disgorge their throngs of rakish noblemen and gentlemen, dissipated men "about town," and the scamps by profession, who hang upon the skirts of the former. Lord Clanrobert, therefore, entered the Sheridan Knowles, a tavern which divides with the Harp the patronage of the actors and others connected with Drury-lane Theatre.

In the parlour, he found Augustus Fitzormond; and, having been supplied with a bottle of wine, he gave a very highly-coloured description of his encounter with Ellen Ashley, which, he stated, was interrupted by a youth, who might have been her brother or a lover, with whom he represented himself as having had a severe contest, which he was obliged to abandon by the appearance of the police. After eulogizing the beauty of the young girl, he offered to reward Fitzormond for finding out who and what she was, and where she lived, which that unprincipled young man agreed to do, and it was arranged that they should meet at the same tavern on the following evening, when Augustus should report to his patron all that he had discovered concerning the dark-eyed Ellen.

CHAPTER LXIV.

NANCY SHRIMP.

NEAR the brow of Windmill-hill, on the gentle slope of which the town of Gravesend is built, are the Tivoli-gardens, which share with the theatre and Tulley's bazaar and concert-room, the patronage of the pleasure-seekers of that pleasant place of cockney resort. Thither did Lord Clanrobert repair one fine evening, a few months after the occurrences related in the preceding chapter, wearied for a time of the dissipation in which he had indulged in London, and in which he had been initiated and encouraged by his reckless associates, Fitzormond and Simpson. The vile plan which he had formed to ensnare the lovely Ellen Ashley had been frustrated by Sam Skelter, whose generosity of feeling and sense of rectitude and honour had not been destroyed by the vicious atmosphere into which the youth had been imperceptibly led. Lord Clanrobert had succeeded in his designs upon the beautiful orphan so far as to forcibly introduce her into a house of notoriously infamous character, close to which he had waylaid her, and his success would have been complete had not the cries of Ellen Ashley brought Sam Skelter to the rescue. He had visited the house in the company of a young lady habituated to promenade the asphaltum of a western street; and, having rescued Ellen from her aristocratic assailant, to whom he administered summary punishment, in a style which would have done credit to a pupil of Tom Cribb, he escorted the young girl to her home, and then returned to the society of his less innocent inamorata.

Lord Clanrobert having been, on two occasions, summarily punished for his audacity in respect to the beautiful orphan, resolved to make no further attempt to obtain possession of Ellen Ashley, and visited the Tivoli-gardens in order to select another intended victim from the numbers of pretty girls who are attracted there by the music, the singing, the fireworks, and the illuminated walks. As his licentious glances roved from one to another, they suddenly alighted upon a neatly-attired girl of about twenty years of age, whose blue eyes and auburn tresses were an irresistible attraction to the youthful libertine. She appeared to be observing the movements of a young man in the garb of a mariner, and a lady, elegantly dressed, who had entered the gardens just before her. He ventured to accost her with the remark that so pretty a girl should not be without a protector; she replied with a lively sally, and in a few minutes the young nobleman was seated with Nancy Shrimp, the blue-eyed maiden who had thus captivated his roving eyes, in one of the bowers.

The fisherman's daughter was walking up Windmill-street at an earlier period of the evening, when she beheld before her a young man whose appearance reminded her forcibly of her father's runaway apprentice, Norman Ashley. Had the young man been alone, she would have overtaken him, and set her doubts at rest at once; but he was accompanied by a young female, attired in a style of equal elegance and taste. She walked a short distance behind them for a little time, and at last became convinced, by the tone of his voice, and a hasty glance which she obtained of his profile, that the young mariner was no other than her inconstant admirer.

She had mourned in secret over what she deemed the faithlessness of Norman Ashley; for, though she was not only possessed of a proud heart, but also of the dangerous spirit of coquetry, yet the tender devotion of a first attachment had rendered her heart yielding and ductile, and deprived her of those weapons of the coquette, of which it may be truly said, as it has been of curses, that, like young chickens, they come home to roost. Nothing can be so galling to the heart of a woman, as to find herself slighted and deserted by the man upon whom she has bestowed her love and lavished her tenderness and devotion; the memory of the past becomes bitter as wormwood, and her pride even is a vain refuge against the galling thought that her affections have been cast away, her proffered

love disdained. It was thus with Nancy Shrimp; but when she saw Norman Ashley in the company of his beautiful mistress, she became devoured with jealousy and resentment, and, acting upon the impulse of the moment, followed them into the gardens.

Every attention or mark of affection which Norman bestowed upon Lolah Hastings was like a drop of oil falling upon the fire which consumed her heart. Envenomed by jealousy, her heart lost the softness and tenderness with which her love for her father's apprentice had imbued it, and encased itself in coquetry and feminine pride. In this mood it was that she was accosted by Lord Clanrobert, and inspired with the desire of showing to her inconstant admirer how independent she was of his attentions—the usual direction of a coquette's resentment—she received his advances with a liveliness which encouraged the libertine peer in the most audacious hopes. She entered with him the bower adjoining that in which Norman Ashley and Lolah Hastings were seated, and few minutes elapsed before the former recognised the voice of the fisherman's daughter, as well as that of Lord Clanrobert.

25

The latter had called for brandy and water, and redoubled his attentions to Nancy as he found his advances received with favour; for all the coquetry of the young girl was roused to action by the proximity of Norman and his mistress, and she was delighted with the opportunity of evincing to him how soon she could obtain another admirer as much a gentleman as himself. But the motive which had at first induced her to receive with encouragement the gallantry of Lord Clanrobert gradually merged into another channel as the incense of flattery intoxicated her imagination; and when she learned that her new admirer was a peer, her heart fluttered, and her mind was dazzled by the perspective which his evident fascination opened to her view. Unsophisticated and unsuspecting, her vanity and coquetry only served to render her more accessible to the wiles of the practised libertine.

By imperceptible degrees, the fisherman's daughter thought less of Norman and his mistress than of her new admirer; and, reading much of her character in her manners and conversation, Lord Clanrobert expatiated so much upon the delights and pleasures of the metropolis, the theatres, the balls, and the concerts, that the young girl's head was turned; and, in proportion as she became delighted by his conversation, she became discontented with the humble position which debarred her from the enjoyment of those pleasures which he described so vividly. Lord Clanrobert feared to lose the advantage he had gained by being too precipitate, but he did not part with the blue-eyed Nancy without obtaining from her a promise to meet him at the same place on the following evening.

At the same hour, therefore, and in the same bower, trellised with the fragrant honeysuckle, did the libertine nobleman and Nancy Shrimp meet on the evening of the ensuing day; and the former, having elicited from the fisherman's daughter that she was about to spend a few days with a relative at the east-end of the metropolis, easily prevailed upon her to commuicate to him the address of the person she was about to visit. This second meeting of Lord Clanrobert and Nancy Shrimp at the Tivoli-gardens was characterised by more earnestness on his part than on the previous occasion, and by stronger symptoms of susceptibility on the part of the fisherman's daughter. She told him that she should be in London on the following day, and when they had again parted, the young nobleman resolved to turn this visit to the furtherance of his views upon the young girl's virtue. He left his mansion at Erith for his town residence in Belgrave-square, and, on the next day, sent to Nancy tickets of admission to one of the theatres for herself and cousin, a young girl a few years the junior of his intended victim. He joined them at a place of assignation which he had proposed in the note which had accompanied the tickets, and, at the conclusion of the performances, took them to the Elysium supper-rooms, with the character of which they were altogether unacquainted. After partaking of wine and oysters, he called a cab and escorted them home, having indelibly confirmed Nancy Shrimp in her love of gaiety and pleasure, and her personal regard for the individual who had introduced her to them.

Nancy availed herself of every opportunity of being in his company, by informing him of every occasion of her visiting any place of amusement or popular resort, so that they were together every day of the young girl's stay in the metropolis. She thought no more of Norman Ashley, but gave all her thoughts to Clanrobert and pleasure. At length the time came for her to return to Gravesend, and her aristocratic lover, having been informed of the period of her departure, joined her on board the steamer, with the avowed intention of escorting her as far as Erith. During the passage down the river, Lord Clanrobert pressed his suit with more ardour than ever; and his tender and impassioned manner soon communicated itself to the bosom of his fair companion. He told her that his guardians would take measures to annul any marriage which he might contract contrary to their wishes before he became legally of age, and besought her to consent to a secret marriage until that period arrived. Nancy at first objected, then hesitated, and at length gave her consent, overpowered by the combined attack of inclination and persuasion upon her yielding heart.

CHAPTER LXV.

FLIRTATION AND RUIN.

NANCY SHRIMP wished to return home, promising to meet her lover for the purpose of a secret marriage, in a few days afterwards; but Lord Clanrobert feared the effect of reflection upon the resolution she had acceded to, and prevailed upon her to leave the boat with him at Erith. He then took her to his mansion in that village, and ordered supper to be served in that apartment in which the mysterious marriage had been performed at midnight, between the late lord and the smuggler's sister, of which he was supposed to be the offspring. In the meantime he ordered the carriage to be got ready, and when they had supped, and partaken rather freely of champagne, they set out for the metropolis again.

It was near eleven o'clock when the carriage, by Lord Clanrobert's directions, stopped at the Brunswick saloon, which he assured his fair companion was a hotel; and there, after overcoming her scruples by a promise of marriage, by special license, on the following morning, they passed the night in each other's arms. Morning dawned, but it brought not with it the fulfilment of the promise which had enabled Lord Clanrobert to effect the seduction of the blue-eyed Nancy Shrimp. He engaged furnished apartments for her at Brompton, and the secret marriage was indefinitely postponed. A ceaseless round of pleasures and amusements engaged the time of the fisherman's daughter, and withdrew her mind from the contemplation of her lapse from virtue, and her equivocal position.

But the time came at length, when her blue eyes, sparkling with vivacity or languishing with tenderness, the sunny hue of her glossy hair and the coquettish smile which wreathed her red lips, ceased to exercise their influence upon the heart of the young nobleman, whose attachments were purely sensual; and when he had become satiated with the charms of the fisherman's daughter, the neglect with which he treated her was speedily followed by desertion. Nancy's infatuation was now over, and she was able to perceive the terrible consequences which had resulted from her flirtation in the Tivoli-gardens. She had flattered herself that she should be Lady Clanrobert, and then how gratifying would be such a means of proving to Norman Ashley that she had lost nothing by his neglect of her. But that dream was now over, and she woke from its illusions to find herself a discarded mistress, the deserted victim of her betrayer.

For a few days she cherished the fond delusion that he would return to her, but this hope soon vanished; and then she resolved to seek him at his own residence. There the domestics informed her that he had gone on a sporting excursion to the moors of Scotland, and this information proved so unequivocally that he had deserted her, that she returned to her lodgings with her last hope crushed, and her bosom agitated by the most conflicting emotions. Love and hate, jealousy and revenge, by turn, held dominion over her heart; but these varied passions gradually merged into those of remorse and disappointed hope. She thought of her parents, and the home of her childhood; but her pride revolted against the first suggestion of her heart, to return to them, for she had written to her parents shortly after her elopement with her betrayer, assuring them that she was privately married to Lord Clanrobert, and would be acknowledged by his lordship as his wife immediately he became of age, and free from the control of his guardians.

She was soon without money, and, to procure some, she was compelled to sacrifice to her exigences a few articles of dress and jewellery, which had been given to her by Lord Clanrobert, in the first rapture of possession. These she took to that general resort of the needy and the dissipated, the pawnbroker's shop, and readily procured money upon them from the usurer of the poor. It was her first visit to the loan-office of the poor man, but it was fated not to be the last by many. She stole in and out again as if she were afraid of being seen; for poverty feels ashamed of its abasement, while crime puts on a countenance of audacity, and stalks unblushingly at noon-day into the shop distinguished by the three gilt balls, the ancient arms of Lombardy.

What a fertile field for the observation of a contemplative mind is afforded by a pawnbroker's shop! Whether we regard the countenances, dress, and bearing of those who enter it, or the heaped-up goods in the warehouse, the scene is alike fraught with interest. The artist may there observe scenes and characters worthy of being delineated by a Hogarth or a Wilkie; the novelist may there gather the materials of a romance, and the politician and the economist obtain an insight into the social condition of the people, which might be looked for in vain through the voluminous Blue Books of parliamentary commissions.

The contemplation of the heterogeneous collection of inanimate objects stored up in the warehouse of the pawnbroker, is scarcely less interesting than that of the men and women, of all classes, but chiefly the poor, who cross the threshold. Every article of furniture, of costume, or of jewellery and plate, seems to be suggestive of its own little history of the penury that concealed itself in obscurity, the pride that strove to maintain an appearance of gentility amid poverty, and the debasing vice that destroyed comfort and self-respect. Here is the black coat of the artisan who has taken the first degree in dissipation, but still seeks to maintain the exterior respectability of a Sunday coat, by regularly pawning it on Monday morning, and redeeming it on Saturday night. Here is a set of tools, pledged by some unfortunate mechanic, who would not sell them even in the extremity of his poverty, because he hoped for better times, and to redeem them with an advance of wages, when he again procured employment. Here is the silver tea-pot, which tells a tale of affluence overtaken by that series of commercial panics which will inevitably reduce the middle-classes to a level with the workmen, whose condition they have so much assisted to depress, unless some organic changes be made in our social system. Here is the wedding-ring of the pale wife of some long unemployed operative, the only article of value they ever possessed, and yet the last parted with, so dear to their hearts were the associations connected with that little circlet of gold.

Nor less does the pawnbroker's warehouse abound in memorials of the vices of the rich. The aristocrat, who raises money upon the security of the title-deeds of his estates, deposited with some wealthy money-lender, is on a level with the man of the people, who borrows a few shillings of the pawnbroker, upon the security of his best coat, or his basket of tools. But it is not always to the usurer that the titled spendthrift applies; the plate and jewellery in the strong boxes of the west-end pawnbrokers does not come there through the improvidence of the poor. There is the casket of diamonds, pledged by some fair patrician, to obtain the means of paying her debts of honour; there the service of plate, upon which money has been raised to save the scion of a noble house from an impending charge of forgery.

From this digression let us return to Nancy Shrimp. Before the supply of money which she had obtained from the pawnbroker was wholly exhausted, she received, through the agency of the impudent Fitzormond, an offer of protection from Edward Ashley, the cousin of Norman and Ellen, who was striving to emulate the profligate example of his fellow-collegian, Lord Clanrobert. Nancy pondered long upon this proposal, which she did not at once accept; she revolted from the idea of disposing of herself to a person whom she had never seen; but, after one or two interviews with the aspirant for her favours, the destitution that rose grimly before her mind prompted her to accept his offer.

CHAPTER LXVI.

THE MARINERS' SALOON.

In the neighbourhood of Ratcliffe-highway is a place of amusement called the Mariners' Saloon, which is much frequented by seamen and the frail sisterhood, and the dissolute characters of Wapping and Shadwell. It is devoted to concerts and dramatic representations, like many similar establishments in various parts of the metropolis, but ranks lower in the scale of respectability than that favourite place of cockney resort, the Grecian Saloon, in the City-road. One evening, more than twelve months after the desertion of Nancy Shrimp by her aristocratic seducer, that young nobleman alighted from a cab, at the entrance of the Mariners' Saloon, accompanied by his dissolute acquaintances, Fitzormond and Simpson; and, after partaking of some refreshment at the bar, passed on to the theatre, where a score of young ladies were pirouetting round the Titania of a fairy ballet. They wore roses in their hair, their round, white arms were bare, and the corsages of their muslin dresses were extremely low, revealing no small proportion of their swelling busts; the skirts were very full, and as proportionately short as the bodies were low, so that the graceful evolutions of the mazy dance left little for the imagination to perform, in judging of the symmetry of those captivating nymphs of the ballet.

The audience consisted principally of sailors and frail women, with a sprinkling of loose characters of every description. Ale and porter and ginger-beer, with nuts, oranges, and apples, were much in requisition; and a thin cloud of light-blue smoke hovered over the pit, curling upward from cigars and pipes of every description, from the blackened "cutty" to the genuine meerschaum, and from the cabbage-leaf Amersfoot to the fragrant Silva or Cabana of the plantations of Cuba.

On the termination of the performances, Lord Clanrobert and his disreputable associates, with a large proportion of the audience, repaired to a long apartment dignified with the appellation of the "saloon," where refreshments of every description were supplied from the bar. Among those who had quitted the theatre for the saloon, was Nancy Shrimp, whose faded and meretricious finery announced that she had sunk to the lowest depth of degradation, and become one of those unfortunates who frequent the low concert-rooms of the taverns of Wapping.

Edward Ashley had soon forsaken her for a pretty Jewess, who kept one of those suspicious-looking cigar-shops on the left-side of Wych-street, going west, and, with fewer scruples than before, she had sought a new admirer. Her career thenceforward was inevitably a downward one, and in a few months she was numbered among the fifty thousand unfortunate females of our mighty metropolis. As she entered the saloon, and her blue eyes glanced round the assembled revellers in quest of an eligible companion, she encountered the gaze of Lord Clanrobert. It was the first time she had seen him since his base desertion of her, and she coloured deeply with mingled shame and indignation as his eyes met hers, and then by a sudden revulsion of feeling, the colour faded from her cheeks, and she became pale as monumental marble.

"Ah, Nancy, my blue-eyed charmer! is it indeed you? Who would have thought of meeting you here?" exclaimed Lord Clanrobert, whose countenance was flushed with wine.

The unfortunate young woman turned away from her seducer, and hurried from the saloon, for this unexpected meeting had roused from the hidden cells of memory a host of recollections which she had sought to smother. As she crossed the threshold, she encountered one whose appearance at that moment roused yet more terribly the thoughts and feelings which her rencontre with Lord Clanrobert had caused to rush tumultuously to her brain; it was Norman Ashley, accompanied by his lawless associate, Shark Slingsby. Again the warm blood sprang to Nancy's countenance, crimsoning even her neck and bosom; for first love is never entirely forgotten, but lingers for life in some secret recess of the heart, often unsuspected even by her in whose bosom the impression slumbers.

"Nancy Shrimp!" exclaimed Norman, evincing some surprise at meeting the young girl in such a place and in such a guise.

But the fisherman's daughter rushed past him without speaking, and in a few moments was in the street.

"She seems frightened, like," observed Shark. "Do you know her, Ashley?"

"I did once, but I have not seen her before for some time," returned Norman, a shade of gloom coming over his countenance at the evident fall of one whom he had regarded with a degree of affection, though not with so ardent a feeling as that which he had inspired in her.

Glancing round the apartment as they entered, Norman Ashley immediately recognised two persons among the revellers present; these were Lord Clanrobert, of whom he took no notice, and James Corbett, the smuggler. The latter had not recovered from the stroke of adverse fortune which had deprived him of his vessel, mulcted him in a heavy fine, and confined him in prison, and his countenance and general appearance bore tokens of the evil days that had come upon him. Seated in a corner, and partially enveloped in a cloud of tobacco smoke, he was regarding his supposed reprobate nephew with a look expressive of mournful interest; but, though the young scapegrace had recognised his uncle on entering the saloon, neither had deigned to acknowledge, in the slightest manner, the presence of the other.

"How go the times with you now, Mr. Corbett?" enquired Norman, stretching his hand across the table.

"Very bad, Mr. Ashley," returned the smuggler, grasping the proffered hand of his former companion with friendly warmth; "but I am glad to see you, lad. What are you doing now?"

"Oh, knocking about along-shore," returned Norman Ashley, in a cheerful tone.

Corbett glanced suspiciously towards Shark Slingsby, and then shook his head in a manner which Norman could not fail to understand. The latter made no comment, however, and the smuggler shortly afterwards took his departure.

Another person in the apartment had recognised Lord Clanrobert, and that was Sam Skelter, who had discovered the name and rank of the libertine from whom he had rescued the lovely Ellen Ashley. He was thinking of that young girl at that moment, for he now lodged in the same neighbourhood, and had frequent opportunities of admiring her peerless loveliness, and convincing himself of the rectitude of her conduct. He was mentally comparing her with the females present, and the contrast caused him to dwell more ardently than before on the image of the dark-eyed Ellen, for whom he had long entertained a feeling of regard.

Let us now leave the revellers in the saloon, and follow the footsteps of Nancy Shrimp. When she left the tavern, after her unexpected meetings with Lord Clanrobert and Norman Ashley, the night was dark and foggy, a cold drizzling rain was falling, and the passengers hurried along with umbrellas, looking as if they wished themselves at home on so comfortless a night. Nancy shivered, and the chill night air again drove the blood back to her heart, for her clothing was light, and more adapted for the saloon than for the streets, and her thin shoes were ill-fitted for walking on the wet and slushy pavement. It was already midnight, and Nancy had yet to obtain the means of subsistence for the morrow; but the streets were nearly deserted, and, unable to endure the thought of returning to the saloon, she walked slowly along the street, in the hope of encountering some sailor, flushed with drink, who might be induced to accompany her to her lodging.

But the rain fell thicker and faster, and none were abroad but the houseless children of destitution, and a few unfortunates like herself, cowering in the shade of arched courts, or shrinking within the shelter of some friendly gateway. An hour was passed by the unhappy girl in the cheerless streets, and then she abandoned her hopeless promenade, and returned wet, miserable, and spiritless, to her humble lodging. Her meeting with her seducer and the object of her first attachment had awakened a train of associations which she had struggled to repress, and now they came upon her in her loneliness with redoubled force; they crowded upon her brain—those teeming thoughts of home, of parents, of her happy childhood, of those halcyon days of innocence she could never know again; and, throwing herself upon her bed, the miserable young woman burst into an agony of tears, and sobbed as though her heart would break with shame and unavailing sorrow.

CHAPTER LXVII.

ELLEN AND THE SCULPTOR.

ELLEN ASHLEY was now sixteen years of age, and the admiration with which she had inspired the young sculptor had grown into a profound regard, on his part, towards the lovely and friendless orphan to whom chance had thus introduced him. Her absence from the study in which he performed his pleasing labours made him feel lonely and unsettled; her presence was the inspiration from which he drew his conceptions of his sublimest works of art; when alone, her image occupied his mind, and she peopled his slumbers with visions of loveliness. Ellen did not perceive the impression which she had unconsciously made upon the heart of the sculptor, until she found a feeling of preference stealing into her own, and then she discovered, with ineffable satisfaction, the state of Leon's sentiments towards herself. But beyond the observations recorded in the sixtieth chapter, Leon Copley had not acquainted her with the thoughts and wishes that were ever uppermost in his mind; but finding at length that the state of his health required a sojourn on the south coast of Devonshire, as was recommended by his physician, he resolved to do so prior to his leaving London.

On the morning on which he had determined to make a declaration of love to the beautiful Ellen, he came into his studio as usual, and sat down before a large and very fine cast in plaster, representing Venus sitting on a panther. He gazed a few moments, with the eye of a master of the divine art, upon the cast of the Paphian goddess, but when he turned his eyes upon the marble busts and statuettes around him, the feelings which his countenance expressed were no longer those of the artist, but the lover; for in every one he beheld the lineaments and contours of the lovely Ellen. Every bust was Ellen's; every statue had her countenance, her arms, and her feet. While he was still thinking of the beautiful original, she entered the studio.

" Good morning, sir," said Ellen, advancing with a modest and engaging demeanour.

" Good morning, Ellen," responded the sculptor. " What do you think of this cast?"

" It would be very beautiful in marble," returned Ellen; " but it would take a long time to execute a work of that size."

" I must decline the order, Ellen, though it is from a good patron," observed Leon Copley. " My medical attendant advises me to repair, for a few months, to Devonshire, the mild, salubrious air of which, he hopes, will restore me to health."

" You have not looked so well lately," observed Ellen, with an air of interest.

" I am glad to find that you feel an interest in me, Ellen," said Leon, rising. " It encourages me to avow the ineffaceable impression which your matchless beauty and goodness of disposition have made upon my heart, and to declare the love with which they have inspired me."

" You do me too much honour by the declaration, Mr. Copley," faltered the blushing Ellen, casting down her eyes.

" Not so, dear Ellen," returned Leon, in an impassioned tone, which called a faint tinge of carnation to his pale cheek. " You have beauty that would adorn a throne, and even the diadem of a queen would derive additional lustre from those love-radiant eyes. Tell me, dear Ellen, may I hope to call you mine?"

Ellen replied not, but raised her lustrous dark eyes to those of the young sculptor, and then suddenly dropped them again, while the rich colour went and came upon her glowing cheeks, and her bosom palpitated with emotions which she had never experienced before.

" You do not reply, Ellen," said Leon Copley, in a tender tone.

" What would you have me say?" said Ellen, blushing deeply as she again raised her dark eyes to those of the sculptor.

" That I need not despair, that your heart is not in the keeping of another, Ellen," returned the ardent young man.

" I fear I should tell you an untruth if I were to tell you that I have still a heart to dispose of," said Ellen, sighing; but no sooner had she spoken the words than she saw the confession she had so naively made, and she blushed deeply.

" If I interpret rightly that sigh and that tell-tale blush, I am not entirely without hope," observed Leon Copley. " Tell me, dear girl, I am not indifferent to you!"

" Oh, no, sir!" replied Ellen; and she raised her dark eyes to her lover's countenance with such a tender expression beaming from their clear and liquid depths, that he no longer doubted of his happiness.

" Thanks, dear Ellen, for that assurance," said he, pressing the small, white hand he had taken in his own. "Many circumstances, which it is of no moment to particularise now, have prevented me from declaring to you my attachment until this moment; but now that I am assured of the mutuality of our sentiments, I feel so supremely happy, that the glow of returning health seems already to animate my frame."

Ellen unconsciously pressed the hand which retained her own, and her soft, dark eyes expressed a tender gladness that she could be in any way instrumental in so desirable a consummation.

"Let us now make our little arrangements for the future," continued the enraptured Leon, passing his arm round Ellen's waist, and taking an unresisted kiss from her ripe lips. "We have known each other long enough to be acquainted with our respective sentiments and dispositions, and a long acquaintance ought, in my opinion, to obviate the necessity of a long courtship. Moreover, the advice of my physician has determined me to take up my residence in Devonshire for a few months, and I like not the thought of leaving you in London, unprotected and uncared for, until my return. I feel, too, that the society of a beloved wife, and her tender care, would conduce fully as much to my speedy restoration to health as the genial salubrity of the coast of Devon, where, my medical adviser tells me, the myrtle and the hydrangea stand through the winter in the open air. These considerations will, I hope, induce my dear Ellen to allow me to fix an early day for our union."

"The reasons which you have advanced are so many claims upon my regard which my heart cannot refuse," replied Ellen Ashley, with a slight blush. "I have no one to consult but my brother; and I am sure that he values my happiness too much to interpose any obstacles to it."

"Then we will be married in the course of the present month, and then proceed to Devonshire," said Leon Copley, pressing Ellen to his heart, and again kissing her.

The kiss was returned; and, before the lovers parted, a day was fixed for the celebration of their nuptials. The young sculptor was overjoyed by the consciousness that the heart of the lovely Ellen was wholly devoted to him, and his vivid imagination drew pictures of marital bliss and domestic felicity of which Ellen was the presiding genius. But the projects with which man busies himself, whether of pleasure or ambition, are often overturned by those laws of the universe which are eternal and immutable; and even when we think we are on the eve of attaining the object of our desires, the cold hand of the relentless king of terrors is often stretched out to seize it as his prey, or to snatch us from it. We often seek to peer into the secrets of futurity, thinking how much more wisely we might regulate our conduct, and what an amount of human blood and tears might be prevented from falling upon the earth, fertilizing it with the dear-bought experience of one generation for the benefit of the next, if we could but penetrate the misty veil which conceals the future from our gaze, and scan, with philosophic eye, the knowledge that lies beyond. But while the actions of mankind are governed more by passion than by reason, we may doubt whether a knowledge of the events which lie hidden in futurity would have any effect upon our progress towards the destiny of our race, and, so far from tending to our happiness, it would be found to militate against it. If we knew the sorrows and adversities which the future may have in store for us, placed by circumstances beyond our own control, we should cease to enjoy the present through our dread of the future, and we should constantly behold the skeleton beside the banquet, and the sword suspended from the ceiling. Therefore it was well that the extatic happiness of Leon Copley was not embittered by the foreknowledge that the hand of death was already extended to mar it.

CHAPTER LXVIII.

THE DEATH OF LEON COPLEY.

ONE delightful afternoon, a few days before that which had been fixed for the nuptials of Leon Copley and Ellen Ashley, the happy pair visited Richmond together, and repaired to the "Star and Garter" tavern, on the hil

made famous by the song attributed to George III., whom we can scarce believe to have had in his soul a scintillation of the poet's fire. There they sat at the open window of the tavern, and never had the young sculptor been happier than at that moment: one arm was thrown around the maiden's waist, the other hand clasped the small white one of the dark-eyed Ellen. Sweet converse held the maiden and her lover—it was an hour of heaven vouchsafed to them on earth. The silver Thames lay before them, the waving trees upon Eel-pie Island casting their long shadows upon his sunlit bosom; and beyond the river were the green meadows and Kew-park, with the deer sporting in the shade of the spreading trees.

"What a delightful prospect," observed Ellen Ashley, as her gaze wandered from the lilac and laburnum-trees near the window, to the more distant objects in that varied landscape.

"River and lake scenery is particularly pleasing to me," said Leon; "and had I devoted myself to painting instead of sculpture, I should have only painted landscapes. A picturesque view without water, is destitute of the greatest charm of natural scenery. I was particularly impressed with the

26

beauty of water scenery when I visited the lakes of Windermere and Ulles-water, and the cataract and stupendous crags of Cross-fell."

" I have never seen the Westmoreland lakes," observed Ellen.

" We will visit them together some day, dearest," returned Leon, pressing her hand. " In the scene before us, beautiful as it is, the presence of so much company, and the villas in the neighbourhood, with the town and bridge, detract in some measure from its picturesqueness; but the tourist who roams at sunset along the shores of Ulleswater, and sees the distant mountains of Borrodaile grow dim and dusky in the gathering shades, or gazes upon the craggy steep of Cross-fell, and listens to the hoarse roar of the waterfall, feels that he is sur-rounded by the works of Nature alone, and his heart holds silent communion with the omnipresent spirit of the universe."

" Are you fond of the sea ?" Ellen asked.

" I care nothing for Brighton," returned Leon, with a smile; " but St. Leonard's is a pleasant place to visit, though less visited by those who repair to watering-places in quest of gaiety and dissipation. Yes, I do love the sea; and often have I stood upon a beetling cliff, and watched it in its wrath, or wandered in the moonlight upon its shell-strewn beach. I love it because, like the glorious azure firmament, man has not set thereon the mark of his usurpa-tion, which the verdant earth everywhere bears witness to. Man has set the stamp of selfish exclusiveness upon the earth, and appropriated even the wild animals of the forest and the moor, and the finny tribes that come and go at pleasure to and from the sea, but he cannot set up his boundary-posts upon the waves, nor draw his divisional lines upon the azure sky. Thus the ocean inspires thoughts of freedom which are repressed and confined when we turn our eyes to the tall hedges and brick walls which mark the odious distinctions of *mine* and *thine*."

" I have often thought that an estimate might be formed of persons' charac-ters by the enclosures of their gardens," observed Ellen, smiling. " Your remarks have recalled the fancy to my mind. When I see an elegant villa stand-ing in a delightful garden, filled with the most beautiful flowers and shrubs, but shut in from the observation of passers-by with a high wall, I conclude the proprietor to be a selfish monopolist, so imbued with the dark spirit of exclusive-ness, that he would engross even the beauty and fragrance of the flowers, and shut them in from all eyes save his own."

" The exclusiveness which manifests itself in thick hedges and high walls, is nowhere so apparent as in this country," said Leon Copley, after a pause. " In France, the fields are divided only by a low mound of earth, or sometimes of stones gathered off the land. There the old feudal aristocracy, the ancient lords of the soil, have disappeared; the revolution of the last century opened its terrible jaws, and chewed them into small gentry."

Ellen smiled at the simile used by her lover to express the operation of those decrees which, under the first revolution in France, destroyed signorial privileges and agrarian monopolies at one tremendous swoop; and, as the golden hues reflected from the setting sun by the placid waters of the Thames were deepen-ing into intermingling shades of purple and rose, they prepared for their return to London.

The moon was rising when the steamer reached the Hungerford-pier, where Leon and Ellen went ashore; and, so calm and beautiful was the night, that, though the air was damp and somewhat chilly, the young sculptor determined upon walking to his residence, first accompanying Ellen to hers. The feelings of love which animated the hearts of both, and the influence of the calm and moonlight hour, caused them to linger on their way; and the night air had an injurious effect upon the lungs of the young sculptor, in which the seeds of consumption were already planted, waiting for the pressure of adverse circum-stances to terminate his existence.

We have heard it stated, upon the authority of medical testimony, that per-sons who have an hereditary tendency to consumption are invariably amiable, gentle, and loving; we would rather believe that the germs of incipient decline foster the growth of a gentle and affectionate disposition, than adopt the alterna-tive that the destroying angel always selects for his victims the gentle and the good; but this we leave to the physiologists to decide. We have merely mentioned it as incidental to our tale, for Leon Copley, the amiable, the loving, the gifted sculptor, was an instance of the singular psychological fact which we have pointed out.

On the day after the trip to Richmond, in which the company of Ellen Ashley had been to him a source of the most unalloyed felicity, Leon found his cough had been increased by his exposure to the humid air on the preceding night; but he consoled himself with the reflection, that he should soon have a tender and loving nurse in the person of Ellen Ashley, and that her solicitude and regard, with the genial air of Devonshire, would restore him to perfect health. But, on the following day, finding himself growing worse, he sent for Ellen and his medical attendant, and, by the advice of the latter, their intended union was postponed. The physician, moreover, advised an immediate removal to the southern coast of England; and, as Leon was averse to leaving Ellen in London, unprotected and unprovided for, it was at last arranged that she should accompany him to Torquay, and engage apartments as near as possible to his own.

This was done; but the premature decline of the gifted young man had been so much aggravated, that he rapidly grew worse; and, in about a week after their arrival at Torquay, the physician who had been summoned to attend him deemed it his duty to inform Ellen that the recovery of his patient was impossible, such rapid progress had the insidious disease made upon the young man's frame. He had no near relations to visit him, and thus Ellen became his only nurse, ministering to his every want as only a loving woman can do, and sitting by his bedside night after night, until the roseate hue that erst had tinged her cheeks began to pale.

She had no hope of saving him, for the physicians had none; but she resolved to remain with him to the last, and, if she could not avert the outstretched hand of death, to mitigate the pangs of dissolution by her tenderness and devotion.

"Ellen," said he, as his wasted hand held that of the young girl, and his debilitated body was supported on the pillows, "if I feel as well to-morrow as I do now, I will try to get down to the beach for an hour; the sea breeze may invigorate me. Do I not look better this evening?"

Ellen looked earnestly at her lover, and returned the pressure of his hand; but she made no reply, and tears gathered in her dark eyes, for the physician had warned her of the premonitory symptoms of approaching death, and these she now beheld in the countenance of Leon Copley; his dark eyes were preternaturally brilliant, and on his pale cheeks dwelt a bright flush, which looked like health, but was not.

"Now I shall go to sleep," continued Leon, "and I shall try to dream that we are spending our honeymoon in Cumberland, and climbing the steep ascent of Cross-fell crags."

A languid smile played upon the features of the young sculptor as he thus gave utterance to an illusive hope, and, closing his eyes, he seemed to fall asleep. Imperceptibly the flush passed from his countenance, a cold sweat bedewed his pale brow, and when Ellen suddenly pressed his hand—beginning to be alarmed by these symptoms—it was quite cold. Leon Copley was dead!

CHAPTER LXIX.

THE PEER AND THE GAMBLER.

LEAVING Ellen to mourn over the hopes that lay buried in the grave of Leon Copley, we must now follow the adventurous career of Norman Ashley, first detailing certain occurrences which were destined to exercise an important influence over his future history. One evening, when he had been absent the entire day, being engaged, with Shark Slingsby, in some minor depredations on the river, a cab drove hastily up to the house in which he and his mistress resided, and Augustus Fitzormond, leaping on the pavement, gave a hurried knock at the door. On its being immediately opened by Lolah Hastings, he informed her, in apparently an excited manner, that Norman had been arrested on a charge of extensive smuggling, and was then in custody at the station-house in Fleet-street, and wished to see her.

Lolah threw on her bonnet and shawl, allowed Fitzormond to hand her into the cab, and away they went at a rapid pace. She knew not the precise locality of the station-house in question, which is situated up an arched passage, and, as the lamps were lighted and the cab proceeded rapidly along, she took no note of where they were going until the cab stopped. Fitzormond sprang out, and, having assisted Lolah to alight, a door was opened, and they entered together. She had not time to observe the appearance of the neighbourhood where the vehicle had stopped, but the street was badly lighted, and a shower of rain having fallen during the progress of the cab, the pavement was slippery with the diluted mire. But the moment she had entered the passage a cold chill struck to her heart, for the appearance of the place was too horribly impressed upon her mind ever to be forgotten; and when she saw Bill Simpson emerge from the room in which she had first beheld him on that night when she became the victim of Colonel Elrington, she became deadly pale, and uttered a faint scream.

" In an instant Simpson's hand was pressed upon her mouth, and while Fitzormond held her forcibly by the arms, the former villain tied his handkerchief over her mouth, and taking her in his arms, partly carried and partly dragged her up the stairs. The recollections which the appearance of that house of crimes awakened, so overpowered her with horror, that she would have been unable to cry out, even if the handkerchief had not restrained her; and when the ruffian had reached the mysterious chamber which had been the scene of so many atrocities, he removed the handkerchief from her mouth, and closing the door upon her, locked it on the outside, leaving the key in the door.

When Fitzormond had surrendered the entrapped victim of his duplicity to Bill Simpson, he entered the parlour which the latter had quitted, in which Lord Clanrobert and Colonel Elrington were then seated. A couple of decanters, nearly empty, and a number of glasses, stood upon the table, and the countenance of Lord Clanrobert, who was engaged in the combustion of a cigar, was flushed with the excitement of inebriation. The countenance of Colonel Elrington wore an air of vexation and perplexity, which evinced itself in his puckered brow; and the occasional nervous quiver of the muscles of his face, while that of Augustus Fitzormond, as he entered the apartment, was radiant with triumph and exultation.

" You must confess that I have won the wager, my lord," said he, sitting down at the table, and pouring out a glass of wine while glancing at Lord Clanrobert. " Lolah is again an inmate of this house, and at your disposal. She ran into the trap I laid for her as easily as a wild duck is decoyed into a net."

" There is the money, Fitz.," returned the reckless young nobleman, throwing a handful of sovereigns on the table. " I made a good bet, though, for the job would have cost me as much without the wager."

The libertine peer chuckled over this idea, which Fitzormond declared was a very good one; and when Bill Simpson returned to the apartment, he threw the end of his cigar upon the uncarpeted floor (for the house was very meanly furnished), and skipped lightly up the stairs.

" When this scapegrace lord has taken his departure, we will proceed to business with you," said Bill Simpson, addressing Colonel Elrington, as he resumed the seat, which he had vacated on the arrival of Fitzormond and Lolah Hastings in the cab.

" I am anxious to complete the negotiation, I assure you," returned the colonel, in a haughty tone.

" Have you brought the thousand pounds?" asked Simpson, in a rough voice.

" I have," was the laconic reply.

" All right, then," returned the ruffian. " Fitz. and I are as anxious as you to settle up, and get out of the country. But—what is that, Fitz.?—a woman's step, I'll swear!" and, in fact, the hurried footsteps of a female were at that moment heard upon the stairs.

Fitzormond and Bill Simpson started from their chairs, and ran into the passage, but recoiled in fear as they encountered Lolah Hastings, brandishing a pointed pair of scissors, which she held like a dagger in her right hand. Before they could recover from their consternation and surprise, she had opened the front door, and escaped into the street. To pursue her was out of the question, and the two sharpers looked at each other with countenances expressive of the most undisguised vexation. Before they had recovered from their surprise, Lord Clanrobert came down the stairs, with a pale and rueful countenance, and interposing his white handkerchief between his satin waistcoat and his shirt, to prevent the former from being stained with the blood which flowed from a superficial wound in his breast, inflicted by the weapon of Lolah Hastings.

Before the entrapped young woman had recovered from the horror which she experienced on finding herself again a prisoner in the very room where the villain Elrington had triumphed over her a few years before, and concerning which she had heard such fearful tales from the lips of Susan Walters, than she heard the quick tread of a man ascending the creaking stairs. The key turned in the lock, the door was opened, and Lord Clanrobert entered the apartment. She had never encountered him before, and was unacquainted with his name and quality, but she knew that his visit could bode no good.

" What is the meaning of this ruffianly outrage, sir? and why have I been deluded hither to become a prisoner?" she exclaimed, in a tone of deep indignation.

" The reason is, my charmer, that you are the loveliest of women," returned the libertine; " and you have been made my prisoner, because there was no other means of obtaining an interview with you. I want to talk to you, my beauty, and to persuade you to some arrangement that will be greatly to your advantage."

" If you wish to have any conversation with me, it must be on equal terms; and that cannot be while I am a prisoner," rejoined Lolah, firmly.

" It is I who am the captive of those bright eyes," said Lord Clanrobert; " and it is for you, my charmer, to decide upon my fate. Say, then, my beauty, will you bless me by becoming mine?"

He attempted to seize her hand, but Lolah indignantly withdrew to a greater distance, and put her hand in her pocket to grasp her scissors, which she that moment recollected, and with which she resolved to defend herself to the last extremity.

" Your proposal is odious and insulting!" she exclaimed, colouring with indignation.

" Proud beauty!" said the libertine peer, brooking no restraint upon his passions, half inebriated as he was with wine, " you shall be mine by right of conquest, since you will not be so by treaty;" and he attempted to seize her in his arms, but Lolah suddenly withdrew her hand from her pocket, and, grasping the scissors firmly, struck him on the breast.

He released her instantly, and staggered back, his countenance becoming frightfully pale, for he had felt the point; and his intended victim seized the opportunity to effect her escape. Still grasping the scissors firmly in her hand, she opened the door, and flew rather than ran down the stairs, where she encountered Simpson and Fitzormond in the passage, as already described.

Lord Clanrobert muttered an oath as he perceived the blood upon his shirt, and staunching it with his white pocket-handkerchief, he slowly descended the stairs. The wound was a mere superficial one, the point of the scissors having struck one of the ribs, and glanced off without inflicting any serious injury, and Lord Clanrobert immediately left the house, vexed at the termination of the adventure, so different to what he had anticipated. Selfish as the profligate always are, he would have cared less for the anguish and misery which might have followed success, than for the disappointment which his licentious passion had received from the spirited conduct of his intended victim; for the wealthy and titled ever consider themselves as the pivots on which society turns, instead of as atoms on the revolving circle, retarding its progress towards the perfect happiness which we believe to be the ultimate destiny of the human race.

CHAPTER LXX.

THE MURDER.

" We must settle this business quickly," said Bill Simpson to his confederate, when Lord Clanrobert had left the house, " or that girl will bring a possé of police about the house."

" The colonel has brought the gilt, and so that is all right," observed Augustus Fitzormond.

" We are right for a thousand, anyhow," said Simpson; "but the old bloke drew out five thousand, and he has got it about him; we may as well have it all, and hook it over to France."

Fitzormond started at this suggestion, but after a moment's pause he nodded his acquiescence, and the two gamblers entered the parlour together. Colonel Elrington rose as they entered, and with a certain nervousness of manner drew from his pocket-book a written paper, and bank-notes to the amount of a thousand pounds.

" Sign this paper," said he, "and the thousand pounds are yours. The paper is an acknowledgment that the accusation you have threatened me with, relative to Lolah Hastings and others, is a mere invention to extort money; I require it as a preventive of such nefarious attempts in future."

" And suppose we refuse to sign it ?" observed Simpson, in a coarse, sneering tone.

" Then I shall keep the money you have demanded as the price of your silence," returned Colonel Elrington, beginning to gather up the notes.

" No, you won't, though !" exclaimed Simpson; and snatching the poker from the fire-place, he struck the colonel a severe blow upon his bald head.

The old man raised his arm to avert the blow, but it was so sudden and heavy, that he fell prostrate and stunned upon the floor. Fitzormond and Simpson immediately snatched up the notes which lay upon the table, and then, stooping down, proceeded to abstract the colonel's pocket-book to obtain the rest of the money, which he had that day withdrawn from the Bank of England to satisfy their demands. Colonel Elrington groaned heavily as consciousness returned, and raising himself on his elbow, he made an ineffectual attempt to recover his property; but Bill Simpson struck him in the face with his clenched hand, and he again fell backward.

" Help ! murder !" cried the colonel, in a faint, gasping tone, struggling with the robbers, and striving in vain to rise from the floor.

" Damn you ! take that, then !" exclaimed Bill Simpson, again seizing the poker, and striking the old man a furious blow on the head. "That will stop your noise, you obstinate old fool !" he continued, repeating the blow.

The blood flowed profusely from the old man's head, and he groaned heavily as he lay motionless on the floor.

" Blest if you haven't killed him !" observed Augustus Fitzormond, as he pocketed the notes taken from the colonel's pocket-book, which made up the amount of five thousand pounds.

" Serve him right," returned Bill Simpson, in a brutal tone. "But now we have got the tin, let us be off before the police are upon us for that affair of Clanrobert and the girl."

" What shall we do with the stiff 'un ?" asked Fitzormond, glancing at the body of the murdered colonel.

" Leave it where it is," replied Simpson; "but let us finish the wine," and the reckless profligate poured the remaining wine into the glasses.

" What was that ?" asked Fitzormond, in a faltering voice, as he raised the glass of sparkling sherry to his lips.

A sound like the creaking of a boot, as if some one was moving in the passage, had reached his ears at that moment.

" I heard nothing," said Bill Simpson, putting down his glass, and listening.

" There it is again !" whispered Fitzormond, turning pale, and this time the miscreant Simpson heard the sound likewise.

" There cannot be anybody in the house, unless it is a stray cat," said the latter, as he advanced towards the door, and, opening it, peered into the dark passage, and called " Puss, puss !"

No feline mew answered, however, but they distinctly heard the creaking tread of some person at the most remote part of the passage.

" Let us hook it," suggested Fitzormond, beginning to feel nervous and alarmed at the ominous sounds.

" I will find out what it is first," exclaimed Simpson; and catching up the candle with one hand, and grasping the poker in the other, he rushed into the passage.

No living creature was visible; he held up the candle so as to throw the light to the farther end of the passage, and glanced up the stairs, but no quadruped or biped intruder could be seen, and he re-entered the parlour.

"Come, let us be off," said he, replacing the poker and the candlestick; and then he and his confederate, Fitzormond, moved towards the passage, but before they reached the door they were again alarmed by a loud knock at the front door.

Even the reckless Simpson turned pale at this new source of alarm; but while the two sharpers looked at one another in fear and perplexity, the knock was repeated more violently than before, and the street door flew open. Simpson and Fitzormond drew back in alarm and astonishment, and Norman Ashley rushed, breathless with haste, into the passage.

"Where is my wife?" said he, in an excited manner, which was evident also in his flushed countenance. "She has been traced to this house—to this den of everything infamous, and if any evil has happened to her your lives shall be forfeited for it."

"You have been misinformed, my good fellow," replied Augustus Fitzormond; "there is no woman here, I can assure you. You are welcome to search the house, if that will satisfy you."

"If she is not here now, it is because she has been removed; but I will satisfy myself before I go," said Norman, and, closing the street door, he drew a pistol from his pocket, and moved towards the back parlour, for as the door of the other room was partly open, he knew that she was not there.

"Our goose is cooked unless we fasten that affair upon him," said Bill Simpson in a hasty whisper to his confederate, at the same time pointing over his shoulder with his thumb to the door of the room in which lay the body of Colonel Elrington. "You fetch a policeman, and leave the rest to me."

Augustus Fitzormond shuddered slightly at the allusion to the murder to which he had been accessory, and then opened the door, and ran into the street, crying: "Murder! help! murder!" On hearing these appalling words, Norman Ashley rushed into the passage, and was immediately seized by Bill Simpson, who had thrown the roll of bank-notes into the front parlour at the moment of his confederate's exit.

"Help! murder!" repeated Simpson, with whom Norman was engaged in a severe struggle, believing it, at first, to be a *ruse* to prevent him from searching the house in order to recover Lolah; but, when the door of the apartment which had been the scene of the murder was flung wide open in the struggle, and he beheld the corpse and the blood upon the floor, he concluded that he was to be made the scapegoat of an atrocious crime.

Fitzormond now returned, accompanied by two policemen, and, in another moment, Norman Ashley was seized and securely handcuffed. One of the policemen entered the parlour, and lifted up the body of Colonel Elrington, but he was quite dead, and a surgeon who had immediately bustled in attempted in vain to bleed him. The cries of Augustus had collected a number of persons about the house, and in a few minutes the passage was filled with people.

"I am innocent!" exclaimed Norman Ashley, in a tone of mingled indignation and amazement. "If murder has been done, my accusers are the guilty parties. I came here to seek my wife, who has been entrapped and brought here for some vile purpose which these men are acquainted with."

"He seems to think that his wife has been seduced and brought here by this unfortunate gentleman," observed Simpson, addressing the police, and indicating the murdered colonel.

"Search the house," exclaimed Norman. "These men have only made this charge to get rid of me."

The two policemen looked at each other, and then one of them went up the stairs; but he returned in a few moments, and stated that every room was empty. During his absence, a man crept cautiously up the kitchen stairs, and mingled with the crowd of curious persons in the passage, but not without being perceived by both Fitzormond and Simpson, as well as by the unfortunate Norman. The two former exchanged a hurried glance of apprehension, and the latter started as if he recognised the person who had emerged from the obscurity of the kitchen stairs, but the policeman descended the stairs at that moment, and this circumstance drew his attention from the other.   He was then searched and deprived of his pistol, which was loaded, and taken to the station-house in the custody of the two policemen, followed by his accusers and a number of people.

CHAPTER LXXI.

EXPLANATIONS.

WE must now explain the cause of the alarm which had seized Simpson and Fitzormond previous to the appearance of Norman Ashley, and the singular and unexpected emergence from the kitchen of the individual who had thus intruded upon the crime-haunted passage of the house of murder.   Our readers cannot have forgotten Peter Tomkins, clerk and sexton of a certain village church not far from Eton; that respectable and mammon-loving individual having come to the metropolis to transact certain matters tending towards the consummation of those ambitious hopes which he had contemplated so complacently on the night when he bartered his probity for gold, such as the receipt of the rents of a number of old houses which he had purchased in the crowded districts of Whitechapel and Bethnal-green, and their profitable investment in the purchase of others, had discovered that the needy attorney whom he had employed to collect his rents, and who was of the Sampson Brass variety of the animal, had absconded with the entire receipts of six months.   This circumstance had such an effect upon Peter Tomkins, that, to drown his rage and mortification, he indulged in such copious potations of diluted cognac, that he became intoxicated, and in this state attempted to find his way to his temporary lodgings in the salubrious locality of Shire-lane.

The house was contiguous to that in which Lolah Hastings had been a temporary prisoner through the treacherous duplicity of Augustus Fitzormond; and, as the houses were much alike, Peter Tomkins, in his present mental obfuscation, was unable to determine which was the right one.   He brought himself to a halt before the house where the two sharpers were then engaged in the dispute with Colonel Elrington, and, after regarding it with a look of drunken stupidity, began fumbling about to open it; it happened that the door had been imperfectly closed after him by Lord Clanrobert, when he quitted the house, and on Tomkins pushing against it the door opened.   He immediately entered, and after closing the door behind him, but as imperfectly as before, he advanced a few steps along the passage, the opening of the door not having been heard by Simpson and Fitzormond, because they were at that moment engaged in the robbery and murder of Colonel Elrington.

The door of the front parlour in which the murderous struggle had just terminated in the death of the colonel, stood partly open, and thus Peter Tomkins became witness to the scene which we have described in the previous chapter. The terrible catastrophe of the murder had the effect of rendering him completely sober in a moment, and as soon as he could recover himself from the horror which it inspired in his mind, he moved with cautious steps towards the door. It was then that his footsteps were heard for the first time by Augustus Fitzormond, and when the latter spoke of it to his companion, Tomkins stood still in a perfect agony of dread.

" I heard nothing," he heard Simpson remark, and this emboldened him to take another step towards the door, but before he could reach it he heard Simpson advancing towards the parlour door, upon which he retreated hastily towards the kitchen stairs, where he hoped the obscurity would conceal him from observation.

When Simpson withdrew from the door to seize the poker and the candle, expressing at the same time a determination to find out the cause of the mysterious sounds, Peter Tomkins retreated down the kitchen stairs, where he lay concealed until the seizure of Norman Ashley by the police, when he availed himself of the opportunity afforded him by the confusion of the moment to mingle with the crowd which had assembled in the passage and outside the house.

This cautious movement, however, had not been effected without being observed by both Fitzormond and Simpson, who were thus made aware of the cause of their alarm, and also by Norman, who immediately recognised Tomkins, having visited him a few months previously, to ascertain the correctness of the statement made to him by his uncle, relative to his illegitimacy. Tomkins failed to recognise Norman in the nervous trepidation of which he could not divest himself until he got some distance from the house.

Owing to the same cause, he did not observe that he was followed by a ragged and singularly ill-looking fellow whom Simpson had accosted soon after leaving the house, and to whom he had whispered a few hasty directions, and given a note which he had scrawled in the street, using the shutters of a shop for a surface to lay the paper on. Tomkins walked some little distance before he recollected that he was going away from his lodgings, for his only object was to be beyond the reach of danger; having at last recovered from his fright, he began to retrace his steps, still followed by the individual above alluded to.

27

" Beg your pardon, sir," said the fellow, touching the rim of a very dilapidated hat; "genelman down the court wants to speak to you."

" What court? what gentleman?" asked Tomkins, eyeing the sinister-looking fellow in a suspicious manner.

" Down here, sir," replied the fellow, indicating the court in which Habakuk Holdfast's chapel was situated. " Genelman in a cloak—wants to speak about some money."

" Oh! about some money?" said Tomkins, a thought striking him that the person who wanted him must be the attorney whom he had employed to collect his rents, and that he wished to give him the money before leaving the country, in consequence of some embarrassing affairs of his own. " Is he a tall gentleman?"

" Yes, sir," replied the other, readily.

" Black hair? hooked nose?" continued Tomkins, in an anxious tone.

" That's him, sir," returned the mendacious vagabond.

Peter Tomkins hesitated no longer, but followed the fellow down the court. Just as they came opposite the chapel, the latter suddenly faced about, and, drawing a heavily-loaded life-preserver from the pocket of his ragged coat, he struck him a tremendous blow on the head, the effect of which was to prostrate Peter Tomkins on the steps of the chapel, stunned and senseless. The ruffian then dragged him close up to the door of the chapel, and walked briskly round to the house of Habakuk Holdfast, to whom he gave the note entrusted to him by Bill Simpson.

" Oh, very well," said the undertaker; " where is he?"

" On the steps of the chapel. You must look sharp, master," returned the ruffian.

" Come in," said Holdfast; and, having admitted the ragged fellow into the house, he forthwith led the way into the chapel.

The door being opened by the undertaker, the unconscious Tomkins was dragged into the chapel, and then the door was closed and fastened; the entrance to the vaults was then opened, and the unfortunate Peter was dropped in among the coffins. Holdfast and the villain who had assailed Tomkins in the court then left the chapel, after replacing the planks which covered the trap through which coffins were lowered into the vaults, and the living and dead were left in darkness together.

After the lapse of a few minutes, Tomkins recovered from the effects of the stunning blow dealt him by his assailant, and, after groaning with the painful consciousness of injury—for his head had been cut by the force of the blow—he faintly articulated :

" Where am I?"

There was no response, and he lay for a few minutes in a state of semi-obliviousness, and then he rose slowly from the damp bottom of the vault, and, pressing his hand upon his bleeding forehead, strove to recall his scattered senses. His head ached, he could feel the blood trickling down his face, and an intolerable stench saluted his olfactory organ. Gradually he recollected being struck down by the ruffian in the court, but where was he now? The place was involved in Stygian darkness; but the faint, earthy smell which pervaded the place made him sick with horror, and he shuddered as he recollected the chapel in the court.

He stretched out his hands, and encountered nothing; he took a step forward, and he kicked against a broken coffin. He stooped down to ascertain the nature of the object which he had struck his foot against; and, as his hand ran over the nails upon the lid of the coffin, a cold sweat broke out upon him, and an irrepressible shudder pervaded his entire frame. His duties as the sexton of his native village had caused him to acquire a degree of familiarity with such objects, which prevented him from being so utterly overpowered by the horrors of his situation as others would have been; but still his confinement in such a place, and his uncertainty of the fate which awaited him, were sufficient to inspire him with a mortal terror. He groped about until he found a coffin to sit upon, and in this manner he resolved to wait for the morning, when he should most probably see or hear something of his persecutors, if it was not their intention to starve him to death; and against that idea he strove to fortify himself by every argument he could call to his assistance.

CHAPTER LXXII.

THE OLD BAILEY.

NORMAN ASHLEY was taken to the station-house, charged with the murder of Colonel Elrington, and locked up for the night in a filthy cell; the vice and misery which he there witnessed being sufficient to banish sleep from his eyelids, even if his mind had not been tortured by his uncertainty respecting the fate of Lolah and the dreadful accusation impending over him. On returning home on the previous evening, he had been informed by the women in whose house he and Lolah lodged, that his mistress had gone out in a cab with Fitzormond, and she repeated the subterfuge of that imaginative vagabond with which Lolah had entrusted her. Knowing the character of Augustus, and that he and Simpson had lately taken the house formerly occupied by Mother Jones, he concluded that some scheme of villany was on foot, and immediately hastened there. The result the reader is acquainted with; but the conspiracy of Simpson and Fitzormond against his life, in order to save themselves from the consequences of their crime, was near being frustrated by the appearance of Peter Tomkins; and their fears lest he should have witnessed the murder of the colonel led to the scene at Habakuk Holdfast's chapel.

On the following morning, Norman was taken before the magistrates, and Simpson and Fitzormond, and the policeman who had apprehended him, were in attendance to give evidence. Simpson swore that he, Fitzormond, and the deceased colonel were sitting in the parlour, when the prisoner rushed in from the street, and accused the colonel of seducing his wife; that high words ensued between them, and that Ashley seized the poker, and struck deceased several violent blows on the head before it could be wrested from him. This tale, which had so much the appearance of truth, was repeated by Fitzormond, and Norman was then asked by the magistrate if he wished to say anything.

"There is such an artful mixture of truth and falsehood in the evidence, your worship, that it would be difficult to disprove the charge without some other evidence than my own," said the calumniated young man. "I went to the house to seek my wife, whom I believed to have been inveigled there by the witness Fitzormond; but I declare most solemnly, that I did not see the deceased until after he was dead, for he had been murdered before I entered the house. As soon as I discovered the murder, I was given into custody by Fitzormond; and while one of the policemen was up-stairs, I saw a man come up from the kitchen, and mingle with the people in the passage of the house. That man I know: his name is Tomkins, and he is clerk and sexton to the church of a village in Berkshire. If that man can be found, I have no doubt that his evidence will exculpate me from this most unjust charge."

Directions were then given by the magistrate for the production of Tomkins, and Norman was remanded for a week for that purpose. It was not until they saw the journals of the next day, that Lolah Hastings and Ellen Ashley were aware of his arrest, and the former was thus released from a most painful anxiety concerning him, only to be plunged into yet more terrible apprehensions for his fate. The week having expired, he was taken before the magistrates for re-examination, when the policeman who had been sent into Berkshire to find out Peter Tomkins, stated that that functionary's housekeeper had informed him that he was in London; that she had given him the address of the gentleman employed by him to collect his rents, and that upon returning to the metropolis he had ascertained that the person in question had absconded.

Norman persisted in his former statement respecting Peter Tomkins, and was again remanded for a week, the police being directed to use all their vigilance to discover the absent witness. Lolah Hastings now came forward, and preferred a charge of abduction against Augustus Fitzormond, and one of assault against Simpson, who were immediately placed in the dock. Lolah was then sworn, and deposed to the facts connected with the subterfuge by which she was induced to accompany Fitzormond, and the treatment which she subsequently experienced from Simpson and Lord Clanrobert, with whose name and rank she was unacquainted. The defendants gave an emphatic denial to the whole of her statement, with the exception of her riding in the cab with Fitzormond, which the latter knew could be corroborated by her landlady, and which he explained in a plausible manner. After a lengthened investigation, the magistrate expressed his conviction that the charge had only been made to shake the evidence of the defendants with regard to the murder, and ordered them both to be discharged from custody.

Again was Norman Ashley brought before the magistrates, but Peter Tomkins was not forthcoming to prove his innocence of the crime imputed to him, and this time he was committed to Newgate to abide a trial for the murder of Colonel Elrington. Lolah Hastings and Ellen Ashley were inconsolable; the latter, since the death of Leon Copley, had obtained an engagement as a professional singer at a tavern concert-room in Drury-lane, where Sam Skelter was in the nightly habit of attending, to drink in the music of her voice and steaming compounds of alcohol and water. On the evening of Norman's committal to Newgate, Sam Skelter called upon Ellen at her lodgings, previous to her leaving for the scene of her vocal exertions, and said that he had come to offer his services in the cause of her brother.

" I have not a doubt of his innocence, nor of the guilt of Fitzormond and Simpson," said he. " I know them both, by sight, as men of the vilest character; and the treatment experienced by Mrs. Ashley, joined to this unaccountable disappearance of Tomkins, go far to prove the existence of a plot. I cannot promise any result, for the abominable web seems closely woven, but I will try to discover Tomkins, and will watch every movement of the scoundrels Simpson and Fitzormond, whose haunts I am well acquainted with."

Ellen thanked the barrister's clerk for the interest which he manifested in her brother's fate; and then Sam took up his hat, and lingered a moment, as if about to speak, but was irresolute as to whether he should.

" Something I could wish to say," said he, looking at Ellen with an admiration which he could not conceal, " but this is not the time. We shall meet again —till then, farewell!" and, bowing gracefully to the object of his adoration, he quitted the room.

In about a week after the committal of Norman Ashley, the sessions of the Central Criminal Court commenced at the Old Bailey, and his trial came on the second day. Peter Tomkins had not come to light yet, and all the exertions of Sam Skelter to make some discovery which might serve the cause of Ellen's brother had been fruitless; but counsel had been retained for the defence, and a lingering hope yet remained. The barrister engaged to defend Norman, laid much stress on the bad repute of the principal witnesses, reminded the jury that the scene of the murder was the notorious den in which the skeletons had been discovered some years previously, and dwelt forcibly upon the mysterious disappearance of Tomkins, whose evidence would have exculpated his client from the heinous crime laid to his charge, which he considered, in conjunction with the absconding of Tomkins's attorney, as the result and the evidence of a vile conspiracy. His address evidently made an impression upon the jury, who retired to decide upon their verdict, and, during their absence, a profound silence reigned throughout the court.

They were absent three-quarters of an hour, and, when they returned into court, Norman glanced anxiously towards them, to read his fate in their countenances. But no ray of hope was there: every one of those twelve men wore on his countenance an expression of deep and earnest solemnity, which told him that he had nothing to hope for; for, however much some of them might have deplored the blind revenge which animates our penal code, they were bound by their oaths to find a verdict according to the evidence; the sentence lay with the judge. He waited not to hear the foreman's announcement, but rested his face upon his hands while that functionary came to the front of the jury-box, and said:

" We find the prisoner guilty, my lord."

Then the judge put on the black cap, and, in the most impressive manner, proceeded to pass the awful sentence of death upon an innocent man, with all the forms and solemnities prescribed by the laws.

CHAPTER LXXIII.

THE ESCAPE FROM NEWGATE.

AFTER his conviction, the thoughts of Norman Ashley were turned to the possibility of escape; for, to be barbarously strangled, in the presence of thousands of persons, for an offence of which he was innocent, was too terrible for contemplation, and the dread certainty of his fate, if he did not effect his escape, nerved him to brave every danger in the attempt. He knew that men had escaped from Newgate, and he thought that what had been done before might be done again. He knew that such a project was less feasible than in the days of Jack Sheppard, when the discipline and regulations of the prison were less strict; but the attempt was worth making, inasmuch as death was inevitable, whether he waited resignedly for his doom or made an attempt to escape and failed. His only instrument was an old rusty nail which he had picked up and contrived to secrete about his person; and with this he had to remove his fetters, and to break through stone walls.

He could not be very sanguine of success, for the prospect of escape with such slender means was very discouraging; but the stake was life, and he resolved to essay his fortune. His only fetters were iron cuffs upon his wrists, connected together by a short chain, and he laboured hard to cut through one of the links with his rusty nail, leaving off whenever he heard any of the turnkeys or other officials of the prison approaching his cell. He succeeded in accomplishing his arduous task about an hour after midnight, and, as the quietest of the hours of darkness was now approaching, he hoped to effect his escape without immediate detection. The freedom of action in which the severance of the chain enabled him to indulge gave increased buoyancy to his hopes; and, after listening attentively at the door of his cell, he planted his table upon his iron bedstead, which stood against the wall, and mounted on the top.

He immediately began picking away the plaster of the ceiling with his rusty nail, stopping occasionally to listen, and then resuming his labour with renewed vigour. At length the plaster was cleared away for a considerable space, and then he proceeded to break the laths; this was effected, and then he found, as he had anticipated, that a stone lay on the joists, which he found to be the hearth of the apartment above. Stopping a moment to wipe the dust and sweat from his heated brow, he raised the stone upon his hands, not without some difficulty, and moved it on one side.

He paused again to listen, but all was still; and, descending from his scaffolding, he again listened attentively at the door of his cell, and then snatching a sheet from his bed, he bade it adieu with a feeling of increasing hope, and, again mounting his scaffolding, emerged into the room above. Without waiting to replace the stone, he glanced hastily around him, and to his great joy found a basket of tools in one corner of the apartment, which had been left there by some workmen employed in the interior of the prison, and which the moonlight enabled him to perceive. There was a door locked, as he found on attempting to quietly open it, but he speedily removed the lock with a screwdriver, taking care to work as noiselessly as possible. He took from the basket a small file, which he consigned to his pocket, and with the screwdriver in one hand and an axe in the other, with which he determined to defend himself should he encounter any enemy to his liberty, he entered the adjoining apartment. It was similar to the one he had quitted; and, having removed the lock as expeditiously as was compatible with caution, the door opened, and he entered a long, gloomy passage.

Groping his way with caution, he paused when he had traversed some distance, finding a current of cold air blow on his heated countenance. He found, upon examination, that it proceeded from a wide flight of stone stairs, leading downwards; but, not choosing to abandon his fate to the chances of where they might conduct him, he kept along the passage until he came suddenly to a termination, and struck his head against the stone wall. He felt the wall on either side, and found a door, the lock of which he removed, and found it open upon a flight of narrow stairs, which, after a moment's hesitation, he began to ascend.

He found the stairs terminate in a narrow door, which was secured by a lock and two formidable bolts; he removed the lock with the screwdriver, drew the bolts, and, opening the door, emerged upon the lower leads of the prison roof. He was free! and for a moment he was surprised at the success which had attended his endeavours; then he clasped his hands with a fervent ejaculation of thankfulness, and proceeded to complete his escape.

The moon rode high in the firmament, now shining out from the deep-blue concave, and silvering the edges of the clouds which floated slowly through the atmosphere, and now obscured for a moment by a cloud passing across her pearly disk. The night air blew cool and refreshing upon the countenance of the escaped prisoner, and not a sound reached his ears as he stood upon those leads where, more than a century before, Jack Sheppard had preceded him.

Laying down the axe as no longer required for his defence, he tore the sheet which he had brought with him from his cell into strips, knotted them securely together, and having fastened one end to the iron *chevaux-de-frise*, which ran round the parapet of the prison roof, he threw the other end over. A cursory survey, which the moonlight enabled him to make of the adjacent roofs, informed him that he was above the tops of the houses in that part of the Old Bailey, and, carefully crossing the *chevaux-de-frise*, he firmly grasped his rope, and descended from the top of the prison to the roof of the adjoining house.

As he alighted on the tiles, the clocks of the neighbouring churches struck the hour of two, vibrating sonorously upon the deep silence of that lonely hour. Norman crawled over the tiles until he reached a skylight in the roof of the back part of a house, being afraid to creep down into the parapets in front, for fear of attracting the notice of some vigilant policeman on the opposite of the Old Bailey. The moonlight enabled him to perceive that the room was empty; and the frame of the skylight being of lead, he had little difficulty in removing a square of glass with the assistance of the screwdriver, used as a chisel, and was thus enabled to introduce his hand, and unfasten the frame.

He dropped noiselessly into the room, and, after listening a moment at the door, he opened it, and cautiously descended the stairs. As he reached the bottom of each flight, he paused to listen; but he had the good fortune to disturb none of the inmates, for at that hour people are in their first and soundest sleep, and he reached the entrance-passage without having excited the slightest alarm. The lamp opposite the front door shone through the fanlight over the door, and enabled him to reach it without creating any alarm by stumbling over anything which might be placed in the passage, which he might have ruined all by doing, but for its assistance. He felt for the fastenings, carefully removed them, and after listening for the last time, and waiting until the echoing footsteps of a policeman on duty in the Old Bailey had died away in the distance, he ventured to open the door. He looked right and left to see if any one was in sight; but the policeman had turned into Newgate-street, and the Old Bailey was deserted. He seized the opportunity to slip out, and, leaving the door ajar, for fear of rousing the sleeping inmates by closing it, he darted towards Ludgate-hill.

He stopped for a moment only at the corner of the Old Bailey, to ascertain if any policeman was in sight, and the survey being satisfactory, he ran across the street, and dived into Creed-lane. Thrusting his hands into his pockets to conceal the iron bracelets and fragments of his chain which yet remained upon his wrists, he walked quickly along until he reached Blackfriars-bridge, which he crossed, passing two policemen without exciting any unusual notice, and immediately into the maze of little streets lying between the Blackfriars and Southwark-bridge roads. These being inhabited almost entirely by mechanics and labourers, who have no property to protect, he encountered very few of the police; and it was to avoid their observation that he had taken this circuitous route to reach Wapping, in preference to passing through the city. At length he reached the foot of London-bridge, which he crossed, and, turning into Thames-street, went on to Wapping, and having arrived at the tavern where he had concealed himself on a former occasion, he readily obtained admission, even at that unseasonable hour.

CHAPTER LXXIV.

THE CAPTIVE IN THE VAULTS.

WE must now return to the unfortunate Peter Tomkins, immured in the pestiferous vaults of Habakuk Holdfast's chapel, where he remained in confinement during the imprisonment of Norman Ashley in Newgate, previous to his trial. It was about nine o'clock on the morning after he had been thrown into that gloomy vault, though the darkness prevented him from forming any idea of the lapse of time, when he heard footsteps approaching the vaults on the same level; and presently he heard a door creak upon its rusty hinges, and a light glimmered in the same direction. Hastily glancing towards the door from whence the light proceeded, he perceived an old man, whose features were concealed by a piece of black crape, and who carried a lighted candle in one hand, and a small basket in the other. Tomkins rose from his seat on the coffin, to address his mysterious gaoler; but the man set down the basket, and withdrew, closing the door behind him. The light flickered a moment upon the damp walls of the horrible charnel-house, and then Tomkins was again in darkness.

Under the impression that the masked visitor had brought him food, he groped his way to the door of the vaults, which, as the reader is aware, were approached below through the undertaker's cellar, and, having found the basket, he quickly rifled it of its contents, which consisted of cold meat and bread and a bottle of beer. The allowance was ample, and the quality of the edibles and beer excellent; there was, evidently, on the part of his persecutors, no intention of starving him. This gave confidence to the mind of the captive, and, when he could reflect more calmly upon his position, he had difficulty in attributing his imprisonment to the murderers of Colonel Elrington, for fear that he should divulge their guilt. He could arrive at no other conclusion after a long and serious consideration of all the circumstances, and, as this view of the matter held out hopes of his release when all inquiry into the murder had terminated with the wreaking of the law's revenge upon the innocent Norman Ashley, he regarded his incarceration as only temporary, and this made him more resigned to his present horrible situation.

True, his release would be consequent upon the public strangulation of an innocent man—a human victim immolated upon the bloody altar of social expediency; but the guiding principle of Peter Tomkins was unmitigated selfishness—the prolific parent of so many crimes. If we were asked what human failing caused the greatest amount of social misery and vice, we would unhesitatingly answer, the grovelling and egotistic love of self. The commonplace sentiment, that self-preservation is the first law of nature is abstractedly a true one; but it is commonly used in a perverted sense, for the interest of all is, rightly understood, the common interest of each individual in society. But how much crime—how much misery, springs from that dark spirit which leads men to pursue their individual aggrandizement and pleasure, with a reckless disregard of the rights of others! Norman Ashley and his sister were disinherited, and branded with the stigma of illegitimacy, through the villany of their uncle and the base subserviency of Peter Tomkins; but the latter cared not for the injustice, for it made him comparatively a wealthy man. Norman Ashley was in a felon's cell, awaiting the dreadful penalty of death for the crime of another; but Peter Tomkins almost longed for the catastrophe—for the legal murder of a man whom he knew to be innocent of the crime imputed to him; for he conjectured that the execution would be the signal for his liberation from that dark and loathsome vault.

The pestilential miasmi which loaded the damp and confined air of his prison not only deprived him of his appetite, but, from constant inhalation of that noxious atmosphere, his lungs became affected, as if the poisonous effluvia had implanted there the germs of decay and death. On the second morning, he begged to be allowed a light; but his masked gaoler assured him that a candle would not burn ten minutes after the door was closed, and the truth of this objection was so painfully apparent to the captive, that he did not repeat the request. When his mysterious gaoler visited him on the morning of the third day of his confinement, to bring him his daily allowance of food, he begged to be removed from the vaults to the cellar, representing that the effluvia arising from so many corpses, in every stage of decomposition, would be injurious to his health; but his request was not complied with.

Thus passed day after day, the daily appearance of the masked goaler with his food alone marking the flight of time in the mental diary of the immured prisoner; and at length the moment arrived when his persecutors thought they might liberate him with safety to themselves. One evening, the evening after Norman Ashley's trial and condemnation at the Old Bailey, Habakuk Holdfast descended to the vault to liberate his prisoner, having had an interview with Bill Simpson the day before, when the latter had paid the undertaker the balance of the sum which he had agreed to pay for Tomkins' detention, and had authorized the unscrupulous manufacturer of economical coffins to release the captive in the vaults, as himself and Fitzormond were about to leave London for the continent, taking with them their respective mistresses. They had no cause for personal animosity against Norman Ashley, and only made him the scapegoat of their crime in order to evade its penalty themselves; hence, the trial over, and the excitement of the inquiry at an end, they were enabled to leave the country without suspicion, which they could not do while the trial was pending.

The undertaker was accompanied by the ruffian who had assailed the unfortunate Tomkins in the court; the latter carried a short step-ladder, and the former a lantern. Tomkins trembled when he saw the undertaker close the door, for his confinement in that horrible place had attenuated his mind as well as his body, and he feared for a moment that they had come to murder him.

"We have come to liberate you," said the undertaker, who wore the black crape over his face, as usual.

"Thank God!" ejaculated Tomkins; and it was perhaps the most fervent thanksgiving he had ever breathed.

"But you must submit to be blindfolded, so that you shall not be able to give evidence against us on account of your imprisonment," continued Habakuk Holdfast.

"I am agreeable," returned Tomkins, who was glad to submit to any inconvenience to obtain his liberation from that horrible hole.

Holdfast then bound a handkerchief over the captive's eyes, and, the steps being planted beneath the entrance to the vaults from the chapel, it was thrown open by the vagabond who accompanied, and Tomkins was guided up the steps. The chapel doors were opened by its proprietor, and the captive was hurried out of the building and up the court; a cab was waiting in the street, into which he was thrust, his ruffianly assailant of a month since seated himself by his side, and the vehicle was instantly in motion.

His companion assured him in an undertone, that instant death would be the penalty of any imprudence, and the cab was driven rapidly along the dirty streets which lie within the square formed by Drury-lane, Holborn, Chancerylane, Fleet-street, and the Strand. After driving about for nearly an hour, the cab stopped, Tomkins was assisted to alight, and the vehicle was immediately driven round the corner of a neighbouring street. At the same moment the bandage was removed from the eyes of Peter Tomkins, and he found himself alone in one of the narrowest and dirtiest streets in the district of Bethnal-green. His guide had disappeared up a dark court, and for a moment Tomkins stood rooted to the spot, almost dazzled by the gas-lights, after having been confined for a month in a darksome vault. He might succeed in discovering the place where he had been confined, but he knew that the attempt would be attended with danger, and he judged it more prudent to return home. He engaged a bed for the night, at a coffee-house near the spot where he had been set down, and on the following morning returned to Berkshire. Here he read through all the details of the murder of Colonel Elrington, and the trial of the supposed assassin, which had appeared in the newspapers; and, though his conscience prompted him to reveal all that he knew of that affair, he was restrained by his fears for his own safety. He heard with considerable satisfaction of the escape

of the condemned prisoner from Newgate; for, now that he was free himself, the stifled promptings of justice and humanity returned, and he felt himself released from the responsibility which had rested upon him for withholding his evidence concerning the murder.

CHAPTER LXXV.

AN IMPORTANT DISCOVERY.

SAM SKELTER had kept his promise to Ellen to endeavour to discover the retreat of Peter Tomkins; but he could only pursue his search after the missing witness of the murder of Colonel Elrington after leaving the office of the solicitor by whom he was then employed; and the reader is aware that, even had this not been the case, the place in which Tomkins was immured would not have been discovered. Sam had conceived a warm attachment for Ellen Ashley, and hence he was disposed to do all in his power to avert from her brother the dreadful doom impending over him; but, unless he could discover the only witness of the murder, besides the assassins themselves, he could do nothing to save him, and the law must take its course. On the morning of Norman's escape from the condemned cell in Newgate, he was sitting in his employer's office, in the gloom and dreariness of Furnival's-Inn, pondering upon the mystery which appeared to envelope the absence of Peter Tomkins, and occasionally reverting to the image of the lovely Ellen, when his fellow-clerk entered, with the morning paper in his hand.

"Ashley has escaped from Newgate!" said he, proffering the newspaper to Sam Skelter,

"Hurrah!" exclaimed the latter, joyfully; and he eagerly proceeded to read the account of his escape given in a second edition of the *Times*.

Sam now ardently wished for evening, that he might avail himself of the excuse afforded him by the escape of Norman Ashley to call upon Ellen, and congratulate her upon the felicitous circumstance. There was little to do in the office that day; and, during the absence of his fellow-clerk in the afternoon on matters of business, Sam sought to amuse himself by reading an old newspaper which he had taken from the bottom of a file of journals, extending over a period of more than twenty years. While thus engaged, his own name happened to catch his eye, and he proceeded to read the paragraph in which it occurred, which ran as follows:

"ACCIDENT ON THE RIVER.—During the storm on Monday evening, a boat, containing five persons, was overset while crossing from the Wapping shore to that of Rotherhithe, and the whole of the party were immersed in the water. A seaman named Skelter, with his wife and infant child, were picked up, and also the waterman who rowed them; but an elderly female who was with them, never rose to the surface afterwards, and her body has not yet been discovered."

Sam had no remembrance of ever having lived at Rotherhithe; and, though the coincidence of the name had struck him at first, he would probably have thought no more about the matter, but for a singular discovery which he made immediately afterwards. In turning over the broad pages of the newspaper a sheet of paper dropped out, which Sam picked up, and which curiosity impelled him to read. The paper was yellow with age, and the writing scarcely legible, from the same cause. It appeared to be a string of business memoranda, and the caligraphy was that of Sam's employer. These memoranda ran as follows:

"*Mem.*—To ascertain for Lord Clanrobert if any child of a year old, or about that age, was lost in the river, between London-bridge and Rotherhithe-wall, on the night of February 10th; or, if any accident occurred on that night by which a child of that age was immersed in the water.

"*Mem.*—The newspapers of Sunday, February 16th, state, that the infant child of a seaman named Skelter was immersed by the oversetting of a boat, but picked up on the evening in question.

"*Mem.*—To find out this Skelter, and to claim the child for Lord Clanrobert."

Sam laid aside the newspaper, and mused for some time upon the evident mystery which these memoranda involved. The date of the newspaper corresponded with that mentioned in the memoranda, which appeared to have been inadvertently left between the folds of the newspaper, and laid by with it.

"What, if I were this child about which the late Lord Clanrobert—for it cannot be the present lord—was so strangely interested?" thought Sam Skelter; and he fell into a reverie upon the matter, becoming every moment more impressed with the idea that he was the child in whose fate the father of the present Lord Clanrobert had manifested so much interest.

The wooden-legged sailor who had brought him up had often asserted that he was not his father; and if the Skelter of the solicitor's memoranda was the old sailor of Ratcliffe-highway, Sam had every reason to believe that he was really the child of some person related to Lord Clanrobert, if not the late lord's natural son. After pondering some time over this idea, he took from a shelf the *Red Book* of the peerage, and, hastily turning over the leaves, came to the following account of the noble libertine from whom he had rescued Ellen Ashley.

" CLANROBERT, VISCOUNT, born February 1st, 1815; unmarried. Succeeded to the peerage on the death of his father, by apoplexy, May 21st, 1816. The late viscount was privately married to Charlotte Corbett, the daughter of a farmer at Erith, who, being dead at the time of his decease, a claim to the peerage was set up by Charles Macrae, Esq., of Brechin, in Scotland. The rival claimants referred the matter to the House of Lords, a committee of which decided upon the legitimacy of the present viscount. His lordship's mother, the late Lady Clanrobert, was drowned in the Thames, just below London-bridge, on the evening of February 10th, 1816, in consequence of the oversetting of a boat rowed by her husband, who, with their infant child, escaped the untimely fate of the lady."

Sam Skelter started as he perused the last four lines, for, coupled with the catastrophe recorded in that paragraph of an old newspaper, and those almost illegible memoranda of his employer, they opened to his mind the most brilliant and exciting prospects. But a moment before, he had fancied himself no more the adopted child of the wooden-legged sailor, but the illegitimate offspring of a peer; and now there were good reasons for supposing himself the rightful heir to a title and estates.

" On a certain night," thus he communed with himself, "two boats are on the bosom of Old Father Thames. One of them contains a peer of the realm, with his young wife and infant child—the other, a mariner, his wife, and their child, rowed by a waterman. By some means, both boats are upset near the same spot, and, though both the children are rescued from the water, in the darkness and confusion which prevail, they become changed : the child of noble birth goes to the humble roof of poverty, the seaman's offspring to the mansion of the peer. The seaman discovers the mistake too late to rectify it, for he has no clue to his missing child ; but the nobleman sets inquiries on foot, which appear to have been frustrated and set aside by his sudden death. That para-graph of an old newspaper and those musty memoranda have given me a coronet ! how I long to place it on the coal-black tresses of the lovely Ellen !"

Sam mused for a few moments upon the brilliant prospect opened to his mental vision by these discoveries, and then cut the paragraph relating to the accident on the river from the old newspaper, and put it in his pocket-book, together with the memoranda made by his employer so many years before. While pondering upon the best means to be adopted for establishing his claim to the title and estates held by the son of the wooden-legged sailor, his fellow-clerk returned to the office, and proposed, as they had nothing to do, to regale themselves with rum-punch and cigars. Sam was so excited by his discovery of his noble birth, that he readily agreed to the proposition, which was too con-genial to his habits ; and the cigars and the requisites for the punch being obtained from a tavern near Furnival's-Inn, the two clerks determined to enjoy their *otium cum dignitate* in their own peculiar way.

In the midst of their hilarity and enjoyment, their employer entered suddenly, and, as the glasses could not be put out of sight before he perceived them, nor the fumes of tobacco dissipated before they saluted his olfactory nerves, he reprimanded them severely. He was a man of violent temper and overbearing manners, and on the present occasion was irritated by something which had occurred to vex him during his absence ; hence, on Sam Skelter, in the exube-rance of his joviality, and the buoyancy of feeling excited by the coronet, which seemed to glitter in the perspective of his prospects, ventured to justify their hilarity and indulgence on the score of having nothing else to do, he at once dismissed him from his employment.

It was evening when Sam Skelter left Furnival's-Inn, and bent his steps towards Drury-lane, determined to seek an interview with Ellen Ashley, and then set about those inquiries which were necessary preliminaries to claiming the title and estates of Lord Clanrobert.

CHAPTER LXXVI.

THE CONCERT SINGER.

On arriving at Ellen's lodgings, Sam Skelter found that she had gone to the tavern where she was wont to charm the hearts and senses of all the law-clerks in Lincoln's-Inn-Fields, and tradesmen's assistants from Holborn and the Strand, by the touching sweetness with which she warbled " Dermot ashore," or "The land of the West." Thither he accordingly bent his steps, excited by the punch he had imbibed in the company of his fellow-clerk, elated by the discovery of his noble birth and brilliant prospects, and with the tide of thought running upon a coronet and the lovely Ellen. The tavern in question was situated in Drury-lane, and the concert-room was a long, lofty apartment, with a raised stage at one end, which was fitted up like the proscenium of a theatre, and forms running across the breadth of the room for the audience.

Sam Skelter took a front seat, as was his wont, and waited with impatience for the appearance of Ellen Ashley. The audience consisted, for the most part, of law-clerks and linen drapers' assistants, tradesmen's apprentices, young females employed in the manufacture of cigars and artificial flowers, and a sprinkling of the humble class of shopkeepers of the neighbourhood. The house not being licensed for musical entertainments, no charge was made for admission; but each visitor to the concert-room received a refreshment ticket, for which he paid sixpence, and this entitled him to liquor to that amount. Smoking, too, was allowed, and a light haze almost concealed the painted ceiling, the gas-lights shining through it like bright stars through the mists of evening.

Just as Sam entered, four shabby-genteel young men took their places immediately below the stage, and began torturing the strings of a bass viol, two violins, and a harp, into the most discordant sounds. When this had lasted some time, and a quart pot had duly passed from one to another of the musicians, they began playing an overture of Rossini's, which they executed in a very tolerable style. Then a pale young man, with black hair and dark-blue eyes, and shirt-collar turned over, *a-la-Byron*, made his bow, and sung a sentimental song. He was followed by a jovial but exceedingly dissipated-looking fellow, whose countenance presented a perpetual grimace, and who amused the audience with a very humourous melody concerning a certain wight called Duck-legged Dick.

Then Ellen Ashley appeared, and, while she entranced the audience with the charms of song, Sam Skelter had eyes and ears for her alone. Ellen was pale, apparently more from excitement than fear or langour, and an air of anxiety pervaded her fine features. She had heard of her brother's escape from Newgate, but she was not yet in possession of any further tidings concerning him. Sam waited till she had sung another song and a duet with the blue-eyed young man, which was the share of the entertainment assigned to her in the programme, and then he quitted the tavern, and waited for her at the door.

" Will you grant me the favour of your company as far as your abode, Miss Ashley?" said he, respectfully, as he proffered his arm to the lovely vocalist.

Ellen hesitated a moment, and then took the arm of her admirer without speaking.

" You have heard the good news, Miss Ashley?" said Sam, in a low tone of interrogation.

" That Norman has escaped? Yes; and if he can but preserve his liberty until the discovery of Mr. Tomkins, he is saved," returned Ellen.

" Miss Ashley," said Sam Skelter, summoning all his moral courage to make a declaration of his attachment—for, paradoxical as it may seem, there is more of that quality required when the impression is real than when it is feigned for dishonourable purposes—" since the first moment that I beheld you, I have felt that my future happiness depends upon you; for if you can give me no hope that our destinies may ever become united, through mutuality of sentiment, I shall be truly miserable. I have had this avowal on my lips before, but the fear of being rejected has prevented me from making it. Say, then, my dear Miss Ashley, if the state of your heart will allow me to hope?"

"The eminent service which you once rendered me, and the interest you have shown in behalf of my brother, command my everlasting gratitude," returned Ellen, after a moment's pause; "but for the present, Mr. Skelter, you must be content to be my friend, without seeking a closer tie. I thank you for the preference you have shown me, but solid reasons exist at present which prevent me from giving you any hope of being more to me than an esteemed friend."

"Would it be too much presumption to ask what those reasons are?—a prior attachment, perhaps?" said the youth, in a saddened and disappointed tone.

"You are mistaken, Mr. Skelter," rejoined Ellen, with a faint smile. "My heart is entirely free; and, since you have inquired the reasons why I cannot accord you more than my esteem, I will candidly inform you. Your devotion to pleasure and dissipation are not unknown to me, neither are your associates; and your own candour will acknowledge that they are not well chosen or creditable to a young man of reputation and honour. A man of pleasure is inevitably a selfish man, and cannot be so capable of feeling, or appreciating the tender passion, as the man must be whom I shall choose for a husband."

"The rebuke is just, Miss Ashley," said Sam Skelter, colouring slightly; "but if you will but deign me one word of hope——"

"Hush! I know what you are going to say," observed Ellen, quickly. "You were about to make a hasty promise of reformation, if I would give you any hope that the proffered love of the reformed and penitent rake would be accepted. This I cannot do; but study to become worthy of my regard, and, though I will not promise it as the result, you will assuredly be a gainer in reputation and in self-respect."

"You assure me that your affections are wholly disengaged?" said Sam, in a faltering voice; for he felt all the force of Ellen's mild rebuke.

"It is," replied Ellen, subduing a rising sigh as she thought of Leon Copley.

"And you will not say that, should I succeed in acquiring your unreserved respect, you will again refuse me, should your heart remain intact?" asked Sam Skelter.

"No; I will not say that; and that is all the hope I can hold out to you at present," replied Ellen, with a sweet smile. "But here we are at my lodgings, and you must now leave me."

"Ellen!" said a low, deep voice, close behind them; and, turning quickly round, the young girl beheld her brother, to whom a black woolly wig and some lamp-black had given all the appearance of a veritable African.

"Dear Norman!" exclaimed Ellen, scarcely able to restrain her tears at this joyful and unexpected meeting.

"Hush! who is this young man?" said her brother, glancing at Sam Skelter.

"The gentleman who rescued me from Lord Clanrobert," whispered Ellen. "He has exerted himself to discover Tomkins, but without success. But why are you in London, dear brother, where there is so much to be feared?"

"I could not venture from my concealment until evening," replied Norman, "and I wished to see both you and Lolah before I leave London, to assure you of my safety. I must not linger here, lest I should be observed and suspected. Farewell!"

Norman pressed his sister's hand, and hurried towards the Strand.

"Farewell, Miss Ashley," said Sam Skelter, advancing, and taking her hand. "I am about to leave London, not precisely like the knights-errant of olden time, to earn the smiles of beauty by valiant deeds of arms, but as a moral Quixote in the cause of justice. Like the Peri of Moore's beautiful poem, I am about to seek the gift which may obtain, for the erring, admission into Paradise."

"I honour the resolution, Mr. Skelter, and hope that it will endure," returned Ellen. "But I repeat that I make no promise, or hold out any hope as an inducement to reformation; to do so, would detract from your self-denial; and the more spontaneous your amendment, the more meritorious it will be.

I shall be happy to see you on your return to London; for the present, farewell!"

Sam Skelter raised the hand he held to his lips, and kissed it, without the fair owner manifesting any displeasure, and then hurried away. His interview with Ellen had strengthened his love for her, and his failings being the result of the contamination of example, joined to a certain buoyancy of feeling and volatility of manner, and more circumstantial than organic, he resolved to shake off all his associates and habits, and, from that moment, to become another character. Such is the redeeming influence of love! With this resolution, and with these impressions, he hurried towards the Strand, following in the footsteps of Norman Ashley.

CHAPTER LXXVII.

THE ALABAMA MINSTRELS.

NORMAN ASHLEY felt a sense of security when he reached the shelter of the old tavern in Wapping, but he longed to see Lolah and his sister, and assure them of his safety; and, moreover, he conceived that the possession of liberty would enable him to discover the absent Peter Tomkins, and thereby establish his innocence of the crime for which he had been unjustly condemned to suffer an ignominious death. He had removed his hand-cuffs by means of the file which he had abstracted from the basket in the room he had passed through in his escape from Newgate, and at night he ventured forth from his concealment, and had the brief interview with Ellen which we have described in the preceding chapter.

He had reached Waterloo-bridge on his way to the lodgings he had occupied with Lolah Hastings before his arrest, after parting with his sister in Drury-lane, when he heard a quick step behind him, and heard his name pronounced in a low and cautious whisper. Turning quickly round, not without an apprehension of danger, he beheld Sam Skelter, who followed in his footsteps through Drury-court and along the Strand.

"Your secret is safe with me," said Sam, seeing that Ashley regarded him with a degree of hesitation, which almost had the appearance of suspicion; "but we cannot talk here; and I have something to say to you."

"Come with me, then," said Norman Ashley, after a moment's pause. I am going to see my wife, and then I shall leave London."

He walked on quickly as he spoke, and Sam Skelter accompanied him; having reached a retired street in Lambeth, Norman desired his companion to wait for him, and knocked at the door of the house in which Lolah Hastings had her present abode. The door was opened by Lolah herself. Norman caught her in his arms, pressed her fondly to his heart, and their lips met in a fervent kiss. Lolah closed the door, and would have led him to their apartments; but he feared detection if he stayed long, and resolved not to go beyond the passage, which was involved in darkness, as Lolah had brought no light with her.

"Listen, dearest," said Norman, in a low voice; "the establishment of my innocence of this murder depends upon the success of my search after Tomkins. You will, probably, not see me until I have succeeded, unless I should have the misfortune to be detected; but we must not think of that. I have seen Ellen, and comforted her with the assurance of my safety. And now, farewell, my own love, and let hope keep those bright eyes from becoming dim with grief."

"Do we meet only to part so quickly?" murmured the weeping Lolah.

"It is necessary for my safety, dearest," returned Norman; and, again pressing her in his arms, and tenderly kissing her, he bade her farewell, and then opened the door, and passed quickly into the street.

He went on without speaking, through the heart of old Lambeth, and past the foot of Vauxhall-bridge, and then he slackened his pace, and said to his companion:

"We can converse now; it is getting late, and there will be few to observe us here."

"Your disguise suggested to me an admirable scheme for concealment," said Sam Skelter; and, as I promised your sister to aid you in discovering Tomkins, and have, moreover, been discharged from my situation this afternoon, its adoption is easy, and calculated to be of much service to us. I propose that we both assume the disguise of negro vocalists, and in that manner we shall be able to pursue our investigations without exciting any suspicion, and at the same time you will be more likely to evade detection. What do you think of my plan?"

"It is not a bad one," returned Norman; but you must procure the disguises; it will not do for me to venture into the vicinity of Drury-lane to procure them."

"Leave the properties to me," said Sam Skelter. "Do you push on to Battersea or Putney, and I will go back to town, and provide every article that is required for our purpose."

"I shall walk all night, for it will scarcely be safe to linger in the neighbourhood of London," rejoined Norman Ashley. "I shall reach Richmond by the morning, and I will wait for you at the 'Fox and Duck,' about a mile from the town, on the road to Ham."

With this understanding they seperated, and Sam Skelter retraced his way to Westminster-bridge, which he crossed, and took the shortest route to Drury-lane, where he made a variety of purchases, and then proceeded to his usual lodging. He rose early the next morning, and, walking down to the Hungerford-pier, stepped on board a Richmond steamer, and was borne rapidly over the rolling waters of Old Father Thames to the place of his destination.

On landing from the steamer at Richmond-bridge, the young man took the road to Ham; and, on reaching the "Fox and Duck," found Norman Ashley sitting alone in the tap-room. He had provided a couple of straw hats, a wig of black wool for himself, some lamp-black for keeping up the sable hue of their complexions, a tambourine, and a banjo. After drinking a pint of ale together, they issued from the house completely metamorphosed, and commenced their perigrinations in the character of negro minstrels.

"We must make our way to the village where Tomkins lives, and in this disguise we shall be able to discover whether he is really absent, or whether it is only a plant," said Sam Skelter. To find him out must be our first object, and, that accomplished, we can return to London with him, and compel him to give evidence concerning the murder."

"He must either be kept out of the way by those vagabonds, Fitzormond and Simpson, or by the influence of my uncle," said Norman Ashley, musing; and then he added: "But you know nothing of that affair; you shall hear it."

He then unfolded to his companion, as far as he could penetrate them himself, the nefarious plots of his uncle to deprive him of the title and property which ought of right to have accrued to him by the death of his father. Sam Skelter returned the confidence of his newly-acquired friend, by relating the discoveries which he had made at his late employer's chambers in Furnivals-Inn, and the prospect which had opened to him of succeeding to a coronet, a seat in the upper house of parliament, and considerable landed and funded property.

By the time these mutual confidences had been brought to a close, they had reached a considerable village, and here Sam proposed that they should commence the professional campaign, both to avoid the suspicion which might attach to them in the eyes of the police if they travelled without exercising their assumed profession, and in aid of their exchequer. Norman therefore twanged a prelude on the banjo, and, being soon surrounded by a crowd of curious and admiring rustics, the two strollers treated them to the following specimen of Guinea song:

De Alabama minstrels come,
Don't you hear our tum, tum, tum?
De twang, twang ob de ole banjo?—
Alabama minstrels all de go!

De Vermont gals are berry neat,
Boston lasses kiss so sweet,

Tennessee gals are berry free,—
But Alabama gals for me.

O, I wish dat I was dere,
Wid Flora May and Dinah Clare,
Miss Lucy Long, and Lucy Neal—
De yaller girl ob Massa Deal.

O, when dis nigger in de street,
Buckra ladies smile so sweet ;
Buckra massas frown and swear,
De minstrels captivate de fair.

Darky minstrels roam and sing,
Happier dan many a king ;
Wid our tum, tum, and our ole banjo,
Alabama minstrels all de go !

This choice effusion elicited the warmest applause, and, judging from the number of hands which were moved towards waistcoat and breeches pockets that the collection would be liberal, Skelter proceeded to sing the following more sentimental melody :

The bright moon is shining on Ohio's stream,
    And silvering the tall cotton-tree ;
The valley lies sleeping beneath her clear beam,
    And Mary, the lovely, is waiting for me.
Shine on, silver moon ! over valley and mountain,
    And guide the lone wanderer by Ohio's stream,
By thy light seeking the red chieftain's fountain,
    Where Mary is waiting beneath thy pure beam.

Oh, where is my Mary ?—dark-eyed creole maiden,
    The ebon-tressed loved one on Ohio's shore !
With blight and with sorrow my song now is laden,
    For Mary, the lovely, will meet me no more.
God of the negro, who speakest in thunder !
    How long shall the white man treat us with scorn,
Sell us like cattle, and tear us asunder ?—
    Better the negro had never been born !

By the feminine portion of their audience, this pathetic melody was received with even more approbation than the other, and the result was a more liberal collection of pence than they could possibly have anticipated.   In this manner they passed from village to village, and from town town, their assumed avocation enabling Norman Ashley to evade detection, until they reached the village, in Berkshire, where Peter Tomkins was wont to exercise the joint functions of parish clerk and sexton.

CHAPTER LXXVIII.

THE WITNESS.

It was at the close of a fine afternoon, when the Alabama minstrels entered the quiet village, and, being speedily followed by a troop of yelling boys, they stopped before the cottage of Peter Tomkins, and began their gratuitous concert with the praises of the maidens of Vermont and Tennessee.   During this part of the vocal entertainment, Peter Tomkins appeared at the window.   He was thinner and paler than when Norman had last seen him, and his countenance bore evident traces of the impress of the horror and dread which he had endured in the vaults of Habakuk Holdfast's chapel, and no less of the pestilential effluvia which pervaded that horrible and revolting charnel-house.   Norman exchanged a significant glance with Sam Skelter, and, when the latter had sung the pathetic air which we have given in the preceding chapter, they made

a collection of pence among their auditors, and then proceeded to the public-house where Peter Tomkins had passed the evening previous to the nefarious transaction recorded in the thirty-sixth chapter, in order to decide upon the steps necessary to be adopted in order to obtain the exculpatory evidence of that functionary, with reference to the murder of Colonel Elrington.

"It is quite clear that, whether voluntary or involuntary, he has been out of the way because he should not be brought into court as a witness," said Norman Ashley, as they conferred together in the tap-room, from the window of which they had a view of the house and garden of the parish clerk. "If he is an honest man, and was kept out of the way against his will by Simpson and Fitzormond, he would have gone to the magistrates, and declared me innocent, as soon as he obtained his liberty."

"He may have been liberated since your escape," suggested Sam Skelter.

"That is scarcely probable," returned Norman. "If he has been kept somewhere out of the way, it is scarce likely that he would have been set at liberty in the last week of my imprisonment: he would have been either

29

released as soon as the trial was over, or not until after the final catastrophe. Even supposing your surmise to be correct, it does not materially alter the case ; for his evidence would remove from me the odium of the crime, and save my life in the event of my being retaken. If his absence has been involuntary, his present atrocious apathy is the result of a vile cowardice."

" We can watch the house from here, and, when he leaves it, we can pounce upon him, and compel him to accompany us to the nearest magistrate," observed Sam Skelter.

" No; we will take him at once to London," said Norman Ashley. " He will not dare to refuse or resist, and he cannot deny his knowledge of my innocence."

The two young men sat in the tap-room of the public-house until it became nearly dark, one or other constantly watching the cottage of Peter Tomkins, whom they at length beheld issue from thence, and walk across the road towards the inn. Skelter immediately rose, and, with a mute signal for Norman to await his return, he watched Tomkins past the bar, and saw him enter the parlour. He immediately followed, and ensconced himself in a corner of the same apartment, in order to keep a close watch upon his movements.

Peter Tomkins had, on his return to the village, given an emphatic denial to the assertion of Norman Ashley, respecting his presence in the house in which the murder of Colonel Elrington had been committed, and accounted for his absence by saying that he had been on a visit to some friends in the north of England. Norman having escaped from prison, Tomkins considered that he had nothing to upbraid himself with—for such men have the narrowest idea of their moral obligations and their duties to society ; hence, the only drawback to the full enjoyment of his pipe and his brandy-and-water was, the indisposition which had resulted from his horrible confinement, and from which he was gradually recovering.

About eleven o'clock, he rose to depart, and Sam Skelter followed in his wake, and, as he passed the door of the tap-room, opened it quietly, and attracted the attention of Norman Ashley by a low whistle. They emerged from the inn together a moment after the departure of Tomkins ; they cast a hasty glance up and down the road, and, seeing that no one was near, they darted across the road, and were in an instant at the side of the startled clerk.

" Your name is Tomkins ?" said Sam Skelter, in a sharp, stern tone.

" Ye—yes !" stammered the clerk, looking from one to the other in a bewildered manner.

" That is enough," said Sam. " You must accompany us to London, to give evidence concerning the murder of Colonel Elrington."

" I know nothing about it," returned Tomkins, endeavouring to assume an air of assurance, though he trembled all the time.

" We have a witness who saw you in the house at the time," said Sam Skelter ; " and, if you do not mind what you are about, my man, you will stand a nasty chance of being transported for life as an accessory."

At these ominous words, Peter Tomkins turned dreadfully pale, and trembled so excessively, that he could scarcely stand. He had not recognised Norman Ashley, owing to his disguise and the darkness ; and the last words of Sam Skelter caused him an agony of apprehension.

" Who are you ?" he at length ventured to ask.

" Perhaps we are *detectives*—perhaps we are not," returned Sam. " At any rate, if you resist, or refuse to accompany us, we can soon obtain the assistance of the police."

" Just allow me to speak to my housekeeper, and then I will go with you, gentlemen," said Peter Tomkins, after a moment's hesitation.

" Willingly," rejoined Sam Skelter ; and he followed the clerk into his cottage, while Norman waited in the road.

In a few minutes they came out, and, having ascertained that a post-chaise could not be procured nearer than Eton, they all three proceeded there on foot, the trembling clerk walking between his sable captors. It was midnight when they reached Eton, and the anxiety of Norman to free himself from the odium of the murder, joined to their fears that Tomkins might endeavour to give them the slip during the night, urged them to hire a post-chaise, and proceed to London at once.

They reached the metropolis just as the rising sun was beginning to warm the pavement of the west-end, and having discharged the chaise at the bottom of Southampton-street, they proceeded towards the police-station in Vine-street on foot.

" Can we see the inspector ?" demanded Sam Skelter of a policeman who was standing in the passage.

" Walk this way," returned the constable, regarding the party with scrutinizing attention ; and they followed him into an office, where the inspector was sitting at a table.

" This gentleman," said Sam Skelter, addressing the inspector, and indicating Tomkins, "has important evidence to tender, concerning the murder of Colonel Elrington, which will entirely exculpate Mr. Ashley."

" You had better attend before the magistrates at Bow-street," said the inspector ; "but of course you are aware that Ashley has escaped from Newgate, and has not yet been re-taken."

" I am Norman Ashley," observed that person, advancing a pace or two ; " and I wish to surrender into custody, confident, of a reversal of the sentence unjustly passed upon me."

The inspector was astonished, and the voluntary surrender of Norman Ashley evidently impressed him with a conviction of his innocence of the crime imputed to him. He conducted them into a private room, where they were supplied with breakfast from a neighbouring coffee-house, Sam Skelter not wishing either to leave Norman alone, or to lose sight of Tomkins ; and, as soon as the police-court in Bow-street was open, the inspector accompanied them thither.

The inspector having intimated to the magistrates that Norman Ashley had that morning surrendered himself into the custody of the police, and that Mr. Tomkins was in attendance to give evidence of an important nature, the clerk was ushered into the witness-box. He had by this time recovered most of his equanimity, and, after relating the manner in which he became cognizant of the facts connected with the murder, he detailed the particulars of the extraordinary means which the murderers had adopted to prevent him from appearing as a witness. His fears of future violence from the assassins or their confederates impelled him to declare his absolute ignorance of the locality of his horrible prison ; but his evidence was so conclusive as to the guilt of Fitzormond and Simpson, and the innocence of Norman Ashley, that the magistrates issued warrants for the apprehension of the murderers, and made an immediate communication of the facts to the Secretary of State for the home department, with the view of procuring the release of Norman Ashley. Peter Tomkins was bound over to prosecute the murderers, when they should be discovered, and Norman was removed to Newgate until an order should be received from the Home-office for his release.

CHAPTER LXXIX.

OAKWOOD HALL.

In a few days Norman Ashley was released from prison, by order of the Secretary of State, his innocence being placed beyond a doubt by the evidence of Peter Tomkins, and thus the administrators of the law were spared the commission of a murder. The verdict of the jury would have been no extenuation of their blood-guiltiness in such a case ; for the laws consider it no mitigation of a murderer's guilt that the person murdered was deprived of life through being mistaken for another. It is only in self-defence that the taking away of human life can be justified, and a case cannot possibly be conceived in which society is placed upon its defence against a single individual. Immediately upon obtaining his release, Norman proceeded to the lodgings of his beloved Lolah, and there he found his sister Ellen, a very warm friendship having sprung up between those lovely girls.

" I shall now," said Norman Ashley, after he had received the congratulations of his mistress and sister, and returned their endearments—" I shall now proceed with the design which I formed some time since for establishing my claim to the baronetcy and property of my father, which I would have carried out while in the country in quest of Tomkins, but for the necessity of first vindicating myself from the imputation which circumstances enabled a pair of villains to cast upon my character. I shall go down to Oakwood, and, by some means or other, possess myself of the necessary documents for that purpose."

" But how, dear Norman ?" said Lolah, with renewed apprehension for her lover's safety. " If you should be detected in the search, your uncle will charge you with burglary, and you will be taken from us again."

" Fear not, my Lolah," returned Norman; " the cause is one of right against usurpation, and it must prosper. Have we not, in the fact of my being now among you, a proof of the power of right to vindicate itself when supported by an indomitable resolution? I will watch for an opportunity of seizing the papers, which I have every reason to believe will prove my right to the property; and, if I succeed, I shall have my uncle too much in my power for him to dare to take any proceedings against me for any burglary I may commit, or for the abstraction of the papers. When a villain shelters himself behind the chicanery of the law, a violation of the law is sometimes necessary to unmask him."

" Suppose the documents have been destroyed ?" suggested Ellen.

" If our uncle had forged a will, he would doubtless have destroyed the genuine one," returned Norman; " but, as he alleges that there is no will, he has most probably merely concealed it—that is, supposing his allegation to be false, which I have every reason to believe. The legitimacy of our birth is another question; but, if we can prove that our uncle has deceived us on one point, we may reasonably infer that he has done so on the other, and I hope to establish that also."

" May you be successful !" said his sister; " but pray be careful what yo do, dear Norman."

" I will, for Lolah's sake and yours," returned Norman; and he kissed them both for the interest they manifested in his designs.

On the following morning he set out for Gloucestershire, and, late in the evening, arrived at Cirencester, where he smoked his smuggled cigars in the tap-room of a public-house until the landlord announced that he was about to close for the night. He then left the house, and walked towards Oakwood Hall, where he arrived about an hour after midnight. It was a dark and somewhat stormy night, and therefore the better for his purpose; for the wind howled and moaned around the mansion of his forefathers, and, as the black clouds sailed through the dull, leaden sky, like the sombre chariot of the demon of the storm, large drops of rain pattered among the foliage of the ancient oaks which grew around the park.

Crossing the fence which enclosed the domain of Oakwood, Norman Ashley strode rapidly over the park, and soon was standing in the deep shadow of the mansion, regarding it with the interest with which we invariably gaze upon the scenes endeared to us by the reminiscences of our childhood. He had provided himself with such implements for effecting an entrance into the mansion as he thought he should require, and these he now proceeded to draw from his pockets. Mounting on the stone sill outside one of the drawing-room windows, which looked upon the verdant lawn, with its parterres of flowers and clumps of evergreen shrubs, he bored a hole with a centre-bit in one of the shutters, the moaning wind drowning the grating noise of the instrument. He was then enabled to introduce his finger into the aperture which he had made, and draw the bolt of the shutter; there was another bolt at the bottom of the shutter, and another hole had to be bored with the centre-bit before it could be drawn.

Having opened the shutters, Norman next proceeded to trace round the edges of a square of glass with a glazier's diamond, and, when he had almost cut it out, he spread his handkerchief against it, and a slight tap at the bottom of the pane caused it to fall outwards without making any noise. There was still the internal shutters to open, and these he knew were only secured by a single bolt at the bottom, and were consequently opened with less difficulty than those outside, after he had passed his hand through the square from which he had removed the glass, turned back the spring, and thrown up the sash. Having at last removed every impediment to his entrance, he listened attentively for any sound which might indicate that the sleeping inmates of the mansion had been alarmed, and none reaching his ears, he entered the drawing-room, and immediately closed the outer shutters.

Having procured a light with a congreve match, he lighted a dark lantern which he had brought with him, and stole cautiously from the room. Having reached the passage, he listened attentively for a moment, and, having taken off his boots that his movements might be as noiseless as possible, he began to ascend the stairs.

Pausing occasionally to listen, and hearing only the low moaning of the wind without, he ascended the familiar stairs with cautious and cat-like steps, and at length found himself at the door of the chamber in which his father had drawn his last breath. He applied his hand to the door, and found it locked. He listened attentively, but all within was silent as the grave. Taking a small chisel from his pocket, he quickly wrenched off the beading which projected over the line of meeting of the door and partition, and then cut out a small piece of the edge of the partition with a circular steel saw, to allow of the door being opened without having been previously unlocked.

The chamber was untenanted, and everything remained in the same position as he had last beheld them. Advancing to the desk from which his uncle had removed the will of Sir Norman Ashley, he found it unfastened. He knew the secret drawer in which the will had been deposited, and eagerly opened it. It was empty; and though he had almost expected to find it, yet the absence of the document upon which so much depended caused him a momentary disappointment. He mused for some time upon the object which had led him to that house, and revolved in his mind all that his uncle had said in announcing to him his illegitimacy and the intestacy of his father; then he considered the various places in which his uncle would probably have concealed the will, if one existed, and then he recollected the ebony cabinet.

He had seen it in the drawing-room as he came through, and, immediately leaving the chamber in which his revered parent had closed his eyes for ever, he cautiously descended the stairs. He was half way down, when he thought he heard a noise. He stopped, and listened: it was only the rain beating against the window at the end of the corridor at the head of the first flight of stairs, and he went on again. He reached the passage, re-entered the drawing-room, and, in a few minutes, had forced open the cabinet with his chisel: it contained a variety of papers. One by one he scanned their contents with a rapid glance, and at length his eyes rested upon a paper on which he perceived the names of his parents.

With irrepressible eagerness and impatience he caught up the paper, and found it to contain the registry of several marriages, among others that of his parents. The pleasure which Norman experienced at a discovery which vindicated the fair fame of his mother from the aspersion of his knavish uncle was increased when, upon comparing the date of the register with his own age, he ascertained his legitimacy beyond the shadow of a doubt. This was the leaf cut out from the parish register by Peter Tomkins, and immediately beneath it he found the object of his search—his father's will. His heart beat high as he made these discoveries, and, having secured the documents about him, he put on his boots, opened the shutters, and sprang out upon the lawn. The rain had almost ceased to fall, but the night was still dark and cloudy, and the wind blew in fitful gusts. He closed the shutters of the window, and, hurrying through the park, leaped into the road, and walked quickly towards Gloucester.

CHAPTER LXXX.

NORMAN'S SOLICITOR.

DURING his dark and lonely walk towards the city of Gloucester, Norman reflected deeply on the discoveries which he had made at Oakwood Hall, and contrasted them with the allegations of his uncle respecting his legitimacy and the intestacy of his father, and the assertion of Peter Tomkins that no marriage had been solemnized at the church in which he officiated, between Norman's parents. One thing was evident: either Peter Tomkins was a party to the injustice perpetrated by the senior Edward Ashley, or the marriage had been solemnized at some other church. In either case, it was clear that his uncle had bribed the clerk to destroy the evidence of the marriage by cutting out, from the church register, the leaf upon which it had been registered. He therefore determined to deposit the documents which he had abstracted from the ebony cabinet at Oakwood Hall in the hands of some respectable solicitor, immediately on his reaching London, and to act upon his advice in the future steps to be taken for prosecuting his claim to the property usurped by his uncle.

He reached Gloucester in time to proceed by the first train to Birmingham, and thence to London, having resolved upon taking this route in order to evade the pursuit that would undoubtedly be made along the road from Cirencester to London as soon as his uncle had discovered the abstraction of the papers from the ebony cabinet. On his arrival at the lodgings of Lolah Hastings, in the York Road, he found his sister there, anxiously waiting his return from Gloucestershire, and eagerly revealed to them the discoveries which he had made.

" I see that you have been successful," observed Lolah, remarking the radiance of his countenance.

" I have," returned Norman, kissing her; "and to-morrow you shall be Lady Ashley. I will procure a licence in the course of the day. I have secured the evidence of our legitimacy," he continued, turning to Ellen, whose dark eyes sparkled with joy; "and here is our father's will."

He drew it from his pocket as he spoke, and read it aloud to Lolah and his sister. It set forth that the testator bequeathed to his son, Norman Ashley, his lawful successor to the baronetcy and the estate pertaining thereto, all his landed property; to his daughter Ellen, the sum of five thousand pounds on her attaining the age of twenty-one, or on her marriage, should she marry before attaining that age, provided such marriage received the sanction of her guardian; to his brother Edward—who was appointed sole executor and guardian—a like sum; and the residue of his funded property to his son, to assist him in the improvement of the estates.

Norman repeatedly kissed Lolah and his sister in the exuberance of his joy, and then set off to consult a solicitor, whose chambers were in Clifford's-Inn— that gloomy solitude in the immediate vicinity of the bustling thoroughfare of Fleet-street. Having stated the circumstances of the case, and placed in the solicitor's hands the stolen leaf of the register and his father's will, he candidly acknowledged the means he had used to obtain them.

" We are often obliged to violate the laws in order to vindicate justice," observed the solicitor, smiling; "and, having obtained our object, we leave the other party to bring his action, if he chooses, and do the worst he can. But you have nothing of that to apprehend in this case, I imagine, though our opponent is in the law; for an action is an uncertain instrument which lawyers seldom like to use on their own account. I will go down to Berkshire, and, by a personal examination of the church register, ascertain whether this leaf has been taken from it. If it has, we shall be able to extort, from the fears of Peter Tomkins, a confession of the participation of Mr. Ashley in the felonious abstraction; if it has not, we must pursue our inquiries at other churches in the neighbourhood. When we have discovered the register from which this leaf has been taken, the law will support you in taking possession of the property, and leaving your uncle to indict you for trespass if he chooses."

" But he will stand upon the authority given him by the will appointing him sole executor and guardian," observed Norman.

" He has abused the trust, and application can be made for the Court of Chancery to appoint another guardian," returned the solicitor. " Moreover, you will soon be of age, I presume?"

" In a few months," returned Norman.

" Then our course is clear," continued the man of law. " You have right on your side; and, when once you have possession of the property, your uncle will not venture to dispute it with you. I will proceed with the case with all dispatch, and, in a few days, you shall hear from me."

Norman Ashley next proceeded to Doctors'-Commons to procure a licence for the union of himself and Lolah on the following day, and then returned to the York-road, to acquaint Lolah and Ellen with the result of his interview with his solicitor. On the following morning, he made Lolah Hastings his wife, according to the law and the church, as she was already by love, in the presence of his sister, who officiated as bridesmaid. In a few days afterwards, he received the following letter from the solicitor whom he had employed to prosecute his claim to the property of his father :

" Dear sir,—I have just returned from Berkshire, and have the pleasure to inform you that I have succeeded in obtaining the information which we required to complete the evidence of your right to the baronetcy and property of the late Sir Norman Ashley, as well as of the disgraceful acts of Mr. E. Ashley. I began by asking Tomkins whether such a marriage had ever been performed there; and, after pretending to consult a duplicate register, he replied in the negative, as he did to you. I then informed him that I was the solicitor employed by you, and paid the usual fee to inspect the church register. On observing to him that a leaf appeared to be missing, he seemed agitated, and, on my producing the leaf, and threatening him with an indictment, he confessed that he had been bribed by Mr. Ashley to cut out that leaf. I wrote down his confession, and he signed it. In a few months, you will attain your legal majority; and, in the meantime, Tomkins will be deterred from making any communication to your uncle, by the fear of a prosecution; wait until then, as such a delay will render our course easier, and obviate the necessity of placing yourself and sister under the guardianship of the Lord Chancellor. Let me know when the auspicious day arrives, and I will accompany you to Oakwood Hall, to take possession of your patrimonial possessions.

I am, sir,
Yours faithfully,
MATTHEW MORTMAIN."

Norman, Lolah, and Ellen now looked forward with joyful impatience to the period which should witness the triumph of right over knavery and injustice, and the succession of the former to the ranks of that minor nobility, the baronetage of England, from which the usurpation of his uncle had excluded him. One of the earliest acts of Norman Ashley, after receiving the letter of his solicitor, was, to make out a list of the merchants and others whose property he had self-appropriated in the exercise of his avocations as a pirate on the Thames, with the view of making complete restitution to those parties, both as a matter of justice and of prudence, lest any ulterior proceedings might compromise his reputation, and reveal to the world that Sir Norman Ashley had been a smuggler and a pirate.

Edward Ashley, his uncle, in the meantime had offered a reward of a thousand pounds for the apprehension of the unknown burglar who had entered Oakwood Hall, and abstracted the papers from the ebony cabinet. The fact that no other property was taken away, proved to him that the object of the burglary was solely to obtain possession of those important documents, and a thousand times he cursed his stupidity for not having destroyed them. But, as week succeeded week, and nothing transpired to induce a belief that steps were being taken to wrest from him the title and property which he had usurped, his equanimity in some degree returned, though he could not divest his mind of the thought that those papers were in the hands of those who would doubtless use them for that purpose; and the reflection that such a use might at any moment hurl him from his present proud position, and brand him with the stigma of crime, was constantly hanging over him, like the sword of Damocles, banishing peace from his breast, and stamping his features with the impression of care's searing fingers.

CHAPTER LXXXI.

THE HEIR OF OAKWOOD.

On the day that Norman Ashley completed his twenty-first year, the crafty usurper of his patrimony sat in the drawing-room of Oakwood Hall, with his eyes raised to the ceiling, in a fit of moody abstraction, while his wife sat opposite to him, the impersonation of worldly-mindedness, and the pride of wealth. It was evening, and the fading beams of an autumnal sun streamed through the gothic windows, and lengthened the shadows of the venerable oaks that dotted the verdant and undulating park.   A few deer were grouped in the shade of the ancient trees, or chasing each other through the sunlit stream which meandered through the park—an indispensable appendage to the dignity of the ex-barrister as a baronet and a landed proprietor, a member of the aristocracy, created by the first of the Stuarts.

" It is strange we have heard nothing of the papers taken from the ebony cabinet," said Lady Ashley, in a musing tone.

" It is nearly three months ago, observed her husband, without lowering his eyes from the ceiling; " and yet they must have been taken by some one in the interest of Norman, or other property would have disappeared at the same time." ——

" It is a pity they were not destroyed at the time they came into your possession," said his wife.

" True, but who would have thought of their disappearing after lying safely in that cabinet for six years?" returned the barrister. " It is a most unfortunate thing, and, whenever I think of it, the reflection that the papers will some day be made use of to wrest the property from us, constantly arises in my mind."

As he uttered the last words, his attention was drawn to a post-chaise, driving up the carriage-road to the mansion, and a presentiment of some approaching evil immediately struck to his heart.   There were two gentlemen in the chaise, but he could only discern the countenance of one, and that was unknown to him.   The chaise stopped before the door, he heard them admitted, and then the servant entered the drawing-room, and announced that two gentlemen wished to speak with him on urgent and important business.

" Did they give their names?" inquired the barrister.

The servant handed him a card, on which was engraved, " *Matthew Mortmain, Clifford's-Inn*," which the barrister passed to his wife, with a look of uneasiness and apprehension; for he knew that the person whose name was thus announced was in the profession of the law.

" Where are they waiting, Robert ?" said he.

" In the library, sir," replied the servant; and thither the barrister proceeded.

Mr. Mortmain and Norman Ashley rose as he entered, and the surprise of the barrister at thus encountering his injured nephew was so great, that he was unable to bid them be seated.   With visible confusion in his manner, he glanced first at his nephew, and then at the solicitor, seeing in their visit the realization of all the fears that had beset him since the abstraction of the papers from the ebony cabinet by the unknown burglar.

" You do not seem pleased to see me, uncle," said Norman Ashley, in a tone which was the least bit ironical. " This is my birthday—my twenty-first birthday, and I thought you would have assembled the tenantry on the lawn to receive their future landlord, and regaled them with a roasted ox and the oldest ale in the cellars in honour of this occasion."

" I do not understand you, sir," returned his uncle, in a cold and rather stern tone; but he did not say any more until he had found out the object of the inauspicious visit of his nephew and the solicitor.

" Then I must refer you to my solicitor, Mr. Mortmain, uncle," said Norman Ashley, throwing himself into a chair, and leaving the men of law to fight the battle alone.

His uncle took a chair, and, motioning Mr. Mortmain to resume his seat, he waited for him to open his business.

The pleasure which good men derive from the consciousness of having performed a worthy action, is one which lasts all their lives, and, to this great and and enviable pleasure, it is now in my power to open a wide avenue to you, sir," began Mortmain, addressing himself to Edward Ashley, who figetted on his chair, and scarce knew what to expect from such a commencement. " To be enabled to perform a meritorious act of justice, is an unspeakable satisfaction

even when some personal sacrifice is necessary to obtain it. I am sure, Mr. Ashley, that a man of your liberality of mind, and keen sense of justice, will consider such a gratification a counterbalance to any regret you may experience at having to surrender such a fine domain as this of Oakwood to your nephew, the rightful owner."

"You are labouring under a mistake, sir," returned Edward Ashley, striving to conceal his embarrassment; "and I think you might have taken the trouble to ascertain the facts of the case you appear to have taken up, before indulging in what seems to me an ill-timed pleasantry. My brother died intestate, and his children have been proved illegitimate."

"I am sorry, sir, that you have dissipated the pleasing illusion I was indulging in," returned Mr. Mortmain, gravely. "But I will adopt the conclusion most favourable to yourself, and presume you to be ignorant of the fact that a will *was* made by the late Sir Norman Ashley, and that that will is still in existence."

"If such a document does exist, it must have been forged to serve the purpose of his illegitimate offspring," observed the barrister, becoming desperate as he foresaw the conclusion of the interview.

"What, sir!" exclaimed Norman, colouring with anger. "Not content with defaming my mother, endeavouring to brand my sister and myself with the stigma of illegitimacy, and depriving us of our rightful patrimony, you dare to accuse me of forgery!"

"I have nothing to say to you, sir," returned his uncle, sternly, "and I am surprised at your audacity in coming here after absconding from the employment in which I placed you, and becoming a criminal, the associate of criminals, and the inmate of a criminal prison."

"My kind uncle apprenticed me to a fisherman at Gravesend," said Norman Ashley, turning to Mr. Mortmain, "and not liking such an amphibious occupation, I engaged in the contraband trade between London and Hamburgh, or Flushing, and having had the misfortune to be taken with the rest of the crew in the Thames, I feel no shame in acknowledging that I became for three months, as my worthy uncle expresses it, the inmate of a criminal prison."

"It is extremely gratifying to me to receive such an explanation of so grave a charge," said the solicitor. "To you, Mr. Ashley, I have to state that I have in my possession a will of the late baronet, which can be proved authentic; you can peruse it, if you please;" and he handed the document to the barrister.

The latter received it with a tremulous hand, and a cold perspiration distilled upon his pale brow as he perceived that it was really the will of his brother. He merely glanced over it in a confused manner, and then returning it to Mr. Mortmain, he observed that the illegitimacy of his nephew debarred him from inheriting the entailed estates appertaining to the baronetcy.

"You are as much mistaken with regard to the legitimacy, or otherwise, of your nephew and neice, as you were with reference to the presumed intestacy of your brother," said Mr. Mortmain, producing the leaf cut from the register by Peter Tomkins. "An inspection of this document will satisfy you of the legitimacy of this young gentleman and his sister."

"What is this, sir?—I cannot understand it!" said Mr. Ashley, with a forced smile.

"Then I will submit another document, which, perhaps, you will understand better," returned the solicitor, drawing from his pocket-book the confession of Peter Tomkins, and handing it to Mr. Ashley.

"The treacherous villain!" exclaimed the barrister, becoming fearfully excited by this evidence of the means possessed by Norman of not only wresting from him the property, but also ruining his reputation, and branding him with the stigma of crime.

"You now perceive that you are at the mercy of your injured nephew, and that your designs have recoiled upon your own head," said Mr. Mortmain; "but my client has no desire to crush a fallen adversary, and——"

Before he could conclude the sentence, Mr. Ashley had rushed in an excited manner from the room, and in a moment after they heard the report of a pistol up-stairs. The screams of Mrs. Ashley rang through the mansion, and Norman bounded up the stairs, followed by Mortmain. There a shocking spectacle awaited them; the knowledge that he was unmasked, and at the mercy of those whom he had injured, had rendered Edward Ashley desperate, and in a paroxysm of temporary insanity he had committed suicide, by blowing out his brains with a pistol.

CHAPTER LXXXII.

THE OLD SAILOR.

We must now return to Sam Skelter, who, as soon as he was assured of the safety and vindicated reputation of Norman Ashley, determined to pursue those inquiries which he had reason to believe would establish his claim to the title and property of Lord Clanrobert. He had a far more difficult task to accomplish than Norman had had, for he had to establish even his identity with the child immersed in the Thames at the time that the late Lady Clanrobert was drowned, and to prove that the child that had been reared as the heir of Clanrobert, was in reality the offspring of the seaman Skelter. His first step, therefore, was to seek out his supposed father, the wooden-legged sailor of Ratcliffe-highway, and gather from him such particulars of the accident on the river, in 1816, as might supply the link required to connect the account given in the *Red Book* with the newspaper paragraph relating to the same affair.

With this object in view he proceeded to Shadwell, on the evening after his return from Berkshire, and sought out the dwelling of the old sailor, from which he had fled several years since, and from which Lolah Hastings, also, had fled from the insane wrath of the infuriated Malay. But the old vagabond no longer lodged there, and no one in the neighbourhood knew anything of his present whereabouts, though all remembered that there was such a person, and had seen him sitting with his pictorial imposture before him, in Ratcliffe-highway, or hobbling home on his wooden supporters in the evening.

Determined not to be frustrated, and to terminate his search only when he found his adoptive father or his grave, Sam proceeded to the gin palace at which the old sailor had been wont to slake his clay in the evening with the potent spirit imported from Jamaica. Glancing round the bar without discovering the object of his search among the infatuated victims of intemperance, whose conduct only differs from that of the wretched devotees who immolate themselves beneath the crushing wheels of the chariot of Juggernaut, in the comparative slowness of their mode of suicide, he entered the tap-room, but he was not there, and he emerged into the street with an air of disappointment upon his handsome countenance.

After some consideration, Sam walked back as far as the middle of Ratcliffe-highway, and sought the information he required of a policeman; but the man, though he knew the wooden-legged sailor, was not acquainted with the locality of his domicile, and advised Sam to make inquiries in Shadwell. Back to Shadwell, therefore, Sam went, and at length found a police constable who was able to direct him to the abode of the wooden-legged hero of the Polar icebergs, which was situate in a court connecting two of the narrow, dirty streets which lie between the High-street of Shadwell and the Commercial-road. He found the old sailor in a miserable little room, with scarcely any furniture, just knocking out, with a deep sigh, the ashes of a pipe he had no means of refilling, while the open door of the little cupboard showed that it was destitute of food.

" What cheer, old tar?" said Sam Skelter, as he entered, and glanced round the miserable room. " What! do you not recollect me?"

" Blest if it arn't little Sam!" exclaimed the old sailor, opening his eyes very wide, and looking at Sam with astonishment.

" How are you, dad?" said Sam, shaking the hand of his adoptive father, and then seating himself on the edge of the greasy and notched deal table.

" Why, I have been precious bad, Sam," returned the old sailor, in a grumbling tone; " and the consequence is, that here I am, laid up like an old hulk as arn't seaworthy, and not a shot in the locker, nor a biscuit in the bread-room. But you seem well rigged and stored, Sam," he added, glancing at the young man's comparatively genteel appearance.

" I am sorry to hear you are so hard up, old tar," returned Sam; " and as I bear no malice for past rope's-endings, I will lay in some stores for you, and help you to splice the main-brace."

Sam skipped down the broken stairs, each of which was thickly encrusted with dirt, and, having been absent about ten minutes, returned, loaded with a plate of cold beef, a four-pound loaf, a pot of " heavy wet," an ounce of tobacco, and a quartern of rum.

" Now, my jolly old Argonaut," said he, placing the refreshments on the table, " polish off these eatables, and then we will blow a cloud over some cold grog, and talk about old times."

The old sailor fell to without saying a word, and, when he had disposed of the beef and beer, with a proportionate allowance of bread, Sam poured the rum into a mug without a handle, filled it up with water, and, after tasting it himself, passed it to old Skelter.

" I have often thought about you, Sam, since we parted," observed the old sailor, as he put the mug down, and began filling his short pipe. " I never could hear where you was gone to, or what you was doing; but, as that little dancing-girl decamped the same night, I reckoned you up to have hooked it together."

"You were wrong, dad," returned Sam Skelter, as he selected a cigar from his case, and lighted it at the old man's pipe. "That young lady is now the wife of a wealthy baronet in Gloucestershire, and I have the honour of their acquaintance, and that of the baronet's sister."

"Ay, I heard some years ago that she turned out to belong to some great folks," observed old Skelter, helping himself to the rum-and-water. "But about yourself, Sam—are you pretty well off?"

"Why, I have seen some ups and downs since the night we parted company," returned Sam; "but I have now been pretty comfortable for several years. Lately I have been put, quite by accident, upon the clue to the discovery of my real parents; for you know you have often told me that you were not my father. Now, if it should turn out that my progenitor was a man of rank and wealth, it will be something to your advantage as well as mine."

Old Skelter bent his eyes to the floor in a meditative manner, and puffed away vigorously at his pipe, while Sam was making these remarks, and then he related as much as he knew of the exchange of infants at the time of the accident on the river. This was a very trivial increase to Sam's stock of knowledge respecting his parentage, and was only important as being corroborative of what he already knew. One thing was certain: the child of the seaman Skelter, and that of the late Lord Clanrobert, had been accidentally immersed in the Thames at the same time; and the child recovered by the seaman not being his own, the only conclusion that could be fairly arrived at, after a consideration of all the facts, was, that it was the child of Lord Clanrobert. Sam had no moral doubt of his being the son of that nobleman, but he was aware of the necessity of obtaining some legal and positive proof of the relationship, and the only persons he could then think of applying to, were the Corbetts mentioned in the *Red Book*. He therefore resolved to go down to Erith on the following morning, and ascertain if any of the family were still residing there; and as no further information could be obtained from the old sailor, he took his departure, with a promise to see him again in a few days.

It was late when Sam Skelter reached his humble lodging in the neighbourhood of Clare-market, and, as he looked out from the dingy window of his little chamber upon the adjacent roofs, the yellow-looking linen hung out to dry upon lines rigged out from back windows with the aid of a broom, and the gas-lights that rendered the filth and wretchedness of the narrow courts more conspicuous, he contrasted in his mind his present situation with that to which he believed himself to have been born, and the contrast excited some beneficial thoughts of how much was in the power of those possessed of wealth and influence to ameliorate the condition of the poor.

"But the aristocracy," thought Sam, "have not the experience which a workman has of the condition of the labouring class; and ignorance combines with self-interest to induce a disregard of that most vitally-important of all questions—how the increasing population of this country is to be fed? The usurper of the soil, and the capitalist who grows rich upon the industry of the poor, can never truly represent the class of workmen, the most numerous and useful, and therefore the most really important of all. As well might the wolves claim to represent the sheep! But there is a good time coming; I wish we knew when!" and, with this reflection, Sam withdrew from the window, and retired to rest.

———

CHAPTER LXXXIII.

JAMES CORBETT.

On the following morning, Sam Skelter went down to the steam-wharf, in Thames-street, and walked on board a steamer that was just about to start for Gravesend; he was put ashore at Erith by one of the boats which convey passengers to and from the steamers and the shore, and, entering the village, made inquiries concerning the abode of the Corbetts. He was directed to the cottage mentioned in an early portion of our narrative, and, looking in at the open door, on the threshold of which two or three children were playing with some wild flowers, he beheld a weather-beaten seaman, of middle age, on one side of the table, and a female, neatly dressed, and somewhat younger than the man, on the other.

" Your name is Corbett, sir, I believe ?" said Sam, interrogatively.

" James Corbett, at your service, sir," returned the seaman, laying down the pipe that he had been smoking.

" You will excuse the questions I am about to ask you, when you understand the importance of the object I have in asking them," said the youth. " You are, I believe, a relation of the Clanrobert family ?"

" Lord Clanrobert is my nephew," returned James Corbett. " The late lord married my sister. But sit down, young man, and then we can converse more at ease."

" Thank you," said Sam, taking the seat offered him by the smuggler. " In perusing an old newspaper, I became acquainted with the details of an accident on the river, near London-bridge, in the year 1816, by which a seaman and his wife and child were immersed in the stream by the upsetting of the boat, but none of them were drowned. At the same time, I discovered some memorandums, made shortly after that occurrence by an eminent solicitor of Furnival's-inn, referring to inquiries set on foot respecting this accident by the late Lord Clanrobert. This circumstance induced me, from motives of curiosity, to pursue my inquiries farther ; and, on referring to the peerage-list, I found that a boat, containing the late Lord and Lady Clanrobert and their infant son, was upset at the same time and place, but all, likewise, were rescued from the water. Now, I am the supposed son of that seaman ; but in reality he knows not whether his own child was drowned, or whether it was recovered by my parents, under the impression that it was their own. In the darkness and confusion— for it was night when the double accident occurred—the seaman and his wife were not aware, until they reached home, that the child which they recovered was not their own. You perceive the aspiring thoughts which these discoveries were calculated to awaken within me, and I have been induced to visit you in the hope that you might be able to throw some additional light upon the question of my origin."

The smuggler had started when Sam Skelter mentioned the supposed upsetting of the two boats near London-bridge ; and when the youth came to relate the discovery he had made respecting the inquiries instituted by the late Lord Clanrobert, and the fact that the child recovered by the seaman was not his own, he became considerably agitated, pressed his hand upon his head, and then rose, and paced the room, while Sam continued his narrative.

" You say that inquiries were made by the solicitor alluded to at the instance of the late Lord Clanrobert ?" said James Corbett, resuming his seat. " Might I ask the nature of those inquiries ?"

" You shall see the memoranda yourself," replied Sam, taking the papers from a pocket-book, and laying them on the table.

" There is evidently some mystery here," observed James Corbett, looking at his wife, after perusing the papers submitted to him by Sam Skelter. " I should be rejoiced to find that a right to the title of Lord Clanrobert could be proved by some one more worthy of the dignity of the peerage and the hereditary house of legislature than the youth who now bears it. But I cannot assist you in any way to support your claim, Mr. Skelter ; for I do not think I ever saw my sister's child, while an infant, more than a dozen times; and children of that tender age are so much alike, that I believe it to be impossible to say which of two young men has grown up from a certain infant."

" If there was any mark, now, on the person or clothes of the infant heir of Clanrobert by which the true lord might be distinguished, our doubts could easily be set at rest," observed Sam Skelter, glancing towards the smuggler and his wife.

" Doubtless there were some initials upon the clothes which you had on at the time of the accident," suggested James Corbett.

" I never heard of them ; and the clothes are not likely to be now in existence," returned Sam Skelter, shaking his head.

"We know the address of the nurse who attended Lady Clanrobert when her son was born," observed the smuggler's wife; "and if there are any marks by which the identity could be proved, she is the most likely person to be acquainted with them."

"Well thought of!" exclaimed Corbett. "The old lady lives at Greenwich, and, if you have no objection, we will set out at once, and see if she can solve our doubts."

"Sam Skelter eagerly embraced the proposition, and accompanied the smuggler to Greenwich, and to the residence of the female alluded to. Corbett acquainted her with the object of their visit; and the old lady, who was proud of having attended Lady Clanrobert, made a number of irrelevant remarks upon her beauty and amiability of disposition before satisfying the doubts of the impatient Skelter and the smuggler.

"Yes," she said, when the subject was again forced upon her attention, "the dear little babe had the mark of a raspberry on his left arm, just above the elbow, as plain as ever I see anything in my life, and I remember my lady observing——"

Before the garrulous nurse could finish the sentence by relating the observation made by the unfortunate sister of the smuggler on the occasion of the mark alluded to being discovered, Sam Skelter had pulled off his coat, and, turning up his shirt-sleeve, pointed triumphantly to a red spot on his left arm, just above the elbow.

"The very mark!" exclaimed the nurse, holding up her hands in astonishment.

"I never knew whether to call it a raspberry, a mulberry, or a blackberry," said Sam Skelter; "but since this good lady has decided it to be a raspberry, I have no doubt of the accuracy of the description, which speaks highly for her knowledge of the botany of the human frame. But seriously, Mr. Corbett, we have recovered another link of the chain of evidence necessary to substantiate my claim, and if some accident should bring to light the identical clothing which I had on when picked up in the river, the chain will be complete."

They then left the abode of the nurse, and after some further conversation they parted, Sam Skelter proceeding by steamer to London-bridge, and James Corbett returning to Erith. Sam then walked in a meditative manner down to Shadwell, and called upon old Skelter, to make inquiries concerning the clothing of his infancy.

"Well, I hope they arn't quite lost, if they are likely to be of any sarvice to you, Sam," said the old sailor; "but I'm most afeared you will never look upon them ag'in; for after the old 'oman hopped the broom with the skipper, and hooked it away, I sold all the old toggery to the man as keeps the rag-shop in the court where we used to live, and God knows what has become on 'em—perhaps converted into tinder, Sam."

This was not very encouraging; but Sam was not easily discouraged, as the reader has seen on other occasions, and away he went to the court in which his earliest years had been passed, and, pausing at a shop distinguished by the sign of a black doll hanging over the door, he made inquiries after the rags that had suddenly become of so much importance to him. The man laughed at the strangeness of the application, but observing the earnestness of Sam's manner, he said that it was impossible for him to say what had become of the things, and probably they had long since been converted into paper.

"No, no—not all of them," said his wife, coming into the shop. "Don't you recollect that some of the things were pretty good, and that Angelina wore the baby's frock that was amongst them?"

"If that frock is still in existence, I will give you a crown for it," said Sam, with some eagerness.

"Well, I really think it must be about the place somewhere," returned the woman, bustling out of the shop; and after being absent about ten minutes she returned with a ragged white frock.

Sam eagerly caught it out of her hand, and having discovered the initials G. M., surmounted by a viscount's coronet, upon it, he immediately threw two half-crowns upon the counter.

"Well, I don't know as you haven't got it too cheap, arter all," said the man, regarding the ragged relic with a glance of curiosity; but Sam made no reply, and hurried out of the shop.

Here was the last link required to connect the various facts he had discovered, so as to form an unbroken chain of evidence in support of his claim to the title of Lord Clanrobert; and before he retired to rest that night, the whole of the papers, and also the ragged frock, were in the hands of a respectable solicitor.

CHAPTER LXXXIV.

THE CONVIVIALISTS.

Two or three months after the occurrences related in the preceding chapter, a convivial party was assembled at the town mansion of Lord Clanrobert, as we must for the present style the young man who has hitherto borne that title. It was the early part of the evening; and the investigation of Sam Skelter's claim to the Clanrobert peerage had been brought to a conclusion that afternoon by the committee of peers appointed by the House of Lords for that purpose; but the habitual indolence of the youthful nobleman, and his indifference to politics, had always kept him away from the scene of hereditary legislature in which he was entitled to a seat, and, looking with supreme contempt on the claims of the plebeian Sam Skelter, he had chosen to entertain his friends on that evening, in the full anticipation of a decision in his favour.

A flood of light filled the apartment, streaming from the numerous silver candelabra disposed upon the table and down the sides of the room, and was reflected from the crystal that glittered upon the table, around which sat a score of gay young men, the scions of noble houses, many of them already verging upon the confines of intoxication. Lord Clanrobert was lounging back in his chair, smoking a cigar; Edward Ashley sat near him, and the countenances of both were flushed with wine. The result of the inquiry at the House of Lords was not then known to the young nobleman, and never had he been more highly exhilarated than on the present occasion.

"But who is this fellow—this pretender to the honours of the peerage?" said young Ashley, the subject having been broached by one of the company.

"Has any gentleman present ever extended his travels so far into the uncivilized regions of the far-east as Ratcliffe-highway?" said Lord Clanrobert, removing the cigar from his mouth, and exhaling a puff of fragrant smoke.

"Not I, faith!" exclaimed one of the lordlings present. "I should be suffocated by their vile smells and fogs, if I ventured beyond Temple-bar, I am sure I should.

"You are right, Villiers," said another. "I once went as far as the Bank on urgent business of a pecuniary nature, and when I descended from the carriage, I was obliged to apply a smelling-bottle to my olfactory organ, to avoid being overpowered by the effluvia with which the atmosphere is laden. It is a smell like nothing else—a vile city smell!"

"I have heard of such a place as Ratcliffe-highway," said another, in a languid tone; "but where it is situated, I know no more than the man in the moon. Which way do you go to it? where do you change horses?"

"I perceive I must enlighten you, and plead guilty to having travelled as far east as Ratcliffe-highway," returned Lord Clanrobert. "It is a long, dirty street, near the docks, and any gentleman who venture the length of it, ought to be placed under a strict quarantine by his friends on returning to the west-end, and be thoroughly fumigated with aromatics, and bathed in rose-water, before entering again into decent society. The horrid smell that pervades it, seems a combination of the effluvia of bilge-water and tar, with the concentrated essence of a city fog. In this abominable quarter, dwelt a characterless vagabond named Skelter, an amphibious impostor with wooden legs, who seats himself by the road-side, and exhibits a picture to attract the attention of the charitable to his legless condition."

"But what has this fellow to do with the impudent pretender to your coronet, my lord?" asked a beardless youth who had been promoted in the army over the heads of the veterans of Toulouse and Waterloo.

"Everything," replied Clanrobert, smiling; "for the old impostor was the progenitor of the young one, who, having by some inexplicable means wormed himself into an attorney's office, has had his inherent genius for imposture sharpened by the study and practice of legal quibbles and chicanery."

"Confusion to all impostors!" exclaimed Edward Ashley, filling his glass. "We will drink that, my lord."

"With all my heart," said Clanrobert, gaily. "Confusion to all impostors!"

The toast was drank, and, before the laughter and applause had subsided, a servant entered, and announced the solicitor employed by Lord Clanrobert to defend the peerage case.

"Excuse me a few minutes," said the young nobleman to his friends, as he rose from the table. "My legal adviser has doubtless brought me the news of the decision of the House of Lords against the claim of that impudent plebeian, the son and heir of the legless mendicant of Wapping."

"You bring me tidings of the discomfiture of that braggart plebeian, the attorney's clerk, I presume," said Clanrobert to his solicitor, as he entered the apartment in which the latter was waiting.

The manner and tone of the young nobleman were as gay and flippant as usual, and a smile of contempt curled his haughty lip as he alluded to Sam Skelter; but it faded away before a vague apprehension of evil, as he remarked the grave and cold demeanour of his solicitor.

"I regret to be the bearer of unwelcome intelligence, sir," said the latter, after a momentary pause; "but the result must be made known to you, and perhaps the sooner the better."

"You surely do not mean that the House of Lords has decided against me?" said the supposed nobleman, a paleness stealing over his countenance, in spite of the haughtiness with which he spoke.

"That is precisely what I do mean, sir," returned the solicitor. "The committee has decided that the young gentleman hitherto known by the name of Samuel Skelter is really George Macrae, the true heir to the Clanrobert peerage and property."

"Distraction!" shrieked the astonished young man, dashing his hand against his forehead. "But you cannot mean it; you are bantering with me; the thing is impossible!"

"It is not only possible, but true," returned the lawyer, with a little asperity. "The shock is doubtless a terrible one to you; and the result of the investigation has surprised most of the profession. I could not have supposed that such a chain of irrefragable evidence could have been brought forward in a case of disputed identity, after the lapse of so many years."

"And I am no longer a lord! my honours, my property, all pass from me to that plebeian wretch, whom I have seen walking with a roll of papers tied up with red tape," said the bewildered young man, in a kind of soliloquy; then suddenly addressing the solicitor, he said: "But who am I? am I anybody at all?"

"Why, sir, you can procure a patent to assume some more aristocratic name than that of Skelter, if you are not pleased with that; but I know of no other to which you are otherwise entitled," returned his legal adviser, in a hesitating manner.

"What!" exclaimed Skelter; "I the son of the legless vagabond of Ratcliffe-highway? I the heir of that wooden-legged impostor?"

"You will excuse me from offering any opinion of my own upon the matter; but such is the decision of the committee," returned the solicitor.

"Horrible!" groaned the young man. "What a height to tumble from! From the peerage to mendicity—from Belgravia to Wapping! What shall I be now? shall I sweep a crossing, or shall I invest all my property, if I can be said to possess any, in the purchase of a peripatetic potatoe bakehouse, and take my stand at the corner of the Victoria Theatre?"

An expression of intense bitterness crossed the features of young Skelter as he made these remarks, and as he concluded, he heard the voices of several persons in the hall, together with a shuffling of feet, as if a number of people had entered together. He advanced with a desperate gesture towards the door of the apartment, and opened it. The servant had just closed the door of the room on the other side, into which he had admitted the persons whom Skelter had heard in the hall, and he announced them to his master in a low voice, and with an air of mystery and astonishment.

"All my misfortunes have come upon me together," exclaimed his bewildered master. "Tell them that I am engaged at present, but will wait upon them in a few minutes."

The servant retired with this message, and his master re-entered the apartment in which he had left his legal adviser.

"Excuse me a few minutes, sir," said he to the lawyer. "Ill news flies fast; and the knowledge of my altered position seems to have made my tradesmen importunate for their several demands upon me."

The solicitor bowed, and the agitated and bewildered Skelter quitted the room; but instead of proceeding to confront his clamorous creditors, he rapidly descended the kitchen stairs, passed through the kitchen—to the astonishment of the domestics—and rushed up the area steps into the square.

The flush of partial inebriation had passed from his countenance, and a wild and reckless expression pervaded his features as he hurried away from the square to shun the glances of his aristocratic friends and the demands of the tradesmen whose confidence he had abused by incurring liabilities which he

31

could never have discharged, even if the decision of the House of Lords had not been against him. He walked fast, not caring and scarcely knowing the way that he was going, but only anxious to get away from the aristocratic quarter in which he had resided. At length the increased number of vehicles and passengers reminded him of his contiguity to the city, and, looking around him, he found himself descending Holborn.

CHAPTER LXXXV.

LONDON BRIDGE.

SKELTER stopped not until he reached London-bridge, for the excitement of his mind carried him along, regardless of whither he was hurrying; and when he found himself on the bridge, he turned into one of the recesses, and leaned over the parapet to rest himself, and cool his heated countenance. The moon rode high in the heavens, silvering the edges of the white and fleecy clouds that flecked the dark-blue canopy of the universe, and her pearly light reflected on the broad bosom of the Thames, whose ever-flowing waters were rolling towards the distant sea, with a dull and melancholy ripple, as the wavelets broke against the massive piers of the noble bridge. The masts and rigging of the shipping on the river, in the docks, and along the wharves, looked like black lines traced upon the sky, and their canvass showed white and distinct in the clear moonlight. Along the Rotherhithe shore, the lights glittered like distant stars; and where the tall warehouses rose along the banks, the river lay in shade; while, in the open channel, and along the opposite shore, the rippling current reflected the pure lustre of the moon.

He stood gazing vacantly upon the moonlit river, his mind completely absorbed in the bewildering occurrences of the last hour, which had come upon him so suddenly, so little expected by him was the decision arrived at by the committee of the House of Lords, that there were moments when he could scarce believe them real. An hour since, he had believed himself a peer of the realm, the lineal descendant of an ancient house, a legislator by hereditary right, and the possessor of large estates; now he was but one degree above absolute destitution, the son of a vagrant, flying from the rage of his duped creditors, and as anxious to shun his patrician friends as his plebeian enemies. His fall had been as sudden and as crushing as the catastrophe to the aerial castle-building of Alnaschar in the oriental tale, and he shuddered at its contemplation.

He was aroused from his reverie by feeling a hand placed lightly on his arm, and, turning round, he beheld a young female, whose attire evinced an attempt at finery in the midst of destitution and misery. He started slightly as he recognised, by the light of the moon, the features of Nancy Shrimp; and as her seducer turned round, and the light of the gas-lamp above their heads revealed to her his countenance, the young girl started also. The smile which the lost one had forced upon her countenance fled at that recognition, and the little colour which misery had left upon her fair cheeks faded rapidly into the blanched and pallid hue of wretchedness and despair; for this meeting aroused so many reminiscences of the past, that she became overwhelmed, for a moment, by the consciousness of shame and degradation.

"Nancy!" ejaculated her betrayer, in a tone of surprise and evident embarrassment.

"Yes, Lord Clanrobert, it is me—the wretched girl whom you betrayed to shame and disgrace!" exclaimed Nancy Shrimp, speaking with sudden excitement. "If there is a life beyond the grave, and a righteous Providence overruling all, tell me, Lord Clanrobert, how you can hope for salvation until you have repaired the deep wrong you have done me?"

"I am not Lord Clanrobert," returned the young man, evading the vehement appeal of his miserable victim. "I was so called once, but I am a lord no longer. I scarce know who I am; I am the shuttlecock of fortune, and shall soon begin to fancy myself the sport of malignant friends. Call me Skelter; that name will do as well as any other," he added, with an evanescent smile of intense bitterness.

Nancy Shrimp gazed at him a moment, as if she thought his mind was wandering, from the strangeness of his words and manner, and then she exclaimed: "Skelter or Clanrobert, you are the man who came like a dark cloud athwart the sunshine of my happy youth, and blighted my future existence, like a foul canker in the bud of the rose. But you have not answered my question; what hopes of your soul's salvation can you dare to entertain while the deep wrong you have done me remains unatoned for?"

"I have misery enough to endure without your reproaches, Nancy," returned Skelter, averting his looks from the despair-impressed countenance of the pale victim of his perfidy. "Within the last hour I have been stripped of rank and wealth, and now I am but a penniless vagabond skulking from the anger of my deluded creditors."

"Have you endured the pangs of hunger?—the pitiless pelting of the rain upon your uncovered head for hours, for lack of threepence to procure even such a wretched lodging as that money will obtain?" exclaimed Nancy Shrimp, with undiminished vehemence. "Have you been forced to veil the real feelings of your heart, shame, anguish, and disgust, beneath a smiling countenance, and to force the laugh of seeming gaiety from the heart that was bursting with its pent-up load? If you have not endured such agony as this, you cannot compare your misery with mine. You call it misery when the creditor, made by your extravagance, demands payment of the money that is justly due to him; I have known what it is to endure the pangs of hunger for want of a penny. You call it misery, when you are obliged to descend from champagne to a humble beverage, but I have been obliged to assuage my thirst at the street pump."

"Why did you not go home, and thus have avoided the misery of which you complain so bitterly?" asked young Skelter, in a tone of vexation and embarrassment.

"Home!" almost shrieked the unfortunate Nancy. "Where was my home? I had a moral claim upon you for a home, but that claim you repudiated and denied. Seduction may be palliated, we may admit extenuating circumstances in every case, but who can justify the subsequent neglect and desertion of the deluded victim of man's perfidy for a fairer face, or perchance for one boasting only the greater charm of novelty? You never loved me, George, and from the moment when first you saw me you designed my irretrievable ruin."

The unfortunate girl sank upon the stone seat of the recess as she uttered the last words, and burst into tears.

"These outpourings of passion are useless, and will draw the notice of the police upon us," observed the annoyed Skelter. "Let us leave the recess, and have something to drink."

"Never!" exclaimed Nancy, speaking with as much vehemence as at first, notwithstanding her tears. "Never will I accept so much as a glass of spirits from you, while the debt of justice you owe me remains uncancelled."

"The past is beyond recall, Nancy, and I assure you that I am now as destitute as yourself!" observed her betrayer, moving away from the recess.

"You have no pity, George—no love—no honour!" sobbed the unhappy Nancy, as her seducer turned away from her, but he kept on towards Southwark, and made no reply.

"The dark waters of the Thames are less treacherous than man, and they will not refuse to receive my weary and polluted body!" exclaimed Nancy, starting from the cold stone seat in the recess, and suddenly mounting upon it; the wildness of momentary delirium gleamed from her blue eyes, and throwing off her bonnet and shawl, she sprang upon the parapet of the bridge, and threw herself head foremost into the dark tide that was rolling through the arch below with a dull and mournful sound.

The rapidity of her fall from that dizzy height deprived her of consciousness before she reached the surface of the river, and she fell into it with a dull splash, and floated down with the tide an inert mass. Several persons who had witnessed the rash act looked over the parapet of the bridge, and shouted to the watermen on the stairs, and two or three boats put off towards the spot where the miserable young woman had disappeared below the rippling surface of the tide.

Skelter had heard the shouts of those who had beheld the suicidal act of his wretched victim, and as the never-failing voice of conscience told him that he was the cause, a shudder pervaded his frame, and a cold perspiration burst out upon his pale forehead. He hurried onward, however, and had reached the foot of the bridge when an exclamation from a bystander involuntarily arrested him.

"Here they come—he has got her out!" was the observation he had heard, and glancing down the stairs he beheld a boat approaching in which a waterman was supporting the unconscious form of a young woman. The man stepped ashore with his inanimate burden, and two policemen carried her to the nearest public-house. Skelter followed with the crowd which such an occurrence speedily serves to collect. The face of the suicide was ashy pale, her eyes were closed, and the water dripped from the dishevelled tresses of her auburn hair. The attendance of a surgeon was immediately procured, and all the usual remedies in cases of suspended animation were resorted to, but without effect; the soul of the unhappy victim of libertinism had taken its flight to that bourne from whence no traveller returns.

CHAPTER LXXXVI.

THE TRUE NOBLE.

Skelter hurried from the spot as soon as he had ascertained that the wretched suicide was no more, as if he would fain have escaped from even the companionship of his own thoughts. His fall from the dignity of the peerage and the senate to a condition little removed from actual vagrancy, the upbraidings of the unhappy Nancy, and the subsequent suicide of that unfortunate girl almost in his presence, had produced such a morbidity of the mind, that he felt completely wretched, and could almost have followed the example of his ill-fated victim. But he was both selfish and cowardly, and to such a man death is something very terrible; hence, though he stopped a moment before a chemist's shop, and gazed gloomily at the globular vessels filled with red and blue liquids in the window, and glanced down the opening to the wharves, which allowed him a glimpse of the moonlit river as he turned into Tooley-street, the idea of suicide was abandoned as soon as it was suggested, and he entered a tavern near Hay's-lane. The parlour was destitute of a single guest, and the gaslight was partially turned off in consequence; this gloom suited the morbidity of his mind, and, having been supplied with a glass of brandy-and-water, he bent his head upon his folded arms, and gave way to his melancholy reflections.

He had sat thus for some time, when the opening of the door aroused him, and the waiter having turned the gas full on before leaving the room, after supplying him with his brandy-and-water, the sudden blaze of light which his eyes encountered when he raised his head prevented him for a moment from perceiving who the new comer was. But when he heard his voice as he ordered some refreshment of the waiter who had followed him in, he recognised it as one he had heard before, and he started up with a haughty flush upon his pale countenance.

It was the despised plebeian, the attorney's clerk, now Lord Clanrobert; it was him whom the reader has hitherto known as Sam Skelter who had thus disturbed the privacy of the false patrician. The recognition was mutual, and the true Clanrobert regarded the false with a feeling of surprise, that they should have encountered each other in that obscure spot, on the very evening that rank and wealth had passed from the possession of the latter to that of the former. Naturally of a frank and generous disposition, Lord Clanrobert would have felt some sympathy for his fallen rival, had he not been so well acquainted with his inveterately selfish and profligate character—a knowledge which only inspired that kind of pity which borders so closely upon contempt, as to be more obnoxious than welcome.

The two young men sat for some time in silence, each absorbed in his own reflections: it was Skelter who first broke the silence.

"I congratulate your lordship upon your unexpected accession to extensive property, and what I doubt not you will value more, the dignity of the peerage," said he, in a tone of bitter irony. "I presume I am the first to do so?"

" Having just returned from Greenwich, I was unaware of the decision of the House of Lords," returned Lord Clanrobert, without noticing the ironical tone of his rival; "but it was far from unexpected, the evidence given having rendered my right indubitable. With reference to your supposition as to my estimate of the value of the title, I beg to assure you that I only value it inasmuch as it affords me the means of promoting, in the upper house of parliament, the welfare of my fellow-creatures."

" I suppose you intend the last remark as a reflection upon me for not attending to my legislative duties?" said Skelter, with a sinister smile upon his countenance, though his heart was full of wrath, malice, envy, and bitterness.

" I intended nothing of the kind, and I beg to decline entering any farther upon a subject that can only be productive of dissension and ill-feeling," returned Clanrobert, mildly.

" You did mean it, though you will not acknowledge it," persisted Skelter. " No doubt you already enjoy, by anticipation, the honours of the senate, and regard yourself as an orator in embryo, as the Mirabeau of the English parliament. Whitechapel will echo your eloquence, and the tap-rooms of Seven-dials will resound with your praises."

" If there are men in the purlieus of Whitechapel, and the pestiferous courts of Seven-dials, capable of appreciating the exertions which may be made for their welfare, all honour to the sons of labour whom poverty compels to take up their abode in those benighted regions," returned Clanrobert, roused to energy by the studied attempts of Skelter to insult him. " It is seldom that governments think of ameliorating their condition—still more seldom that the ministers of religion are found in their miserable abodes. Such shafts as that you have just thrown fall harmlessly upon me; take care, sir, that, like the boomerang, they recoil not upon the hand that hurls them."

" The landlord ought to think his parlour highly honoured by being made the scene of the first attempt at oratory of the *parvenu* Lord Clanrobert," observed Skelter, with a malignant sneer.

" Mr. Skelter," said Clanrobert, who still preserved his equanimity, "your object is evidently to insult me, and fasten a quarrel upon me; though what you promise yourself from such a despicable course, I cannot imagine. It was you who forced your conversation upon me—it was you who instituted the comparison between your own conduct as a peer and a legislator, and what you prognosticated of mine. I regard legislative power as given to the nobility of this country for the benefit of the people—as a trust with which they are invested by the constitution. You held this trust for some time : what account can you give of your stewardship? your conduct as an individual has been that of the aristocracy as a body. Powerless for good, your proxy has been at the service of the people's enemies when the purpose was evil. Proud, without having ever performed an action of which a man should be proud, selfish, profligate, uninfluenced by a single generous sentiment, you stood prominently forth as the type of your order. Pleasure, and often vice, was the business of your life—sharpers and swindlers were your habitual companions."

" This insolence is not to be borne !" exclaimed Skelter, rising suddenly from his chair, and his manner changing from irony to uncontrollable rage. " I demand satisfaction !"

" Satisfaction !" retorted Lord Clanrobert, with a contemptuous smile. " Take care that you do not receive such satisfaction as you compelled me to administer on a certain occasion some time ago."

" Such conduct may be fitted for the society you have been accustomed to," said the enraged Skelter; "but such an evasion shall not serve you. I demand the satisfaction of a gentleman."

" To descend to your own language, Mr. Skelter," said Lord Clanrobert, " your present conduct may be fitted for the society you have been accustomed to, but men of honour do not assume the manners of the gladiator; they chastise the insolent as they would a snarling cur, and appeal to the laws when a bravo menaces their life."

Skelter bit his lip at this severe and well-merited reproof, and before he could recover from its effect, Lord Clanrobert had quitted the room. Left alone, the excitement of anger which had sustained him during his quarrel with the young nobleman who had interposed between him and the possession of rank and wealth speedily subsided, and he again sank into that morbid despondency from which the entry of Lord Clanrobert had roused him. His glass was empty, and, not wishing to still further diminish his slender exchequer by having it replenished, he quitted the public-house.

He knew no one to whom he could apply for pecuniary assistance, for those who adulated the peer cared little for the man, and the army suggested itself to him as the only resource open to one who was ashamed to beg, and knew not how to work. In this mood he encountered a sergeant wearing a uniform which struck him as differing from any worn in the British army, and on accosting and questioning the man, he found that he was raising men for the service of Don Carlos of Spain, who was then engaged in a sanguinary civil war, for the purpose of wresting the crown of that country from the brow of his niece, Queen Isabella. In the service of the would-be despot, Skelter accordingly enlisted, and in a few weeks was landed at Bayonne, with a number of others, and sent from thence to Hernani, the head-quarters of the Carlist army. The partizans of the Bourbon pretender had recovered from the defeat at Fontarabia, and the result of the skirmishes at Hernani and Irun had inspired them with renewed confidence. Shortly after Skelter's arrival in the Spanish camp the movement was made on Andouin, which resulted in that disastrous slaughter of the British auxiliaries of the Christino party, which was but the prelude to the disorganization of the legion of General Evans; and here we leave him for the present, to follow the fortunes of more amiable characters.

CHAPTER LXXXVII.

SIR NORMAN ASHLEY.

ABOUT a week after the decision of the House of Lords in the Clanrobert peerage case, Sir Norman Ashley was superintending some improvements near the hall, when a carriage with a crest and coronet on the panels rolled up the wide avenue, and Lord Clanrobert sprang out, and grasped the proffered hand of the young baronet with friendly warmth.

"I am rejoiced to see your lordship," said Sir Norman Ashley, "and Lady Ashley and my sister will be equally delighted by this visit. My uncle seems to have contemplated the necessity of resigning Oakwood at some time, for he does not appear to have expended five pounds in making the alterations and improvements which were required during the six years that he held his usurped possession."

"You have a fine prospect of the Cotswold-hills from here," observed Lord Clanrobert, looking around him in an admiring manner, "and by felling a few trees there, you have opened an equally fine vista in that direction."

Lolah now came forth from the hall to welcome the visitor, accompanied by Ellen Ashley, and as they advanced across the smooth and verdant lawn to the spot where the two young men were standing, Lord Clanrobert would have been as puzzled upon which to bestow the prize of beauty as was the shepherd-prince of Troy upon the pine-clad hill of Ida. The young nobleman advanced to meet them, and was received by Lolah with sisterly friendship, and by Ellen with a frankness and cordiality that inspired him with the most ardent hopes.

"I have been admiring the beauty of the adjacent scenery," said the young nobleman; "for Oakwood seems placed in the midst of all that is worthy of admiration in the county of Gloucester."

"We must detain you for a few days, that you may have leisure to observe its beauties," said Lolah, for Norman had proposed to her that morning to invite the young nobleman to Oakwood."

"I shall accept the invitation with pleasure," returned Lord Clanrobert.

"That is the window by which I entered my own mansion as a burglar, after an absence of six years," observed Norman Ashley, as the party returned to the hall; and with this preface he related the circumstances which had attended his search for the contents of the ebony cabinet, and his subsequent visit, accompanied by Mr. Mortmain. Mrs. Ashley had returned to London after the funeral of her husband, and had made no attempt to disturb her nephew in the possession of the property.

On the following morning Norman Ashley accompanied Lord Clanrobert over the estate on horseback, and pointed out to him the improvements which he intended to make, at the same time relating the alterations which he had made in the management of the property; all of which had been made with a view to the better cultivation of the soil, the greater prosperity of his tenants, and the improvement of the condition of the labouring population. He had found the arable land in a very defective state of cultivation, the farmers discontented, and the labourers in an abject state of poverty; for his uncle's sole care had been to raise as large a revenue from the estate as possible; disregarding the oppression, discontent, and misery to which this policy gave rise. His first thought was to reduce the rent paid by his tenants for their farms; but his steward represented that they paid no more than those upon other estates, and that a greater boon would be to give them a tenure, affording greater security and advantage. Acting upon this suggestion, he gave all his tenants leases, which secured to them all the improvements they might make upon their farms, and also gave them permission to destroy the game that fattened upon their property. This made him many enemies among the neighbouring gentry, but it had the effect of inducing them to discharge their gamekeepers, for they found it expensive to preserve the game for Sir Norman's tenants to destroy. Having found that the smallest farms were usually the best cultivated, he resolved never to give a lease to holders of more than a hundred acres, and when the larger farms were given up on that account by the tenants, he divided them into smaller ones, and by this means the land became better cultivated, and the value of the property considerably enhanced, besides giving employment to a far greater number of labourers. His next care was to introduce a better system of agriculture, for he found that his tenants frequently used six or seven horses in ploughing, without performing the work so well as is done by the Scotch farmers with only one horse. In order to effect such a desirable change, he took one of the farms into his own management, and by studying the most approved modes of culture, and consulting his steward as to their applicability to his own land, he rendered the farm a model for the example of the county.

This statement of the changes effected by Sir Norman Ashley upon his patrimonial estates is partially prospective; for at the time of Lord Clanrobert's visit, he had not had time to carry out all the plans which he had conceived, and which had so beneficial an effect alike upon the tenants and the labourers.

In the evening, Lord Clanrobert, missing Ellen from the drawing-room, sought her in the garden, being anxious to learn from her own lips the progress which he had made in her good opinion. He found her in a bower, trellissed with honey-suckle and clematis; a slight blush suffused her lovely countenance as he entered the fragrant retreat, but it passed away in a moment.

"Some months have elapsed, Miss Ashley," said the young nobleman, as he seated himself by her side, "since we spoke upon the subject that then, as it is now, was nearest to my heart. I had the temerity to ask for your affection; you forbade me to hope that I could ever gain it, since such hope might be doomed to disappointment, but you did not deny me your friendship. But I still hoped on; for could I have been deprived of hope, I should have been miserable—wretched. While you lived, while I believed your affections to be disengaged, as you then assured me they were, all my hopes of happiness to come were fixed on you, as strongly as those of the mariner upon the beacon light that marks the haven of his destination. You bade me reform my habits of life, in which I acknowledge there was scope for reformation," continued the young nobleman, after a moment's hesitation; "and though the period is short since you kindly, and in the true spirit of friendship, gave me that recommendation, yet the guerdon which I hoped for would have been sufficient to urge me to greater sacrifices than the conquest of vicious habits, acquired from pernicious examples. It may be deemed an evidence of vanity for me to say that I have succeeded; but will you, Miss Ashley, receive my assurance as to the period since we parted in London, and my promise as to the future?"

"I will," replied Ellen; "and believe me, your assurance gives me great pleasure."

"May I now hope, Miss Ashley, that my unalterable attachment and adherence to the good resolutions I have formed will obtain me the reward of your love?" asked Lord Clanrobert, taking her small white hand in his own, and looking earnestly into the clear depths of her dark eyes.

"Might not the world say that I refused Mr. Skelter and accepted Lord Clanrobert?" returned Ellen, in a hesitating tone, but without withdrawing her hand.

"Why should we regard the world, Ellen?" asked the young nobleman, speaking in a more impassioned tone, as he drew confidence from the tone and manner of his beautiful companion. "The opinion of the world should be regarded only by worldlings. It is of too chamelion-like a complexion to be looked upon with deference by the votaries of truth."

"I admire those sentiments, and they show that the contagion of vicious examples has not reached your heart," returned Ellen, raising her fine dark eyes to her lover's countenance, and immediately withdrawing them again, as they encountered his impassioned glance.

"If I were Ellen Ashley, I would dare to act in accordance with every principle that I deemed worthy of admiration," said Lord Clanrobert, smiling.

"I dare do so," returned Ellen; "for I was led to the remark, not by any deference to the world's opinion, but by a fear that you might deem me influenced by such a selfish and ignoble motive, if I received the suit of Lord Clanrobert more favourably than that of Mr. Skelter, the attorney's clerk. It was this fear alone which made me hesitate in my reply, or I would have said: 'George, receive the reward of your constancy and resolution, in the assurance of my regard.'"

"Do I hear aright? you really love me, Ellen?" exclaimed Lord Clanrobert, pressing to his lips the hand that he retained in his own.

"Yes, George—you only," returned the blushing girl; and ere the words had scarcely left her lips, they were warmly pressed by those of her enraptured lover, who could scarcely believe in the reality of his happiness.

The conversation that followed Ellen's avowal of her reciprocation of Lord Clanrobert's attachment, we shall not place before our readers. We can assure them, however, that they will lose nothing by the omission; for a report of the conversation of lovers is seldom very edifying, save to the parties concerned, as those who have loved—and who has not?—can bear us testimony. It will be sufficient, as our narrative approaches its termination, briefly to state that, in less than a month after the preceding conversation, the lovely Ellen became the bride of Lord Clanrobert, whose subsequent conduct has not given her the slightest reason to regret the choice which her young heart made.

CHAPTER LXXXVIII.

THE DISCHARGED SOLDIER AND THE STROLLING PLAYER.

WE must now pass over the two years subsequent to the incidents recorded in the preceding chapter, during which nothing of importance marked the tranquil existences of the families of Sir Norman Ashley and Lord Clanrobert, save the birth of an heir to the title and property of that young nobleman. By the generosity of his newly-found nephew, James Corbett was made the owner of a fine brig, and, renouncing the illegal and hazardous pursuits of the contrabandist, he embarked in the West India trade, and in time accumulated a competence. These brief notices enable us to pass on to the year 1839, and introduce the reader to the tap-room of a public-house in Bow-lane, near the East India docks.

It was near midnight; and the only person in the little smoke-begrimed room, was a young man, sitting in a corner, and gazing vacantly at the almost extinct fire which glimmered in the rusty grate. His features were not unhandsome; but on his sallow countenance were prematurely traced the lines made by the combined effects of dissipation and vicissitude; there was a settled gloom upon his brow; and his long, disordered hair and exuberant whiskers imparted to his countenance an expression of mingled wildness and ferocity.

His dress consisted of a very battered and napless hat and a drab great-coat, which, being open, showed beneath it a tattered red jacket, the yellow cotton lace of which hung in shreds; his trousers were dark-blue, with a yellow stripe down the outside seam, and were in the same condition as the jacket.

A short pipe and an empty pint pot stood on the table near him; and the decaying fire and the half-extinguished gas increased the gloomy appearance of the smoky room. The stranger's reverie, of whatever nature it was, was interrupted by the entrance of another young man, who stopped abruptly on the threshold, and gazed at him in undisguised astonishment. The new comer was fair and rather pale, with curling light-brown hair straying over the greasy collar of a black dress-coat in the last stage of seediness; a white hat, in perfect keeping with his coat, surmounted his curly sconce, and inclined very much to the right side. His cravat consisted of a piece of black ribbon; and as his coat was buttoned up to his throat, the existence of a shirt and waistcoat would have been somewhat apocryphal, had it not been for the appearance of the latter below the front of his coat, and the line of rather yellow linen which the short-

32

ness of the sleeves of that garment rendered visible. His trousers were of a large tartan pattern, and tightly strapped down, which effected the two-fold object of concealing the holes in his dirty stockings, and keeping together the soles and upper-leathers of his shoes, which would otherwise have dissolved partnership, besides enhancing the fit of those nether encasements, which seemed to cling with desperate tenacity to the young man's legs.

"Angels and ministers of grace defend us!" exclaimed the new comer, with a melo-dramatic start. "Art thou a spirit of health or goblin damned? Bringest thou airs from heaven or blasts from hell? Be thy intents wicked or charitable?"

"Stow that nonsense, Ned Ashley," returned the man in the military habiliments, with an air of vexation; and then looking intently at the young man, he added: "You do not seem in much better feather than myself."

"All the world's a stage, and every man and woman merely players!" sighed Edward Ashley, shaking his head, as he sat down, and called for a pint of porter. "A mantle of ermine to-day, a robe of serge to-morrow: such are the vicissitudes of life! But who would have thought of us meeting in this crib, when we parted two years ago in Belgrave-square!"

"Do not speak of it, Ned," returned the other, who, as the reader has doubtless conjectured, was Sam Skelter. "That night I enlisted in the service of Don Carlos, and have only returned a few weeks from the Peninsula. You have taken to the sock and buskin, it seems?"

"Yes," said Edward Ashley; "our company is at present performing in this neighbourhood, and I dropped in to slake my thirst with a cooling draught of double X, 'my custom always in the evening,' little expecting to meet the old acquaintance whom I last met over champagne. 'What a falling off was there!' But drink, man; humidify the clay of your humanity with this humble beverage; and, 'if any pain or care remain, drown it in the bowl.'"

"I wish I could take it as easy as you seem to do," observed Skelter, as he took the pewter vessel handed him by Ashley, and drank eagerly.

"Why not?" responded his companion. "Since 'life's a bumper, filled by fate, let us guests enjoy the treat.' There is no philosophy like that which teaches us to enjoy the present while we may; and even when fortune frowns, to laugh to scorn the arrows of adversity. Ho, without there!"

He struck the pint pot forcibly on the table as he spoke, and, on the appearance of the waiter—a pale, unhealthy-looking lad—he saluted him with:

"E'en such a wight, so wan, so woe-begone, drew Priam's curtains in the dead of night! Fill this tankard with the beverage called, by the vulgar, 'heavy wet,' and take care that it be mild as a zephyr and cool as the snows of frosty Caucasus. This mood of mine, my noble friend," he continued, turning to Skelter, "does for me what whistling did for the plough-boy in passing through the churchyard: it prevents me from dwelling too long and deeply on the harsh realities of life. It is a lottery in which all cannot draw prizes; but that is no reason why we should embitter the enjoyment that is left us, by useless reflections upon what we have lost. 'Begone, dull care!' let us drink and be happy."

"Drink, and be happy, when the draught is humble malt?" observed Skelter, bitterly. "Custom may have reconciled you to it, Ned; but I have drank nothing but wine and brandy in the Peninsula and in France; and, if it had not been for an unfortunate affair that Fitzormond, Simpson, and I were engaged in at Paris, I would have remained there."

"And what has become of those superlative rascals?" inquired young Ashley.

"Working in the dockyard at Toulon," returned Skelter.

"Clothed, lodged, and fed at the expense of the state, and taken so much care of, that they work with a chain about their legs, to prevent their running away: is that the ticket?" inquired Edward Ashley, in a satiric tone.

"Yes; so much the worse for them," replied Skelter. "I met them at one of the hells in the Palais Royal, after leaving the service of his catholic majesty, on account of not getting my arrears of pay, and we concerted a plan of quartering ourselves upon the good citizens of Paris. The plan reflected great credit upon the fertile brain of Fitzormond; but the laws called it swindling; and, one fine morning, the police introduced my confederates, much against their inclination, to the prefect of Paris. I took the alarm, and disappeared; but Augustus and Simpson were sent to Toulon, to improve their minds, by contemplating the billows of the Mediterranean, and acquire a more correct perception of the principle of *meum* and *tuum*."

"To such base uses may we come, Horatio!" said Edward Ashley, in a soliloquising tone. "But 'tis now the witching hour of night, when church-yards yawn, and graves give up their dead; and I begin to feel the want of 'tired Nature's prime restorer—balmy sleep.' I must away!"

He rose as he spoke, and was about to leave the room without any other parting, or any farther manifestation of interest in the well-being of his former intimate acquaintance, when two policemen entered, at sight of whom Sam Skelter betrayed visible uneasiness. He rose from the settle, and would have quitted the room in the company of Edward Ashley, but one of the policemen seized his arm.

"We want you," said the policeman, laconically.

"What for?" exclaimed Skelter, looking sternly at the constable, though a keen observer might have seen that the expression was only assumed, to hide his confusion.

"That little affair of the watch," returned the policeman. "You must come with us to the station-house, and if you can prove your innocence to the magistrates, of course you will be set at liberty."

Sam Skelter saw that it would be useless to offer any resistance, and suffered himself to be led away by the police.

"That's the cove as prigged the lady's watch t' other day, as she stood gazing up at the Monnyment," observed the cadaverous waiter to Edward Ashley.

"This should teach us there's a divinity that shapes our ends, rough-hew them how we will!" murmured the strolling player, as he stood at the door of the tavern, and looked after the forms of his quondam friend and the constables until they disappeared.

Sam Skelter was tried at the Central Criminal Court, and was sentenced to seven years' transportation; what became of him after the expiration of his term of punishment, which he underwent on board the *Justitia* hulk at Woolwich, we know not, nor is the matter of much importance.

The old wooden-legged sailor gave up the ghost a few years since; and Shark Slingsby, when last we heard of him, was on his way to South Australia, where the authorities had insisted upon his taking up his abode for the rest of his life.

Edward Ashley for some time followed the career of a strolling player, but on the death of his mother, a few years since, he retired from the vagrant profession, and, with the little money which the intemperate habits fallen into by his mother, after the suicide of her husband, had enabled her to leave him, he purchased a cab and horse, and now plies at one of the railway-termini, frequently regaling his fares and brother "cabbies" with choice morsels from the Swan of Avon.

EPILOGUE.

OUR task is ended, and the phantasmagorial figures evoked by our spells from the world of shadows, fade from the drapery of mist which canopies the ever-rolling tide of Old Father Thames.

The rising luminary of day, shining redly through the fog, gilds the gothic tracery of Westminster's ancient abbey, and causes the flame-tipped summit of the Monument to glow like the fire with which the priests of the Mexitili greeted the beneficent deity of the national worship. The waters of the German Ocean, thrown back from the shores of the northern Peninsula, rush in mighty volume through the arches of the six bridges which connect the twin cities of the metropolis with the boroughs on the southern bank of the Thames, and roll onward far beyond the western limits of the modern Babylon. Would that they could bear to the towers and terraces of Windsor the tears, and sighs, and groans with which they are laden!

For the waves of Old Father Thames flow past the wretched abodes of the toiling workman, whose incessant labour scarce keeps his family from starvation;

and the unwilling idler, looking on with folded arms and moody brow, and the breeze which passes over his rippling surface, bears, from the cold cell of the imprisoned patriot, his sighs for the ruined hopes of his country, and his fervent aspirations for the reign of right.

Was it for this, Old Father Thames, that thy silver waves reflected the sheen of the steel armour of the barons who dictated Magna Charta to the tyrant John on the field of Runnymede? Was it for this that thy ancient bridge echoed the trampling march of the followers of Tyler and Cade? Well does London carry on her shield of arms the bloody dagger of the treacherous Walworth! for it is a fit emblem of the unrelenting enmity of her citizens to the suffering and down-trodden labour-class!

Would that thy glassy surface was a mirror in which we could read the future, and know how long the tree of freedom shall be fertilised with the blood of her martyred worshippers, ere her branches spread themselves out as a canopy formed by Nature for all her children, and its fruits and flowers hang within the reach of all!

Roll on, silver Thames! tyranny cannot destroy the beauty of nature; and recollections of the romantic scenery of thy verdant banks shall soothe the mind of the incarcerated patriot, and birds shall twitter at his dungeon grating, and whisper words of hope that shall reanimate his soul, and inspire him to resume the struggle with oppression the moment its frowning portals have closed behind him, and he breathes again the free air, and feels the refreshing breeze upon his pallid countenance.

Old Father Thames! when the shivering child of destitution cowers beneath the protecting shelter of the landward arches of the bridges which span thy broad channel, and feels the bleak wind freezing the current of his blood, sees darkness above and around him, irradiated only by the lamps which glimmer through the fog, the hope that sustains him in his bitterest hour of extremity arises from the knowledge that morning will succeed that night of cold and cheerless darkness, that he will again revel in the light and warmth of the resplendent sun.

So should it be with us: we stand in the gloomy shadow of antiquated institutions, we feel within our hearts the benumbing influence of the withering breath of power; and the light of heaven and the beauty of earth is obscured by the black pall which tyranny has spread over the land, illumined only by the sparks cast from the half-extinguished torch of freedom, crushed beneath the iron heel of the oppressor; yet faith in humanity sustains us, and already on the horizon we see the red glow which announces the coming day of universal justice.

Then, Old Father Thames! thy ever-rolling tide will no longer flow between palaces and hovels, churches and prisons; for when the minds of the people are under the dominion of reason, crowns and mitres, coronets, sceptres, and crosiers, will be rejected as the toys and baubles of the nation's infancy, and they will perceive that inequality is not order, but anarchy.

The mists of morning, when they rest upon thy bosom, ruffled by the breeze, will no longer be burdened with sighs, and tears, and groans; for happiness will be equally diffused among all, when the conditions which enable man to obtain and enjoy it are brought within the reach of all. Society will no longer resemble the ant-hill, in which there is a master-class and a slave-class, but the bee-hive, in which the enjoyment of each is in proportion to the labour of all.

Old Father Thames! thy waves rolled on as now when the painted Briton chased the deer and the boar through the forests, whose green branches dipped into thy stream, where now stand warehouses, stored with the merchandise of the world; and thou knowest that the free savage was happier than the civilised slave of capital. Men surrendered their natural liberty, and entered into a civil compact for their mutual advantage, exchanging the independence of nature for the common dependence of civilisation. But the social compact has been broken, and if it were always to remain so, better for the poor man if he had remained the lone hunter of the woods and wastes.

What has civilisation done for us? In what is our condition preferable to that of the Red Indian? The savage has his hunting-grounds, his rivers teeming with fish, and the spontaneous fruits of the forest and the prairie, but what have we? Absolutely nothing! The soil that we bedew with our sweat, the labour that gives value to everything, it is not our own.

Such, from the crowded districts of the metropolis, from the factories of Manchester, from the quays of Liverpool, from the blighted fields of Ireland, is the ominous cry of discontent that now surges upward in sullen roar.

Yet London is the capital of civilisation, the chief mart of commerce, the grand emporium of wealth. What a singular paradox! In the richest city in the world, men die of hunger! In close proximity to splendid palaces, men are frozen to death on door-steps! In a country whose factories clothe the world, men shiver in rags! In a country which imports, annually, millions of quarters of corn, while our own fields lie half-uncultivated, men stand, with folded arms, lacking employment! In a country where a thousand fanes are dedicated to the religion of peace, buildings rise in startling contiguity, in which men are taught and practised in the art of war; nay, the fluttering emblem of nationality under which they go forth to war, is blessed and consecrated by the priest of peace!

And this is order! this is civilisation! These are the evidences of the excellence of our social system! These are the things we are told to respect and cherish!

FINIS.